BOOK ONE OF THE WATCHERS TRILOGY

The WATCHERS OF EDEN

T.C. EDGE

Table of Contents

1
Pickers

When I wake I think of my mother. It's like that every day. When someone you love is dying, you'll be just the same.

She sleeps next door to me, in the room she once shared with my father. I wish most days that he was still here to care for her. I wish most days that I could remember more about him; the sound of his voice, the way he looked when he smiled.

We only have one picture of him, but he's not smiling in it. He's grimacing. It was the day he was taken from us.

It's still dark when I creep to my mother's room and cup my ear to the door. Sometimes I hear movement; the sound of her dressing, of her muttering to herself like she always does. That's not a symptom of her illness. It's just how she is. Somehow she finds solace in talking to the walls.

On other days it's deathly silent in there, and those are the days that scare me. Today is one of them, so I quickly click open the door and guide my eyes to her bed. She lies on her back, her chest moving steadily up and down. I can see glimmers of sweat beading on her forehead, a grimace of pain on her face. It's rare to see her with another expression these days.

It's not always physical pain, though. Today, I know it's different. Today, I'm to be tested. Tomorrow, I'll get the results. It's the same for every school leaver across the mainland regions. We're told it's the same for those who live on the sea cities too. So every parent is suffering the same this morning. None of them truly know where their children will be when next week dawns.

I watch my mother for a moment before lightly shutting the door and returning to my room to dress. I pack my school uniform into a bag – long grey shorts that fall below the knee, a simple white shirt, scuffed black shoes – and dress in my Pickers' gear: hardy but light clothes intended for manual outdoor work, but breezy enough to remain comfortable under the sweltering sun.

I'm not actually an official Picker. That's my mother's duty, but most days she's too ill to work. Our Leader, Bette, lets me fill in for her to keep up her quota. Otherwise, she wouldn't get her rations and she'd starve. That's how it is here. Everyone needs to have a use. If they don't, they're considered expendable.

Before I leave, I check my look in the cracked mirror in my room, tying my long golden hair back into a ponytail. I get some funny looks at school these days, because I'm starting to resemble an adult already with my tanned skin and sparkling hair. Most kids stay inside during the day out of the sun, but as a fill-in Picker for my mother, I've seen my fair share of it over the last few years. It's already given me a slightly more weather beaten look than most kids my age, and a brighter golden tinge to my hair as well.

There are bags under my eyes too. They probably don't look so stark because of my golden colouring, but they're still clear enough. Symptoms of early mornings, late evenings, and a woeful lack of sleep for a girl my age.

During the summer months it's too hot to pick during the day, so we all have to start work just after sunrise, and then get back to work once the heat of the day has subsided. That means an early shift for me, then school, and then back to the orchards and fruit fields for another shift in the evening. Sometimes I feel like I'm going to pass out by the end of the day, but I need to keep going. If I don't, my mother won't get her rations and I won't have enough to trade for medicines. So it's not really a choice. It's a duty. That's pretty much how everything works around here.

Our living quarters are small and in a building shared with others. It's more like a long, single level structure, with a flat roof covered in solar panelling to generate electricity. Apparently it was once used for housing soldiers and was called a barracks. But we just call it The Block.

My mother's room is adjoined to mine as part of our two room housing allotment. Hers is the only real bedroom, intended as the marital room. Mine isn't a bedroom at all, though. Rather several rooms stuffed into one. Inside is a kitchenette, sink, storage units, and triple bunk beds. My brother and sister used to join me in them before they left for their duties, but now I have a choice of where to sleep. I generally choose the bottom one.

I step out into the corridor and walk towards the front door of the building, passing several other doors as I go. They're marked with surnames indicating the families that live inside.

Marshall.

Pietersen.

Slattery.

Ours says Drayton. That's my surname. I've never cared much for it, or my first name. My mother named us all with a 'C' at the beginning like her. So my brother was Carson and my sister was Cassie. I've always thought I pulled the short straw when she called me Cyra.

The corridor is already active at 5.30 in the morning. I hear frantic activity as people dress for their duties inside their apartments, see doors opening up ahead as they step out in their uniforms. Many in this block work as Pickers, but there are a couple who are Breeders and Labourers.

I join a group of Pickers out in the square outside the building. It's enclosed by several other residential buildings and is mainly used as a pick up point for different groups. During July the Pickers get picked up at 5.45 to be taken to the orchards for the morning shift. That changes through the year depending on when it's light. During winter, when it's not quite so hot, all workers tend to work through the day to make the most of the available daylight.

There's a gathering of different age groups around me. I'm the youngest, because I'm still in school and aren't an official Picker. There are others who were assigned last year when they finished school. They're only 17. Then the ages gradually increase all the way up to Madge, who's 78. Not many people get as far as her, mostly because they either die or have family willing to take care of them when they can no longer work.

Madge has no family, however, so unless she works she won't get her rations. For someone leading such a bleak existence, she always seems remarkably upbeat. Her smile is one of the only things that keeps me going some mornings. This morning is one of them.

At 5.45 on the dot, our solar powered bus silently pulls up into the dusty square. Bette sits behind the controls, her face craggy and weathered from too many summers. She's got this croak to her voice when she speaks, a result of spending much of the day bleating and barking orders at people. The orchards where we work are close to the crop fields where huge harvesting machines chug across the landscape. They're loud, so Bette's needed to shout over them for the last 30 years.

If I didn't know her better I might be a bit intimidated, but she was always close to my mother, ever since they went to school together. That's why she's allowed me to step in for her when another Leader might have sought out a full time worker to help them meet their quota.

It's all quotas here. Quotas for the Pickers. Quotas for the Leaders. Quotas for the Supervisor who oversees the entire town. All the way up to the top of the tree. Everyone's accountable to someone else. That's what keeps people in order.

"On the bus," croaks Bette, her voice even more creaky in the morning.

We all pile on and silently sit down. No one has much energy for chit chat in the mornings. The orchards are about 2 miles from our town of Arbor, so it doesn't take long to get there. When we arrive, we march out and set straight to work. Within 10 minutes the worker chants have already started. They're supposed to help with both productivity and motivation. Sing a song and you'll forget you're picking fruit all day. I suppose Pickers aren't the brightest people in the world or they'd have been assigned somewhere else.

The sun hots up as the morning progresses, and by 8 AM everyone is allowed a short break. They immediately scuttle to the nearest shade for some respite from the sun, soaking their shirts in water from a trough and draping them back over their bodies. The sight of steam rising from weary limbs as the clothes quickly dry creates a small cloud of fog over the apple trees.

I don't join them though. It's not that I'm antisocial, it's because I've got to get to school. I see Bette nodding at me from across the orchard and go fetch my bag from the bus, where I change into my school uniform. Eyes linger on me jealously as I go. Their fate is set, yet mine is still open. I bet half of them are expecting me to join them all full time next week though.

The walk to school takes about 30 minutes cutting

through crop fields. People are busy at work wherever I go, tending the fields and animals, processing the food in the large factories and warehouses that line the edge of town. Our town of Arbor is one of many in Agricola, the region dedicated to farming and agriculture. *Feed the World.* That's our motto. That's our duty. I wonder if it will be *my* duty too. For my mother's sake, it has to be. I'm the one who needs to take care of her.

There's a buzz when I get to school. It's a nervous energy, rather than one of excitement. My eyes search for one face through the crowd, but I don't see him. I look over faces brimming with anxious smiles, and those hung in deflation. Most will already know their fates. They'll have seen their mothers and fathers already living them. They can expect to stay in Agricola, whether in Arbor or elsewhere. It's not a life that warrants any particular enthusiasm.

I feel a hand touch my back and turn to see my best friend, Jackson, right behind me. It always amazes me how quietly he can creep up on me like that. He looks particularly weary after several days away from school. Coming from a family of Leaders who work the fields, Jackson's always had exemption from attending a lot of school so he can work and learn the trade. He knows, more than anyone, that his duty isn't going to change.

He's got a rugged appearance and arms packed with sinewy muscle, making him look much older than he is. When he does appear in class, he looks like an adult coming to sit in with the kids for the day. Like the adults, his skin is golden and weather worn by the sun, and his hair a sparkling blond. To say he's old beyond his years would be an understatement. He accepted long ago that his future lay in tilling the earth and growing food to keep everyone else alive.

When I turn to face him I get the feeling he wants to pull me in for a hug. He steps forward a touch before glancing around with his eyes and moving back. Any sign of affection among minors is counted as a strike, even a hug among friends. It's only in our quieter moments together that we're able to show any sort of intimacy beyond a smile.

"You all set for today?" he asks me.

I nod, peering around at our gathered classmates. "I'll do as badly a I can. Then it's just the final test."

"It'll be OK, Cyra. Your mum will have support whatever happens. Don't worry too much about it."

I shake my head. "No, no, I'm not worried. Even if I'm sent to a nearby town as a Picker I'll still be able to visit and can have some of my rations sent back."

I see the briefest downturn in Jackson's eye that tells me he's not quite so sure. "I mean, people never get sent away, right? I've lived my entire life in Arbor and have helped as a Picker for years, on and off."

Jackson nods and makes sure to keep eye contact with me this time, but the inflection in his words still doesn't convince me. "Absolutely Cy, let's just wait and see what happens, shall we? Just, you know, keep with the plan. It's only the last part that you can't control."

A loud creak sounds behind me and I turn back to

12

the crowd. The large double doors to the school open and the Principal stands in the doorway, flanked by a couple of uptight looking women in matching light grey suits. Both have their dark hair pulled back into bobs, their faces stern and severe. Two women from the testing board no doubt.

Principal Lewis speaks first, raising his arms to calm the chattering crowd.

"Right now everyone, today is the day. Just relax and do as well as you can. As we know, if it's meant to be, it will be. These two lovely women will address you first in the main hall. Please file in sensibly and take your seats. Boys to the right, and girls to the left."

Jackson and I glance at each other and smirk. As if we don't all know that by now. Boys and girls are always separated, whatever we're doing. In class, in the hall, during lunch. It's a wonder they don't have separate schools to teach us in.

Gradually everyone files into the main hall, taking their positions. I steer myself to the back, as does Jackson, so that we can find a spot near to each other across the walkway going down the middle of the hall. I've always chosen to sit at the back, whether in the bus going to the orchards, in class, or in the hall. I guess I like to know what's in front of me at all times.

Once more Principal Lewis steps forward at the front of the stage to formally introduce the two testers. It must be fairly hard for him, having to do this year after year. He looks straight forward down the gap between us as he speaks, trying not to run his eyes over the sea of glum faces. By now there are probably tears being spilled here and there. Tomorrow will be worse though. That's when we get our results.

When he's done, he steps back and sinks into a chair at the side. I watch as he wipes his brow and lightly shakes his head. Then the two women appear, standing straight, one looking over the boys, and the other looking over the girls. From this distance they could be twins, but for their differing height.

The taller one speaks first, her chin upright and eyes set over the boys. I catch Jackson out of the corner of my eye trying to stifle a laugh at her appearance. You get no one like them out in the fields. By the look of their white skin, they'd probably shrivel into a crisp after a day under the sun.

"Good morning, boys and girls," she starts, her voice as shrill as her appearance. "Today is testing day for the Duty Call. Tomorrow you will be assigned your duties. Please don't be nervous. As your principal says, if it's meant to be, it will be."

I see a motion of dropping heads as she speaks the de facto mantra for the regions. I suppose some people believe it. That we're all born for something, to fit a role in the world. For me, it's more like a prison sentence. Stuck doing the same thing for life. In some ways I'd rather be banished. Die, get ill, get caught by the rebels. At least I'd be free.

"Now, where you get assigned will be based on three things. Firstly, your performance throughout your schooling life, as well as any other factors outside of it." I know that here she's talking about situations like Jackson's, where he's literally been trained to work in the fields already. Me too, working as a Picker for my mother. That will also be taken into consideration.

Now the other woman speaks, her voice a little softer but still no less grating. "Secondly," she says, looking specifically over the girls, "you will be tested today. Physical and aptitude tests. These are your final opportunities to show what you can do."

"Finally," says the tall woman again, "you will go through the genetics test. Now don't be alarmed if that sounds unusual to you. This is merely a way for us to examine your inner 'blueprint' to discover any untapped potential you may have. Remember, we aren't always gifted at school, but may have a whole treasure trove of wonders to unlock within."

A murmuring sounds around the room, which I find odd because we've all known how the three stages of testing works for a long time. You'd think that half the hall had only just found out.

"So, even if you haven't had the most auspicious career at school, or if you don't perform well in the physical and aptitude tests, it doesn't mean it's the end. It's quite common for us to find a rough diamond who may even be assigned to Eden. You just never know."

Now the murmuring has grown to a light rumble of chatter. I can even hear distinct excitement among the audience. Again, I look at Jackson and we simultaneously shake our heads and roll our eyes.

"Right, the girls will start with their physical and aptitude testing first, with the boys having the genetics test. If the ladies would follow me, we can get started."

"And please, gentlemen, if you'd accompany me we can all get going," says the tall woman. "The sooner we finish, the sooner we can break for lunch."

The sound of scraping chairs fills the room as the boys and girls begin filing out in opposite directions. I turn to see Jackson hop quickly towards me and slide his hand over my palm. "Good luck," he says quietly. "Do your worst."

Then he hops back just as quickly, a smile dancing on his face, and joins the back of the boys.

Do my worst. That's precisely the plan.

2
The Testing

Once Jackson's left, I turn to join the back of the girls filing out of the hall by the left passage. There's a bit more spring in everyone's step now, after the testers' assurance that the final genetics test might be their ticket to a better life elsewhere.

It's true that some people have hidden qualities that their school lives and exam results don't show up, but for most it's little more than a dream. And clutching at hope will only make things worse come tomorrow, when everyone gets assigned their duties.

I trail in behind a few girls who are now giddily discussing the possibility of where they might be sent. Aside from the regions on the mainland, there are some nicer places on the coast, although they're generally populated by ship-builders, marine engineers, and traders. You generally need a sharp mind to be sent there, and our school in Arbor isn't particularly known to churn out geniuses.

Then there are the sea cities. They were built a long time ago to cater to the growing need for space as the world became overpopulated and underfed, and the earth grew parched and dry. Only the most important are sent there to perform the most important roles. Politicians, scientists, the wealthy and famous. Those that run the country and push it forward. Those in control. I don't know of anyone from Arbor who's been sent to a sea city before. I think the last was before my time.

We move down a passageway towards another part of the school, populated with study rooms and social chambers for the different school years. They're all separated, of course, between the boys and girls.

The smaller tester stops outside the social chamber for our year and steps to the side, before ushering us all into the room. As usual, I make my way to the back to find a place to stand.

"We're going to start by splitting you into two groups. Letters A through M will start with the physical tests and letters N through Z will begin with the mental aptitude tests. Please, split into your two groups now."

A few confused looks are passed around before people realise she's talking about our surnames. I see a friend, Amy Appleby, move to the right and follow suit. After a bit of shuffling we've all gathered into two roughly equal sized groups on opposite sides of the room.

"OK, group A through M, please proceed down the corridor towards the main gym. You know the way. I will be taking care of the aptitude testing, but we have brought our own gym master to supervise your performance for the physical tests."

At that she shoos us away with a light flutter of her hands until we're all out of the room.

The gym is only a short walk to the end of the corridor, where it opens out into a large room filled with various types of equipment. I don't quite know what the point of physical testing is, but am sure it's not as important as the others. I suppose it's testing more than just strength, but things like spacial awareness and coordination, although quite what use such things have are still beyond me. I guess the testing board know what they're doing.

When we reach the gym there's another tester waiting for us, this time a man. He's dressed in light grey, like the others, although his outfit is more like a boiler suit. His skin colour is, like the others, pale, and his hair dark and closely cut to his scalp. I'm beginning to get the impression that these testers don't see the sun all that much.

The first thing he does is instruct us to go to the changing room and dress in the appropriate outfits there. They're similar to his, grey and dull and with a funny smell, like they've been used several times before without a wash. When we return, he calls upon us to get into alphabetical order, before sending us back into the changing rooms to wait our turn. A quick look down the line tells me I'm in 7th position.

I can see the other girls twitching nervously as my friend, Amy Appleby, steps out. When she returns 10 minutes later, her cheeks have turned a special kind of crimson and her blonde hair is dark with sweat. She gives me an abbreviated smile before stumbling towards the shower facilities at the back.

It takes about an hour before I'm called up, at which point I happily skip to my feet. Unlike the other girls, I'm not nervous. No, this is going to be the quickest ten minutes of my life.

The test goes just as I expect. Speed drills, strength tests like clambering across bars and doing push ups. I perform spectacularly badly, of course, although even if I'd tried my best I doubt I'd have done much better. I decide half way through that this form of testing is more specifically aimed at the boys in an attempt to discover who might be fit for certain labour duties. I know that when Jackson steps up, he'll ace it. Half his life is spent at work already.

When I walk out I'm hardly even out of breath, and I get a look from the tester that says he knows what I'm up to. I'd imagine that a lot of people try to under perform during the physical stuff to avoid being sent for hard labour anywhere. For the majority of the boys, though, there will be no way to avoid it.

Next up are the mental aptitude tests, which I'm sure will be equally easy to fail at. Our group is taken to a room full of computers and odd equipment I've never seen before. It looks as though it's all been brought in just for today.

For the next two hours I carefully make sure I get just about every answer wrong. Some I get right on purpose to make things look real, and others I miss out altogether. I spend half my time glancing at the other girls, their foreheads creased with frowns, their heads shaking lightly with resignation as they encounter a puzzle they have no chance of getting right.

Logic, problem solving, strategic reasoning, the

ability to assimilate information and learn new skills. Just about every corner of someone's mental capacity is being probed at here. Yet all this is pointless for these girls. All their parents are Pickers and Labourers, Breeders and Planters. That's all they're going to be as well.

I guess it's different for me. I don't dream like the rest of them. I don't hope that some test is going to alter my life. I don't even want any of that. I want to stay here, with my mother, where I can take care of her. Where I can go to work full time and save enough rations to eventually buy her some proper medication. Not the stuff that just keeps her symptoms at bay, but the real stuff. The stuff that will cure her.

At lunch I manage to catch sight of Jackson chatting with a bunch of the boys. I don't know what he's saying, but it's commanding their attention. He's always been like that. I suppose it's the fact that he seems so much older than everyone else, so they hang on his every word. I just know that every girl in school is hoping to be Paired with him. If they're going to be destined to life in Arbor, being Paired with Jackson Kane would be a great silver lining.

His eyes raise to mine across the tables and he gives me a look of 'how's it going'? All I do is nod at him and smile. All the boys look in good spirits, though, so I suspect the genetics test is just as the tall woman said – nothing to worry about.

If it's meant to be, it will be.

I hate that damn mantra. It all just seems so draconian to me. The entire point of Pairing is to put two people who are similar together. They marry and their kids will grow up learning the same trade. When those kids finish school at 16, they're assigned to what suits them best, which is almost inevitably going to be what their parents have been doing.

So, how is that fair? *If it's meant to be, it will be.* Right, but it's all manufactured isn't it? A huge set up to keep people where they belong. There's no way of escaping the rut that your life becomes. No way of bettering yourself or doing something you actually enjoy. Pickers' kids become Pickers. Planters' kids become Planters. It's all like one big carousel, and around and around she goes.

My thoughts are broken by the sound of the tall, shrill woman, clapping her hands and demanding our attention. She orders the boys to follow her through towards the gym for the second round of testing, while our tester leads us off for our genetics test.

We once again arrange ourselves alphabetically before she begins reiterating what she and her stretched out doppelganger told us earlier in the hall.

"All you need to do is relax and lie back. There's nothing you can do here. You have no control over this particular test."

She smiles a sickly smile, although I know it's meant to appear friendly, and slides her eyes over every girl in the room.

No control. That rings a bell. No one has any control over anything here.

"Now, the machine is intended to examine your

inner 'blueprint', as we like to call it. It will decipher any particular abilities you may have that might set you aside from the crowd. You really never know what you might find in the most unlikely of places."

Now she's telling us a story about a boy from Fossor, a mining region to the north. His parents were Miners, and each of their parents too. Two brothers, a sister. All worked in and around the mines. This boy, of course, was found to have some fantastic ability that no one saw coming, blossomed, and flew the nest. I begin to lose interest in her story as she tells it, and don't catch the end. Frankly, it all sounds like made up rubbish intended to give people hope.

Hope. It's meant to keep order, but I don't look at it that way. It's just another way to subjugate people, to keep them under the boot. This test, for all I know, is just another method used to distract us. Smoke and mirrors designed to appease everyone and make them think that, yes, this is precisely where they belong. They're Miners. They're Pickers. They're Labourers and Builders. That's all they are and ever will be.

All the while those folk on Eden, the central hub of power, are laughing at how stupid we are. Designing new ways to keep us down and doing the jobs they don't want to do. They pair us with each other, design a system that is meant to ensure the future of our nation, one designed to push us forward. Make sure that everyone is doing what they're best at. *If it's meant to be, it will be.*

Total and utter rubbish.

I tune in again just in time to see our short, stubby tester finish her tale with "so, you just never know where you might end up."

I've half a mind to stand up and argue back to her. To tell her that, for as long as I know, nobody from this school has escaped the mainland. That the hundreds I've seen go through the Duty Call have all ended up either staying in Agricola or, if they're super super lucky, being sent down towards the coastal regions.

But I say nothing, because really, there's no point. In fact, I don't even know why I'm grinding my teeth so hard as I listen to her. As I watch her smile with this false warmth at us. All I care about is staying near my mother so I can care for her. Everything else is irrelevant to me.

We go into the testing room one by one. Our tester tells us that it will take about 5 to 10 minutes for the machine to 'read' us. The idea that any machine can know what someone's potential might be is slightly ridiculous to me, although I really have no idea what those scientists over on Eden are cooking up. As far as I've heard, there's almost an entire level dedicated to scientific research there, which is hard to believe given the city's size. All I've seen are pictures, but from the outside it looks like an enormous platform in the ocean, spanning several square miles with several levels, some of which are apparently underwater.

For me, it's like reading some science fiction book. I've never even seen the ocean, so the thought of giant platform cities being built out to sea is as odd as going to live on the moon.

The girls file in one at a time, starting with Amy Appleby. I wonder if she'll become a teacher at the school here, or maybe somewhere else in the region. She's always had this way with people, an ability to help them learn or guide them to a conclusion without giving them an answer outright. In class she's always been the brightest spark. If anyone was to leave the region, it would be her. At the least, she shouldn't be out toiling in the fields, she's too delicate for that. And her father's a teacher here, so I suppose it's in the family.

She reappears after about 10 minutes with a smile on her face. That doesn't really say much. She's always smiling, like old Madge out in the orchards. The girls start asking her how it all went, so she stands ahead of them, giving them the outline to help them stay at ease. I can tell that some, despite the tester's assurances, are still a bit worried.

"It's nothing, really," she says in her sweet, comforting voice. "All you do is lie down on this bed and a large scanner hovers over you. That's all. You don't do anything else."

"Does it hurt?" asks a girl.

She shakes her head. "No, no, not at all. It's quite relaxing, actually. It makes a nice humming sound."

Several girls go in before me. Their stays last differing amounts of time. Some are there only about 3 or 4 minutes, while others stay for up to 10. Before long, it's my turn to step up.

When I enter through the door, I see the bed and the hovering scanner, just as Amy described. Again, this equipment is alien to me, and must have been brought by the testers.

"Please lie down on the bed miss, er, Drayton," says the stubby woman, glancing down at her electronic tablet to check my name.

I walk over and do as ordered. The bed's warm from the bodies before me.

"Now, this should only take a few minutes, Cyra. Just lie back with your head in the mould and relax. It won't hurt, but you may feel a warming sensation from the scanner."

I do as I'm told once more, lying with my head facing up as the scanner glides into view. I can still see the tester, out of the corner of my eye, controlling the machine using the tablet in her hand. She glides her finger over it and the scanner continues to move until it's positioned exactly over my body.

"OK Cyra, are you ready?"

She doesn't wait for a reply. She taps a button again and immediately the screen above me starts glowing to life. I see patterns of what look like electrical currents shooting over its pale yellow surface as it starts to purr gently. Like Amy said, it is quite soothing.

I feel my eyes beginning to relax as I stare at the screen. The sparks of blue electricity are soon joined by red ones. Then purple. They dance together above me creating a rhythmic, entrancing, show of lights. I've never seen anything quite so mesmerising.

I begin to slip, almost into a dream. Flashes appear

in front of my eyes, like pictures on a wall, snapshots in time. I see the ocean, lapping against the shore. There are giant ports, huge warehouses nearby housing massive ships under construction. I see the coast again, but this time from the sea. Then a towering platform, giant waves churning against massive pylons launching it above the water. I see a wall, sprawling and cutting across a wasteland, as far as the eye can see. There are men there, men in uniform, standing atop it like silent guardians. Then I see a face, captured in a moment of pain. People surround her, holding her hand. Her eyes are lifeless. People weep.

It's the face of my dead mother.

I snap my eyes open and suddenly it's crackling lights of blue and red and purple that I see again. The outline of the screen comes into focus and the fog beyond it clears. In the corner of my eye I can still see the tester, sitting silently in her chair. I arch my head slightly and look at her. She's lost in her tablet as before, her eyes locked to it, unblinking.

As I stare at her I feel the warmth of the scanner begin to fade, the calming hum grow quiet. She shakes her head lightly from side to side before raising her eyes up to me. She seems surprised to see me staring at her, and immediately plants that rehearsed smile back on her face.

"Well, Cyra, I think we're all about finished here." Her words are more jumpy than normal. "Please sit up and let me look at you."

I feel unexpectedly drained as I pull my body up to sit on the edge of the bed. The tester moves around in front of me and puts her hand to my chin. She lifts it, gently, before leaning in and staring into my eyes.

"Um, is everything OK?" I mumble.

"Oh, yes, quite all right. It's protocol to check the eyes after the test."

I don't ask her why. Frankly, I don't actually care.

"I saw things," I say. She immediately leans back and her eyes focus on mine.

"Yes?" she says, nodding.

"Is that normal? I saw things I've never seen in real life before." Right now the only thing I have seen is that expression on my mother's face. That grimace of pain. I see that almost every day. Those lifeless eyes are what I'm most afraid of seeing each morning.

"Um, yes. It does...happen." Her tone is hardly convincing.

She steps back once more, before picking up her tablet. "OK Cyra, if you'd send the next girl in, that would be lovely."

When I stand my body feels heavy, so heavy I almost stumble. It feels like I've been up for days without rest, like that scanner sucked just about every ounce of energy from my body. Maybe that's what it does to 'read your blueprint' or whatever they told us. But then, none of the other girls seemed tired when they walked out.

I'm ushered to the door by the tester, who I still catch looking at me in a sort of curious way. "OK Cyra, I'll see you tomorrow at the Duty Call. You're free to go home, if you wish."

Home. Yeah, right. I've still got a Picker shift to get through before then.

I pace sleepily down the hall and back into the waiting room to instruct the next girl to go ahead. When I enter, I encounter more odd looks and wonder if I look funny in some way. That maybe the scanner made me go red all over or that my hair's suddenly turned blue and red and purple like those lights.

They stare at me in unison as I walk in, following my footsteps. I hear whispers as the next girl in line steps up and moves past me to the door. Before I have a chance to ask anyone what's going on, I lift my eyes to the back wall. On it hangs a clock, its hands endlessly ticking round and round.

But they have to be wrong. It's got to be broken. When I went in the time said 2.30. Now it says 3.35. *It will only take between 5 and 10 minutes*, she told us.

And I took over an hour.

3

Roamers and the Woods

I wake the next morning following a night of dreams. I can only remember sparse details: crashing waves, structures emerging from the middle of the sea, a sunset over the desert. Most of all, however, I recall the face of my mother, lifeless and still. It's the same image I saw yesterday under the scanner.

My usual routine is to immediately check on her, afraid that during the night she'd have taken a turn for the worst. But this morning I don't need to. This morning, it's her who's checking on me.

She's there when my eyes crack open, her weary face lit up by the splinters of sunlight cutting in through the curtains. She's grown more pale these last few years, and more haggard too. It pains me sometimes when I remember how beautiful she was. Those big blue eyes have turned grey with her affliction; her golden hair and skin have gone pallid.

Yet I still see the light of who she was shining inside her. When she smiles she still lights up the room, brings a glow to my heart that only she can do. I can't remember the last time I woke to see her face like this. Before she grew ill, it would be every morning, kissing each of us on the cheeks before she set out to the orchard. Now, though, it's me who checks on her.

"Big day today," she whispers.

I can see a sadness on her face, hidden beneath her smile. I've seen the same look before on the day of my brother and sisters' Duty Call. Both were sent to other parts of Agricola, where there was a need for more workers. It's the hardest day of a mother's life. For some, it's the last time they'll ever see their children.

I nod as I sit up on the bottom bunk and hold my hand to her forehead. She's warm, but not as hot as some days.

"How are you feeling today?" I ask, staring into her cloudy grey eyes.

She reaches to my hand and brings it down to her lap before gripping it tight between hers. I can see a tear forming in the corner of her eye as she says: "OK."

She turns her head from me in an attempt to conceal her watery eyes. I wonder how long she's been there, beside my bunk, just looking at me. Thinking that this might be it, the last time we see each other. Carson and Cassie are rarely able to visit. If I go, she'll be left all alone.

It's only now that I notice she's wearing her Pickers outfit. It doesn't quite fit her like it used to, the fabric looking slightly more baggy against her withered frame.

She answers the look on my face without me saying a word. "It's OK honey, I feel well enough to work today." It's been several weeks since she was last out in the fields, and that was only a single shift.

"You shouldn't have to think about working today."

"But I don't mind, really," I say. The truth is that I actually quite want to go to work. The last thing I want is to dwell on the Duty Call. Dwell on what happened yesterday at the testing. "You should rest mum. You're in no condition to work right now."

Her face stiffens slightly at my words. "No, Cyra, I need to do this. I have to stop relying on you. By the end of today, it may be just..."

"Don't say it," I cut in. "Don't even think like that. I'm not going anywhere."

My mother nods, but I know she doesn't believe it. She's already seen her first two children get dragged off, so why not me?

The sound of activity reaches us from the corridor outside. Doors opening and shutting and the murmur of morning greetings as people shuffle off into the square outside to wait for their pick ups.

"It's nearing 5.45 honey. I need to go. I'll be at the school later."

My mother gives me a kiss before I can protest and slips out of the door to join the march. I move to the only window by the front wall and watch as she emerges into the morning light. People surround her, no doubt asking her how she is. Usually their questions would relate to her illness. Today they could just as easily be about the Duty Call.

I watch as Madge shuffles up towards her and gives her a hug. For the first time in a while, there's no smile on her face. It's more a look of condolence, and brings my mother to tears. I watch from the window, helpless, as she breaks down in old

Madge's tanned, leathery arms. Some come and say kind words of support. Others glance over and turn back to their conversations. Seeing a mother breaking down is no great surprise on the day of the Duty Call.

I turn away, unable to watch any longer. It's the same each year. Mothers falling apart in the street, unable to cope. They'll be crumbling this morning; out in the fields, in the sorting warehouses, across Agricola and all the other regions.

By the end of the day some of those tears will be of happiness. Delight that their children will be assigned nearby, or perhaps that they've been given a duty that is safe or carries some esteem. Others will be inconsolable, losing their kids to arduous duties hundreds, even thousands, of miles away. Knowing that they may only see them rarely, if at all, or that they're assigned work so dangerous that their life will most likely be cut short.

The room is spilling with the light of dawn when I decide I can't be there any more. I dress in my school uniform and make my way across town towards the outskirts, passing through the merchant sector where the rations are exported. We only export food here, sending it away to the other regions and sea cities. Crops, fruits, vegetables, livestock. They're all grown and manufactured and turned into food, which is then exported all over. That's why they call our region the *Breadbasket*.

There's a bustling merchant sector in every major town through Agricola. Food exported out and other goods brought in. The currency we all live with is food. It's the true currency of the world now. I guess, in some way, that gives us a bit of power. If we all put our hands up and said 'nope, we're not doing it any more' I don't know what would happen. I've read about things called *strikes* that people used to do a long time ago. They'd stop working until their demands were met. Maybe that's something we should arrange.

Beyond the merchant sector is more residential housing, primarily for Labourers and Animal Handers. Most of the field labour is done on this side of town, and the livestock is cared for and nurtured in huge pens stretching for miles across the landscape beyond. There are old farms here that were built centuries ago, made from stone and brick and strong wood. They're so much more beautiful than the converted military barracks most people live in. Our building is very much built for purpose, not pleasure. Here, though, there is at least some beauty.

One farm houses Jackson and his family. They actually occupy the entire thing, which amazed me the first time I heard about it. Both his parents were assigned to be Leaders, and since then he and his brothers have been groomed for the same work. Two of them are older and already live there with the girls they were Paired with. The other is younger, but, like Jackson, gets exemption from school sometimes to work the fields.

I always feel nervous when I creep towards his house. Leaders are generally fierce people, and no one is meant to spend time with anyone of the opposite sex outside of school. The thought is that it will cause upset when people are Paired, and may make it more difficult for the new pair to bond.

That didn't stop us, though. I was only a little girl when he stumbled across me in the fields. I'd tripped on a jutting root when playing and badly twisted my ankle. He found me and helped me back to my house several miles away.

Since then we've always had this bond. We'd look at each other across the class at school and communicate with secret smiles and eye movements. As we grew we learned how serious an offence it was to spend time together outside of school. None of the other kids were doing it, even if they wanted to, and yet it didn't stop us. There was something special about having a forbidden friendship that appealed to both of us.

Over the last couple of years, though, it's become more difficult for us to keep our desires at bay. There's something more than friendship between us, but we both refuse to act upon it. It will only make things harder when we're inevitably Paired with other people.

It's still early morning when I reach the downstairs window occupied by Jackson. I know that all of his family, except perhaps his younger brother, will be out working their duties already. If it wasn't the morning of the Duty Call, he'd be out there too.

I tap lightly on the glass and wait for him to appear. I've never been inside, but have seen through his window on a couple of occasions. The first time, I almost fell over at the size of his room. It's about the size of mine and my mother's entire living quarters, and it's only him in there. His family get better rations as well, being Leaders. As far as things go, that's not a bad deal for the region.

He looks bleary eyed when he appears and I can't help but laugh at his appearance: blond hair sticking out at funny angles, eyes squinting at the bright morning sunshine, lips chafed and cracked from the heat. He looks at me with a feigned annoyance for being woken up. This is one of the few days he actually gets to sleep in, and I've gone and ruined it. He tells me all that with a joking stare through the glass, before pulling the curtains shut, and leaving me staring at my reflection.

I retreat to a safe distance from the house and wait for the front door to open. A few minutes later he appears, hair put back in order, face now brightly lit with a smile. He paces casually towards me, staring up at the big blue sky, his hands locked into his pockets.

"Nice day for a Duty Call," he says. We've learned that it's easiest to try to make light of the situation. When you end up dwelling on it, that's when the crying starts.

"I'd prefer it to be raining," I respond. "Then everyone's tears will be hidden!"

Jackson laughs and checks to the left and right as he reaches me. There's no one around. He slips his hand out of his pocket and slides his fingers gently over my palm. It's a sign of affection that people use in the region. Somewhere between a warm smile and a tender hug. It's pretty much all we can get away with, unless we know we're completely alone.

"The Grove?" he asks, and I nod in reply.

It's a place we go when we want to be alone. The only place we can actually meet outside of school without people getting suspicious. We used to meet there a lot, before his and my duties became more of a burden. Now we're lucky if we can spend more than a fleeting hour together every week or two.

It takes us about 20 minutes to walk there along a track that runs adjacent to some corn fields just off the edge of town. Out here, there are no Custodians, the men and women tasked with making sure things run smoothly in each town and region. Some of them are stationed at specific posts, like those in the warehouses and granaries who make sure no one steals any rations. Others are assigned to roam freely, making sure that no criminal acts are performed. I don't know what their official titles are, but they've become locally known across the region as Roamers.

Out here, however, I've never seen one. They generally stick close to town and will wander to the more populous areas like the merchant sector, or even the orchards, to keep an eye on everything. The one good thing about them is that they're easy to spot. Their uniforms are made from white reflective material that is meant to keep them cool, so often they catch the light and you can see them glinting in the distance.

At the end of the corn fields there's a small section of woodland that is considered to have no real use. Time will tell whether it will be chopped down for wood, but for now it's still standing. It's what

Jackson and I call the Grove, and for all the years we've gone there we've never run into anyone else. Amid this world of flat lands and open fields, it's the only place where we can see each other in private without the eyes of the world looking in.

There's a large log about halfway in that we sit on. It's the remains of an old tree that must have fallen down in a storm some time ago, and creates a small clearing in the centre. It's always so peaceful in there, with only the fluttering of leaves and the whistling of birds disturbing the silence. We know, in the middle of that thicket, that we can talk freely without fear that a Roamer will see or hear us.

Today, despite our attempts at making light of everything, I know that this might be the last time we sit here together. It's a sobering thought, and one that's hard to escape. For months, years even, we've moved towards this day, one neither of us can escape. It was right here, several years ago, that we made the plan for me to perform poorly in school once my mother got sick. Every time we've spoken, it's been a hot topic of conversation, something I've worked towards for years. Stay close to my mother. Stay close to Jackson. Beyond that, I never considered anything. Not the potential arduousness of a life as a Picker. Not the fact that Jackson will almost certainly be Paired with someone else, and so will I. I suppose there's a small chance that we might be Paired together, but it's so remote that it's not something we've ever bothered to talk about.

We sit, as we always do, straddling the log and looking at each other. Most times we meet we have plenty of questions for each other, plenty to say. Not today. Today we sit for a while in silent reflection, intermittently catching eyes with each other, but predominantly looking around at the foliage enclosing us, sparkling under the low morning sun.

Eventually Jackson breaks the silence with the topic that's troubling me the most.

"So, how did everything go yesterday?" he asks, his voice a little strained. Clearly he's noticed the look on my face. By now he's had plenty of practice reading my facial expressions.

I don't lie to Jackson. I never do. He's the one person I'm fully truthful with, the one person I confide in over my mother and family and everything else in my life. But today, of all days, I break the trend. Today I don't want to tell him the truth because, I suppose, I don't know what the truth is.

Until the Duty Call later, all I can do is speculate as to what happened during my genetics test. And there's no way Jackson can help me come to any conclusion about why I was in there for so much longer than everyone else. As to why I saw such vivid images of things I've never seen before. As to why the small tester woman looked so curiously at me. All those things give me a dull feeling in the pit of my stomach. A feeling that today might be my last day in Arbor. My last day with my mother. My last day with Jackson.

"It went fine," is all I say.

Jackson gives me a probing look.

"Are you sure? You seem a bit...I don't know. A bit quiet."

"Well, it's just...today. It's all been leading to today."

He knows what I mean. Every single person involved in the Duty Call has a right to be quiet or angry or scared on this day. No type of behaviour or emotion really needs an explanation.

"How about you though? Did you find all those physical tests as pointless as me?"

"What do you mean?"

"Well," I say with a derisive laugh, "what does it matter how fast we can run and how many push ups we can do. I still can't believe that that part of the testing process is still going."

"Is that all you did?" he asks. "Push ups and running?"

"Well, more or less. There were a few other things to test co-ordination, I guess, and reflexes. Not exactly going to be helpful for the people around here. Who needs to be able to run like a cheetah when all they're doing is picking or packing fruit all day?!"

I laugh, but Jackson doesn't join me. In fact, he's got this questioning look on his face, like what I'm saying makes no sense.

"So that's it? You didn't do any virtual reality testing?"

Now it's my turn to be confused. "Um, no. We were in there for about 10 minutes each and that was it. I did think that maybe the whole thing was more for the boys, but had no idea about any virtual reality test."

"Yeah, I had no idea coming into it either. I told my brothers when I got home and neither of them had done it. Seems like it's a new thing. I guess it was only for the boys."

"Weird. So what happened?"

"It was bizarre Cy, really strange. They had this machine that you lay down in and they put this headset on you. I swear I felt like I was in there for hours, but when I came back out it had only been a few minutes."

I'm starting to realize why Jackson looked so exhausted when I woke him up.

"And what did you do in there?"

"Loads. Teamwork exercises. Leadership exercises. It all seemed so real. They had these other virtual characters that were just like real people. I had to work with them, lead them, all this sort of stuff. The weirdest thing is that it was kinda like a dream, but a really vivid one. I can only remember certain elements, but nothing too clear. Just the same as a dream."

"So why do you think it was just for the boys and not the girls?"

Jackson shakes his head and shrugs his shoulders. "No idea. I mean, maybe they're recruiting more boys to be Leaders or something."

"Could be. But then, why test you for team-working as well?"

"Because to be a good Leader you need to know how to work in a team. That's what my parents always tell me."

"So I guess you did well then?"

Jackson isn't the sort of boy to be arrogant. Around here, arrogance doesn't really exist. It's just a word we hear describing the people who live on the sea cities. What he does do is tell it as it is and speak his mind. So when he tells me he's done something well, I know it's the truth.

"I did well, yeah." There's no doubt in his mind. If anyone at school was a born Leader, it would be Jackson. It's part of who he is. It's in his blood.

The fact that more boys might be trained as Leaders doesn't surprise me. They already outnumber the girls a lot in that respect, especially with certain duties. Jackson was always going to follow in his family's footsteps, and this will only strengthen that case.

We decide to change the subject and talk about less important things. Right now all I want is to laugh and smile, to walk through the woods and listen to the chirping birds and clicking insects. To make the most of these last fleeting moments where I'm actually still considered a child, and before the burden of adulthood stamps its foot down on me.

All across town, across the region and beyond, I know the kids will be doing the same. Doing what they love the most while they can. Enjoying a last day of freedom before their fates are sealed.

The hours will tick by mercilessly until everyone is summoned together in the hall at school. Children at the front, their parents at the back. All waiting to hear their fate. All with hearts pumping and hands shaking at the prospect of being dragged from their homes.

Before I know it, it's time for us to go. Time to leave the tranquillity and privacy of the woods and step back into the world of watchful eyes and glum expressions. A world of routine and hard labour. And today, in particular, a world of great sorrow and misery.

On the edge of the woods, I stop Jackson and pull him towards me. We only hug each other here, on the boundary of the trees, before we part again until our next meeting. Every time it's like a dagger in my heart, knowing it will be a week or more until we're here again. This time, I hug him tighter than ever.

This time, it might just be our last walk in the woods.

4

The Duty Call

The school is already growing busy when I arrive. There's a much greater sense of nervousness in the air today than there was yesterday. A dull murmur floating above the crowd as parents try to keep their children calm. For some, I can tell, the pressure is already growing too acute. I can see tears glinting in the sunlight as they fall down cheeks, eyes reddening and heads shaking as parents speak comforting words to their offspring.

Some children stand alone, or in small groups, their parents yet to arrive. I see Amy with her father, still smiling, if only faintly now. It grows brighter when she catches sight of me across the crowd, before giving me a thumbs up. Her infectious nature makes it impossible for me not to return the compliment.

About five minutes after my arrival, Jackson turns up. We made sure to leave each other on the boundary of the woods and come separately for fear of being seen by a Roamer or, perhaps worse, Jackson's parents. I've told my mother about Jackson many times before and, although I don't think she approves, she certainly understands. Jackson's parents aren't the same. The best way to describe them would be that they fit the system, and are happy to see it adhered to. If they knew about their son's secret friendship, they'd have made sure to shut it down immediately. As Leaders, that's their role.

Right now, though, Jackson's parents aren't here, and he stands alone. Immediately, a few other single boys gravitate towards him, encircling him like planets around a star. They look up at him with puppy dog expressions, as if he's their stand-in father until their real parents arrive. I see them nod in unison as he speaks and turns to look at each boy individually, perhaps offering some words of reassurance that today will go well for them all. Looking at him, I know he'll make a fantastic Leader.

Gradually the crowd grows, bolstered by parents arriving from their duties to stand with their children. I wait, eagerly, for my mother, my eyes searching constantly for her withered frame. I've told her time and again that she doesn't need to come. That it will only make things harder with her being there if I've been assigned somewhere else. I'm sure a lot of the kids feel the same, but all parents are required to share the burden. It's a rite of passage that all school leavers take, and one that all parents are meant to witness.

And yet, when the doors to the school finally open, and the crowd begin to filter in, I'm still standing alone. I follow inside, and take my place on the left side of the hall with all the girls. To our right are the boys, and behind us all, the parents. The grating sound of chairs scraping on the floor fills the room as people sit, followed by a chorus of fidgeting as Principal Lewis steps forward from his seat on the stage.

"Welcome ladies and gentlemen, boys and girls," he starts, his voice booming through a small microphone attached to his ear. "Today is the day of the Duty Call. It is the day that all children's lives lead towards. The day that all of you," he says, referencing the students with his hands, "become adults."

A light applause flows through the audience, started from the front by the two testers from the previous day.

"This day is a momentous day in all of our lives. For all of you before me, it marks the end of one thing, and the start of something else."

I notice how carefully he chooses his words. How he doesn't openly state the fact that this day is, for many, the worst day of their lives.

"Good luck to all of you and remember, if it's meant to be, it will be."

Another flutter of applause fills the room as Principal Lewis returns to his seat and the two testers step forward. Both smile widely and move to either side of the stage, as before, their chins high and eyes wide with hope and promise. They hold just about the opposite expression as everyone else in the room.

Once again they speak, taking turns to contribute a little more of their rehearsed address to the audience. They talk of the history of the Duty Call. About how this nation of ours, Arcadia, that has seen so much trouble and strife, has now been rebuilt on its principles. How the symbiotic nature of our society makes for a better world. How each of us having our own little role creates harmony and a better future for our children, and our children's children.

I keep an eye on the door at the back the entire time, furtively glancing behind me whenever another applause begins. My mother's face, however, remains elusive amid the throng of parents.

The address continues as the testers speak of the honour of holding any position, from the lowliest to the most esteemed. How every duty is as important as the next. How each and every one of us should be proud today wherever we end up. How Arcadia is mother to us all, and we should all do everything we can to serve her in the best way possible. That, we are told, is what the Duty Call is all about.

Eventually the address is brought to a close with the words: "and now, without further delay, let us begin the Duty Call."

I can feel the nerves building around me now. There's a stiffness and a silence as the two testers step back to their seats, pick up their electronic tablets, and return to the front of the stage.

"We will start with the girls," says the shorter tester. "I shall read your names out alphabetically, along with your duty and where you will be assigned. Remember, you will go where your skills take you, and where the nation most needs you. Please stand when I announce your name."

The entire audience takes an intake of breath and a

sudden hush quiets the hall. I search with my eyes to find Amy, who will be first up, but can only catch the back of her head through the crowd.

"Amy Appleby."

Amy stands straight, and all eyes fall on her.

"You are to be a Teacher in Oakmont. Congratulations."

An applause starts again, and I see Amy turn to find her father. Oakmont, I know, is close by, and being a Teacher is considered of high honour in the region. It's a good result, and her smile says so.

The abbreviated applause dies down as Amy sits, before the tester announces the next girl.

"Bethany Astor."

I look down the line of girls next to me to see Bethany stand. Her face is wrought with nerves and I can see her hands shaking as she tries to hold them tight to her side.

"You are to be a Packer here in Arbor. Congratulations."

Bethany lets out a small gasp of air as she sits. I can't tell whether it's one of disappointment or relief, but given that her mother's a Packer, and she gets to stay here, it's probably the latter.

Again, an applause rings out as the tester states her congratulations, and Bethany looks around to see her parents.

The next few girls receive assignments that are just as predictable. They follow in their mother's footsteps, just as they can have expected, and generally are assigned nearby. When the girl before me is announced, my pulse has accelerated to an unprecedented rate.

"Selina Dawson."

Selina stands.

"You are to be a Breeder in Equo. Congratulations."

Selina looks to her parents before collapsing into her chair in tears. Equo, I know, is a town on the other end of the region, hundreds of miles away. She may never see her parents again.

As the applause fades, leaving only the light sound of Selina's sobs, I hear my name being called.

I look up and see the tester looking at me curiously, just as she did yesterday.

"Cyra Drayton," she says, her eyes locked onto mine. The room once again hushes.

I stand, and can immediately feel every eye in the room burrowing into me. My knees feel suddenly weak beneath me as I attempt to lift my chin and steady my breath. My head swells, my eyesight blurring. I feel as if I'm about to collapse.

I'm so disoriented by the whole experience that the words of the tester fail to register. For a moment I think I'm dreaming, or that I'm under that scanner again, weird images being sent into my mind. The raging sea. Huge pylons rising from the tumult. A monstrous city in the ocean.

My mind begins to return to the hall, my eyes clearing once more, and I hear the tester repeat her words once again, as if disbelieving it herself.

"You're to be sent to....Eden. Your duty will be

assigned to you there. Con....congratulations."

The room falls silent. For a moment you could hear a pin drop as I stand in front of everyone, trying to make sense of things.

But this time there's no applause. No obligatory clapping to usher in the next announcement. Only a murmur, a state of shock that gradually grows louder as each person turns to the next and asks the same question.

Why is she being sent to Eden?

I dare to scan my eyes over the room and see a range of expressions. Shock. Disbelief. Anger. Jealousy. Even Jackson's face is written with a look of total bewilderment.

I see shaking heads and all I want to do is bury my own into my lap and block everything out. Then I remember my mother and arch my neck around to check the back of the room. Dozens of sets of eyes stare at me from the parents behind, but I don't see the cloudy grey of my mother's. Only those of sparkling blue. No grey. No withered frame and weak smile. My mother isn't there.

The murmuring continues for so long that the tester has to call for everyone to quiet before continuing to announce the rest of the girls. Even as the next girl stands, I can feel everyone staring at me, still wondering why I've been given such a great privilege. Still wondering what my duty will be. Still wondering why it wasn't them.

I can't take it. My stomach begins to churn, to turn over and over, my breathing growing heavy as my mind stumbles in a thousand directions.

When the next applause begins, I stand, suddenly, and start pushing past the girls next to me towards the exit. I see Jackson, in a split second, his eyes filled with worry and confusion, make a move to stand and come towards me. But he checks himself and stops, before retreating back down into his chair.

I hear the voice of the tester, calling me to sit back down. But I don't listen. I need to get out. I need fresh air.

All eyes are back on me again. I rush faster, stumbling along past the girls as they shuffle to move out of my way. Soon I've made it to the walkway down the middle of the hall and I'm running, straight to the back door. I pray that my mother's outside, waiting for me, to give me a hug, tell me it's going to be OK.

But she's not. I burst into the sunshine and immediately throw up, dropping to my knees and retching into the warm dirt. My head swims, spinning and beginning to turn inward. I can feel myself losing consciousness, a blackness engulfing me, closing in on my eyes as I kneel in the dust.

I hear more applause inside, but it sounds so eerie and distant now. My hands give way beneath me, and I collapse into the dirt, my eyes still wide open but seeing nothing. Then images reach me, clear as day. Things like before. Things I've never seen. The coast and the ocean and the great city in the sea. The great city of Eden.

When my eyes open again, I have no idea how long I've been lying there. I sit up, the fog clearing, and turn back to the hall. Once more I hear the sound of applause and the faint voice of the taller tester calling out a name, followed by more obligatory applause.

I manage to get to my feet and gingerly stumble back towards the door. I listen carefully for the next announcement and hear the name of Jason Cusiter. They must already be onto the boys.

My mind remains cloudy when the next name is called. Cyra. I listen more closely and hear it again, but it makes no sense.

Then I realise it's not coming from inside the hall. It's coming from behind me. I turn and see a figure rushing towards me, hair golden and skin browned from the sun. Her voice grows clearer as she continues to call my name. Then I hear that familiar croak. The cracked and broken voice of our Leader, Bette.

I move towards her as her face comes into focus ahead of me. I see an expression on it that I've never seen. A look of pain and anguish.

Beads of sweat drip down her face as she pants my name again. My own voice croaks when I speak, a confusion setting inside me.

"Bette?" I say. "What's going on?"

She reaches me and stops short in the dirt, and it's only now that I see those drips of sweat down her cheeks aren't sweat at all. They're tears.

"It's your mother Cyra. You need to come with me, right now."

5

Changes

My mother lies in her bed, Madge dabbing her forehead with a cloth. Her breathing is weak, the grey of her eyes more cloudy than ever as she slowly arches her neck to look at me. I stand in the doorway, quickly drying my own tears to remain strong, and step forward.

I take her hand and force a smile onto my face. She returns the look, the pallid skin lifting at the corners of her withered mouth.

"I'm so sorry I wasn't there today, Cyra," she says, her voice only a croaky whisper.

"It's OK, it's OK. You should be resting anyway."

I hear a couple of sniffs behind me and turn to see both Madge and Bette standing at the edge of the room. They look at me with sullen eyes before stepping out and shutting the door to leave us alone.

"Bette tells me you collapsed in the fields."

My mother nods, tears now building in her eyes. "It's....the heat. It got to me."

I grip her hand tighter. We both know it wasn't the heat.

"It's OK, mum, you can rest for now. Don't worry. I'm here to take care of you."

She shakes her head slowly and stares at me with

those silver eyes. "No, Cyra, you won't. I know you're better than this place. I've always known."

"No....I'm not going anywhere," I say, trying to convince myself.

"What was your assignment Cyra?" she asks me.

"It's...here. Just the same as you," I lie.

Her mouth arches in a smile once more. "I could always tell when you were lying. Ever since you were little. Tell me, Cyra. Tell me where you're going."

A tear rolls down my cheek. I know this is it. Whatever I say, I know I can't stay here. I can't just swap my place with another Picker and stay with my mother. I'm bound for Eden, and there's nothing I can do about it.

"Eden," I say, my head dropping. "I don't know why mum. I'm scared to leave....to leave you."

Her hand reaches to my cheek and brushes away a tear. Her palm is cold, her fingers shaking slightly. "I always knew you were special, sweetheart. You've always had a special glow about you. I'm so happy for you."

"No, I don't want to go! I want to take care of you."

"And you have done, sweetheart, for far too long. It's time you lived your own life now. You can change your stars."

My face is warm with tears now as I stand. "No, I don't want to leave you. I can't lose you. I can save for medicines when I'm Paired. Together we'll have enough to get you the cure."

"No medicines can save me now. I'm too far gone."

"But....but no. The medicine you've been taking has kept you stable. I...I'll get you the cure in Eden. I'll send it home for you."

Her voice is so weak now, her eyes fading. "Look in the bottom drawer, at the back."

My eyebrows arch in confusion. "What? Why?"

"Just do it."

I walk to the series of compartments at the side of the room and open the bottom drawer. In it are a pile of cloths and rags and other old garments. I move them to one side and reach to the back. My hand clutches small boxes, their corners pricking at my skin.

I pull them out and stare at the contents of my hand. Boxes of medicine, of pills, for my mother's illness. I open them up to see that they're full, that the pills are still locked tight in their packets.

"What's this?! But...your medicine."

My mother's voice creaks across the room. "I haven't been taking it, Cyra."

"But...but why?" I say, my breathing growing heavy, as I stand and pace back towards her. I look into her eyes and see the tears trickling down her cheeks, creating sparkling lines down her ashen skin.

"Because of you, Cyra. I want you to live your life. I want you to be happy and not have to think about me. I'm just a burden on you, holding you back. I know you've been doing badly at school on purpose. I can't have you here, sharing your rations, doing my work, when there's so much potential in you."

She coughs, and blood shows on her hand when she brushes her mouth.

"Mum," I say, reaching for her.

"No," she says, pulling her hand away. "This is how it was always going to end, sweetheart. Whether by this illness or starvation, this day was always going to signal the end for me. Without you, without Carson and Cassie, without your father - I see no point in living anyway."

I take her hand now and can barely see her through my tears. "No...please don't do this. Please take your medicine. I'll get the cure in Eden, I'll send it back. I promise. Please...you can't do this to me."

Her hand shivers in mine, her mouth coughing up more blood. "I'm not doing this *to* you, Cyra," she croaks. "I'm doing this *for* you. You'll realise one day that it was for the best."

Tears cascade down my cheeks now, dripping onto the edge of her bed. I watch her breathing begin to grow more shallow, the blood building in the corners of her mouth, her eyes losing focus.

"I love you, mum," I whisper.

A bloodied smile forms on her lips and her eyes refocus on me. "And I love you, sweetheart. Your father would have been so proud to see the girl you've become."

And those are her last words to me. Her last words

to anyone. For the next hour I sit with her, watching her body gradually give way, watching as the deadly virus that decimated the world all those years ago finally finishes her off.

The last look I see on her face is that familiar grimace of pain as her heart gives out. Her lifeless dull grey eyes staring at the ceiling, her lips curled in suffering. I wipe her mouth with a cloth to clear the blood, and there I see it. The same snapshot I've been afraid of seeing for years. The same vision I saw under the scanner and in my dreams. The face of my dead mother.

I stay awake all night that evening, sitting by my mother's body, whispering to her everything I ever wanted to tell her, but didn't get the chance. Without even realising it, the break of dawn soon cracks through the heavens, bringing a solemn glow into the room. For one final time I kiss my mother on the forehead and tell her I love her, before stepping out into my room and shutting the door gently behind me.

All I want to do right now is collapse and forget the world. To wrap myself in a blanket and close myself off from everyone and everything. I've prepared for the death of my mother for years. Even lived it before in my dreams. But this morning, despite all of that, it hurts more than I could have imagined. The hope that I'd be able to care for her, to save her, to cure her, is gone. Hope. I've always hated the word.

But I don't lie down. I don't wrap myself up and shun it all. Instead I pack what mementos I have into a bag and wait for my summons: the picture of my father before he was taken; several others of my brother and sister and mother; a diary, unfilled, that my mother managed to get me for my birthday; a small wristwatch that she used to wear before it was broken. It was a cherished heirloom of her family, and one she always kept safe, even though she might have sold it for extra rations.

I pack clothing and some food and anything else I think I might need. Part of our preparation classes at school gave us a list of things we might need if we ever did leave home. Right now I can't remember them, so I just take whatever I have.

It's still early when I hear a knock at the door. I had several visitors through the evening after my mother passed. Mainly Pickers and others who live on the Block and around Arbor who had known her. They would usually have waited a couple of days to pass on their kind words. Perhaps during her cremation. But not on this occasion. By now everyone knows of my assignment, and that last night was my final evening in Arbor. Their last chance to tell me sorry. To tell me what my mother meant to them.

My summons today mean I won't be there at her funeral. I won't be around to speak prayers in her name and talk of how wonderful she was. In some ways, I don't mind. I've never been one for an audience, and I'd rather say goodbye alone in my own way, like I did last night.

Another knock sounds softly on the door and I move towards it. When I open it I see the face of

Jackson in front of me, creased with worry and looking as solemn as my own. I can't help but cry again when I see him there, and wrap my arms around his neck. He grips back, hard, and rubs my back, kicking the door shut with his foot.

"I don't know what to say, Cy, I'm so sorry."

I sob into his shoulder for a while before pulling myself together. Jackson's never seen me cry before.

When I pull back and look at him, though, I realise that this will probably be the last time I ever see him as well. The thought threatens to break me down again, so I turn and continue busying myself with my packing.

"So what happened with you then?" I ask, my voice deeper than normal as I tighten up my emotions. "I wasn't there to see what happened."

"Um...well it's not just you going away Cy."

I stand and turn back to him. "You're not staying here either?" A foolish sense of hope springs up inside me that maybe Jackson's being sent to Eden too.

His eyes tell me my hope is unfounded. There's a sadness in them that goes beyond what's happened to my mother. It's a disconcerting expression.

"No. It turns out the whole virtual reality test was for an important reason."

"What? What's going on?"

"A lot of the boys have been recruited, called up for service. I guess they're strengthening the military at the Divide along Knight's Wall."

"What! You're being sent to the Divide!"

Jackson nods glumly. Military service used to be quite common for the best physical candidates when leaving school, but in recent years there's been little to no recruitment across the regions. A large push usually indicates that something is going on beyond the boundary of our nation that the powers in Eden aren't happy with.

"I'm going to be trained as an Officer there," he says. "It's basically like a Leader here, so I'll be in charge of some of the other guys."

"And...is the service still set at ten years?"

He nods again. Ten years stationed along the Divide, the great fortress wall, defending against the Deadlands outside. Ten years without being Paired, without having the opportunity to start a family. A selfish thought crosses my mind that at least Jackson won't be Paired with anyone, but it's short lived.

I see on his face now the same look my dad had when he was taken. The look he's got in the picture in my bag. The one he had the day he was dragged away to defend Knight's Wall. He'd been working for years already in Arbor as a Labourer, happily in a marriage with my mother, three young kids to take care of. That was when the virus first hit, and those beyond the boundary line began getting ill. Across the regions the virus wasn't so damaging, but beyond the boundary wall it ravaged the rebel populations. For years they fought to migrate to Arcadia, but we repelled them.

Eventually, they were all wiped out. Most by the virus, the rest in attempts to cross the boundary. Now, no one in the regions really knows what's going on over in the wasteland where the old cities used to stand. The central and western states of the Old USA are now lost to the parched earth and barren lands, unwalked and untrodden by the millions that used to live there.

That was the last I saw of my father. My mother was told he served 7 years of his service before he was killed. We only got official word of that several years ago. So now, looking at Jackson, I see the same look, and the same thought crosses my mind. That this will be the last I see of him too. That he, like my father, like my mother, is about to be ripped from my life.

"So, Eden," he says, trying to lighten things somehow. "How about that..."

"Yeah," I say. "It's gonna be different from Arbor I guess."

Jackson smiles for the first time and huffs. "I'll bet. Have they told you what you're doing there yet?"

I shake my head.

"Well, maybe you'll become important and can get me away from the Divide in a few years."

I know he's joking. Not about me, but about him. Jackson's not a coward, not by a long stretch. Once he's there, he'll do his service to defend the people. If that's where he's needed, he'll commit.

"Or maybe they just need people to shine shoes over there or something," I say. "I really have no idea why I'm going."

"Well, I guess you'll find out soon."

The brief levity is already fading. Frankly, neither of us have ever experienced such change before. It's hard to joke about anything on a day like today, despite his best efforts to cheer me up.

"So," he says tentatively, turning his head to my mother's room. "Are you allowed to stay, you know, for the funeral?"

I shake my head. "I haven't asked."

"But they might let you, you know. They might let you go out in a few days instead."

I shake my head again. "I want to leave today."

His tanned forehead cracks in a series of creases.

"Don't look so shocked, Jackson. I've said goodbye to her in my way. I want to leave this town behind now, and never look back. It's given me nothing but pain," I finish with a whisper.

"I understand. Why delay things, right."

"Right."

An awkward silence falls between us as the light continues to brighten outside. I don't want to leave things on an awkward note with us, but in some ways, maybe it would be easier without a drawn out goodbye. We'll still have all those memories of our time spent together to warm us on bitter nights. What does a single goodbye matter?

It's almost as if Jackson's reading my thoughts, because he stands on cue.

"I guess I should get back. You know, to my family and packing and everything. The train to my outpost is leaving in a couple of hours."

"Sure. I guess you've got more goodbyes than I

do."

We walk to the door together and he moves to open it. I feel a heavy pang in my gut as his hand slides over the handle, wondering if I'll ever see him again after this.

"Jackson," I whisper.

He turns and sees my shining eyes, wet again with tears. Then he steps closer to me and kisses me, my first ever kiss.

"That's my goodbye, Cyra. I'll never forget about you."

And before I can tell him how I feel, he's gone, slipping out of the door and away into the hot morning sun.

6
Road to New Atlantis

It's soon after Jackson leaves that I get another knock at the door. When I open it, I see the stiff face of the short tester woman standing before me, her white skin already beginning to glisten from the morning heat.

"Good morning, Cyra. Are you feeling a little better today?"

I stare at her blankly.

"Well, you were ill were you not, during the Duty Call? That's why you ran out. Don't worry, dear, it does happen quite often. It's the nerves, you see."

I nod, but still don't answer.

"May I come in?"

I glance around to make sure the door to my mother's room is shut. I know they'll be coming to pick up her body soon, but would rather this woman not see her. I doubt she even knows she's just died.

I move back and shut the door behind her as she steps into the room. There's a metronomic way in which she walks, almost like she's a robot. Perhaps she is.

She briefly looks around the interior of my living quarters and gives off a funny sort of exhale. "Things are truly about to change for you, young lady. Your quarters in Eden will be far nicer than this."

I want to smack her in the mouth, but all I do is clench my fist by my side. I don't think she means it spitefully. I think it's just a statement of fact from an objective point of view. Frankly, most living quarters are likely to be nicer than what we have. For me, though, it's home.

"When do I leave?" I ask, my voice empty and shallow.

"Well, that's what I'm here for. Right now, actually."

I nod my head. It's fine by me. The sooner I leave, the better.

"Now, before we go, we need to assign you your code. Hold out your left arm please."

I know what's coming. Every new adult is assigned a code so that they can be kept tabs on. It's like a barcode, written onto your wrist. Each day when you turn up to perform your duty, it's scanned. If you don't work, you don't get the same amount of rations. Those who regularly miss work will get strikes. Too many of those, and they can be banished outside of the Divide to fend for themselves.

Apparently it's a fair system where people only get paid for what they do. In this society, everyone is expendable if they're not contributing. Having a barcode written into your wrist is the most efficient way of knowing just who's carrying their weight, and who isn't.

I hold out my arm, as instructed, and the woman

lifts a small contraption from her bag. She presses a button and it clicks open into a large metal wristband. She slips it over my hand and presses another button. This time it clamps shut, closing tight around my left wrist.

"Now this will sting a little bit," she says, before activating the device.

I feel an immediate sensation of burning on the bottom of my left wrist. It's intense, but lasts only a few seconds before quickly cooling. I watch as the device glows a strange colour of red before turning blue.

"Right," says the woman, raising her eyebrows. "All done."

She unclips the device and neatly packs it back into her small bag.

I look at the underside of my wrist, which is now written in a strange series of black lines and dots.

"That's unique to you," she says. "It's part of your identity now."

"Great," I say.

"OK, there's a hoverbus downstairs waiting for us now. It's going to take us to the coast. There are a few people we'll be picking up and dropping off on the way, so we really must get going."

Us. Fantastic. So she's coming too.

"By the way, my name is Leeta. If you're to be an Edenite, you should really know my first name."

She puts out a hand and I begrudgingly take it. "Nice to officially meet you, Cyra, as a brand new member of Eden."

I have nothing to say in reply. *Member of Eden.* Like suddenly I'm special enough to warrant an official introduction, just because I'm going to Eden. And what about each duty being as important as the next? What about each person being as important as each other?

Unfortunately, my mother taught me too well to be polite, so I shake back and return the compliment. "And you, Leeta."

She smiles. "Excellent. Now let's get going. Time is ticking."

With that, she steps back towards the door, pulls on the handle, and moves out into the corridor. I follow, fetching my bag as I go.

"Oh, you won't need that. You'll be provided with everything you need in Eden."

"I'm taking it," I say, my tongue a little sharp. "They're my personal things."

"Oh, right. OK, that's...fine. Bring it if you wish."

As she marches off down the corridor, I feel myself locked in place. Locked in the doorway outside my living quarters, my eyes glancing back at my mother's door. Soon they'll come and fetch her body to be prepared for her cremation. They'll be no special service. Just a few gathered people, saying their own prayers and perhaps a few words for her as her body is burned to ash.

I hear Leeta calling my name behind me, telling me we're in a rush. I take a final deep breath and glance around the room. The place I've lived my whole life. The place where I knew my father, where I loved my mother, where I grew up with my brother and sister, laughing and playing when the world was more simple.

One final look at my childhood. One final look at my family. And then the door shuts tight in front of my eyes.

When I turn I see Leeta hurrying me on with a frantic gesture of her hands and I begin moving towards her. I don't rush. I don't run. I won't do what this woman tells me.

I reach her and we move together out into the sunlight. It's oppressively hot, as it is most days, and Leeta quickly unfurls an umbrella to shade us over the very short trip to the floating craft ahead of us. I've only ever seen a hoverbus, or a hover vehicle of any kind, on a couple of occasions. Usually when someone important comes through town to check up on things.

Today will be my first time inside one though. It sits just above the ground by a foot or so, gently swaying up and down as blue lights blaze beneath it. Leeta steps up first before folding up her umbrella and giving a wide smile to the driver.

"OK, Cyra, please make yourself comfortable somewhere."

I climb on as she sits down just behind the driver and begins quizzing him on the journey. The change in heat is immediate as I step inside and the door slides shut. It's so cool, as cool as a winter's night, and I feel an immediate shudder run through my body.

Inside I see a few familiar faces from school, as well as many I don't recognise from other towns.

They each sit in plush grey cushioned chairs, set against the white interior of the bus. Those that recognise me give me the same looks I got yesterday at the Duty Call. Some offer resentment and jealousy, yet others pity, most likely because they've heard about my mother.

I carefully walk down the middle of the bus as it whirs to life and gently rises higher above the dirt.

"Sit down before we start," I hear the driver say. I turn to see his eyes staring at me in the mirror, waiting for me to find a seat.

I move towards the back, shielding myself from staring eyes, until I hear a sweet voice sounding from the rear.

"Hey, Cyra!"

I look up and see Amy Appleby sitting right at the back with a spare seat next to her.

"Sit with me, honey."

I find it impossible not to smile when I see her. She stands and gives me a hug, before taking the bag from my shoulder and stowing it in a compartment above our heads.

Another shout from the driver forces us to quickly take our seats, which are impossibly comfortable and soft against my legs. I look over to see a holographic image floating in front of Amy's eyes, shining out from a small bead of light on the seat in front of her.

She reaches forward and presses a button, and immediately the image of a man and a woman dancing disappears.

"Have you used one of these before?" she asks.

I shake my head. We didn't even have a television in our house.

"You'll get used to them where you're going I reckon," she says. Unlike others, I think she's genuinely happy for me. She must be the only one.

"So, are you nervous?" she asks.

I guess I am, but my nerves are hidden deep within. Deep beneath the numbness that's currently engulfing me.

"A bit. I don't know what to expect really."

Suddenly I feel the hoverbus move. It glides silently through the town square, slipping past people as they set about their duties for the day. I can see, in the distance, the orchards and picking fields where I've spent so much time. By now they'll be taking a break under the trees, dousing themselves in water to stay cool under the intense sun.

We reach the boundary of the town and start cruising down an open road, picking up pace. If I wasn't looking outside I'd hardly know we were moving, it's so smooth. The bus I take to the orchards is the opposite, bumping over rocks and kicking up dirt and dust behind it. In there you feel everything, but on this thing I might as well be sitting on a cloud.

"It's amazing isn't it? This bus. Shame I'm only on it for a bit."

"Oh, yeah, you're going to Oakmont aren't you? That's good. You'll be close to home and your dad."

Her grin widens as she nods her head. I know now that she can't have heard about my mother. She'd have mentioned it by now. I'm glad. I don't want to talk about it.

"Yeah, I'll see him sometimes which is good. I'm just happy to be a Teacher. It's what I've always wanted."

"And you'll be great Amy, you really will. No one's better suited to anything."

She hugs me again as the bus reaches an intersection, linking onto a massive wide highway that stretches from north to south. I can see other vehicles cruising along it, mainly old solar powered buses and cars like we have in Arbor. There are other vehicles, though. Hoverbikes and cars and massive carriers transporting goods from the various regions.

I stare open eyed out of the window. I've never seen a road like this. In fact, this is about as far as I've ever got from Arbor. Already it feels alien to me, and I'm still in Agricola. I look up the bus and see that every pair of eyes is glued to the window. Every child staring as vehicles they've never seen before storm up and down the road.

"Right everyone," I hear the driver say. "Make sure you're all strapped into your seats."

I look over at Amy, who's quickly pulling two belts down from behind her. They criss-cross over her chest and fix tightly into locks either side of her hips. I begin fiddling behind me in an attempt to copy her until she helps me and fixes my belts in place.

Then I look up to see Leeta moving up the bus, checking we're all locked in. She nods at each of us before returning to her seat and putting on her own safety belt.

It's something of an anticlimax when we continue to glide gently out onto the wide road and join the vehicles speeding up and down. Perhaps it's the law to wear these harnesses when on the major highways cutting up, down, and across the nation?

A moment later, my thoughts are quickly interrupted by a loud growling beneath my feet as a rumble runs up through from the base of the bus. It grows for a few seconds before, suddenly, the bus bursts into life, shooting quickly down the road at several times the speed as before. I feel myself pinned back into my seat as I glance out the window and see the world flying by in a blur.

"It's the Fast Track," Amy says, looking over at me. "My father told me about it. It's intended for the fast vehicles so they're not caught behind the slow ones."

"I guess we'll be getting to Oakmont quickly then," I say.

She nods and her perennial smile fades a touch. "I'll miss you, Cyra. I'm sure you'll do amazingly on Eden, whatever you do. If you ever come back to Agricola, drop in and see me, will you?"

"Of course," I say, without any real belief that I'll be coming back.

After only a few minutes the bus begins to slow once more, before pulling off down a smaller track. "This is it, I think," says Amy. "My new home."

Around us I see large areas of woodland and massive pens filled with animals off in the distance. It's more scenic here than in Arbor, yet the land is still flat and expansive, stretching off for miles into the distance but peppered with thickets of trees and shrubbery.

Soon the bus pulls up into a town square and Amy gives me a final hug and words of encouragement, as is her way, before disembarking with several others. Outside, several men and women stand waiting for them. Most likely Leaders for their given duties. I watch as a woman, probably the school Principal, greets Amy with a warm handshake before leading her off away from the bus.

So, there's another person I care about who I'll probably never see again.

The next hours pass without great incident, leaving me with time to dwell on my mother. In a way, this journey into the unknown is the best thing for me right now. If I was just out there today, picking fruit with everyone's consoling eyes constantly lingering on me, I'd feel even worse. I'd get words of support and grief at every break. For days, weeks even, people would treat me differently, tiptoe around me as if a harsh word would break me.

At least out here, no one knows me. There's nothing to remind me of what I've lost. A clean break from my previous life. My journey to adulthood across a vast ocean I've never even seen. Every day will bring something new. A new challenge. A new sight or sound or person entering into my life. Everything will be a distraction from my grief, a mask for me to hide behind. Then, as time goes by, maybe I'll truly heal.

My thoughts churn around in my head as I fall into a troubled sleep. My dreams are once again more vivid than I can ever remember them being. I see a clear sight of towers reaching above the sea, connected by a series of tunnels. I see a huge ship, rising many stories above the tiny waves below, drifting gracefully out into the ocean. I see that familiar platform in the distance, a colossal structure locked to the ocean floor with columns hundreds of feet wide.

I'm awoken by the sound of my name, as if brought to me by the wind. When my eyes open, I see Leeta standing up beside me, lightly shaking my shoulder.

"Cyra, are you OK?"

I blink the haze from my eyes and cough. "I'm fine."

Once more I see that curious look on her face, the same one she gave me during the genetics test, the same one I saw across the room during the Duty Call.

"Right," she says. "Bad dreams?"

"I don't remember," I lie, turning my eyes to look out of the window. By now the landscape has grown more industrial. Large swathes of smoke cough up from huge factories in the distance, painting the sky a heavy shade of grey. The sun has made way for fierce looking clouds, black with rain and ready to spill. I see no trees, no natural beauty of any kind. Just massive buildings as far as the eye can see;

people milling like ants around them.

I turn back to Leeta, who's followed my gaze out of the window, her eyes more sunken than I've seen before.

"What is this place?" I ask.

She continues to stare beyond me as she speaks, her voice lacking its usual grating enthusiasm.

"It's the region of Arma," she says. "It's the industrial region."

"What do they make here?"

"Everything. Whatever the country needs, they provide."

I turn back to look out at the view. The buildings here dwarf the sorting and packing warehouses we have in Agricola. I thought they were large, but these are several times as tall and wide. They tower into the dark sky, looming high over the thousands of people moving around outside of them.

Massive vehicles rumble past on concrete roads, trucks filled with materials of various kinds. Other smaller ones zip past them, carrying people between stations. It's a true hive of activity like I've never seen before. Suddenly I feel so grateful to have grown up in Agricola. *If it's meant to be, it will be.* And these guys got the rough end of the stick.

I turn back to Leeta, who's still staring at the factories as they pass.

"Is it only men who work here?" I ask. They're all I can see, although from this distance I can't be sure.

"No," she answers. "Men do the rougher jobs, but there are women here too. They'll be inside the factories and doing various other roles around the region. These men need to be paired with someone."

Of course. Paired so that their children can also grow up to live in this land filled with smoke fumes and hard, endless, labour. I remember hearing that the average lifespan here is several years shorter than elsewhere. No wonder really.

"I've never liked this place," says Leeta, somewhat out of the blue. "It's lifeless. Has no colour."

I find that an odd thing for her to dislike. I've only ever seen her wearing grey. Even her lipstick is grey to match her pallid skin tone and dark black hair.

"You know, Cyra, you have no idea what a privilege it is being sent to Eden. You shouldn't feel guilty for being sent from your home. It's a great honour."

"Right. Great for me. Great for my children and my children's children," I say sarcastically.

Leeta's eyes drop to her lap briefly. "Not always."

"How do you mean?"

"My son. He was sent here. He's out there working, right now."

"*Your* son. But, you're from Eden. I didn't think anyone could be send somewhere like this from there?"

"Some people can," she says, "if they have nothing to offer on Eden. My son...had learning difficulties. This was the best place to utilise his assets."

Suddenly I feel a heavy pang of pity for this woman, and understand why she hates coming here so much. To cruise by inside a luxurious hoverbus, knowing her son is out there in the heat and smoke and dirt. It must be hard.

"I'm sorry," I say, with genuine sympathy.

She shakes her head and plants a forced smile back on her face.

"Don't be, Cyra. We all have our place in the world. This is my son's place. Eden is mine, and will be yours."

"You believe that?" I ask.

"Of course I do. It's my role to believe it. That's my duty, and I wouldn't be very good at it if I didn't."

She smiles briefly at me again before changing the subject. Somehow I get the feeling she doesn't completely believe what's she's saying. With a son out here, how could she?

"Anyway, Cyra. We have things to discuss."

For the next hour or so she begins telling me about Eden protocols. About how people dress and behave, about the structure and its history. About its importance in our nation and the great strife we've suffered.

It was initially built to cater to the growing population when they could no longer be sustained on land, she tells me. The earth grew warmer, and the seas began to grow higher, gradually reducing the landmass of what used to be the USA. With less land for people to live on, and fewer areas where crops and food could be cultivated, the sea cities were built to house people so that the land could be used more efficiently.

Eden became the centre of it all, the centre of the new movement as the structure of the nation changed. Civil wars were fought, cities lost to the fighting, and eventually the nation of Arcadia was born, with Eden as its capital.

A dividing wall was built, cutting Arcadia off from the barren and scorched earth beyond its boundaries where rebels remained a potent force. The place known as the Deadlands. The wall stretched South from what used to be the bottom of Lake Michigan, all the way down to the Gulf of Mexico. Beyond lay a wasteland where crops could no longer exist on the barren landscape, and where rebel factions continued to live, attacking the border and seeking to loot and pillage stores of food and weapons.

Then the virus hit. It killed in the millions, especially beyond the Divide where they had no means of devising a cure. On the mainland of Arcadia the population was less affected, although many still lost their lives before a cure was spread throughout the population.

But it didn't work for everyone. For years people who had been given immunity against it kept falling ill and dying as the virus grew more aggressive. More powerful cures were created to combat it, but they weren't handed out as before. Before, it was an epidemic, threatening to destroy the population. Now it was only killing a few people, and they had to pay for the privilege of keeping their lives.

My mother was one of those people. The

medication we could afford only kept her going. It was a band aid on a serious wound, a quick fix that was never going to cure her for good. She lost her life, like so many others before her, because she didn't have enough money to pay for the cure. Her life wasn't deemed important enough to save. Just a lowly Picker in Arbor. So much for every person, every duty, being as important as the next.

As Leeta recites the history of Arcadia and Eden, the landscape outside continues to morph into things I've never seen. Gone are the giant factories and smoky skies, the huge vehicles and flat, expansive concrete lands. Instead, I see mountains and hills for the first time. Mounds of earth rising towards the heavens, fog and cloud and mist floating between them in deep valleys. Forests pepper the slopes, dark green trees scattered over the earth as far as the eye can see.

There are settlements and towns too, hidden in small clearings among the trees and down in the valleys. Smoke rises in places, and everywhere are patches of felled trees, only their stumps still stuck in the ground.

"These used to be called the Appalachian Mountains," says Leeta, noticing I've grown bored of her history lecture. "That was hundreds of years ago, though. Now this region is known as Lignum. It's an ancient word for wood."

"So what do they do here?"

"They're mainly Choppers and Planters. Trees are important, Cyra, for many things. Over the last few centuries a lot of the woodland here has been cleared to make way for taller forests and trees. It's a constant cycle of chopping them down and letting them grow back."

"Well, how long does that take? For them to grow? Isn't it years?"

"It used to be years, even decades, to reach maturity. The seeds we plant have been genetically enhanced on Eden to grow more quickly. Now they only take months."

"So why don't they do that with our crops and fruits and vegetables? Grow them quicker or bigger or something?"

"Ah, you are perceptive. Actually, that's something they're currently working on. There's a lot of things happening on Eden that are very exciting."

I turn back to the window as we climb over a hill. The sky is beginning to darken now, the sun blotted out by heavy clouds that linger overhead. It's so different here to home. There it's all flat lands filled with fields. Oranges and yellows and reds fill the landscape. Colours that match the searing heat. Maybe it's just being inside this cold bus, but outside it just looks cooler and wetter here. Shades of green and brown paint the land, giving it a more earthy and rustic tone. I can imagine, looking out over the hills, that living here wouldn't be so bad.

The night is steadily advancing when the rain begins and Leeta moves back to her seat at the front. I see her talking with the driver, perhaps working out the logistics of our next stop off point. For the entire day we've been stopping periodically, dropping off people and picking them up. It's a strange sight, seeing someone, completely alone, walk off the bus to start their life in a new town or region. And just at the same time, someone steps on, leaving the town they know, their family and friends, to start a life elsewhere.

By now, no one who was originally on the bus when I got on is still with me. It's changed its entire cargo several times over. All except me. All except the special girl bound for Eden.

The people I knew from school left long ago. Four of them were dropped in a nearby town, not long after Amy said goodbye. A couple of others went a bit further, but that was it. Since then it's been new faces and few smiles. Most climb on, their eyes ripe with fear and nerves, and drop into a seat. I feel sorry for just about every person I see.

When we reach a small town in a misty valley between two hills, Leeta stands and announces that this will be our last stop for today. Two boys step off and are greeted by a tall and muscular man outside. No doubt they're to become Choppers.

A timid looking girl climbs on and sheepishly searches for a spare seat. There are plenty by now, roughly half the bus now sitting empty. She shuffles towards the back with a small bag over her shoulder and takes the two spare seats across from me.

She looks young, younger than 16. There's a freshness to her face that perhaps I don't have. Spending so much time under the sun will do that to a person. Her skin is unblemished and pale, although not quite to the same extent as Leeta. As she sits down I see a flash of green in her eyes. It matches beautifully with her hazel brown hair. Green and brown. Just like the trees and the earth around here. She must, I suppose, come from a family of Planters. Most likely that will be her duty, perhaps in a nearby town where there's greater need for her.

Just as she's stowing her bag, Leeta climbs back onto the bus and addresses its remaining occupants. She claps briefly, demanding our attention, before smiling and putting on that irritating softly spoken voice that she only seems to offer in public.

"Now, everyone. This is our last stop for this evening. The Supervisor here has kindly allowed us to park here for the night. Please, step off the bus so we can prepare it for sleeping."

We all wearily clamber off the bus, no one quite knowing what Leeta is talking about. "It's going to transform," I hear someone whisper. "I've seen it before."

A loud whirring sounds from inside the bus as several legs extend out of the bottom, propping it up in the earth. Moments later, the blazing blue lights beneath it go out. Suddenly, the windows fade to black, and various hisses and clanks and electronic buzzes fill the night air. This goes on for a few moments as each of us share looks of confusion.

"Right, all done," says Leeta, just as the clicking and clanging stops.

The door opens once more and she steps on, taking a look inside. "Perfect. Right everyone, back on the bus."

When I step back on it's like I'm in a completely different place. I can't quite believe that I've just spent the entire day inside this thing. The seats are all gone, replaced or morphed into bunk beds. They line up along either side of the bus, which looks so much more like a building now.

"Choose a bed please."

I move immediately to the back where I was sitting before. Everyone else does the same, returning to roughly the same spot they previously occupied.

"The lights will be going out in one hour. First, follow me towards the mess hall in town where we're kindly being treated to a local dinner. I believe they catch a lot of deer here."

The next hour drags along like a dead weight behind us all. No one is in any mood to speak to each other much or socialise. Really, what would be the point when we're all going to be in separate places by tomorrow? I choose not to share my final destination with anyone for want of getting more jealous stares. Everyone here is to be a local Planter or Chopper or perhaps something in a nearby region. They won't look kindly on someone bound for Eden.

I notice the young looking girl down the table saying nothing at all. She just sits with her head low and eyes peering up every so often. This is her home town, and her mother and father probably live just around the corner. How she must want to run back to them rather than being here with us. But she, like all of us, needs to let go of that now.

When we return to the bus, I'm happy to crawl into my bunk. There's plenty of space, so no one sleeps above me. Just like it's been for the last few years since Cassie left home.

I fall into uneasy dreams and find myself waking often. When I do I don't know where I am in the pitch dark of the bus. In my hand I clutch my mother's watch, feeling my fingers along the cracked glass, and a tear rolls down my cheek.

But I'm not the only one crying. In the silence of the night I hear a whimper across from me. Light sobs in the darkness. The tears of the young looking girl, about to be torn from her home.

7
The Graveyard

The next morning we're awoken early by Leeta's orders to get off the bus. Outside we gather, a host of confused 16 year olds with blurry eyes and funny hair, watching as the strange vehicle transforms into its previous form.

As we get back on I can't help but notice the young looking girl with brown hair, her eyes red and puffy, staring out towards a patch of wood. It's probably where her mother works.

Leeta's calls force her eyes around and she climbs back on, head down, and creeps into her seat at the back. For the next couple of hours I don't see her turn her gaze from the window. Periodically, I see her reflection, though, and know that those green eyes are once more filled with tears.

The day moves on as before as we hover through the hills and mountains. Lunchtime quickly comes and goes, Leeta passing out our rations to eat as we travel. By early afternoon we've left the mountains and are returning to flatter lands, passing through old towns and settlements that no longer look to be occupied. Some show signs of battle: crumbled walls, bullet holes, craters in the ground. There are old vehicles, rusted and beyond repair, lying everywhere.

The further we go, the worse it gets. Old unoccupied towns become rubble. Unused cars become metal shells. A grey mist seems to hang over the land. No trees or bushes grow. No signs of life exist. It must be the place known as the Graveyard. It's a place that every kid knows about.

It happened during the civil war a long time ago at the height of the fighting. The rebels managed to steal a nuclear weapon and dropped it here, close to the coast, on what used to be a highly populated region. Thousands died in the blast, and many more followed in the months and years that followed. Ever since that day the land has become toxic, unused by Eden and left as a memorial for the victims.

It's a large barren blip on the mainland of Arcadia, and a reminder for everyone of what the rebels were capable of. At a time when people were divided, questioning the morals of fighting their own countrymen, it brought people together under a united goal. The war didn't last much longer after that, and the world came together to sanction the decommissioning of all nuclear weapons. Just so nothing like that could ever happen again.

Leeta begins sermonising once more as we pass through the old ruins, standing up at the front and dragging our attention to any particular points of interest. I wonder if she does this every year, educating her latest troop of school leavers as they pass through to their final destinations.

It takes a while before the earth begins to show signs of life again. Trees spring up in the distance, buildings appear on the horizon. The further we go, the grander they get. Soon Leeta is excitedly telling us that we're approaching the coast.

"Has anyone seen the sea before?" she asks, an uncharacteristically genuine smile on her face.

I see a series of heads shake ahead of me.

"Well, it's magnificent....no, no I won't spoil it for you, I'll let you see it for yourself. We'll be coming into the fishing city of Piscator soon. Um, Mr Hansen, Mr Dawler and erm," she says, looking down at her tablet, "Miss Kepple, you're all disembarking here."

She looks up towards the back of the bus. "Cyra and Ellie, you'll be coming with me."

I look to my left to see the green eyed girl gingerly turn her head in my direction. A nervous smile arches at the corners of her mouth. "Hi. My name's Ellie, like she said."

"I'm Cyra, like she said," I say, smiling wide to make her feel at ease. "So, you're leaving the mainland as well?"

She nods her head quickly. "Yeah, I don't know why. They're taking me to Eden." She seems embarrassed as she says it. I know the feeling.

"Wow, really? Me too. I guess we'll be travelling together."

Her smile loses its cloak of nerves and suddenly brightens. "Oh...that's great! I thought it would be just me."

"There's a lot of that going around," I say, laughing. "I didn't think anyone went to Eden from the mainland."

"No, neither did I. No one from my town has ever been picked."

I reach forward and extend my hand. "Well, Ellie, I guess we're the special ones," I say, half mocking, half genuine.

She slips her small hand into my own and I shake it lightly. Her skin is as soft as her features, which are pretty and almost childlike. She's got this sweet smile and button nose. There's an innocence there that makes her seem younger than she is.

"So, did you get your duty yet?" she asks. The way she says it suggests she hasn't been given hers either.

"No, they just said I was going to Eden. Nothing else. I guess maybe they need some people to do manual tasks there. I'm no scientist or engineer."

"Me neither. I was never very good in school."

"Well there's gotta be a reason. I don't think Leeta even knows."

"Oh, is that the woman at the front?" she asks.

"Yeah, her name's Leeta. She took my testing. She's odd, but actually OK when you talk to her a bit."

"They're all like that I think. All the people from the testing board. They all look the same too."

"Yeah, tell me about it. It's all grey and black. Not the friendliest colours are they!"

"I like your colouring," she says, nodding her head at me. "I'd love to have skin your colour. And your hair's so bright. I look more like them really."

"No, your hair's lovely. And...is that green in your eyes?"

She nods. "I guess. I haven't really seen my reflection much. We don't have many mirrors where I'm from."

"Well take it from me. They're beautiful. Much nicer than Leeta's, although don't tell her I said that."

She giggles as we both look up to see Leeta talking to the remaining people on the bus. Just the two boys and one girl left other than us. I'm glad to have a companion for my onward journey to Eden, though. Maybe we'll have the same duty? Just knowing that there will be someone else from the mainland there makes everything just that little less intimidating.

"OK, we're nearing the city of Piscator now," Leeta announces from the front. "Everyone, please prepare yourselves to disembark."

The bus begins to slow as I stand and remove my small backpack from the storage compartment above my head. I slip my mother's watch inside a secure pocket and tighten the zip, before sitting back down and waiting for the bus to stop.

We seem to be entering the residential part of the city. The buildings here are long and narrow, yet tall. They look like the Block back in Arbor, only with several of them piled on top of each other. Floor upon floor of small living quarters for those working in the city and down at the port.

The bus pulls to a stop in a square surrounded by these tall, narrow buildings. The two boys and girl disembark first and are greeted by their waiting Leaders. One meets with the boys, and the other with the single girl, before guiding them away out of the square.

"Right ladies, are you ready?" asks Leeta from the front.

Ellie and I share a quick look before nodding and standing with our bags. When we step off, a smell that I've never experienced before quickly fills the air. It's salty and pungent and stings the inside of my nostrils. I raise my fingers to my nose and start rubbing, and look over to see that Ellie is doing the same.

"Yes, the smell is a bit unpleasant isn't it?" says Leeta, who doesn't seem to be having the same trouble as us. "It's the same whenever I pass through."

"And what is it?" I ask, searching with my eyes for the source of the stink.

"Fish, mainly. And the smell of the ocean. Come now girls, you'll get used to it in a few minutes."

Leeta begins marching off through the city and we follow. The sun shines bright in the late afternoon sky, yet there's a greyness to the buildings, similar to the industrial region of Arma that we passed through. Strangely, however, there are no people around, and we walk for several minutes without seeing a single soul. When I ask Leeta why, she tells me they're all either down working on the docks or out at sea on fishing trawlers.

Gradually we move through and away from the maze of tall, narrow, buildings and into an area of warehouses and factories. A tremendous cacophony of noise sounds from inside each one, making it hard for us to hear as Leeta explains where we are. I just about hear that this is where all of the fish are packed and processed. It's basically a much larger version of the sorting and processing warehouses we have in Arbor.

Inside one I hear hundreds of voices, singing together in unison. It reminds me of the productivity songs they sing out in the orchards, although on a grander scale. From outside I can't make out any of the words, but once again Leeta is on hand to tell us that it's an old fisherman's song from centuries ago. It has a strange, haunting quality that is in contrast to the sweet melodies we'd sing out under the morning sun in the picking fields.

Beyond the warehouses and factories lies a sprawling series of ports. Huge ships lie stationed on the docks, with others either embarking out to sea or returning from a voyage. For the first time in my life I see the ocean beyond. An endless blue blanket stretching all the way to the horizon.

"Beautiful, isn't it," says Leeta, her eyes dancing at the sight of the sea.

I nod in agreement, but feel I must be missing something. To me, it's terrifying. An unending expanse of water towards a completely unknown world beyond. It's the opposite of my safe haven back home. Of the golden fields and green woods. Here it's all grey and blue and sickly tones. It doesn't smell of the harvest, or of the sweet apple and orange trees, but of death and decay. Standing there, looking out over the enormous ships and the tens of thousands of people in their grey overalls and heavy boots, I feel more lost than I ever have.

When I turn to Ellie, I see that she's thinking the same. She's used to woods and mountains and beautiful, earthy colours. She scans the landscape ahead and her brows begin to furrow more deeply. Then she mutters something under her breath, something I can't make out over the din and rumble of giant ships and busy factories.

Leeta looks to have misconstrued the looks on our faces as those of wonder and amazement. In truth, there's an element of that in there. It would be impossible not to marvel at the sight ahead of us. At everything I've seen so far on this journey across the mainland. Yet all that is secondary to the feeling of homesickness, of loneliness. Having never left my little town, all of this is more than a bit overwhelming.

By the looks of things, Leeta brought us through this part of town purely so that we could see the bustling port and noisy industrial sector, because it's not where our boat is. She tells us that it's further down the coastline through the city in the merchant sector.

"This is the busiest harbour city in all of Arcadia," she says. "This is the fishing sector, but merchant trade is brought in at another port. There's also a military port in the other direction that I'd just love to show you, but time is pressing I'm afraid."

"That's a shame," I say, hardly attempting to hide my sarcastic tone. She takes it as genuine though, making me think that perhaps sarcasm isn't used much among Edenites.

The merchant sector feels more familiar to me, and looks just like a huge version of our trading area in Arbor. All sorts of items appear to be changing hands, from cloth and fine materials to food delicacies and luxury items like cigarettes and alcohol. Away along the docks are massive container ships being loaded with crates to be delivered to the sea cities. From what I can see, the vast majority of trade is going out, with little coming in. Food, fuel, clothing, and a huge number of products produced in the industrial region of Arma are continually manufactured, packed, brought to the harbour, and sent out to sea. And all the mainland regions get in return is food and protection against the threat of rebels beyond the Divide. I wouldn't call that a fair deal.

Leeta continues to educate us as we go, explaining the history of Piscator and its geographical importance. Hundreds of years ago, all of this would have been land, she tells us. That beneath the waves lie old towns and cities stretching for miles out to sea, submerged when the water began to move inland, drowning much of the coastline in the East.

"This city has seen continual growth ever since it was founded," she says. "It's now the most important port along the coastline and is a gateway to all the sea cities, Eden included."

She opens her arms out as she speaks, and gestures towards a huge ship stationed on the dock. "And this, girls, is the vessel that will take us there."

Our eyes follow her hands as they point at the juggernaut of a ship docked against the harbour. Under the sun it gleams white, its front end pointed like the tip of a knife to cut through the ocean. The body grows wider as it extends back, the rear of the ship flat and covered in a series of massive circular turbines that glow blue. On the top, massive solar sails extend from the upper deck, capturing the sun's rays to power the huge machine, and all down the sides are hundreds of smaller panels, sparkling in the sunlight.

When we move closer, the ship looms ever larger, standing dozens of stories high above the water. Inside I see people at the windows, looking out over the docks and the city beyond. At the bottom, thousands of people continue to board, with vehicles and various other items of luggage being fitted into massive container areas in the belly of the ship.

"Who are all these people?" I ask Leeta as we approach. I can tell from the various ages that they're not all school leavers assigned to Eden.

"All sorts," she says. "Many will be Supervisors from the various towns and cities throughout the mainland regions. They're required each year after the Duty Call to report to Eden for a debrief."

"A debrief?" asks Ellie, finally finding her voice. It's the first question she's asked of Leeta all day.

"Yes Ellie. It basically means they're required to update Eden on their town, its progress, where their school leavers have been assigned, and to get new orders for the coming year. It's all just part of the system."

"And everyone else?" I ask.

"Well, there will be a lot of Testers, like myself, as well as some assigned to Eden, like yourselves. And other diplomats and political figures and military personnel going back and forward. A lot of them will just be those on vacation as well."

"Vacation?" asks Ellie again. "What's that?"

"It's basically like a long Sunday," I tell her before Leeta can speak. "You have Sundays off, right?"

Ellie nods. As far as I know, Sunday is the one day people have off across the regions. It certainly is where I'm from.

"Well, vacation is maybe a whole week off, maybe even two." I look over to Leeta, who nods.

"Yes," she says, "one or two weeks is the norm. People from Eden like to see the mainland when they can, or perhaps visit relatives on other sea cities or....elsewhere." She trails off, and I know she's thinking of her son back in Arma.

"So will we get vacation?" asks Ellie excitedly.

"I'm not sure," says Leeta, her voice now more withdrawn. "It depends on your duty."

"Which we'll hear about when?" I ask a little curtly.

"When you reach Eden. I've already told you that, Cyra," she bites.

She falls silent for a second before leading us towards the queue outside the ship. We join the back and wait, a slight awkwardness hanging in the air. Ellie seems to have moved on from the slump she was in for much of the morning, her eyes no longer red or blotchy, but wide and bright. I think it's the thought that she'll be able to visit her family, her home, if she gets vacation.

I find myself reaching into the pocket of my bag containing my mother's watch, and sliding my fingers over the cracked glass. There's no going back to Arbor for me. Not any more. There's nothing there for me now. Not my mother. Not Jackson. Not any of the other friends I had in school, limited in number as they were. If I returned now it would be to a ghost town, full of memories and pain. It's the last place I'd think of visiting.

It takes us no time to get to the front of the queue. When we get there we are asked to roll up our sleeves for our barcodes to be scanned. When it's my turn, I see a brief screen flash up with my information in front of a guard. I see an image of myself, my vital statistics, and various other pieces of information I can't decipher.

I'm ushered through additional security as Ellie has her own code scanned. There's some sort of x-ray machine that deciphers the contents of my bag without me needing to open it, and my own body is also scanned to make sure I've got nothing dangerous on me. I get through without a problem, and Ellie follows after me.

By the time we meet Leeta on the other side, she appears to have lightened up once more. She leads us straight inside and into a lift, which quickly shoots us up onto the 12th floor of this floating behemoth. When we step out, we enter into a large social area filled with comfortable seats. At one end is a long bar serving drinks and all sorts of food. At the sides, viewing areas provide expansive views through large glass windows.

I drift towards one and move up close to the glass, staring down at the incredible sight below. From up here, I can see everything: the merchant docks and fishing port next door; the factories and warehouses and tall residential blocks. Beyond, a little way down the coast, I see what Leeta told us was the military harbour. Several huge ships lie against the docks, with several others seemingly under construction.

My eyes scan the landscape beyond the city, all the way up away from the coast towards the Graveyard. I can just about make out the sight of vehicles crawling along the road leading through it, many bringing supplies to be exported and traded down at the port. In all my life, I've only ever stepped a floor or two up from the ground. Now, it seems, the entire world lies at my feet.

I hear Ellie by my side, exhaling in wonder as she joins me by the glass. "I've never seen anything like it," she says, her eyes unblinking.

"Just wait until we reach Eden." I turn to see Leeta behind us, staring over our shoulders. "There's a whole wide world out there girls. More than the regions you come from. It's time to spread your wings and fulfil your potential. Because I know you both have great potential, deep down inside."

She smiles at both of us before slipping her electronic tablet from her bag. "OK, we'll be in Eden by evening. Both of you feel free to enjoy the space up here, but don't leave this floor. You're not authorised to go anywhere else, OK."

She waits for us both to answer. We do so by nodding.

"Choose any seat you can find if you want to relax and rest, and enjoy any drinks and food over on the tables at the front."

Ellie and I look at each other, our eyebrows drawn down in confusion. "What do you mean? We can take whatever we want?"

Leeta nods and smiles. "This is an Eden boat for Eden residents. Enjoy what you wish."

With that, she steps quickly away and over towards the other side of the room. I watch as she approaches what appears to be a group of other Testers, all dressed in grey and with slicked back dark hair. I wonder if that's part of the criteria to become one. *Must have black hair, pale skin, and an annoying enthusiasm for just about everything.*

I feel Ellie tug at my arm and drag my attention back towards the promise of food and drink. "Did she really mean that? That we can have anything?"

"I guess so," I say, glancing over at the bar as people casually peruse it. "You wanna check it out?"

She nods quickly, as if she's just been given permission to do something by her mother, and quickly skips over towards it. I follow behind, gradually growing wary as more sets of eyes linger on me.

I must look so out of place with my golden skin

and hair. I see few people with anything more than a light splash of colour on their cheeks. Most have black, grey, or dark brown hair, with the lightest shades nothing more than a murky blonde colour. Perhaps it's the sort of colour my hair would be if it wasn't constantly exposed to sunlight.

When I arrive at the long table, covered in plates of food I've rarely, if ever, eaten (and many I've never even seen), I'm feeling incredibly self conscious. Ellie, however, seems lost to her own cravings, and is hastily piling a plate full of cakes and chocolate muffins and other such treats that only appear on birthdays back home. I suppose people just think she's a bona fide Edenite, with her light skin and brown hair. Perhaps the precocious daughter of a family returning from holiday. I doubt many would place her as a school leaver. She really doesn't look old enough.

I follow behind Ellie, who's suddenly burst from her shell amid her desires for such rare foods. She's acting like this is going to be her one chance to eat like this. Maybe she really thinks that's the case. That perhaps she'll arrive at Eden and she'll be back on the rations she's used to having.

I lose what little appetite I have when I realise that won't be the case. That this is how Edenites live day in and day out. So we bust a gut out in the regions and get paltry rations for our efforts, while here they're all chowing down daily on delicacies generally saved for the most special of occasions back home.

I know what Leeta would tell me if I challenged

her on it. That those on Eden are doing the most important work, and therefore get the best food and drink and comfort and just about everything else in between. Then I'd say that during her speech at the Duty Call she said the opposite. That every duty, every role, was as important as the next. I'm sure she'd come back with some defence, some reason to try to make me understand, and in the end where would I get? Nowhere. She'd probably say I should be happy to be in this position. That I shouldn't moan when I'm the one reaping the rewards.

And I wouldn't answer her, because they'd be no point. All I'd do is think of people like Madge back home. An elderly woman, picking fruit all day just to survive. When she can no longer work, she'll slowly starve to death, and no one will do anything to help her.

And on that same day, perhaps a few years from now, I'll be gathered at a table like this, choosing from between hundreds of different sweet and savoury foods. By that time, maybe I'll have forgotten her. Maybe I won't give it a second thought. When that day comes, I'll be a true Edenite.

It's a thought that makes me sick to my bones.

8

Eden

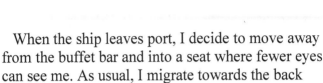

When the ship leaves port, I decide to move away from the buffet bar and into a seat where fewer eyes can see me. As usual, I migrate towards the back and collapse into a large, white, chair with padded arms and a footrest. Immediately the cushioned fabric moulds itself to my body and reclines as I lean back. Sitting in it, I feel almost weightless.

High up and towards the front of the ship, I barely feel the rumble of the turbines at the back. The ship runs, according to Leeta, on a sort of jet propulsion both over and beneath the surface of the water. Below, huge rudders steer its direction, with additional propellers used to provide an extra burst of speed when needed.

Ellie joins me after a few minutes, looking slightly more sluggish than before and holding a plate overflowing with food. I don't think she quite understands the implications of it all. The disparity of life where she came from and life here. Or maybe she just doesn't care. I really don't know her well enough to judge yet.

She offers me the chance to share her plate, but I tell her I'm not hungry. "It's motion sickness," I say, despite the fact that, in this floating giant, you really can't feel a thing.

I find myself drawn to the window on more than one occasion as we go. The first happens only a few minutes after the engines start rumbling. Close to where I'm sitting I spy an empty viewing window, so quickly take my position up against the glass. I watch as the harbour city of Piscator grows smaller in the distance, before eventually fading almost completely from view. Within 15 minutes, miles and miles of coastline have been revealed, fishing, military, and ship-building settlements lining their banks.

After an additional 15 minutes, I can see nothing but open water in every direction. Among the crashing waves I spot much smaller vessels cruising along the water and thank God, at least, that I'm not on one of those. I've spent my entire life on dry land and have never even learned to swim. Back home, there's little need for it, and it's not exactly part of daily life there. So the idea of shipping out to sea in a vessel any smaller than this hulking beast doesn't exactly fill my head with happy thoughts.

My second trip to the window, after a short period away from it, is brought on by Leeta, who has by now returned from her impromptu meeting with the other Testers. She approaches both myself and Ellie, who now appears so full she can barely move, and asks that we follow her back towards the glass.

When we reach it, I see dozens of rectangular towers rising out of the ocean at varying heights. Some rise a couple of stories above the waves; others many more, stretching high into the heavens. Tunnels and walkways connect them together, on which people walk and vehicles drive. At the edge, many ships sit in a sea harbour, busy with tradesmen and merchants.

"What is this place?" asks Ellie, her face pressed up against the glass.

"It's known as New Atlantis," says Leeta. "It was once a great city called New York. These towers you see were huge skyscrapers, some over a hundred floors high. All you see now are their tips above the water."

I search my eyes to the base of the closest tower and see a shadow beneath the surface, stretching down into the depths below.

"They're called seascrapers now," says Leeta, following my eyes. "People live and work in them, even below the surface. Many have at least a few underwater floors with clear glass. One, I've heard, takes you all the way down to the ocean floor where it's so dark outside you'd think it was night."

"Have you ever been there? Down in the city I mean?" asks Ellie.

Leeta shakes her head. "My duty doesn't take me there, no. There are no schools there, no children, no Testing and no Duty Call. It's primarily a merchant city and, well, it's a city of vice."

We both wait for her to continue, which she duly does after a brief pause.

"It's a place where travellers go. Merchants and politicians and military personnel to relax and be entertained. It's more of a free city, you could say."

"And how does that sit with Eden?" I question.

"They tolerate it. It gives people some means of

release, which is often important."

"Well, I know where I'm going on vacation," says Ellie, although I'm not sure she quite understands what Leeta is saying. I'd imagine sordid women and drinking and smoking and other intoxicants are what you'll get down there.

"OK girls, come with me. There are a few people I want you to meet."

Leeta now leads us away from the window and towards the back where I saw her greet all those Testers. *Please don't tell me she's going to introduce us to them*, I think to myself. I'm not sure I can stomach a bunch of Leetas right now.

In a small gathering at the back, however, are a group of girls and boys, presumably school leavers assigned to Eden. They talk excitedly among themselves, each with a beaming smile on their face and shining, hopeful, eyes.

Leeta introduces us around, reciting each of their names one by one as we shake hands. When she asks each to tell us their duty, they happily announce that they're Scientists and Healers and Engineers.

"These are the best of the best from the mainland, girls. You see what company you're with?"

I nod and smile along, but when asked about our duties neither Ellie nor myself can offer a straight answer. When we tell them that we haven't been assigned yet we're met with varying looks of confusion, bemusement, and fascination.

We speak to them for a few minutes before returning to our seats where I plan to settle in for the

104

remainder of the journey. Leeta hovers nearby, though, telling me once again what a privilege it is to be assigned to Eden.

"That's how you should be behaving girls. You should be over there, socialising and getting excited. You see how they were? No frowns and fears. Happiness and excitement. That's the way it should be."

I nod a few times before closing my eyes and lying back in my seat, before Leeta huffs and wanders off again. Frankly, she can't tell me how I'm supposed to feel. I feel how I feel. That's it. Nothing she says will change that, although part of me appreciates what she's trying to do.

It looks as though the sheer weight of food Ellie took on not so long ago is having an effect on her. I turn to see her lying back in her seat, her eyes beginning to fade as she falls asleep. Outside, the windows are starting to grow dark, streaks of rain slashing across them. Storms, I know, are common out to sea. Back home they're rare as a blue rose.

It grows quieter as the hours trickle by. I suppose many people are afflicted as Ellie is, relaxing in their seats and enjoying the remainder of the journey. A light chatter still sounds as groups talk here and there, and the distant, but continuous, rumble of the engines murmurs constantly in the background. Outside, I hear the lightest patter of rain against glass, and notice the distant flash of lightning far away across the ocean.

Ellie groans at my side, and I turn to see her eyes flickering as she sleeps. Her mouth moves, too, which I find slightly more unusual, her lips whispering words I can't make out. I lean closer to try to hear, but it all sounds like garbled nonsense; random words cobbled together that have no clear meaning.

Gradually, she grows slightly more frantic, her head and entire body starting to twitch, her words growing louder. People begin to notice, turning from the seats in front of us and shooting disapproving stares at me, as if I'm the one making all the noise and am somehow responsible.

When it gets too much, I reach over and shake Ellie by the shoulder, waking her from her nightmare. Her eyes open wide almost immediately, her body growing suddenly still.

"Bad dreams?" I ask her.

She nods, but doesn't say anything, before standing and rushing away towards the toilet behind us. She returns a few minutes later and tells me she was feeling ill. I'd believe her, given how much she's eaten, if her eyes weren't red. It's obvious that she's been crying again.

Soon I see more lights out the window, but this time they're not flashes of lightning but stationary. I move over to take a closer look and notice hundreds, maybe thousands of lights twinkling in the distance. Some are brighter and larger than others and create a shape against the black night. The shape of a long dome, miles away on top of the ocean.

I stay put by the window as the ship continues to chug closer. Slowly, the city of Eden comes into view, and for the first time I see in real life what I've been seeing in flashes in my dreams. Those huge black pylons, that towering platform, the massive walls protecting it from the driving waves and fierce weather.

We move closer, and extra details emerge. Docking points for ships of various sizes at different levels above the surf. A giant domed roof that covers the entire city. Guns and various lookout points fixed to its extremities.

Again, I hardly notice when Ellie and Leeta join me, my eyes transfixed to this impossible structure. "How deep do the columns go," I whisper to Leeta.

"Not as far as you might think, given how far off shore we are. I think it's only a few hundred feet, actually. Beneath us, there's a raised portion of the ocean floor. That's why this spot was chosen."

"A raised portion. Like an underwater mountain?" asks Ellie.

"Yes, exactly. The other points of the ocean here are much deeper. All of the sea cities that are far out into the ocean are built on suitably high foundations. Otherwise, it would have been impossible."

"Impossible," I whisper, still staring at the structure. "It all seems impossible to me."

"Yes, quite a feat of engineering and architecture. When you're inside the city walls, however, you'd hardly even notice you were at sea. There's no rocking, no rolling in the waves. Unless you're near the edge, you can't even see the ocean."

"But does it smell as bad there as it did in the last place?" asks Ellie.

"Oh, of course not," says Leeta chuckling. "Eden is a paradise on earth. The only smells are those of beautiful flowers and delicious foods."

"Even in the scientific labs?" I ask bluntly. Her smiley nature really grates on me sometimes. "Or how about the hospital? I assume there's a hospital there, given how one of those kids we met earlier is going to be a Healer."

"It's a figure of speech, Cyra, don't be so antagonistic. All I'm saying is that it won't smell bad in Eden, OK."

"Yeah, I'll bet the toilets smell of roses too," I say, turning back to look out of the window.

I hear Leeta muttering something behind me along the lines of "rudeness like that won't be tolerated in Eden," but don't respond.

We're getting close now, the ship beginning to turn sideways to dock against a long tunnel extending from the city walls. It looks like there are many of these to cater to ships of different heights and allowing for easy passage into the city without having to be exposed to the elements.

The tunnel continues to extend from the wall before stopping in place as the ship gracefully glides into position next to it. I feel a steady rumble through the floor as the connection is made and people begin gathering their things to depart.

"All regular passengers disembark from the 8th floor," comes an announcement, before repeating several times over until we get the message.

"Right, come on," says Leeta, leading us away

towards the lifts. The crowd gathers around and once more I see people looking at me. Amid that throng of drab colours I must stick out like a sore thumb.

Within a few minutes we've made it down to the 8th floor and are stepping off into the inside of the tunnel extending from the city. People march forward, eager perhaps to get back to their homes and beds before starting work the following day. Yet here I don't see the long faces and weary expressions I'm used to. People walk briskly, their faces lit with smiles, chatting happily with each other as they go.

At the far end of the tunnel people start to bottleneck, working their way through security. Once more we have our barcodes, bags, and bodies scanned, before Leeta directs us through the outer wall and into the inner perimeter of the city. This stretches all the way around its boundary, providing people with an easy way to move around the inside of the wall.

It's cavernous and wide, with tracks going up the middle for a form of public transport called a tram. It's super-quick, and can go right round the entire perimeter of the city in only a few minutes without stopping.

I search to the left and right with my eyes, expecting to see a couple of Leaders step forward. One for me, one for Ellie. Or perhaps just one for the two of us. But I see no one approach. People continue to bustle forward, stepping eagerly on trams as they shoot at speed from the left and right.

They're so fast I can barely see them coming, suddenly appearing in front of me as if out of thin air.

"There are crossing points beneath the tracks," says Leeta, pointing to a section of tunnel that descends under the tramlines about 30 metres to our right. "Don't ever consider trying to cross over at this level or you'll get hit."

As she speaks, another tram quickly materialises in front of us. Its doors open, and Leeta steps on. "Come on," she says, ushering us frantically with her hands, "get on."

We pass through the doorway and the opening slides quickly shut just as we're in.

"Jeez, that was close," says Ellie, checking to see that her backside hasn't been cut off.

"The doors are sensor activated Ellie, don't worry. They won't shut if they sense someone approaching or in the doorway."

At that point the outside world suddenly turns to a blur, but it feels like we're not even moving. It's as if the entire city is spinning quickly and we're the ones who are still. Then, within only a few seconds, the space outside the tram grows clear again and the doors open with a hiss of air.

Ellie looks as dumbfounded as me as this occurs several times, people stepping on and off at each stop. I'm so lost in it all that I hardly even notice the people around me, with their sharp clothes and perfectly trimmed hair. Their white teeth, bright eyes, and often rounder physiques. Back home, seeing an overweight person is like seeing a unicorn. Only some of the Leaders and the Supervisor are able to eat enough to have fuller shapes.

After about five stops Leeta ushers us to the front and escorts us off the tram. I'm still getting funny looks from just about every person I pass, although I'm beginning to get used to that already. If they want to stare, they can stare. That's their business, not mine.

We pass under a passageway beneath the tracks and appear on the other side where there's a large bright opening. It looks to be about 20 metres tall and about the same in width, yet beyond it's so bright I can hardly make out anything.

When we pass through, however, the view grows clear, and I feel my knees growing weak at the sight. I see colour and flowers and curved white buildings. Beautiful paved walkways wind this way and that, tree lined gardens and beds of flowers dotted in sections between them. My eyes drift up at the high walls that stretch towards the clear domed roof, which sparkles with the lights of a thousand stars.

Railway tracks link the buildings above my head as strange, snake-like trains slip along them. They pass into a building before appearing a moment later on the other side. People move around the street, dressed in sleek clothing that remind me a little of the Roamers back in Arbor. They wear strange suits of silver and white and black, with only a small smattering of colour along the edges and borders of their arms and legs.

Vehicles pass by, aerodynamic and smooth,

shining under the many lights dotted along the paved roads and up the side of buildings. They all shimmer blue underneath, like the hoverbus, as they carefully weave their way up the immaculate streets.

I turn to see Leeta, her eyes glowing as bright as the city ahead of us, a smile gradually broadening on her lips. "Welcome to Eden," she says. "Welcome to your new home."

9

Watchers

I'm back on the mainland, but I don't know where. I turn and see a giant wall, standing high against the parched earth, the sun setting at its summit, and realise I'm at the border of Arcadia. Silhouettes swarm in the face of the sun on top of it, flashes of light following one after another in the gathering gloom.

I move forward, my body light as air, and begin to rise above the ground. I float high, swept up by the wind until I'm level with the top of the wall. Then higher I go, rising and rising until I can see beyond it.

Standing in the distance in a shroud of darkness stands a man, cloaked and covered in tattered cloth. He raises his arm, high into the air, before dropping it quickly back to his side. A thousand flashes light up the sky behind, illuminating an army of men, and my eyes open wide.

I blink in the cold light of morning and look quickly around the room, my heart beating fast. Slowly my vision comes into focus, and all I see is white. The walls, the curtains, the carpeted floor, all shades of white and light grey. When I step to the floor I feel a shiver run through me, right up my spine. It's cold here. Much colder than I'm used to.

Then a voice reaches my ears. The voice of a woman, soothing and electronic, that appears to come from nowhere in particular.

"Your heart-rate is high, Cyra, and you're shivering at an abnormal level. Would you like me to raise the room temperate?"

I quickly twist my neck in just about every direction, searching for the source of the voice.

"Who said that!" I shout, my voice cracking with an early morning fog.

"I did," comes the voice, once more out of nowhere.

"Well, where are you!"

"I'm everywhere," comes the voice.

"What do you mean, everywhere?"

"I mean I exist everywhere around Eden. I'm officially designated as artificial intelligence, or AI for short. Shall I increase the room temperate for you?"

I continue to look around the room, my head still foggy and filled with lingering memories of my dreams.

"Um...yes please, I guess."

I feel an immediate change as the floor beneath my feet grows warmer.

"I have calibrated the appropriate temperature," says the voice. "I shall set it as the norm for your room."

"Er, thanks," I say. "So, do you control everything in the room?"

"Yes. Whatever can be controlled, that is."

"So, if I wanted the curtains to be opened, you could do that?"

Immediately the curtains slide open, bringing a bright natural light into the room.

I shield my eyes and the windows suddenly darken a few shades. "Is that better for you?" asks the voice.

"Much better, thanks. Do you have a name?"

"I activate to the name Eve."

"Right, Eve, thanks. I'm Cyra," I say, feeling a little bit stupid for introducing myself to a computer.

"Nice to meet you, Cyra. Please call on me if you require any help with anything."

"Sure," I say, staring up to the ceiling at a random point as if I'm talking to a God.

I move towards the window, still thinking that perhaps I'm dreaming. A talking computer who can understand me and control the room. And I thought yesterday I'd seen it all.

Outside, the city is alive. Snake trains slip silently between buildings. People zip about in their hover vehicles on the streets below. From where I am, up on the 10th floor, I can see hordes of workers stepping through the large opening into the perimeter and getting on trams. People pour on, but no one comes off. I guess this must be a purely residential area of the city.

Last night, when we arrived, Leeta did little but lead us to our living quarters. I was so drained from everything I'd seen over the previous two days that I barely registered how clean and large my room was. Even now, looking out upon the city, the room hardly has an impact on me. I suppose I'm already beginning to grow desensitised to such things. Even being introduced to a talking computer hasn't sent me fainting to the floor as it might have done a few days ago. If only Jackson could see me now. He'd almost certainly laugh at the sight of me talking to the ceiling.

A knock on the door sounds and I move towards it, wearing nothing but a light night gown that was on the bed the previous evening. As I approach, an image of the outside appears on the wall next to the door. I can see Leeta, standing upright and in her usual grey attire, patiently waiting for me to let her in.

She knocks again, and I watch the image as she speaks. "Cyra, wake up now. There's lot's to be done."

I give it a few more moments and watch her grow increasingly agitated outside. Just for my own amusement, nothing more. Eventually I relent and pull the door open with a click. She steps right in past me and does a little twist.

"Didn't I tell you, Cyra. Isn't it much nicer here than your old home?"

I glance around at the large, bare space, and find myself disagreeing. "Well, it's a bit empty isn't it. There's only a bed."

Leeta shakes her head and chuckles. "Silly girl. Everything is voice activated. I told you this last night. Have you not met Eve yet?"

I nod and shrug my head at the same time. I literally have no memory of her telling me about any of this the previous evening. It's not overly surprising. I have developed a habit of zoning out sometimes when Leeta talks.

"Eve," says Leeta. "Would you activate the wardrobe please."

Immediately the wall on the other side of the room begins clicking as a wardrobe unfolds in front of my eyes, sprouting as if from nowhere. Leeta moves towards it, opens it up, and pulls out the sort of white outfit I've seen various other people wear since I got here. "They're all your size in here, all the clothing. You can activate other furniture too. Sofas, desks, chairs. Do I really have to tell you this again, Cyra?"

I shake my head. "No, it's OK, I'll work it out."

"Right. Now get those on quickly and come along. And try to smile more. You'll stand out if you don't smile. And not in a good way."

Sure, it's the not smiling that will make me stand out. Not the fact that my skin is the colour of the sunset and my hair as bright as the stars.

I dress quickly before stepping out into the corridor, where Ellie is already waiting with Leeta with a beaming smile on her face.

"Leeta says she's taking us to the same place. So, our duty is together!" she cries.

"That's the spirit," says Leeta, referencing the smile on Ellie's face. "You'd do well to follow her example Cyra. You'd think someone had just died the way you're always frowning."

117

I shot of pain rushes through me, but I keep my eyes up. With everything I've been seeing, it's hard to believe that my mother only died a few days ago. I fear that my grief is only lying dormant for now. Soon, perhaps, it will hit me.

"So," I say, quickly changing the subject, "you know what our duty is?"

"Still a no I'm afraid. But, no matter, you'll find out soon enough."

"Is that normal, though? I mean, why don't you know? Why is this all being kept from us?"

"Come now, Cyra, if it's not my duty to know, then it's not my business. I just turn my own little cog around and around as part of that big machine. Asking questions isn't part of that. But, to answer your question, I don't know if this is normal or not. I've always been assigned to the Testing on the mainland regions, and have never had anyone assigned to Eden before. You two girls are my first."

We move down through the building in a lift that takes just a split second to reach ground level. Just like the trams, everything seems to work at lightning pace. Why waste time travelling when there's such important work to be done, I suppose.

A short walk takes us back towards the perimeter wall, where we pass under the tram tracks and onto the other side. There, I see a series of lifts. We step in and I notice buttons on the wall numbering 1 to 8 next to the letter S, and 1 to 6 next to the letter U. The 'S', Leeta says, is for Surface levels and the 'U' for Underwater levels. Overall, that makes 14 levels beneath the deck level used primarily for residential buildings and living quarters.

Leeta presses the button for U5 and I gulp air as if we're about to actually dive under the surface. I see levels flash by in front of me as we descend, before the lift pulls to a quick stop at Underwater Level 5. I gingerly step out of the lift and take a look around, feeling like the walls are about to cave in and flood at any moment. It's an odd feeling, knowing I'm currently deep beneath the raging sea, and makes my head spin a little.

As with the deck level, there's a rail running to the left and right in front of us. I'd imagine there's one of those at each level to offer quick transport for the people working there.

"OK, girls. This is as far as I can take you."

"You're leaving?" asks Ellie, almost longingly. Leeta has, for all her irritating quirks, become the closest person we have to a friend out here.

"I have to. I don't have access to this level. Don't worry, though, I'll see you both again soon."

She steps back into the lift and smiles at us. "Be good, girls," she says, just before the doors close and she's swept back up out of sight.

Ellie and I look at each other, not quite knowing what to do. We're in a sort of tunnel in the perimeter, although the ceilings aren't as high and cavernous down here. Unlike above, the trams don't rush by every minute either. Instead it's quiet and eerie. In both directions it seems darker and more shrouded in shadow, where above it was all brightly lit and bathed in natural sunlight.

Then the sound of footsteps fills the air, echoing from our right. We turn to see a shadow moving through a passageway beneath the tram tracks. In the quiet of the tunnel, it's almost unnerving, and I feel Ellie shift her weight to my side.

Then we hear a voice, deep and precise, as a man moves into view. He wears black, his entire body covered from neck to toe in a sleek suit that seems to suck the light from around him. In the gloomy tunnel, he appears almost as a silhouette against the setting sun, only the outline of his body visible as he moves towards us.

"You must be Cyra and Ellie. We've been waiting for you," he says as he looms closer.

His face comes into view, pale and chiselled as if from a chunk of grey stone. His eyes pierce from beneath black eyebrows, cold and dark as the night.

He stops short of us and looks us both up and down. Wearing white and with my shining blonde hair and golden skin, I must look about the complete opposite of him.

"Follow me please," he says, turning and walking back in the direction he came from.

We follow, as instructed, in silence, although I can see a slightly concerned look on Ellie's face. We go under the tram tracks, as on the upper deck, and onto the other side. Unlike the upper deck, however, there's no large opening and bright light beyond. Only a long wall stretching as far as I can see in either direction. Along it are doors and passageways leading towards the centre of the level. Inside it must be a maze of passages and corridors and unknown rooms where unknown things are being done.

We walk along the wall for a moment before turning left along a long passageway. It stretches inward, into the distance, as far as the eye can see. For several minutes we walk along it, the darkness ahead seemingly never-ending, until finally a door begins to slowly appear. It's large and metallic, gleaming silver under a series of lights shining down from above. There seem to be warning markings around it. They tell people that this is a restricted area. That there are dangers beyond the door.

I feel my heart racing as we approach. *Restricted area. Dangers beyond the door.* Where the hell are we being led? What is all of this?

The man begins to pull up his sleeve as we near the door and I see a small hole leading into the wall. He slips his hand and wrist into it, before a red light begins glowing. A moment later, it turns green, and the seams of the door start hissing as it slowly slides open at the middle.

Coming into view beyond the wall is a large space, like the sports hall back home, only many times the size. The place is almost entirely empty, though, except for an area to the immediate left. We walk in, and I see several other faces staring back at us. Young faces. Faces filled with fear and wonder and confusion. Faces of people like me, of people like Ellie. The faces of school leavers, assigned to Eden.

I count eight; six boys, and a couple of girls. They

sit in chairs in the middle of the open space, patiently waiting for the two of us to join their ranks. The man tells us to sit in the available two seats at the back, and we once again do as ordered.

Among the nervous faces I see one of complete calm. A boy turns around, in his seat, and runs his eyes over us. It's a look I've grown familiar with over the last few days. The sort of look people were giving me at the Duty Call. Anger, maybe. Disgust. I can't really tell. It seems, though, I'm seeing for the first time the arrogance long associated with this city. The feeling that those from the mainland are inherently inferior. I never knew if that was true or simply a rumour. Right now, I'm guessing it's the former.

His eyes seem to linger on me most of all, before turning back to the front. I suppose it's my unique look around here. None of the others share it, and I can quickly tell that there's no one else here from Agricola. By the way everyone's brown and black hair is so neatly cut and styled, I'd assume the majority are either local to Eden, or from other sea cities.

"Right, everyone," says the man in black, standing ahead of us and gracefully running his eyes over each individual, "welcome to the Grid. This room will be your home away from home for the next few months. My name is Commander Ajax, but Ajax will do just fine."

I look over at Ellie, who's already turned her eyes to me, her face riddled with nerves.

"Many of you have travelled a long way to get

here," he continues, looking up towards Ellie and I. "Others have lived here their entire lives." I look towards the arrogant boy, and see a smile creep up the corner of his mouth.

"But all of you," Ajax says, raising his voice, "are now equal. Here in the Grid, we will train together and eat together. We will grow together and improve together. You are all now one big family."

He looks over each of us again, his voice growing more intense.

"Your duty is to Eden. It is to Arcadia. And it is to each other. Because all of you...."

I stare, hardly breathing.

".....are to become Watchers of Eden."

10
The Grid

In front of me, faces turn to each other, etched with looks of confusion. I turn to Ellie first, expecting her to be looking to me, but she's just staring forward. There's a seriousness to her face that I haven't yet seen, an intensity written into her green eyes.

So many questions rush through my mind as I raise my eyes back up to Commander Ajax. He stands there, looking over each of us, waiting for us to give him our complete attention.

"I can tell by the looks on your faces that you don't know what a Watcher is?" he asks.

I scan the room again and see heads shaking. All except two. To my side, Ellie remains still, her eyes locked on Ajax. Ahead of me, the boy from Eden sits casually, a petulant look on his face.

"Well, that's good," says Ajax. "Watchers aren't known to the general public. I wouldn't expect you to know about them."

"So, what are they?" comes a gravelly voice from a boy at the front.

Ajax walks slowly forward, addressing the boy directly. "Tell me, Link, when was your genetics test conducted?"

I lean closer in to catch a better glimpse of the boy. His hair is dark, yet longer and not as perfectly trimmed as the others. There's a scar running down the side of his face, up his jaw and across his cheek, that gives him a roughness that the others don't have. I can tell, just at a glance, that this boy's from the mainland too.

"A few days ago," he answers.

"And since then, have you been dreaming more than usual?"

I see Link's eyes crunch up in a frown. "Yes...I have."

"And those dreams. What have they been about?"

There's a complete hush around us now. I look between pairs of eyes to see them staring intently at Link, waiting for his answer.

"I can't remember them that clearly," he says. "Fragments of things mainly."

"Things that came true? Things you had never seen before?" asks Ajax.

I watch as Link nods, slowly.

Now I'm retracing my own dreams. All the flashes of things I've seen over the last few days. Ever since my genetics test my sleep has been filled with images of things I'd go on to see a day or two later. The sight of the ship that carried me to Eden. The image of the coastline from the sea. The pylons holding the colossal domed platform above the surf. The face of my dead mother.

I trace my eyes over those ahead of me once again and see that they're doing the same. The realisation that those hazy fragments were more than just the imagination. They were the future. Visions of reality, yet to unfold.

Ajax's voice brings all eyes back up to him, putting words to what is already rushing through everyone's minds.

"Those things you've been seeing, Link – the things that all of you have been seeing – is what we call premature reality. More commonly, you might think of it as the future."

"We can see the future?" asks one of the girls.

"Exactly," says Ajax coolly. "Your genetics test unearthed a mutated gene inside each of you. How long did your tests last for?" he asks, looking around the room.

I hear a series of answers.

Thirty minutes

Forty minutes

Three quarters of an hour.

"The reason you all took so long is because the scanner was opening up your pathways so that you can tap into the Void. It's what we call the period between now and the visions of the future you see. We each have that mutated gene, although the extent to which you can control your Watcher abilities will vary."

"Abilities?" comes another question. "There's more than one?"

"There are several. Although you won't all be able to develop them. It really depends on the person and their potential. Watchers cannot control the visions they have. They come most commonly during sleep, when our minds are most active, and vary in their scope. In general, Watchers can only see a few days or weeks ahead, and only events nearby to where they are currently located. Our main responsibility as Watchers is to oversee the policing of Arcadia and the safety of its people."

I look over to Ellie, who now looks about as lost as everyone else. The boy from Eden, however, just looks disinterested.

"There are Watchers assigned all over the nation. Their visions help prevent accidents and catastrophes, crime and attacks from rebels. The clearer the vision, the better prepared we are to prevent it."

"But last year four people died in one of the factories where I'm from. Why wasn't that prevented?" asks Link, his voice dry.

"It's not a complete system or a perfect system," responds Ajax. "Sometimes the vision is too obscured to know where it takes place and when. Sometimes there are enough details to prevent such things. There simply aren't enough of us to blanket the whole country right now, so we do our best with what we have."

I watch as Link sits back, arms folded. I know what he's thinking. That there is no Watcher assigned near where he's from because it's not important enough. Something tells me that most Watchers are assigned to offer protection on the sea cities and the more important regions. I can't ever remember seeing one in Arbor, although I guess I wouldn't know it even if I had.

"I understand that all of this is hard to take on at once," continues Ajax. "There's a lot to learn and discover, and it will take time for it to sink in. Over the coming weeks and months, we will try to unleash the full extent of your abilities, and will train you to use them..."

"But you said they couldn't be controlled," says Link again, cutting Ajax off.

Ajax's face grows suddenly stern, his stone jaw clenching. "Please don't interrupt me again, Link," he says, a menace to his words. "I understand in Fossor that life is different, but here you must observe etiquette."

Link nods and slinks slightly back into his chair.

"But your question is valid. The visions you have cannot be controlled, but your ability to see marginally into the Void can be. Not all Watchers can do so, but those who can are able to look a few seconds into the future around them. When this happens, premature reality overlaps with the present, giving the Watcher an additional ability."

"Which is?" asks the boy from Eden, who suddenly appears more interested.

Ajax smiles. "I think, Theo, it's easier if I show you all."

He begins moving away from us, walking towards the door into the hall before speaking in a loud voice. "Eve, would you simulate a battlefield situation."

"Yes, Commander Ajax," comes the voice of the

AI.

Immediately the large open space ahead of us begins to change. Broken down walls and old buildings begin springing up from the floor. The ground grows heavy with rubble and other debris. I see soldiers appearing as if from nowhere, hiding behind whatever they can find. Within only a few moments, most of the hall resembles a war torn town.

Ellie's eyes have bulged at the sight, and I can see Link also looking around in bewilderment. None of the others seem to bat an eyelid, though. They just watch the room morph as if it's the most natural thing in the world.

Then Ajax asks for Eve to put up a protective screen, and a long see-through sheet appears down the left hand side of the battlefield.

"Please go and stand behind the screen," he says, turning back to us. "And Eve, on my command, activate live gun fire."

Everyone stands from their chairs and begins moving towards the screen, and for the first time I get a good look at them all. Link stands tall and strong, his black hair falling casually over the front of his face. He reminds me a bit of Jackson in how old he looks compared to the others. If I had seen him at any other time I'd put him as older than 16.

Walking at the front is Theo, the boy from Eden. He moves fluidly with a stroll as the other boys from the sea cities follow in his wake. They hustle behind, trying to move up to his side, and gather together as we reach the protective screen. I can hear them whispering, wondering perhaps what exactly is about to happen, as Theo stares ahead, out towards the battlefield.

Ellie walks beside me, staring wide-eyed at the rusted cars and broken down buildings. The other two girls walk together, their hair a strange colour of dark red. They speak as they go, their voices carrying a similar tone, and I quickly realise that they're twins.

At the front of the hall, Ajax stands, patiently waiting for us all to move into place. Everyone's eyes fall to him as a sudden hush runs over the group. Then he shouts, calling to Eve to simulate an attack, and begins running forward into the battleground.

The noise that fills the air is unlike anything I've ever experienced. Even back home near the huge harvesting machines and factories, I've never heard such an explosion of sound. Guns begin firing from a dozen locations in the simulated town, bullets whizzing through the air at Ajax. Lights flash as the weapons fire, the bullets ripping into buildings and cars and other debris lining the floor.

I see Ellie shield her eyes and turn her face to the ground, expecting to see Ajax's body ripped apart by the barrage of firepower ahead of him.

But he keeps coming, keeps running forward, moving further and further into the town. He twists and turns as he goes, moving to the left and right, ducking and jumping through the storm.

The bullets keep firing, the room still raging with the sound of war, flashing constantly as sparks fly all around. I look briefly down the line of faces next to me, and see only wide eyes and open mouths as Ajax keeps going, on and on, passing by soldiers as they fire at him.

He doesn't slow. He just keeps on running, shaping his path towards the other end. Soon he's nearing the other side, the bullets still fizzing through the air after him. Then, as quickly as it all started, the firing stops and the room falls silent, leaving only a heavy ringing that bounces around the room.

Ajax turns to us, not a hint of fear or panic on his face. He begins walking back in our direction as the entire hall begins to return to its original state, the buildings and broken walls and battered cars disappearing back into nothing. The protective sheet ahead of us slides back into the floor and, just as Ellie finally raises her head back up, the room returns to normal.

Not a word is spoken as Ajax continues his approach, his footsteps now the only sound echoing around the hall. Everyone just stares at him, awestruck, wondering what they just witnessed.

Link is the first to speak, shaking his head as he looks at Ajax. "That was fake, right? Just a simulation. They weren't real bullets?"

It's not Ajax who answers, but Theo. I hear his voice down the line, his tone mocking. "Of course it was real," he says, looking at Link as if he's an idiot. "Did you think all those walls were crumbling for no reason?"

"All right wise guy, so what do you think

happened?"

Theo laughs and shakes his head, rolling his eyes. "You mainlanders are so simple. Were you not listening to him before? He can see where the bullets will be before they're even fired. Why do you think he was jigging this way and that? It's not a dance contest."

I can see Link's fist beginning to clench by his side, his tall frame extending to its fullest height. Ajax's voice quickly cuts him back down.

"You don't want to do that Link," he says. "Hitting him won't get you anywhere."

"Yeah, but it'll make me feel better," says Link, shooting a stare at Theo, who just smiles back at him.

"And Theo, don't antagonise people. Or were you not listening earlier either? I said that down here we're all one big family. Trust me, you're going to need each other before long."

Theo sneers but doesn't reply.

"But," continues Ajax, now addressing us all. "Theo is right about what just happened. When you're able to control your abilities, you'll be able to see things a few seconds before they happen. So, essentially, you'll be able to dodge bullets. Or, to be more accurate, you'll simply be avoiding their future paths."

A chorus of disbelief rumbles between us. "For real?" asks one of the boys, his hair a murky blond.

"That's yet to be seen. Not all Watchers are able to do so. Some only have visions, while others are able to control the Void for a limited amount of time, as you just saw me do. That may be a second or two, or perhaps a bit more. It depends on each of us, so don't expect to be able to do what I just did."

"And you? How far into the Void can you see?" I realise, before I know it, that it's me who's asked the question.

Everyone's eyes turn to me before shooting back to Ajax. "I am more gifted than most," he says, without offering anything more. "Our training in the coming months will reveal the extent of your ability to see into the Void. For now, though, I want to speak with you each individually."

Ajax leads us back to the seats near the entrance to the Grid and asks us to sit down. For the rest of the morning, he tells us, we will get to know each other. Each will speak with him one on one as the rest socialise with the other trainees. Strong social ties, he says, are an important element of life on Eden.

I notice that Theo and the other boys and girls from the sea cities are aware of this point. In fact, it looks to be more directed at myself, Ellie, and Link, who appear to be the only ones from the mainland. Life on the sea cities, it would seem, is more social than elsewhere. They probably grew up with more free time on their hands to actually enjoy it, although I know that relationships between boys and girls are still forbidden before the Pairing, even on Eden.

It's the blond haired boy who is first to speak with Ajax alone. They walk to the other side of the hall where several walls suddenly sprout from the floor to provide some privacy. The rest of us remain in our seats, unsure of exactly what to do. Ellie seems to have retracted back into her shell, becoming that shy girl I first met once again. She sits, head low, intermittently peeping her eyes up to see what the others are doing.

It's Theo who is the first to act. He stands up and walks to the front where Ajax had been addressing us, and casually creeps his eyes over each of us, one by one.

"As the only one here from Eden, I suppose it's down to me to organise something," he says.

The other sea city boys immediately sit up as if being spoken to by a teacher, while Link remains relaxed in his chair, a scowl on his face.

"Let's each come up to the front and introduce ourselves to the rest of the group. I'll go first."

I see Ellie shrink further back into herself, her chin dropping even lower to her chest.

"My name is Theo Graves," Theo starts, his voice calm and clear as it rings out through the hall. "I am, as we all know by now, from Eden, and my parents are both members of the Council." He speaks proudly, a smugness growing on his face. "Link, why don't you go next?"

Link stays put for a moment, before grudgingly standing up. He doesn't stand to the front though, but merely stays by his chair, ready to drop back down into it once he's done.

"Thanks Theo," he says sarcastically. "So, I'm Link. My parents aren't members of any Council or nothin'. My dad's dead and my mum's a factory clerk from Fossor. That enough, Mr Graves?"

"Oh, I am sorry to hear about your father," says Theo, insincerely. "How did he die?"

Link's face screws up a little more. "Factory explosion," he says, before tightening his jaw and falling back into his chair.

"Right," says Theo, still directing things. "How about you two twins. You must be from Gaia with that hair?"

The twins stand together and answer in unison. "Yes, that's right Theo. We're Lorna," says one, "and Larna," says the other, "and our parents are Healers."

"For anyone who doesn't know," says Lorna, looking specifically to myself, Ellie, and Link, "Gaia is a very colourful city, so hair like ours is common. It was actually much redder before, but we had it toned down when we learned we were coming here."

"And a good thing too," says Theo. "Hair that's too bright is *unpleasant* for Edenites." He glances at my hair as he speaks, and I can't help but duck my head slightly out of embarrassment.

"How about you?" he says. I lift my eyes to see Theo looking at me. "You look like you're from Agricola?" His words are innocent, but the way he says them makes a jolt of anger run up my spine.

"Yes," I say, "I'm from a town called..."

"Well stand up, stand up," he cuts in. "When you speak to an audience in Eden, you stand."

I reluctantly stand and now know exactly how

Link must be feeling. All I want to do is smack the guy in the mouth.

"I'm from a town called Arbor and my name is Cyra," I continue, making sure to speak clearly and confidently. I don't care who this boy is, I'm not going to have him looking down on me. "My father was called into service and died a few years ago. My mother is....was..."

I stop, my voice caught in my throat. I can feel all eyes on me again, burning through me, just as they did at the Duty Call, on the hoverbus, on the ship from Piscator.

"Yes?" says Theo. "Your mother was a, what?"

I feel my heart beginning to pound, my head starting to ache, my vision slowly blurring. I drop down into my chair again and see images flash before my eyes. Flashes of glowing orange sunsets and mighty walls in the desert. Of soldiers and weapons and howls of pain. I blink my eyes quickly and feel a cool hand across my forehead, the blackness framing my eyes starting to clear.

"Cyra," says a sweet voice, "Cyra, are you OK?"

I see the soft features of Ellie in front of me, her fearful eyes staring into mine.

"I...I'm fine," I say, sitting back up straight. "I don't know what happened."

Gradually the faces in front of me grow into focus and I see all sets of eyes staring at me. "Are you sure you feel all right?" says one of the twins, I can't tell which. "We can check you over if you want. We know how. Our parents are Healers, as we said."

136

I shake my head. "No, thanks, I'm fine. I just....don't like speaking in front of people, that's all."

I hear Theo give off an arrogant huff just as footsteps begin echoing from across the hall. We all turn up and see the blond boy walking back towards us.

"He wants you, Theo," he says as he gets closer.

I share a quick look with Link, whose face is still written in a scowl. He shakes his head and moves over towards me and Ellie.

"Don't like public speaking huh?" he asks.

"Yeah, never have," I lie.

"Well, that guy ain't helping. One of these days he'll get what's coming to him. I'll see to it myself if I have to."

I laugh as Theo begins strolling off to the other side of the room. "So, your father was killed too?" I ask, happy to find someone who might understand my grief.

He nods. "Last year. Accident at his factory."

"You mean...the accident you mentioned earlier? The one the Watchers didn't see?"

His dark grey eyes remain stony and hard. "Yeah, it happens a lot where I'm from. I never knew about all this Watcher stuff. Maybe now I'll be able to prevent some of them."

Without Theo there, everyone seems to fall back into their own private conversations. Link remains at the back with myself and Ellie, who's still keeping herself to herself, while the other boys begin forming into their own little gang up at the front. After about 10 minutes, Theo comes strolling back and sits with the boys, who immediately surround him and begin asking him how it all went. I can't tell whether it's the fact that he's from Eden or if he's actually some big shot around here, but they seem to lap up every word.

One by one, the boys meander off towards the other end of the hall while Theo stands and continues to lead the introductions. The murky blond boy stands next. Rupert, from the second largest sea city of Caprico. Then the final three boys I don't know: Anders, Kyle, and Amir, all of them from the fishing sea city of Aquar.

Link is the last of the boys to pay a visit to Ajax before it's the turn of the girls. The twins go first, just as Theo demands Ellie stand and give her introduction. She does, nervously rattling off the scant details of her life, before melting back into her chair as Theo remarks on how poor mainlanders are at speaking to groups.

Soon it's Ellie who wanders off to see Ajax, returning a few minutes later with her eyes reddened once again. I ask her what happened, but all she does it shut down once more, refusing to tell me.

I have no time to dig for the truth, though, because I'm the only one left for Ajax to see. I walk across the hall and towards the newly formed room, fitted with a door and solid walls. I knock and am called in, finding Ajax sitting in a chair with a spare seat a few feet opposite from him.

He tells me to sit, before explaining exactly what

this is all about.

"Cyra," he says, holding a large tablet, similar to Leeta's, in his hand, "how are you finding Eden?"

I shrug my shoulders. "I haven't really had a chance to get to know it yet. I'm not sure about some of the people though," I say impertinently.

"Theo is highly bred and comes from a long line of powerful people," says Ajax. "But down here, we're all the same."

"How did you know I was talking about him?" I ask quickly.

"Intuition," he says. "I understand he can rub people up the wrong way, but he'll settle in once he's got it out of his system. Just ignore him for now."

"I'll try," I say, "although I can't vouch for Link."

He smiles and looks down at his tablet. "Right, I'm talking to you individually to speak about your genetics test, as well as any visions you may have had since then. Tell me Cyra, what can you remember?"

He looks up from his tablet, his eyes resting on mine.

"Um, well I saw glimpses of things along my journey here. Like the city itself, the boat that took me here, Piscator on the coast."

"Anything else?"

I take a gulp. "My mother. She...she died the night before I left. I saw her face during my genetics test."

His face suddenly loosens, his hard features softening. "I'm so sorry to hear that, Cyra. How did she pass?"

"The virus."

"That's terrible. You must be having a hard time right now?"

I nod but don't answer. I'm afraid if I do my voice will crack.

"It is during times of emotion and trauma that our visions grow clearest, Cyra. The illness and death of your mother may explain why your visions have been more far reaching than the others."

"Far reaching?"

"Yes. Arbor is a long way from Eden, yet you say you saw clear sights of the city. That's rare, Cyra, very rare. As I said earlier, visions are usually confined to areas close to where you are at the time. You, however, have seen thousands of miles."

"Because of my mother?"

"That will be a factor, yes," he says. "There's also your IQ, which is high. Those with higher IQ's dream more, and in the same way, their visions are often stronger and more clear. We'll know more in the coming weeks and months."

"I've seen something else?" I say. "I've seen Knight's Wall at the Divide."

His eyes raise quickly from his tablet. "Knight's Wall? What have you seen?"

"Soldiers, a sunset," I say.

"Yes, and?" he asks quickly, his eyes narrowing.

"Gunfire," I continue, "and flashes of light. And beyond it....an army."

Commander Ajax shuffles his weight in his seat, his face growing grave, his voice turning quiet. "An army...that's not possible."

"I suppose, maybe I was dreaming. My father died at the Divide and a friend of mine has just been sent there, so it's sort of on my mind."

Ajax's face fails to soften this time. He doesn't tell me he's sorry for my father's death. He doesn't offer any consoling words. He just looks at me, almost straight through me, his dark eyes glinting under the light.

"Is that all you saw. Any details? Any faces? Anything else?"

I shake my head. "No. It was kinda blurry, nothing specific or clear."

"Listen to me, Cyra. If you see anything again, anything at all, you come to me immediately. I don't care what time it is, I don't care what you're doing or where you are. You come straight down here, OK."

I nod, his sudden intensity unnerving. "I understand."

"Good."

Then he stands, and orders Eve to dismantle the room, which she duly does. "That's all for today, Cyra. Tell the rest to return here tomorrow at 8 AM. And get some rest. Tomorrow we start your training.

And with that, he begins marching in the other direction, to the other side of the room, before slipping out of another door and disappearing from sight.

11
Fear Training

The afternoon of our first full day on Eden is spent with Leeta. She guides Ellie and I around the upper deck of the city, showing us the entertainment quarter and the commercial district. Both are hives of activity, only growing more busy as the afternoon grows late and the evening approaches.

People sit at cafes and restaurants, eating and drinking a range of foods I've never experienced. Fish and lobster and exotic meats imported from the regions. Fruits and vegetables and soups and breads fill their tables, many hardly touched and going to waste.

My nostrils fill with smells that make my stomach rumble, only for it to turn at the thought of such decadence. I ask Leeta about the staff who clear the tables of used plates and uneaten food. About those who clean the city and keep it smelling and looking like a bed of roses. The sort of role I expected to be given when I arrived.

Those people, she says with an element of guilt, live on the floor below the deck level on Surface Level 8. She doesn't elaborate, but I immediately know that their rations will be similar to what we get in the regions. That their living quarters will be basic compared to my own.

In the entertainment quarter I see things I've only ever heard about. There's an old movie theatre in Arbor, although it doesn't operate any more. Here, there are many, filled with various screens showing the latest holographic pictures. Elsewhere are live action productions, where actors dress up and perform a story in front of an audience. The thought that some people here live for such a purpose baffles me in a world where everyone needs to fill a role.

Again, Leeta says that entertainment is important to help people relax after fulfilling their duties for the day. That, as Ajax had told us, the social aspect of life on Eden is crucial to its structure and for the mental health of the people.

I think of the sort of entertainment we get back home. Playing in the fields as children. Reading what scant books are available in the dilapidated town library. Watching old recordings on television, if you're lucky enough to have one. I remember my mother telling me how they used to erect a screen in the town square during certain times of year. But that was only when I was a child, and hasn't happened in over a decade. It hardly compares really.

That evening, Leeta takes us to the centre of the upper deck as it gets dark, where a huge square marks a popular meeting point in the middle of the city. At the heart of the square is a grand fountain, spraying water high into the air. It sparkles under the moonlight, droplets of water sprinkling down into a large pool surrounding it. Around it people smile and sing and dance, eating at restaurants and perusing the shops bordering the square. Above, buildings stretch high into the night sky, housing some of the most sought after residences in the city.

Only the most important people are provided with living quarters here, where many politicians and powerful officials enjoy unspoilt views across all of the upper deck and beyond across the ocean. I know that Theo's parents, members of the Council, will be among them.

When I ask Leeta about it, she almost falls over from shock.

"Theo Graves is doing the same duty as you?!" she exclaims. I quickly regret telling her, realising that it's not right for me to even speak about my role as a trainee Watcher. Leeta probably doesn't even know what a Watcher is, although I suspect those on Eden, if not elsewhere, are likely to have some idea about them. Certainly, when Ajax revealed our duty earlier in the day, Theo didn't seem surprised or confused at all. He was just glum and disinterested.

In any case, Leeta doesn't ask what the duty is. She merely tells me that she doesn't want to know anyway, and that it's not her duty to pry or ask questions on the matter. What she does do, however, is tell me a little bit about who Theo actually is.

"The Graves are two of the most important members of the Council who run Eden and, by extension, Arcadia," she says. "Theo is their only son, and is known throughout the city. I thought he'd follow them into politics, but obviously not."

"So that explains why he's such a jerk," I say.

"Cyra, wash your mouth out!" says Leeta, quickly glancing around us. "You can't speak about someone like that, especially not someone like him."

I look at Ellie, who's laughing next to me. "But he is," I say. "I've never met anyone so arrogant."

"Well arrogant he may be, but there's a reason for that. The kids here, they all behave like they're up on a pedestal. They'll all grow out of it in the end though."

"And were you like that?" asks Ellie. "You know, arrogant and rude to people from the mainland."

Leeta shakes her head. "Of course not. You may not believe this, but I wasn't born on Eden. So, I know what it's like to be an outsider."

"You're not originally from here?" I ask. "Where are you from then?"

Leeta lifts her chin. "A small region in the north, along the coast. It was a manufacturing region. Mainly ship building. Right, now come along girls, it's getting late."

She hurries off away from the square and back towards our building near the perimeter as Ellie and I chase after her. "I guess that's why she loves the ocean so much," Ellie says. "Because she grew up next to it."

It doesn't take long to get back, at which point Leeta says goodbye and tells us she'll continue our tour another time. She seems strangely reserved as she departs, and I can almost see her eyes glistening slightly as she turns and walks away.

I say goodnight to Ellie, who I've discovered is in the room next to me, and re-enter my own chambers. Inside it's warmer than outside and just about everywhere I've been, owing to the recalibrated heating that Eve set up. I ask her to darken the windows and shut the curtains, and she does without answering.

Then I crawl into bed, my head aching wildly with everything that's happened today, everything I've discovered and learned. I'm so wired that I don't think I'll sleep at all, yet within minutes I'm out like a light, dropping into a deep sleep like I haven't enjoyed for an age. A sleep uninterrupted by dreams and visions and thoughts of my mother and Jackson.

I wake without any feeling of drowsiness either. The curtains have already been opened and the windows are growing more transparent, slowly losing their cloak. Light spills into the room, growing brighter as the minutes pass.

Outside my room, Ellie already waits, although she seems to have had a rougher night. I ask her if she's OK but don't get much of a response. I'd imagine she's worried about the day ahead. I know I am.

It's a funny thing, not knowing what to expect. There's a comfort in knowing what's coming your way, even if it's scary or nerve racking. At least you'd know, so can prepare for it mentally. Right now, neither Ellie nor I have any idea of what to expect from not just today, but the weeks, months, and even years, ahead. Beyond this training, beyond learning to control these so-called abilities we're supposed to have, we have no idea where we'll end up. By the sounds of it, Watchers are assigned all over, destined to watch over others for their entire lives. Right now, the dreams I've been having have often woken me up in a sweat. I can't imagine that continuing for the rest of my life. In fact, the very thought of it terrifies me.

When we arrive at the Grid, we scan our wrists and the door slides open with the usual hiss of air. Like yesterday, we look upon the faces of the other trainees, sitting in their seats. Unlike yesterday, however, there is no long, wide, expansive hall stretching into the distance. In fact, we seem to have walked into a small room with little in it but a few seats and tables with water and fruit on top.

"Ah, that's our full compliment," says Ajax, his eyes scanning over me as we enter.

We find a couple of seats before Ajax briefs us on what we'll be doing.

"I hope you all slept well last night," he says, "because today, and for the weeks to come, you're going to need all your strength."

"Now, let me ask you all a question, and I want you to answer it truthfully." He waits for us all to acknowledge him. "What do you know of fear?"

No one answers.

"Let me re-phrase the question. What are you most scared of?"

His eyes scan us and stop on Link, always one to give his opinion.

"I guess, fire. I've never liked fire."

"Good. Thank you, Link. Anyone else?"

The twins put their hands up. "We both hate

flying," they say together.

"Thank you Larna and Lorna. How about you Ellie?"

"Um, I guess I'm afraid of snakes. I was bitten once, back home in Lignum."

"Yes, snakes are a common fear for mainlanders," says Ajax. "Theo, what scares you?"

Theo shakes his head. "Nothing scares me."

There's a rumble of approval from the other sea city boys. Link and I just look at each other and roll our eyes, just like I'd do with Jackson.

"Everyone is scared of something," says Ajax. "Don't be shy, you can tell us."

"Nothing, all right. What would *I* have to be scared of? What about you, Ajax? You're so tough. What's your major fear then?"

There's a short silence as Ajax and Theo stare at each other, a tension building in the air. "Drowning," he says eventually.

"All right then, I'm scared of drowning too. That good enough?"

"Well, we'll find out soon enough," he says, before turning back to the whole group. "Your fear will be your ally. You need to learn to embrace it, to use it. Fear and emotional trauma are the fuel that allow us to use our abilities."

He walks towards the wall that, presumably, leads into the hall beyond. "Beyond this door your fears will be realised. In order to train, you must learn to live with the things that scare you the most. The more you can master your fear and hold onto that trauma, the stronger your abilities will become.

"But be aware that this won't be easy. Fear is the thing people try to avoid most. Today will be hard, and the days and weeks to follow will be too. But remember why you're doing it. Hold onto that thought every step of the way. Because as soon as you let it go, as soon as you give in, you'll break."

The room falls silent as Ajax's words fall like heavy weights to the floor. Already, I can see people's faces coiled up with anxiety and dread. And none of us have even passed through the door yet.

"Theo," says Ajax, "why don't you go first. Show everyone how it's done."

"Go first? I don't even know what I'm doing!"

"You don't need to know. Enter the Grid and you'll find out."

In a flash that cocksure expression melts off Theo's face, replaced with one of dread and anxiety. He stands from his seat and puffs out his chest, though, trying to appear confident. I think everyone, even the other sea city boys, can see straight through him.

"Go on Theo, show us how it's done cap," says Rupert.

"Yeah, you're the man, Theo," chips in Anders. "You've got this."

Their words of support, I know, are intended to get him to go first. No one ever wants to go first.

Theo makes his way to the door, Ajax moving over towards him. I hear his voice, low now, speaking quietly just to him. "Whatever you see in there will be real. Remember yesterday, with the gunfire. It's all real, Theo."

"And what will be in there?" asks Theo, his bravado gone, his voice filled with nerves.

"I don't know," says Ajax. "But you'll understand when you enter."

I can feel my own pulse racing now as Theo opens the door. Beyond, I see nothing but a black room, the deepest black I've ever seen. Theo stops in the doorway, his hand still clutching at the door handle.

"Go inside, Theo," whispers Ajax. "Embrace your fear."

Slowly, Theo walks in, the door falling shut behind him. There's a silence now, as everyone waits, looking at each other, not knowing what to do.

"How long will it take?" asks Lorna.

"As long as it needs to," comes Ajax's cryptic reply.

So we wait as the minutes pass. No one speaks, no one makes a sound. All eyes stay fixed to the door, watching and waiting.

It must be 30 minutes before there's a sound, and the door finally clicks open. Theo's face appears, pale and sweating, his hair ruffled and out of place. I can see his chest heaving, his hands shaking, as he walks through and slumps into a chair. Ajax walks towards him and puts his arm around over his shoulders, lifting him from his seat and ushering him towards a door at the side of the room. They walk in together, before Ajax comes back out once again a few moments later.

"So, who's next?" he asks, looking around the group. Instinctively, everyone ducks their heads and avoids eye contact with him. Then Link's voice rings out in the room.

"I'll go," he says. "If he can do it, so can I."

Link stands from his seat and walks confidently towards the door. He grasps the handle quickly with his hand and, without delay, pulls it open. Once more I get a brief glimpse inside. I see high walls and machines everywhere. I see people working, dressed in grey clothes and covered in soot and dirt and fumes. Then, just as quickly as the door opened, it shuts behind him.

Now Ajax is moving back towards the other door where he guided Theo. He disappears inside for a few minutes before they both reappear, Theo now looking a little more perky. He walks in confidently again, that smirk returning to his face, and sits casually in his seat. To me, it all looks like one big act.

Again we wait, a silence descending on the room but for a few questions directed at Theo. He brushes them off and tells everyone to wait their turn, then they'll know for themselves. Most probably he just doesn't want to talk about it.

When Link returns, he's sweaty and dirty looking, his clothing singed in places and his face covered in soot. He coughs as he enters, Ajax once more guiding him through into the other room.

"Agricola, why don't you go next?"

I look over to see Theo staring at me. "I think it's

time for a girl to give it a try, don't you?"

A general rumble of agreement sounds through the boys, while the other girls just look at me, waiting for my response.

"You don't have to," says Ellie. "All the boys should go before the girls."

"Tighten up your tongue," bites Theo. "We're all in this together, remember. There's no gender inequality in here."

I turn to Ellie, ignoring Theo's presence entirely. "We've all gotta do it Ellie, so I might as well get mine over with."

"That's the spirit. Maybe you mainlanders aren't as pathetic as I thought," says Theo.

I ignore him again and start walking to the door, just as Ajax reappears. "Cyra, you're going in?"

I nod.

"Good girl. Remember, fear is your ally. Embrace it in there, don't run from it."

I lift my hand to the door handle, my heart quickening. I twist and the door opens a crack, bright sunlight pouring through it from beyond. It grows brighter and more intense as I pull the door open and step through, the door shutting quietly behind me.

I turn and the door has gone, the wall vanished. The ground beneath my feet feels soft and uneven now, not hard like the solid floor. I squint in the sudden light and, gradually, the world grows clearer in my eyes. I see shapes of hills in the distance, undulating mounds crossing the landscape.

Everywhere it's yellow and brown and orange, the sorts of colours I'm used to.

But I've never seen this landscape before. Not in reality. The ground is made up of sandy patches mingled with hard, parched earth. Nothing grows except tangled bushes and sharp cacti. I catch glimpses of vermin scuttling through the brush, hear the sound of a snake rattling close to my feet.

I turn in every direction and see a desert, a barren, broken landscape, stretching far and wide. Then I see it, appearing through the shroud of sand blowing on the wind. The huge fortress wall, standing high into the air, built of solid rock and metal. I hear the sounds of gunfire ringing out over the wasteland, see shadows of people rushing along the top of it against the glowing orange of the setting sun.

I begin moving forward, my feet sinking into patches of sand as I go. The noise grows ever louder, the sounds of cannons and artillery and huge weapons exploding from the defensive bastions stationed at intervals along the wall.

All around me the earth shakes, animals scurrying in the opposite direction. The darkening sky flashes with light as hundreds of weapons fire at once. A strong wind drives at me, holding me back, as I continue to fight my way forward. Sand fills my eyes, my nose, my ears, obscuring my vision and senses.

I drive on towards the wall, the details of the soldiers growing into view. Many look young, their faces fresh and innocent. They rush this way and that under orders from their Officers, who point and direct, shouting loud above the din.

My eyes fall on one, his arms strong and tanned, his hair blond and shining under the dying light. He stands tall, a weapon locked against his shoulder, shouting down the line at his men.

I see people shot, parts of the wall exploding under enemy fire. Soldiers fall with a slump, dropping where they stand. Others are blown from the top as explosive shells rip into the upper level. I hear screaming as an incendiary device blankets an entire section in fire. Soldiers, too young to die, burst into flames as the fire licks at their skin, cooking their flesh.

I can hardly look now, but am unable to turn away, as if my eyes are locked in place. They direct back to the blond man, still shouting and shooting from behind a rampart. Bullets whiz by, leaving trails of light in their wake, as he ducks his head for cover.

When he raises it again, I see it immediately jolt back. His body goes limp, his arms falling to his sides, and he falls backwards against a railing. Over he goes, his momentum carrying him over the top, his weight dropping storey after storey and hitting the earth with a thud.

I'm drawn forward to the very base of the wall, my eyes locked to the body on the ground. He lies face down, his helmet awkwardly skewed on his head, his arms and legs bent in unnatural ways.

I lean down to him, the world ending around me, and roll his body carefully over. I peel back his helmet, a bullet hole torn through it, and feel my hands begin to shake, my heart begin to drum.

I wipe the blood from his forehead, straining his beautiful skin crimson. His blue eyes stare vacantly, bright as the morning sky, yet lifeless and empty. I can hardly breathe, hardly think, as the tears begin rolling down my cheeks.

The final person I care about. The final person I love. Taken from me, like everyone else.

I'm looking at the face of Jackson.

12
Fight or Flight

My eyes are still wet when the world around me changes. I hardly notice it. Just the colours of red and orange and brown fading in the corners of my eyes, replaced with the dark grey tones of the large open hall. The last thing to fade before me is Jackson, his body slowly overcome by darkness until he's completely gone.

I'm left, on my knees, my hands still red with blood, my body still covered in dust and sand, my head still filled with the sight of Jackson's dead body. I stay there for minutes, shaking and unable to stand, until I manage to muster the strength to rise to my feet and turn back to the door.

Around me now, the hall is as long and wide and empty as it was yesterday. Nothing remains. No open landscape. No desert and tundra. No wall, no soldiers, no death and destruction.

My legs are feeble beneath me as I return to the door and compose myself. When I open it, I see fearful faces raise up to meet mine. They look upon me as I looked upon Theo and Link as they returned. Frowning at the sight of me, covered in the stains of the desert, my hands caked with red blood and dark brown dirt.

Ajax is quickly by my side, leading me towards

the other door, guiding me through and into the room beyond. It's like the room from yesterday when he spoke to us individually: lifeless and plain, with only two seats sitting opposite each other.

He sits me down before positioning himself opposite me, my head hung low, my chin quivering above my chest.

"Was all that real?" I ask, my voice trembling. "Was it a vision?"

Ajax's words are soothing yet firm. "Not a vision, no. Just a manifestation of your greatest fear. Tell me Cyra, what did you see."

I raise my eyes to his. "I saw the same thing again. The desert, the wall, the soldiers. They were fighting someone on the other side. It was....chaos," I whisper.

"What else?" asks Ajax. "Was it just a battleground you saw?"

I shake my head. "I saw him die," I say. "My best friend."

Ajax looks at me quizzically. "Your best friend....is a boy?"

I understand his puzzlement. Just revealing to him that Jackson is my best friend might get me in trouble. Somehow, that doesn't seem relevant right now.

"He was," I say. "He was assigned for service at the Divide."

"And you watched him die?" Ajax asks again.

I nod. "It's my greatest fear, isn't it?" I ask. "Watching him die."

Ajax thinks for a moment before answering. "Yes, but it's more than that. Your greatest fear is losing everyone you love. You've lost your father and your mother, you've been dragged from everything you know. Your friend is the last remnant of your old life, of how you define yourself. Your greatest fear is losing him, and losing yourself."

There's a knock at the door, and Link appears. "Commander Ajax," he says, his clothes still tattered and burned and face covered in soot, "Rupert is going in next. I thought you'd better know."

"Yes, of course," says Ajax, standing quickly. "Thank you, Link."

He walks to the door and disappears beyond it as I share a nervous smile with Link. I begin to wonder what he saw, what horrible experience he went through. He said he was scared of fire, and his scarred clothes would suggest he truly lived that terror. Like he told me, accidents are common where he's from. His father even died in one. Perhaps a fire in the factory he worked in. I can imagine, after what I've just been through, how terrifying that must have been.

When Ajax returns, he asks me more questions, squeezing as much detail as possible as he can from my experience. It's the fear of losing Jackson, he tells me, that I have to embrace. I need to learn to use that fear, to let it fill me up and, in time, learn to control it. Only then will my visions grow clearer and more complete. Only then will I be able to develop the other Watcher abilities.

Back in the room, Ellie waits for me, her face a picture of worry and concern. One by one, they go in. Amir and Anders, the twins and then Kyle. Each time they reappear, some of them drenched in sweat and pale like Theo was, others showing visible signs on their clothes and uncovered skin of what they've been through. Tears and rips and patches of red. But no one ever returns injured, not seriously at least.

I give Ellie a short pep talk as her time approaches. I tell her it's not actually real. That it's all just a simulation. What I don't tell her, however, is the truth. That inside it *feels* real, that every sound and smell and sight is as real is the world around us right now. That inside, you wouldn't know any different.

When she goes in, I imagine what she must be seeing. Snakes, she said, were what she was most scared of. I wonder if that's true. I wonder if she'll find herself in the forest, snakes surrounding her, unable to fight her way out. Will they bite her, attack her, bringing back memories of when she was bitten as a child?

She walks out like the others, face colder and greyer than normal, eyes a little wider, lips shut tight together. Like all of us, Ajax leads her in for a debrief before they both return together a few minutes later. By now, the entire room is drained and lost to their own thoughts. No one speaks. No one smiles or stands up to fetch a glass of water. We all just sit, as one, absorbed in our fears.

Ajax moves ahead of us as Ellie sits down, his eyes cold and filled with intent. "This will be the worst day," he says. "Nothing will be harder. Remember this feeling, bottle it, use it. If you run from it, you will fail. A Watcher must learn to hold onto their fears and treat them as their ally. If you cannot do that, you will never become a Watcher."

A voice creaks from one of the twins. Everyone looks at her as she raises her head, her sister's arm tightly wound over her shoulder. "But what if we....don't want to be a Watcher?" she asks, her voice brittle.

Ajax's face hardens, his chin rising, his eyes narrowing. "Being a Watcher is not a privilege," he says, "it is a duty. Your gift helps save lives. That is your purpose."

"But..." croaks the girl again.

"But nothing," says Ajax. "If you fail, you will be reassigned. But if you walk away, if you don't even try, you will be banished."

I look into Ajax's eyes, a fierceness in them that he hasn't yet shown. His appearance is tough and intimidating, yet so far he's appeared nurturing and fair. Now, though, I'm seeing him in a different light. He, just like everyone else, is part of a system, and this is part of his duty. You will either sink or swim, but if you fail to even jump into the water, there will be dire consequences.

"You wouldn't banish me." The voice comes from the back, from Theo, staring up at Ajax. "My parents wouldn't allow it."

"Your parents?" says Ajax, his words oozing menace. "You have no parents now. I don't care who you are. You answer to me, and me alone."

Theo stands, his chair thrust back behind him. "You have no idea who you're talking to, do you?!" he barks. "My parents are close with High Chancellor Knight. Would you deny him as well?"

"I assure you Theo, the rules apply to you too. They are the rules set down by Chancellor Knight, by your parents. They would not break them for a spoilt brat, too afraid to face his fears."

Theo steps forwards quickly, moving up to confront Ajax, his face a vision of thunder. He stands ahead of him, his fist curled into a ball, as if he's about to strike. But Ajax's face remains like stone, his body a statue. He doesn't flinch, he doesn't move. He just stands, staring, waiting for Theo to act.

They stare at each other for a moment, until Theo speaks, his mouth twisted into a snarl.

"I can't listen to this any more," he says, before quickly turning from Ajax and storming out of the door.

A silence descends into the room as the remaining recruits awkwardly look at each other.

"I apologise for that," says Ajax, regaining his composure. "I should not have spoken like I did. But believe me, you will try, or you will find yourself beyond the Divide." He glances at me. "Now go, and all of you take a long look in the mirror."

He begins walking towards the door leading into the Grid. "I'll see you back here tomorrow morning," he says, opening the door and walking through. Beyond, I see the sight of raging water approaching, just before the door slams shut.

13
Surface Level 8

When we return to the Grid the following morning, we're short one person. We wait patiently for Theo to arrive, but he never does. Eventually, Ajax flows into his routine and the day begins.

One by one, we each enter the Grid again. This time, however, there's an even greater sense of fear in the air, so intense it's palpable. When Ajax asks for a volunteer to step up, not even Link answers the call. As a result, he turns to nominating people, calling for Rupert to go in first.

The wait for my turn is excruciating. I know that what's happening in there isn't truly real, but when you're in the thick of it, it might as well be. Somehow the entire manifestation makes you believe it's happening, like stepping into a dream. You never know you've been dreaming until you wake up, and while you're in the depths of your subconscious, you're at its mercy.

When I enter this time, I walk into a different situation. It's not like before. There's no desert, no wasteland and soldiers. There's no war, no flash of lights and sounds of gunfire. This time, it's just me and Jackson.

It's dark all around, but for the form of a body under a light ahead of me. I follow into the darkness and kneel by Jackson's side. He's frail and weak looking, his skin pallid and eyes grey. I know, immediately, that he's infected with the virus.

He croaks weakly as we speak. I tell him I miss him, that I miss our secret meetings in the woods, our glances across at each other in class. That I miss his voice, his devotion to his family, to me. That I think about him every day, that he's all I have left that I truly care about.

I tell him everything I never got to tell him before. Everything I was too afraid or proud to say. He smiles, his face withered and older than I remember, and holds his hand to my cheek. Then his eyes glaze over, and he dies in front of me once more.

I return from the Grid just as dazed as before. Ajax tells me it will take time to adjust, that each time I enter the Grid things will be different. That this time my grief for my mother was also a factor. That I'd linked together her death with the fear of losing Jackson.

The days pass, and each time it gets more difficult to go inside, knowing what awaits me. Yet we all keep going, day after day, subjecting ourselves to these horrors in the hope that soon they'll grow easier.

It's the end of the week when, finally, Theo re-appears. He walks in, tail between his legs, and stands up in front of everyone to apologise to Ajax and beg him to let him continue training. Right then and there, my respect for Ajax triples.

He doesn't rub it in or humiliate Theo. He merely thanks him for his apology and tells him he's welcome back. He also tells the entire group that what we're all experiencing is natural, but that things will get easier in time.

For the rest of that day, Theo's face looks as though it's about to erupt in another outburst, but he stays quiet. It's hard to know who forced him back down here, but clearly he thinks he's above it all. As Leeta told us, everyone expected him to follow in his parents' footsteps, perhaps join the Council in years to come. To have some influence on the future of Eden and live in the lap of luxury.

Some small part of me feels sorry for him. He may not have been ripped from his home and family in the same way as me or Ellie or anyone else, but he's been ripped from the life he knew, the path he expected to walk. In that sense, he's just like the rest of us. Stuck with this power that's more like a curse. So, during my weaker moments when he's not looking down his nose at me or making a snide comment, I still feel for Theo, just like I do for the others.

I don't know if it's a blessing or a way of punishing him, but Ajax makes Theo wait all day before sending him into the Grid. Over the last few days, it's become increasingly common for people to volunteer early to get it out of the way. Better that than waiting around, hour after hour, watching the others come and go. Watching them disappear behind the door and return in various states of distress.

For that entire day Theo says nothing. He just sits there, in the corner, lost in his own world. When his time comes up, he's already visibly shaken by it all. I wonder with him, more than others, what exactly he's seeing in there.

Gradually, people begin to open up, though, Ajax telling us that vocalising our experiences is helpful in accepting them. I speak to Link a lot, who admits what I've already suspected. That his time in the Grid generally involves fire and destruction and often the burden of reliving the death of his father. He quickly develops a thick skin to it, though, his outlook more positive by the day. Soon, he's telling me it's a good thing, that every time he goes in, he comes out that little bit stronger, that little bit more hardened to his fears. As he speaks, I notice Ajax in the background, nodding his approval.

By the sounds of it, people's fears are as varied as they are terrifying. The twins go in individually, but both suffer similar manifestations relating to their fear of flying and fear of heights. Amir, it seems, has the worst of it, though. He tells us he grew up suffering from night terrors, dreams so horrifying they seemed real, filled with murder and death and strange creatures. After several days, he admits to me that his main recurring dream involved his father killing his mother in a horrifying way. Now, when he goes into the Grid, he's forced to relive it all over again.

Ajax continues to lead us away after each experience. At first, speaking about it is difficult and I just want to shut myself off from the world for a while. Gradually, however, it becomes easier to describe what I saw and what happened, and I begin to realise that this training is more than just learning to control our fears. It's also learning to explain the visions we have. Learning to pick out the tiniest of details so that they can be acted upon when it comes to the real thing.

It's about two weeks since we arrived on Eden when I spend the evening being guided around Surface Level 8 by Leeta. I'd requested she take me, and she'd agreed, although she didn't seem too happy about it.

"Only the people who live there go there," she tells me. "You're not officially authorised to enter that level."

I brush off her concerns and say I'm going anyway, with or without her. The truth is that there's a large part of me who feels beholden to find out how the other side live on Eden. Whether there really is such a disparity here as there is with the mainland. So, after a bit of persuasion, Leeta relents, despite hardly knowing the area. We spend several hours walking through the cramped level, the walls fitted busily with door after door. Inside, singles and pairs and families live, mostly in overcrowded living quarters like the one I grew up in.

It smells funny too. That stuffiness that too many bodies can bring. That smell of sweat and body odour that seeps out from each room and infects the corridors and passageways. Leeta holds a cloth to her mouth and nose as she goes, careful not to breathe in the *fumes*, as she calls them. I stuff the cloth back into her hand when she offers me a spare.

I talk to some people and ask them what life is like here. They're mostly positive, happy to live on this great city when they might be on the mainland with a much harsher life. Many can tell I'm from Agricola, just from the sight of me, and often I end up fielding more questions than I ask. In truth, however, my skin is already beginning to fade to a paler shade of golden brown, and my hair has started to lose some of its shine. When I look in the mirror now, I can already see the girl from Arbor starting to dim.

When Leeta and I return to the deck, she finally pulls the cloth from her nose and sucks in a large breath of clean air. I look at her and wonder how much she must have changed over her years here. She doesn't say it aloud, but I can tell she looks down on these people. It's as if she's been indoctrinated to how Edenites think, each year losing more and more of who she truly is underneath. I promise myself, right there and then, that I won't let myself be the same. That I'll always see everyone as equal.

When I return to my room, I hear a light sobbing next door. I knock and hear no answer, so call out Ellie's name. I wait a moment as the sobs die down, before the door opens. She stands in front of me, her eyes red, holding a small picture frame in her hands.

When my eyes drop to the frame, I see the face of a woman. She's beautiful, her hair tightly curled and a deep shade of brown, her eyes green like the grass. Ellie backs off and lets me through, before quickly putting the frame into a drawer.

"Your mother?" I ask.

She nods, wiping her eyes.

We sit together on the bed, and I wrap my arm over her small shoulders. I understand now why I've been finding her in tears so often. Why she goes quiet at times and regresses into herself. She's thinking of her mother, of home.

I tell her that it will get easier. That she'll be able to visit her, that she may even be assigned nearby as a Watcher once she's finished her training. Yet when I speak the words I intend to be comforting, she merely breaks down once more, tears spilling from her eyes.

I squeeze her tighter until her tears relent, and finally her voice croaks as she tells me the truth.

"I'll never see her again," she says.

"You may yet," I respond quickly. "You might get vacation or be assigned there, like I say."

She shakes her head wearily. "You don't understand. I'll never see her again because I know she's going to die soon."

My voice now loses its comforting tone, a realisation dawning on me. "You've seen it?" I whisper, and she nods.

"I didn't know what it was before coming here. I had dreams of her out in the woods, attacked and killed by a bear. I...I thought they were just nightmares."

"Visions?" I say. "Do you have them often?"

"Not here, not any more. Ajax says I'm too far away to see it now."

"Well, can't we warn her...or assign a guard to her or something?"

Ellie lets out an exhalation of air, a sound of deflation. "I asked Ajax that," she says. "They can't help her, though, unless I can give them a time or date or exact destination. It was only blurry. It could be anywhere, at any time. She might," she says, her voice cracking again, "be dead already."

I wrap my arms around her as a fresh stream of tears flows down her cheeks. The words of Ajax begin running through my mind. *In general, Watchers can only see a few days or weeks ahead.* That's what he told us. *And only events nearby to where they're currently located.*

Ellie would have had these visions weeks ago now, before we even set sail for Eden. They would have faded as we moved further from her home, further from her mother. I can only imagine how hard it must have been when she found out those nightmares she had when she slept were more than dreams. That they were visions, destined to come true. That now, being far away from her mother, she'd have no way of helping her.

I think of her crying after her first meeting with Ajax on the first day. How she will have told him what she saw, begged him perhaps to help her. I know what he will have said. That without any exact details, there's nothing they could do. That unless there's a Watcher in the area who may have seen the same thing, this vision of premature reality, of the future, will be impossible to alter.

I think of home. I think of the deaths that occur across the regions. People killed under harvesting machines. Those killed by wild cougars and other dangerous animals. I think of the explosion in the factory when I was young. I think of what Link had told me. That where he's from, factory accidents are common.

Yet each time, there's no one there to see it. No one there to stop it. The deaths of a few paltry mainlanders doesn't warrant the need for a Watcher. Ajax told us they're spread too thin, that there aren't enough of them to cover such a huge area. Perhaps that's true, or perhaps the reality is that those in power just don't care.

I sit with Ellie for a while that evening, letting her vent her emotions and feelings. Letting her curse the world and get it out of her system. Eventually, as the small hours of night approach, she passes out on her bed, and I tuck her under her covers.

My sleep that night is filled with death and destruction. I see bodies littering the golden earth, blood seeping through the dirt. I see flames and explosions, hear screams of pain and suffering. Yet all of it comes in flashes, all blurred as if I'm seeing and hearing it through water.

When I wake, I remember little of the events. They're so blurred and indistinct that I barely even know if they're dreams or visions. I still tell Ajax, though, as he'd instructed me to, when I go down to the Grid. His stony visage crinkles as I tell him, his frown deepening, yet he says nothing but what he told me before. To tell him whenever I see anything else, whatever it happens to be.

Our training continues, and it grows apparent that some are finding it easier than others. Link, whether through sheer bravado or bravery, always walks into the Grid confidently, and comes out with his head held high. I see him speaking more often with Ajax now. Clearly, Ajax has found his star pupil.

Others don't fare so well. Ellie remains immersed in her grief, walking here and there like a zombie. Amir often comes out in the worst state, panting heavily and with wide, staring eyes. One of the twins, Larna I think, appears to be slowly cracking too. They both seem like such gentle souls, but I'd put Lorna as the more dominant twin. She spends much of her time comforting her sister, coaxing her through the worst of it.

Everyone else, including Theo, are in varying states of acceptance, each day growing stronger and more numbed to their fears. Ajax talks to us all individually, as always, noting our mental state, asking us questions, always telling us that things will become easier.

For me, seeing Jackson die, day after day, feels like my soul is being chipped away, piece by piece. I fear that soon they'll be little of me left. Little of the girl from Arbor, picking fruit under the morning sun. The girl who cared for her mother and had a forbidden friendship with a boy. The girl with golden skin and shining blonde hair who used to play in the fields as a child.

What's left of me will be corrupted beyond recognition. Broken down, bit by bit, until I'm nothing more than an implement for Eden to use as it wishes. I look at Ajax and wonder what he must have been like when he first came here. Young and fresh faced, not knowing what lay ahead of him. I wonder how long it took for him to control his own fears. How long it took for him to morph into the man ahead of us today, uncompromising and devoted to his duty.

My mother returns to me in my dreams now. She comes to me, night after night, telling me to be strong. Telling me that I was always special, that she knew I'd be destined for something great. I see her face so clearly, full of colour and beautiful as she once was, before the virus stripped her bare. Her blue eyes shine, her hair sways in a light breeze, and her white smile lights up the room as it used to.

Each time I wake, I feel my mother's old watch in my hand. I run my thumb over the cracked glass and squeeze it tight, a tear trickling down my cheek. Then I stand, dress, and return to the Grid to face my fears.

14
Breaking Point

When I look upon the faces of the other trainees, I see different people to those I first met. Faces have grown staunch and resolute. Eyes have narrowed and intensified. People walk into the Grid, heads high, and walk out with cold eyes and gritted teeth. Day after day they harden, all except one.

It's about a month after we started our training when Amir steps into the Grid. He's grown more introverted each day, more scared of his own shadow. I catch him talking to himself sometimes, whispering words of support that others aren't giving him. I try to help, but he only tells me he's fine.

I know he's a proud young man, and showing weakness is considered a major flaw of ones character here. So he soldiers on, pushing through the pain, stepping up each and every time he's asked to. I can tell Ajax is watching him closely, his eyes missing nothing, yet he doesn't intervene. He watches and waits for an outcome. Either he'll sink, or he'll swim.

That day, Amir spends longer than usual in the Grid. As the minutes tick by a growing tension builds among us. His fellow recruits from Aquar, Anders and Kyle, are most vocal, calling for Ajax to open the door.

"This can't be right," says Kyle. "Something's got to be wrong in there."

Anders moves to open the door, but Ajax stops him, his hand dropping to his wrist and ripping it from the handle. "There's nothing you can do," he says. "Only he can find his way out."

The minutes keep turning, yet nothing happens. It's silent among us now, each of us waiting with bated breath for the door to open, for Amir to reappear. We share nervous looks with each other, but Ajax does nothing. His eyes just stare at the door, waiting for it to move.

After what seems like an eternity, there's a click. All eyes turn quickly to the metal handle, which rotates slowly down. Then there's another click, and the door falls open a crack. Ajax is the first to move, followed by Anders and Kyle, who jump in behind him from their seats.

I stand at the back, but all I hear is a thud. Through the crowd I see a body, lying face up on the floor beyond the door as everyone rushes forward.

Ajax is quickly on his knees, his fingers reaching for a pulse. I hear sobs from the twins, see Kyle and Anders' faces contort in worry. Amir lies, eyes wide open and staring straight up towards the ceiling, arms flat by his sides.

Ajax is calling to him now. "Amir, can you hear me. Amir, come back to us."

Nothing happens. Ajax calls again, louder this time, shouting into Amir's ear.

"Is he dead?" cries Larna, once more in her sister's arms.

Ajax lifts Amir's body, his strong arms easily moving him off the ground, and begins carrying him back through the door.

"Is he dead?!" comes Anders' voice, echoing through the hall.

Ajax shakes his head. "He's not dead," he says. "He's broken."

He carries on towards the main door, which slides open with a hiss, and disappears out into the corridor, leaving us all behind.

There's a state of shock in the room, the silence only peppered by shouts of disbelief and the sobs of Larna. Ajax returns after several minutes, his face sombre.

"What's happening?" calls Anders. "What did you mean, broken?"

"The mind can only take so much. Some people run, and when that happens, they may never return."

"Never return?! What the hell does that mean?!" Anders asks again in panic.

"Amir's mind is lost in the Grid now, lost to his fears. He ran from them, so they engulfed him. You must never run, never hide, or you can become lost forever."

Ajax walks towards the door to the Grid and slams it shut. "I told you all that in there, it's real. You have to master your fear, not run from it. This is not a game, this is not fantasy. What happens in there can break you if you let it."

"What will happen with him now?" asks Theo, his voice emotionless.

"They'll try to help him, try to bring him back. If they succeed, he'll be assigned somewhere else. But he'll never be a Watcher."

"And if they don't succeed," I ask.

"Then nothing can help him." says Ajax.

That afternoon we all return together to the deck level, a weight hanging above all our heads. I get the sense, in some strange way, that Ajax is pleased with what happened. That he let Amir keep going and going until he broke just to teach the rest of us a valuable lesson. To show us that there's no turning back now. That we either become Watchers, or break like Amir did.

In the following days he appears to show no remorse over what happened. We just continue as always, now with the stakes even higher than they were before. The loss of Amir hits Anders the most. They were friends on Aquar before they were sent here and had known each other for years. Now he, like myself, like Ellie and Link, has to deal with the grief of losing someone he cares about on top of everything else.

In my private sessions with Ajax I'm not afraid to question him further about Amir. I ask him if he saw it coming, but he tells me he had no idea it would happen, and that Watchers cannot have visions about things that go on in the Grid because it isn't true reality in there. I'm finding it harder and harder now to know if he's lying or not. The extent of his own abilities are unknown to me, and I truly have no idea whether he's letting us in on everything he knows.

I spend my evenings with Ellie and Link most of all. We often walk together, through the city, feeling so out of place yet looking, at a glance, like we belong. When people hear us talk or get close enough to see Link's scar, however, they immediately know we're not natives of the city. Sometimes we catch sight of others like us. Those from the mainland who have been assigned to Eden for other duties. One night, I see some of the mainlanders that Ellie and I met on the boat. Trainee Scientists and Engineers, laughing and enjoying the city like most people would.

For us, however, it's all like a dream. Gradually it becomes harder to know what's actually real and what isn't, caught between visions and dreams and strange manifestations in the Grid. It all just blurs and bundles into one. One long hallucination that it's impossible to wake up from.

These times with Ellie and Link are the few moments of respite I have. We bond as a trio, telling stories of home and letting each other in on our fears. I hear of Ellie's love for the woods and the rolling hills, how she misses the sound of rainfall dripping down through the trees. Link tells us of the harshness of his world in Fossor, of the mines that go deep into the earth. He tells us about his little sister, Abby, who's only a few years away from the Duty Call herself, and how he longs more than anything to see her assigned somewhere clean and safe where she can be happy.

Once a week, Leeta continues to check in on Ellie and myself. I don't know if it's part of her duty or whether she just wants to see us, but she makes it a weekly thing. Mostly, she continues our education of Eden and the other sea cities and regions across Arcadia. She takes us to places around the city that we might never see, always speaking with great passion and enthusiasm. Her aim, I suspect, is to try to make us learn to like it here. Perhaps indoctrinate us as she was. As time goes by, I can tell it's starting to work on Ellie.

One evening we reach a part of the deck we haven't seen before. At the opposite end from where we live is a closed off portion, high walls and gates protecting it from possible intrusion. Soldiers patrol its borders, protecting what lies within. I can see, set back beyond the gate, a grand building, ornate and elegant, embroidered with statues and beautiful carvings. One stands taller than the others, fixed to an arch above the main doorway. The statue of a man, perhaps in his early 40's, dressed in a long cloak that hangs to his feet.

When I ask Leeta what this place is, she tells me it's the home of the High Chancellor, Augustus Knight. The statue that catches my eye, she says, is him.

"So this is the ruler of Eden's house?" asks Ellie, staring wide eyed towards the great structure. "Is it right that he's over a hundred years old? He doesn't look too old in the statue."

"He's nearly one hundred and thirty actually," says Leeta.

179

I nearly choke. "How old?!"

"Nearly one hundred and thirty," repeats Leeta calmly. "There are gene therapies here that slow and even prevent ageing. That's why he still looks quite young."

"So...there are people around here that old. How old are you?" asks Ellie.

Leeta seems dismayed by the question, and shuffles on her feet. "That's not a polite question to ask, Ellie. But if you're wondering, no I haven't had any gene therapy and I never will. Only the richest and most powerful have them. Most of the Council members are much older than they may look."

"Right, that makes perfect sense," I say with a heavy dose of sarcasm. "So the powerful stay young and nothing ever changes. The whole mainland's going to be under their boot forever."

"Well, a lot of Knight's policies have been very successful actually, Cyra. The Dividing Wall, his wall, is highly effective. The Duty Call and Pairing work very well. He's brought this nation back from the brink of destruction. I think he deserves some praise and credit."

I shake my head and turn away from her disapproving eyes. Frankly none of those policies sound good to me. Just means of control, but Leeta will never see it that way. Even if she did, she'd never admit to it. So, I change the subject, guiding my eyes back to the grand mansion beyond the high gates.

"So, the big boss lives here then..."

"Yes, this is where he lives," says Leeta, happy to

get back to her lesson. "Rumour has it there's a lift somewhere in the house that descends right to the bottom floor."

"Why?" asks Ellie.

"Because that's where the Council gathers. That's where the decisions about Arcadia are made."

"Have you ever been down there?"

Leeta looks at us as if we're mad. "Me, oh gosh no. No one is allowed down there but the most important people. That's certainly not me."

"So there's an entire level just for a few people to meet and talk about things. That's a bit of a waste of space, isn't it?" I say.

"Truth is, Cyra, no one really knows what goes on down there. And, no one really questions it."

I think about all those people crammed into Surface Level 8. All those thousands of people squashed into small living quarters when elsewhere there's so much space. Even down on Underwater Level 5, beyond the Grid, I have little idea of what the space is used for. Empty rooms, probably, stretching into the distance in every direction.

Leeta tries to explain, but even she isn't completely sure about what each level is used for.

"There's the science level, used for research and development," she says. "That's Underwater Level 3. Then there's the military level where soldiers train and live. That's Underwater Level 2."

"How about Underwater 4?" asks Ellie.

"I'm not exactly sure," says Leeta. "I think that may be for science as well. Experiments and things like that. I have heard they keep a huge range of animal and plant species down there for their tests."

"Jeez," says Ellie, "I'll want to avoid there then. They've probably got lots of snakes I'll bet."

"I'd say that's a fair guess, Ellie. Now, Underwater Level 1 is engineering. Um, then there's the Surface Levels."

"Yeah, well we know what's on 8 don't we," I say bitterly. "What about the other 7?"

"Um, well there's a worker level on 7. That's things like laundry and food preparation and things like that. Below that, on Level 6, there's food storage."

"An entire level for storing food?" asks Ellie. "Now I *would* like to go there!"

Talk of food always seems to perk Ellie up, regardless of her mood. I swear it's amazing how she stays so small and slim the amount she eats.

"I know that Surface Level 1 is used for running Eden. Power and computers and all that sort of stuff, although I confess I don't understand any of it."

"OK," I say. "So what about Levels 2 to 5?"

"Well, 2 is more storage. Pretty much anything is stored down there I think. And then there's just 3, 4, and 5 which, well, I'm not so sure about to be honest. I think they might be fairly empty."

"Empty?! I exclaim. "Are you kidding me. And you've got all those people squashed into Level 8!"

"Well, Cyra, it's not my doing. I suppose those levels are used for something. I just don't know what they are, all right? You must learn to stop asking so many questions, you really must. Just focus on your duty."

I shake my head at how vacuous she can be. It's like she doesn't question anything beyond what she's told. Even Ellie doesn't seem to mind all of this. I feel sometimes like I'm the only one with a conscience around here. I'm sure if I talked to Link, he'd feel the same as me.

When I return to my room that evening I ask Eve about the various levels, but she offers me no answers whatsoever.

"You are only authorised to enter Underwater Level 5," she says in that soothing, ethereal voice.

"So how did I manage to get to Surface Level 8 then?" I question.

"There are no security protocols on Surface Level 8," she says. "You are not officially authorised to go there, but there are no measures to stop you."

"And the other levels?" I ask

"All other levels have security protocols."

So that makes perfect sense. Why would anyone want to go to Level 8 anyway?

"Eve, what can you tell me about Chancellor Knight?" I ask.

"I am not authorised to tell you anything."

"Well, is it true he's really old?"

"I am not authorised to tell you."

"Jeez, why not?! I'm not breaking the law or anything. I just want to know more about the big boss. It's not like it's secret knowledge is it. What exactly can you tell me?"

"I am only authorised to follow commands regarding control of your room."

"Wow, that's all. So, you're a bit useless then aren't you?" I say. To any real person, that would be antagonising. For Eve, it's a genuine comment, to which she responds with all of the ways in which she is useful to me. Halfway through I get bored and tell her to shut down.

I drop off to sleep quickly that night, as I always do. I guess it's the intensity of everything; the training, adapting to a new world. It just drains you to the point where you just pass out as soon as your head hits your pillow.

I dream of Jackson, as I often do, but when I wake I can't tell if it was a dream or an aftershock from my training. It's as though I've grown completely desensitised to seeing him die by now. I've experienced that so many times that I hardly seem to care any more.

Ajax tells me that's the entire point, that I've crossed a line. When your fears are no longer scary to you, that's when you know you've mastered them.

That frightens me more than anything. I wonder how I'll feel if ever I find out that Jackson is really dead. Will I care? Or have I grown unemotional and cold? If I held him in my arms now, breathing his last breath, would I shed a tear? Would I just watch as his heart gives out and his eyes fade in front of me?

Even thinking about it now, I don't have that same pang of emotion. I don't feel that stab in my heart at the idea. Already, I can tell, I'm starting to lose myself, watching as the girl from Arbor dims even more, her light flickering and threatening to go out.

Soon, perhaps, we'll all become nothing but empty shells. Nothing inside us but our desire to fulfil our duties. Clones, sent out into the world to see death and suffering in our dreams. Nothing but blunt tools, devoid of any life or emotion.

Before I lose myself completely, I take out the diary that my mother had given me and begin writing my thoughts down in my room. I write down everything I used to love back home. I describe in as much detail as possible my feelings for my mother and father, my siblings and Jackson. I write about Arbor, about life in Agricola, about everything I love, and everything I hate.

I write about the disparity of the world and how much I loathe it. About the Testing and the Duty Call, about how that horrible mantra – *if it's meant to be, it will be* – is loaded with so much contradiction it makes my blood boil beneath my skin.

I write about everything that has meaning to me and everything I feel passionate about. All in the hope that, one day, when there's nothing left of me, I'll be able to read my words and maybe, just maybe, remember who I was.

15
A Fear Realised

Over the next week it becomes clear that several of us have crossed a line.

There's a cold, iciness to the faces around me now that reminds me of Ajax. People no longer shake as they enter the Grid. They don't rush to get their go out of the way. They still return showing signs of what happened in there: ripped clothing and minor cuts and bruises; dirt and blood and soot. Yet their faces are no longer twisted with anguish, no longer pale and beading with sweat.

The only one still struggling is Anders, who hasn't been quite the same since Amir left. He was making good progress, yet seeing his friend, his mind broken in front of him, has left a scar that is failing to heal.

One evening I follow him and find him sitting down a cold passageway on Underwater 5, his head buried into his hands, knees tightly clasped to his chest. When he sees me he stands, quickly, and brushes things off, but I know he's not how he was.

He tells me he's been visiting Amir each evening in the hospital on Underwater Level 3 where the scientists work. Apparently, that level is also home to all of the city's medical supplies and Healers. I ask him how he got access, knowing that we're not authorised to enter the other levels, and he says he got special dispensation to visit his close friend. Apparently, it was Ajax who arranged it.

He asks me if I want to go along as well, so I do. I liked Amir, but it's my curiosity to see more of Eden that truly spikes my interest.

When we reach Underwater 3, I find myself blinking at the bright lights. Beyond the tram tracks are wide open spaces, many with see through glass walls and doors, stretching away into the distance. Inside I see scientists, all dressed in white, busying themselves with experiments I could never hope to fathom.

Each entry point has the sort of security scanner I've grown used to seeing around the city. The sort of scanner used to determine whether we're authorised to be at any particular place. Naturally, our barcodes don't allow us entry, but Anders has a special keycard that he's able to use to provide him with limited access.

As with the other levels I've seen, there are endless passageways and corridors leading inwards across the level, peppered with security points to gain access to the different areas. I see various signs as we go, directing people to the appropriate areas. Agronomy, Botany, Cytology, Epidemiology, Genetics, Marine Biology, Medical, Meteorology, Physics, Seismology.

Some of the signs I don't even understand. One sends a shock through me: Epidemiology, the study of disease. I tried, in vain, to learn as much as I could on the subject when my mother got ill. Of course, none of it helped.

We continue in the direction of the Medical section, where Anders tells me there's a hospital that deals with all illnesses, diseases, and accidents on Eden. When we reach it, Anders enters his keycard, the doors slide open, and I'm immediately surprised by how empty it seems. There are few Healers and Medics and Nurses, and hardly any patients. According to Anders, few people grow ill on Eden, and there are very few accidents.

When we reach the ward marked Mental Health, we find the room where Amir is being cared for. He sits, upright in a chair, his body tense and fastened to the frame with various belts and buckles. His eyes stare blankly ahead, his lips moving, whispering indiscernible words.

"Any change?" Anders asks the nurse in the room as she checks a series of computer readouts.

She shakes her head. "Sorry, Anders. Nothing yet. We still have hope, though." Her words are hollow and unconvincing.

She leaves us alone with Amir for the next half hour as Anders sits near him. "They say a familiar voice might help him find his way back," he tells me. Then he starts whispering to Amir, the same words over and over again, the same words Ajax used when we first found him in the Grid,

"Amir, come back to us," he says, repeating it several times. "It's Anders, can you hear me. Come back to us, Amir."

Amir does nothing but stare vacantly forward, hardly blinking, hardly moving but for the fluttering of his lips and the illegible words that flow from them. I sit to his other side and repeat the same words with Anders, but it has little impact.

After half an hour, the nurse returns and says we need to leave. Before we go, Anders tells Amir that he'll be back tomorrow, that he'll be back everyday until his friend is OK. He speaks with such pain, his own soul tortured at seeing Amir lose himself in the Grid. I fear, looking into his eyes, that he may be losing himself too.

In the following days, Anders spends a lot of time with Ajax. He now appears so contrasted with the rest of us. Link was always strong, but now he's been joined by those I deemed weak only a few weeks ago. Larna, in particular, and Ellie also, have grown hardened and determined. Theo, despite his smugness and egotism, has now grown used to the training.

Anders, though, is slowly falling apart, so much so that Ajax calls a halt to his training to give him time to recover. The next day, he doesn't appear. When one day becomes a week, we all know that he won't be joining us any more.

Ajax announces to the group that he's going to be assigned elsewhere, that the burden has grown too heavy for him to bear. He could have kept pushing him, like he did with Amir, but he doesn't. Not this time. Perhaps, in the end, Anders is the lucky one, although none of us know where his reassignment will take him.

There's a look of distress on Ajax's face when he tells us. I don't think it's any sort of caring for

Anders, any latent remorse over what happened with Amir. It's simply the fact that now there's one less recruit. One less Watcher. And there are far too few of us already.

Each night I return to my diary. I keep it by my bed, not in a drawer or cupboard that's going to retract into the wall or floor, but in the old bag I brought with me from home. Inside it joins my mother's watch, which finds its way into my hands most nights, and the pictures of my family.

Before I sleep, I lift the diary from the bag and read over the pages I've written in the hope it will keep me human. Then I write a little more, anything I can think of, to nourish that side of me. Every night, I fall asleep with the diary dropped to the floor or lying on top of my lap, thoughts of my mother and Jackson still dominating my dreams.

My sleep is now peppered with other visions as well. I suppose the training must be having an impact, because they grow in clarity as the days go by. For several days in a row I see a great storm brewing in the ocean, overturning a boat laden with people. It comes to me night after night, the visions growing clearer each time.

I tell Ajax and he says what he always says. That I need to look for details, anything specific that will reveal the particular ship or the day it occurs. That night, as people plunge to the depths of the sea and the ship rolls over under the force of the waves, I see a name written onto its side: Adonia.

It's only a couple of days later that the storm that would have sunk the passenger ship Adonia down to the bottom of the ocean begins to rage. But, of course, the same ship had been alerted and, as a result, took a different path to its destination. With the help of the Meteorologists down on Underwater Level 3, my vision meant that the ship was safely diverted away from the oncoming storm. It's hard to know how many lives would have been lost but, in the end, every single soul survives.

Ajax congratulates me when the news comes in, yet I get no other recognition. It's the way of the Watchers, he tells me, to help others with no thought to their own end. There are no grand parades to honour those who save lives. No medals given out. It's the same in the military. Those who achieve great things aren't provided with any special treatment. It is, in the end, all part of our duty.

Some of the other trainees have some success as well. Larna manages to save a man from falling to his death whilst performing some structural work on the city walls. Link sees a gas explosion, all the way over on the sea city of Caprico, which would otherwise have killed several people. It turns out that another Watcher had seen the explosion as well, but nevertheless the additional details Link provided were important.

After two months, Ajax announces that we're to go through an evaluation process to learn how far we have come. For those who pass, the next stage of training awaits. That, Ajax tells us, will involve learning to tap into the Void, as he did the first day we all arrived at the Grid.

He gathers us together before explaining what lies

ahead. "Today," he starts, "we will all learn how much progress you have made. You will undergo two stages of evaluation. A psychological evaluation and a physical evaluation. This time, your physical tests will be real. We will not be using the Grid."

I look to Ellie and Link, a resolve on both their faces. After going through what we've all been through, little fazes us now.

"First of all, let's be clear. Up until now, your experiences in the Grid have been simulations. As much as we attempt to replicate your truest fears, they will never be quite the same as real life. Yes, you can be hurt in there, and yes, you may come out dirty and blooded, but you can never become seriously injured, and you can never die."

"But I got burned. I got cut," says Link, and I see several heads nodding.

"You told me it was real," Theo adds. "The first time I went in, you said it was real."

"I told you that because it's what you needed to believe and, to a certain extent, it is real. The cuts and the burns are all minor injuries which can be sustained to help create the illusion of total reality, but your physical wellbeing is not under serious threat. Eve is constantly monitoring your vital statistics when you're in there. She controls the simulation and it's impossible for you to get truly hurt."

"And today? What happens today?" asks Lorna.

"Today you will face your fears for real. Today, if you run, you may not only break like Amir did, you may die."

A murmur runs around the group, but I don't see those looks of dread and anxiety as I once did. Faces crinkle with minor concern, eyes narrow with intensity, jaws clench with resolve. I see young men and women who know what's coming, who have experienced it daily. Crafted by their fears, I know that no one here will take a backward step, whatever they have to face.

We start with our psychological evaluations, which take place on Underwater Level 3. When we arrive, we step onto the tram and shoot halfway around to the other side. Once there, Ajax leads us towards a sector marked Psychological Testing. He tells us that it's used for soldiers, primarily, to prepare them for the hardships they might experience in battle.

When we arrive, we are all placed into different rooms. Ajax tells us that we will not have any social contact with each other for the rest of the day. We will be called for our evaluation, and when we return to the room, instructions will be provided by Eve on where to go next. We need to follow these instructions exactly, he says, before telling us good luck, and that he'll see us all tomorrow.

As I sit in my room, waiting for the call, my mind begins churning out possible scenarios for my physical evaluation. I know it will be related to what we've been going through in the Grid. It will, in some way, highlight our major fears, force us through them. Ajax told us that injury and death were even possible. That this would be real life, no longer a simulation.

So, perhaps they'll put Ellie in a pit with lots of snakes, forcing her to move through them to escape. Maybe Link will be tasked with saving someone from a burning building somewhere, and the twins forced to climb the highest tower in the city.

Their fears, I think to myself, are more tangible, more definitive. Snakes, fire, heights. But what about me? My greatest fear is losing Jackson and losing everything I know and care about. What possible physical test can they design for me that will test me against that fear?

When the door finally opens, I see a woman standing in front of me. She wears a white coat and holds a tablet in her hand. "Miss Drayton," she says, "would you come with me."

I follow her down a corridor into a room marked 'Testing Room 12' and sit in an upright chair. She lifts a small needle from her pocket and approaches me.

"Lift up your sleeve please," she says, before sticking the pin into my vein.

"What is it?" I ask, watching the clear liquid squeeze out of the syringe.

"It's a truth agent," she says. "It will ensure that every answer you give me is real."

"So you think I'd lie to you?" I ask.

"I don't know you, Miss Drayton, so I can't answer that question."

She pulls the needle from my arm and places it on a counter, before settling into a chair. I can already feel a strange sensation running through me, my eyes growing heavy and sleepy, the world blurring slightly.

She holds her tablet on her lap, lightly touching it in places with her fingers. "OK, Miss Drayton, confirm that I have administered the drug please."

I nod without thinking.

"Vocalise it please."

"Yes," I say. "You have administered the drug."

"Excellent. Thank you."

Now she's asking me all sorts of questions, questions about my upbringing, about my life in Arbor, about my brother and sister and mother and father. I answer her questions, almost without thinking. It's as though I'm watching myself from across the room, slumped slightly in the chair, eyes hazy and speech a bit slurred.

She asks me about my visions, and I tell her everything I know. She asks me about my feelings towards Eden, towards the Testing and the Duty Call, about how the country is run, and I give her my honest opinions.

Then, she starts on Jackson and my experience in the Grid.

"Jackson is your best friend, is he not?" she asks.

"He is," I say.

"Is he more than that?"

I don't answer.

"I'll ask again. Is he more than a friend."

"Yes," I hear myself saying.

"Do you love him?"

My answer is immediate, so quick is surprises even myself. "I do."

"And if you knew he was dead, would you care?"

"Yes." Once more, my answer is immediate.

"Are you scared that he'll die?"

I don't answer. Inside, I can feel a war raging.

"I'll ask again. Are you scared that he'll die?"

"No," I say. "I'm not scared that he'll die."

I see the woman smiling and looking over her tablet. "Good. That's what we want to hear. I think, Miss Drayton, that that's about enough. You will receive your results from Commander Ajax during your debrief."

She tells me to stand and return to the room I came from, the drug still lingering in my system.

"It will pass in a few minutes," she says, as I stumble out of the door, my vision still slightly blurry and legs strangely weak.

When I return to the room I see a screen immediately start glowing on the wall as Eve's voice comes ringing out.

"Hello, Cyra. How are you feeling?"

I slump onto a bench at the side of the room opposite the screen. "Drained," I say. "So what's next?"

"Nothing, for you. You are not required to undergo a physical evaluation."

I shake the remaining drug out of my head. "How come?"

"I do not have that information. Please, return to your living quarters."

"So, that's it for me? There's nothing else?"

"I do not have that information," she says again. "You are to return to your living quarters."

"OK, OK, that's fine by me," I say, slightly surprised to have such a stroke of luck. The way Ajax had spoken earlier I'd have thought I'd be in mortal danger in an hour or so.

I stand and start making my way back towards the deck, purposefully walking around the level rather than using the tram. As I go, I notice one of the Scientist recruits I met on the ship. I see her, through the transparent wall, dressed in her white coat and fiddling with some strange liquids and test tubes.

A large entry point says Epidemiology, and I know her life will be dedicated to finding new ways to prevent disease and illness. So, she'll be saving lives like I will.

I continue on around the boundary of the level, watching the Scientists at work beyond the see-through walls. I pass various sections, tasked with improving life in their own special way. I stop, briefly, at the Agronomist section, a place where soils and crops are studied.

I remember Leeta telling me about how they're working on enhancing the crops so that they grow quicker, more nutritious, and larger. It's funny to think that the work being done here will have such a serious impact on life across Agricola.

Soon I'm back at the main entry point where we

arrived. I enter the lift and return to the deck, step out into the bright sunlight, and suck in a deep breath of fresh air. It always smells so sweet here, despite the fact that we're out at sea. Nothing like that salty sensation that crept up my nose in Piscator.

I get an immediate surprise when I step back into my room. As soon as I take a seat on the bed, my hand almost instinctively reaching for my diary, the wall opposite me begins to come alive, glowing a funny sickly yellow colour. I ask Eve what's going on, but she doesn't answer. I ask again as a hologram begins to shine out of the wall, and still hear nothing.

The image in front of me is similar to what I've seen before. It's a desert setting, orange and red and dry. Yet it's nothing like what I've seen in my sleep. This time, it's as though the footage is real, coming from a fixed position mounted on a wall. A security camera, perhaps, capturing real time events.

I see young men, dressed in battle armour, heavy automatic weapons lifted to their shoulders. They move forward, seemingly through a training ground, passing by obstacles as they're fired on by turrets and fake mechanical soldiers.

One of the men gets shot, and his armour begins flashing red. He stands to his feet and turns to leave the battlefield. It's merely a training exercise, and they're being fired at by phony rounds that simply disable them, not hurt them.

The recruits, however, are using live fire. Their bullets rip into the mechanical soldiers, knocking them down as they progress through the torrent of gunfire. I see one stop, his weapon jammed. He drops to his knee behind cover and begins fiddling with the gun, trying to fix it.

I notice the man leading the charge, an Officer, carefully retreat to his side. Everyone else takes cover behind barriers and broken down walls, waiting for orders.

What happens next causes me to almost fall backwards on my bed. The entire hologram flashes suddenly, colours of orange and yellow and red mixing as an explosive cloud of dust and smoke obscures the battlefield. I hear shouting and screaming as the cloud starts to clear, then the sight of crimson chunks and splattered blood fills my eyes.

I see several young men, bodies mangled, limbs blown off, lying prostrate and helpless in the dirt. People rush in, trying to help, but there's nothing they can do. The hologram moves forward as the helmets of the men are removed, their features growing clearer as the dust parts.

I see the Officer, his hair blond and skin a golden brown. Blue eyes, lifeless and empty, stare up into the sky. Blood trickles out of his mouth, staining his lips red. It's a sight I've seen so many times now. One I thought I'd grown used to.

Yet today, I feel my body trembling more than it ever has. Today, my vision begins to blur, and a blackness closes in around me.

Because today, the sight of Jackson, lying dead in the sand, isn't only a manifestation of my fear.

Today, I've watched Jackson die for real.

And today, the sight overwhelms me to the point where I collapse onto my bed, hoping never to wake up.

16
A Line Crossed

I hear the sound of a sweet voice in my ear. It calls my name, cries for me to wake up. A battle rages inside me. I want to open my eyes but can't. I hear more people in the room, feel my body being lifted and carried away. I hear noises, feel sensations, but nothing is clear, everything is cloaked in a shroud of darkness.

I'm laid down on a bed, feel needles injected into my skin. There's a commotion around me, several voices calling at once. My eyes flicker and a silence dawns. In flashes I see people looking at me. Ellie, Link, Ajax, several others in white coats. They're blurred and unfocused, their voices muffled. I try to speak, but my words are mumbled. I try to move, but can't. I'm locked in my body, my mind drifting, as my eyes close shut again.

I see Jackson now. He's alive, dressed in combat gear, looking like a hero. He's speaking to a group of young men, addressing them as their commander. They look up to him, respect him. I try to reach out to him. Try to call his name, scream it at the top of my lungs, but he doesn't see me, doesn't hear me.

I watch as he and his men begin moving through the training battleground. Fake bullets fly at him, real ones are returned. I call again, try to warm him of what's coming, but I can't. Then, the explosion tears through his body once more, and I sink to my knees in the earth.

I'm lost in darkness, seeing nothing now. I hear that sweet voice again, over and over, calling my name. I fight my way towards the light, trying to escape from this prison. I hear my mother's voice, telling me to be strong, telling me to wake up.

My eyes open.

The haze in front of them clears. I see colours again, defined shapes in the room. Machines hum around me, I hear the beeping sound of a heart monitor. Then movement, and the face of Ellie appears in front of me.

"Cyra," she calls, "can you hear me. Nod if you can hear me."

I nod, and her eyes open wider. She calls for aid, and several people rush into the room. Now another voice calls to me, the voice of a man I don't recognise.

"Cyra, can you understand me. Can you speak."

"Yes," I croak. My voice feels feeble, like it's never been used. "What happened?"

"You had a mental break," comes the voice. "You're in the hospital."

"I'm so glad you're awake," says Ellie, her voice breaking with emotion. "I thought you'd be lost like Amir."

"How long have I been here?" I ask, my throat dry and raspy.

"A few days," says the man. "How much do you

remember?"

I shut my eyes, my face crinkling. "Everything," I say.

"OK, that's good, very good," I hear the Doctor say. "We're going to keep an eye on you overnight, but if everything's in order, you'll be able to leave tomorrow."

I watch as he turns to Ellie and tells her to leave so I can rest. She smiles at me warmly before kissing me on the cheek and leaving the room. "I'll be back later," she says, before disappearing out through the door.

Rest. I don't need any rest. I've been resting for days. What I need are answers.

When the Doctor leaves I don't waste any time. I quickly slip out of the bed and down the corridor towards the exit. I notice immediately that I'm in the same place as Amir was, so am able to easily navigate my way out. Thankfully, the place is so quiet I'm able to get back out towards the perimeter of the level without detection.

It's late when I reach the lifts and hit the button for Underwater Level 5. It's quiet now, most of the level bathed in darkness and only a few lingering people still at work.

I descend and step out into complete silence. Underwater 5 is always quiet, especially where the Grid is. Perhaps in other areas of the level it's a little busier, but I've never explored it to find out.

I walk under the tram tracks, and around the perimeter until I reach the long passageway that leads to the Grid. It's eerie and dim, something I'm used to by now, as I step quietly down the corridor. When I reach the end I slip my arm into the security scanner and feel the warm sensation run over my wrist. Then, with that familiar hiss of air, the door slides open.

Inside, the Grid has returned to its full size. I no longer see the small waiting room that's been our second home for the last two months. I step out into the large, cavernous hall, stretching into the darkness in the distance, and scan the entire area with my eyes, but see no other structure.

I begin walking forward, into the centre of the Grid. It's odd, being in here without having to suffer some painful manifestation. Without having to watch Jackson die. Now, I'll never have to again.

I stiffen my jaw, and shut the thought out of my head. Through the darkness I see the back of the hall, and the door that leads out of it on the other side. I march towards it, my footsteps echoing, my pulse beginning to quicken.

The door has no security scanner. No buttons to operate it. There's a handle instead, which I twist down until the door clicks open. It swings forward as I step into the blackness, and a light suddenly brightens the room.

I squint and hear a voice, deep and cold. "Who is it?"

"It's me, Cyra," I say.

"You're out?" comes the voice again, my eyesight beginning to clear. "I'm glad to hear that."

Ajax's tall frame appears in front of me, dressed in sodden clothes. His hair is wet, water dripping down his face. "Excuse my appearance. Please, take a seat," he says. His voice is so calm, so poised, so unemotional. I'd have hoped seeing me return would make him at least a little happy.

He guides me to a chair and I sit down as he towels his hair dry. I look to see a bed in the corner and little else.

"You live here?" I ask.

"Not permanently, no. Just when training the new recruits."

"And so you can use the Grid yourself?" I ask. "It's drowning you fear, isn't it? So you live that each night."

He nods. "I used to fear it, very much. Now it's as much a part of me as my arms or my legs. It's what gives me my strength."

"And is it worth it?" I ask. "Growing so cold, so...inhuman."

"Losing your fear doesn't make you inhuman, Cyra. It makes you strong, makes you tough. It doesn't mean you lose other emotions."

"Then why are you like that?" I ask, my words accusatory. "What are you so cold?"

"Because I have to be," he says. "It's part of my duty, as a trainer, to remain detached, to show no emotion. Not all Watchers are like me, Cyra."

"And Jackson dying, was that all a set up to teach me a lesson, to make me conquer that fear? Like how you let Amir break, just to show us how serious it is in the Grid? Do you not care about that at all?! Do you not care that I nearly broke too?!" My words grow louder as I speak, spitting out of my mouth like venom as tears build in my eyes.

"Jackson's death was an accident, Cyra. He died several weeks ago. Your test was watching it, knowing that it was real for the first time. You failed that test. You haven't yet let go of that fear."

"And I won't have to now, will I!" I shout. "Because now he's dead, and you've got what you wanted. Now, there's nothing I fear!"

I stand, my heart raging, and storm towards the door.

"Stop," come Ajax's voice behind me.

I stop in the doorway and turn.

"I'm sorry for his death, Cyra, I truly am. But there was nothing you, or anyone else, could have done. It was an unfortunate accident, nothing more."

I stare at him, a hatred building inside me. Not for him, not for anyone in particular. Just a burning hatred for the world, for Eden and everything in it.

"What time do we start tomorrow?" I ask, as calmly as possible. Inside I feel dead and numb, like nothing matters any more.

"Take a few days, Cyra," he says. "Come back next week."

Then I turn and storm out, slamming the door behind me.

Ellie finds me back in my room, having already gone down to the hospital to find that I'd absconded. When she knocks and comes in, I hastily drop my diary back down into the bag next to my bed and brush a tear from my eye.

She asks me what happened, telling me that no one informed her as to why I'd blacked out. I give her the barest of details, finding it almost impossible to speak about it out loud. My eyes grow wet, but inside I feel paralysed, my heart and soul crushed into dust. An empty vessel, now shaped into a tool for Eden to use as it wishes. I guess that's what they wanted all along.

She does most of the speaking, though. I think she can tell that I'm in no condition to go into any detail about what happened. She says that she was by my side, everyday, just like Anders was with Amir. Link would come too, on occasion, to lend his support. I see her welling up as she tells me how she thought I'd never wake up. How she thought I was broken beyond repair, just like Amir.

She describes her own physical test and how she almost died herself, bitten by several snakes as she attempted to reach the anti-venom that would save her. She tells me, though, that she felt no fear as she did it. How those same snakes that used to haunt her dreams are now nothing to her.

Apparently all the others passed their tests too, and for the last week they've moved onto a different type of training. Already, she says, Link is able to see slightly into the Void. Although she admits that she's made no discernible progress herself, nor has anyone else.

I hardly say anything as she speaks, my mind still trying to catch up with everything that's happened, everything I've missed. When she leaves, I lie there, staring up towards the ceiling, my diary clutched tight to my chest. Soon Eve begins to darken the room, and I say nothing. I just let the light fade, slowly into the blackness, hoping that I never see the light again.

I fall into strange dreams. I can now tell the difference between what's a dream and what's a vision. Dreams are more obscure, less clear. When you wake from one you know it's not real, just a manifestation in your mind. A vision is different. It's clearer, more intense. Somehow, when you wake from a vision, you know it's real. You can just feel it inside you, creeping closer as it threatens to become reality, repeating in your sleep night after night.

That night, no visions come to me. Just dreams of everything I've lost. My mother strokes my head as I lie there, curled into a ball, crying until my eyes run dry. She whispers into my ear, telling me to be strong, that I'll get through all of this. Jackson joins her, and they stand side by side, drifting away from me, fading into the blackness.

I wake with a start and sit up in my bed. The room has grown light already, the sound of the city waking up below, carrying on as it always does, day after day after day. Ellie comes to check on me before going to the Grid. She's so sweet like that, and it's nice to see that her sensitive side hasn't been beaten out of her. Maybe Ajax is right. Losing your fear doesn't make you cold and inhuman. It just strengthens you and gives you this confidence and resolve.

Only my fear was different. My fear didn't involve moving past something restrictive, something unpleasant like snakes or fire or a fear of heights. My fear involved the death of everything I love. If anyone is going to grow cold and inhuman, it's me.

I spend the day walking around the upper deck, which is always much quieter during the daytime. When the evening begins to dawn, I retreat to Surface Level 8, a place I feel most at home. I walk through passageways as they fill with workers having completed their duties for the day. Watch as they meet their husbands and wives and hug their children. Happy, despite having so little, to be together.

People look at me as I pass, walking aimlessly across the level. But they don't stare like they do up on deck. They just look at me like I'm one of them. Another young girl, plucked from the mainland, lost and alone.

Down a passageway I see a door ajar. Inside is an unused room, filled with nothing but a bed and a sink. It's not like my room, though. I can't just summon Eve to unfold the wardrobe, or order food to be delivered from a hole in the wall. No. I know, down here, that Eve doesn't exist. That this entire floor is filled with basic rooms like this one, and that rations are given out, just like back home.

I step into the room and shut the door. Inside is a lock, which I turn up, shutting out the world. The bed is uncomfortable when I lie on it compared to my own. Yet it's what I want. It reminds me of home.

Around me I can hear noises through the wall. A man speaking loudly to someone. A child's laughter.

A baby crying. I close my eyes and imagine I'm back in the Block, my mother in the next room, Jackson a short walk away through town. I think of the Grove, of our meeting point at the old log in the middle. I think of how we used to laugh, how we'd hug when we parted, how it felt to have his strong arms wrap around me.

I think of the night my mother died, of how all I wanted was to leave and never look back. Of the kiss Jackson gave me, his way of saying goodbye. I knew, then, that I'd probably never see him again. Now that fear has become reality, one that leaves me empty and hollow, as barren as the landscape he died on.

I lie on that bed for hours. Soon, those hours become a day. Then two. I think of following my mother, following Jackson to the grave. Of letting my growing thirst overcome me. I wonder whether they're looking for me, how long it would take for them to find me. How worried Ellie must be, and perhaps Link too.

But somehow, I don't care. I just lie there, wasting away, my mind consumed by thoughts of my past, thoughts of those I love. I have nothing now. Nothing to live for. Nothing to fight for. Everything in my world has been crushed and destroyed. I might as well follow.

When the door is kicked open off its lock, I hardly even move or react. There's a heavy thud, and a crack as the lock is broken, and the door swings wildly open. I arch my neck up and see Ajax standing in the shadow of the doorway. He rushes towards me, eyes sunken with a mixture of anger and concern, and lifts my head with his hands.

He stares into my flickering eyes and quickly rushes towards the sink, returning with his hands cupped with water. He pours some of the cool liquid down my throat and I feel immediate relief. Then he checks my body for injuries, running his eyes over me.

"Are you hurt?" he asks.

I shake my head. "How did you know I was here?" I croak.

"I saw you," he says. "Last night I saw you here, wasting away. What the hell are you playing at, Cyra?!"

"A vision?" I ask.

"Yes, a vision. Why are you doing this? You have everything to live for."

"I wasn't going to die here," I say weakly. "I just needed time to myself."

"Time without eating or drinking. You were going to die, Cyra, I saw you."

"Well maybe you should have left me. What's the point in carrying on."

"The point is you have a gift and....a responsibility. Your life is too valuable to just give up. What about all the people you'll save? Don't they count? What about your friends here, Ellie and Link. Don't you care what they'd think?"

I roll to my side so that he can't see the tear trickle down my cheek. I know he's right. I know I'm being selfish, that whatever has happened in my past, I do have an obligation to help people. I think of what my mother would say. How disappointed she'd be with me for giving in like this. What Jackson would tell me. To keep going, to fight through the pain and move on.

I feel Ajax rolling me back over, his face softening at the sight of my tears.

"Cyra," he says, his voice quieter now, "I understand what you're going through. We all lose people we love, we all have to suffer change. You have to be strong right now. I'm not going to give up on you and I'm not going to let you self destruct like this."

He takes my hand in a rare moment of tenderness and squeezes it tight. "If ever you need someone to talk to, I'm here for you. If you need support, just ask for it, don't carry the entire burden yourself."

I lightly nod my head as tears start rolling. "I'm sorry about the other day," I say. "I know its not your fault. None of this is your fault. It's just....hard. No one can understand what it's like, seeing the person you care about most dying every day, knowing they're now gone forever. I know it's stupid and I know I probably wouldn't have seen him ever again anyway but....I can't help how I feel."

"It's not stupid, Cyra. And you're wrong about no one being able to understand." His eyes glint with a painful memory. "I understand."

"You lost someone?" I ask, searching his eyes.

"My wife," he says, "and my little girl."

I think of Ajax walking into the Grid, water rushing towards him. I think of seeing him the other day, drenched from head to toe. Every night he goes in there and relives something horrible, something horrific. He relives the deaths of his family.

"They both drowned at sea," he says. "I see it night after night now."

"But....why?"

"Because it gives me my strength, helps me remember what I do this for. Every person I save, every recruit I train who goes on to save people, it makes it all worth it."

I sit up onto the bed, my head feeling light and dizzy. "You must think I'm so stupid," I say, dipping my eyes down.

Ajax lifts my chin. "Not one bit. You're strong, Cyra. You've been through more than any recruit I've ever had, and you're still here. I know it's hard, but you're here for a reason. Everyone has a destiny."

"If it's meant to be, it will be," I whisper. "Do you truly believe that?"

He nods. "Yes, but not in the way you think. I believe there's so much more to people than the roles they're given. People can do amazing things when you let them. I've seen it time and time again. This world we live in isn't fair, Cyra. It never has been, across history. But some of us are put here for an important reason, and you're one of them. That, I truly do believe."

"Thank you," I say, "for coming here. For saving me."

"Don't mention it. Now come on, let's get you

home."

Then he lifts me to my feet, wraps my arm over his shoulder, and supports me all the way back to my room on the deck.

17

The Void

It's a week since my breakdown when I stand, facing forward, a busy street in front of me. I walk, not quite knowing what to expect, when suddenly I see a car rushing in my direction. It comes from around the corner, at a tremendous pace, people jumping out of the way as it hurtles right at me.

I have no time to react. No time to move. I grimace and brace for impact, but it never comes. The car stops, suddenly, and fades in front of my eyes, only a foot or so away from me.

The rest of the street fades as well, and I'm left looking at an empty hall. Or, part of it at least. The Grid has now become portioned off into four separate zones, broken up by clear partition walls. I see, in the zone ahead of me, Link rushing through a battlefield, being sprayed at by fake bullets. They hurt when they hit you – I've experienced that much already – but they can't do any serious harm. He dodges through them, similar to how Ajax did on our first day here, although one still manages to hit him. I can see he's not happy about it.

I turn to the left, where Ellie and Larna are engaged in some sort of hand to hand combat. They look slightly awkward as they fight, their faces obscured by protective headgear, their hands locked inside padded gloves. But it's not their appearance that's odd. It's more their fighting style, which remains extremely amateur. Not that I can judge them much. I'm not exactly brilliant myself.

At the far end of the hall in the final quarter, Theo stands with Lorna, Rupert and Kyle. They crouch behind a low barricade, various weapons lined up on the wall next to them, firing at targets that sprout from the ground and disappear just as quickly. That section is purely used for weapons training.

Ajax walks towards me, shaking his head.

"You're not concentrating hard enough, Cyra. I know you can do this. Link can do it, even Theo has his moments. And I know you'll be able to as well."

"It came out of nowhere! I had no idea that was even going to happen."

He sighs. "That's the entire point. If you knew it would happen, you wouldn't need to see it coming. You should know that car's going to come towards you before you even see it for real. Then, you'll have no trouble avoiding it. Go again, and this time, forget everything else that's going on in your head and focus."

He steps back and, once more, my section of the hall begins morphing in front of my eyes. This time, however, I'm not up on the busy streets above, but am in the woods, surrounded by thick green trees and heavy foliage. I begin walking, as before, trying to follow Ajax's advice.

"It's all about personal survival. Some Watchers have an ability to sense danger to themselves before it occurs. Focus on your surroundings, on what dangers you might face. Concentrate, and you'll see it before it comes."

Ajax has always had a cryptic way of explaining things, and I sure don't understand what he's been telling me for the past week. I've been inside these simulations day after day, and have found myself getting battered and bruised each time. None of the others have had much success either, which makes me feel a bit better. Well, except Link, at least. He's already being shaped into a serious weapon.

Because, in effect, that's what we all are. We're not only used to report on our visions. We're not only tasked with saving people from potential disasters. Some of us have other abilities that make us useful to the military as well. Those Watchers who can see into the Void make up a special military unit that, during times of war, can be called upon to fight.

According to Ajax, that hasn't happened for some time, yet the contingency is always being prepared for. So, that's why we're having to go through weapons and combat training. That's what this part of the training is all about.

I keep moving through the woods, listening for any unusual sounds or the sight of someone holding a gun in my direction. Yet there's nothing. Just the usual tweeting of birds and clicking of insects, the light swaying of the breeze as it brushes through the trees.

I'm reminded of the Grove, and Jackson once more pops into my mind. He's there most days still, although I've been doing everything to keep myself busy and keep him out. I imagine him walking alongside me, talking as we used to. Then, I hear him whisper in my ear: "Watch out for the wolves."

I know it's happening before I hear or see them. It's hard to explain. They're there, rushing towards me from all sides, but they're not really there. They appear more like ghosts, like apparitions, shooting out from the foliage. I react immediately, turning to the nearest tree and jumping up to grab a low hanging branch.

I swing my legs up just as the growling starts and the wolves come bursting from the bushes, following right in behind their ghostly precursors. They pour forward, about a dozen or so of them, running up the bark and snapping at my feet. I'm just out of reach, but climb higher, my heart pounding hard, as they circle beneath me. Then, as quickly as it all started, they fade away, along with the woods around me. All that remains is me, and the tree I happen to be hiding in.

Claps echo across the hall and I look over to see Ajax walking towards me, a smile cut across his face.

"Now that's how to do it, Cyra. You can come down from the tree now."

I carefully drop to the floor and the tree disappears behind me.

"I don't even know what happened," I say, panting slightly. "They were like ghosts, followed in by their real bodies."

"That's exactly it. That's what it's all about. When you learn to control that ability, you'll see all dangers coming your way. In effect, you'll be able to defy death at every turn."

"Well, how often are you expecting me to be in such situations?" I ask. "Defying death is great and all, but I'd rather not tempt fate if at all possible."

"It depends, Cyra. If you're called upon, you might have to go to some very dangerous places."

"Right, that's great. I'd prefer I couldn't see into the Void if that's the case."

Ajax frowns and puts on his more serious voice. "Remember what I told you. This is a duty, it's not a privilege. You should feel honoured to have this ability. Not many Watchers do."

I still can't get past the thought that this is all just one big curse, but I don't say that to him. Link might embrace it all, might love the idea of being this protector of the people, but that's just not me. I'd rather a simple life somewhere. I wish most days, despite wanting to leave so desperately when my mother died, that I could just return to Agricola.

When we change to new stations, I find myself lying alongside Ellie and Link, a heavy automatic weapon in my arms. Behind us, Theo, Rupert, and Kyle are now engaged in combat training, while the twins are working through their simulations.

Link gets straight to it, firing relentlessly at the targets as they appear. He's a good shot, filling them with bullets until they disappear, then quickly moving onto the next as it sprouts from the ground. Ellie, meanwhile, is a little slower and more tentative, and I have little interest in shooting at all. I'm not a soldier and never want to be, so learning how to fire all these weapons isn't going to be overly helpful.

When Ajax appears, however, I'm forced to show willing at least. To my own surprise, I'm actually quite good, and have been improving each day. Now, after only a week, I'm able to shoot a moving target from over a hundred feet. When I started, I spent my entire time spraying at the wall behind them.

I've noticed Link and Ellie getting close recently. Ever since we all began spending time together, it became clear that there was something between them. They make a funny looking pair. He's so tall and strong looking, assertive and confident. She looks about 14 years old and, despite everything we've been through, maintains some of that sweetness and innocence that she had when I met her.

He helps her now, as we fire, to use the weapons and shoot straight. She giggles at his little jokes and I see her smile as his hand slides over the top of her own. When I turn back, I notice Ajax watching from across the hall. He misses absolutely nothing, and I begin to wonder whether his ability to see into the future goes beyond just dangers to his personal well-being. It's like he's got this sixth sense that alerts him to just about everything going on around him.

I turn back and continue firing, knowing that he'll be watching me too. After a while, we change stations again, and I move to the combat quarter to spar with Lorna. She's actually the best fighter of all the girls, and seems more naturally athletic than her sister. She manages to kick high and punch hard, rocking me back as her blows crash against my protective clothing.

I notice Ajax hovering nearby, his eyes burning into me, and focus on the fight. I've got little technique but, as Ajax tells us, when you can see into the Void, you don't need good technique. I focus hard and see the wisps of Lorna's arms coming towards me, followed quickly by her real fists.

I fail to avoid the first few, but eventually am able to dodge through her punches, seeing them a split second early. She grows frustrated, punching and kicking harder, yet I avoid them all. Then, as I step away from an oncoming right hand, I move quickly forward and send my own fist right into her face. She fails to see it coming and I connect with my full force on her nose. Blood immediately spills out from underneath her mask and she drops to the floor, her face in her hands.

"Good, good!" shouts Ajax, smiling at me once again. He kneels down and pulls the mask off Lorna's head to see blood spurting from her nose.

"Ah, I think it's broken," he says. "Right, let's get you down to the hospital to check you over," he says, oblivious to Lorna's sobs.

"Sorry Lorna," I say as she's taken off, but all she does is respond with a glare. Ajax, meanwhile, has never seemed happier.

"Always causing problems, aren't you?" I look over to see Theo, emerging from one of the simulation stations. "It would have been better for everyone if you'd just broken for good."

"What did you say?" says Link, marching across the room.

Theo turns to him. "It's got nothing to do with you, scarface. Go back to playing with your little girlfriend."

I see Ellie's eyes duck a little in embarrassment. I don't think she realises how obvious they are together.

Link continues to storm forward. "You want to say that to my face? There's no Ajax around to protect you now."

Theo huffs. "It's always violence with you, isn't it. I wouldn't expect anything less from someone from Fossor. I've heard it's the most simple of all the regions. Full of dunces like you."

Link comes storming forward now, lifting his fists. Somehow Theo manages to duck away from the first punch, backing off quickly. He stumbles over his feet, tripping to the floor, Link towering above him.

"Say one more thing, and I'll knock your head off," growls Link, staring Theo down.

Then, out of nowhere, Rupert's fist comes crashing into the back of Link's head, knocking him down. He clatters to the floor as Ellie runs forward, screaming. I hold her back, her legs kicking out as Theo returns to his feet.

"Now that's more like it," he says, looking down on Link. "That's just where you belong. At my feet."

Link seems dazed on the floor, a cut on the back of his head now dribbling with blood. Ellie scrambles from my arms and runs towards him, quickly sliding to the floor and tending to his wound.

Rupert, meanwhile, stands to Theo's side, his pathetic, subservient lieutenant. He rubs his fist and keeps his eyes on Link, making sure he doesn't get up.

"So, you got anything to say," says Theo, turning back to me. "You got any spine at all?"

I can feel my insides burning with rage now, my heart pounding.

"No, I thought not. At least you know your place," he sneers.

What I do next I don't expect. It comes like a flash, before I can even think. I dart at him, so fast he barely has time to react. My fist swings and catches him in the jaw, knocking his head sideways. I hear him roar in anger as his own balled fist comes swinging at me, but I see it all coming a moment too soon. I duck below the ghostly fist and send my own back into his nose. I feel the crack, and see the blood, just as Ajax storms back into the room.

"WHAT THE HELL IS GOING ON IN HERE?!" he roars, storming forward and catching me before I can inflict any more damage.

Theo drops to the floor, his hands filling with blood. "What have you done to me," he says, his voice shaking. "My face..."

Ajax is quickly at his side, lifting him to his feet. "Come on, Theo, let's get you to the hospital too." He stares at me, his eyes dark as the night. "And you, stay here. I'll see you after. Alone."

"But, it was all him. He started it..."

"I don't want to hear it. Everyone else, clear out and I'll see you tomorrow. Cyra, stay put."

Theo is still mumbling something about his beautiful face and how I'll regret it when Ajax drags him off. Link, thankfully, has managed to get back to his feet, and is now laughing as Theo stumbles out of the Grid. Then he sends his eyes at Rupert, who turns sheepish and scuttles out of the door.

Ellie, Link and I share a few giggles as Larna and Kyle wander out of the Grid.

"Good shot," says Link, his eyes still a little dazed. "He had it coming."

"Thanks. You'd better get that cut checked out though."

Link waves it off. "It's nothing. I've had a lot worse."

"It's all right, Cyra. I'll take care of him," says Ellie. "Are you OK, though?"

"Never better," I say, smiling. "You two should go, Ajax will be back soon."

They nod to me as they leave, a silence dawning inside the hall as the door slides shut behind them.

I know what Ajax is going to tell me. That Theo Graves, as unbearable as he can be, is nevertheless the only son of two members of the Council. Even if he wasn't, I'm sure Ajax would want to reprimand me for fighting with another recruit.

"You have to learn to control your emotions," I can almost hear him say.

Yeah, well that's hard when you have to spend

your days with someone so hell bent on antagonising anyone from the mainland.

I walk around the Grid, slipping from station to station. I still can't quite believe this is my life right now. Only a few short months ago I was out there, picking fruit in the orchards, listening to those worker songs. Rushing home to check on my mother, negotiating down at the merchant sector for her medication. Meeting Jackson in the Grove, talking about how I'd make sure I stay in Arbor.

Now they're both gone, and I'm stuck here in a place I don't belong. A place where I get funny stares just walking down the street, where I'm teased and taunted for being different. Yet I hardly see the girl who left Arbor in the mirror any more. That girl with shining blonde hair and golden skin. Now my reflection tells of someone fading from who they were. Brown skin and bright hair dimming. Blue eyes losing their shine.

The sound of the door sliding open turns me on my heels, and I see Ajax storming back towards me. He wears a scowl so intense it could kill, his jaw snapped shut like a crocodile.

"Look, I'm sorry, OK. I know I shouldn't have done that. I know I need to control myself. But you didn't see what happened before. You didn't see him taunting me and Link. You didn't see Link get hit in the back of the head by Rupert..."

He continues forward, marching on.

"I don't know what else to say, all right. I swear I won't do it again."

"Stop talking," he says, shutting me off. "What

happened happened, and there's nothing you can do about it now."

"Oh, right. So, you're not mad?"

"I don't care what happened down here. People from different parts of the country always clash, it's nothing out of the ordinary. What I *do* care about, however, is what happens from now on."

"I know, I know. I swear I won't rise to it again."

"I know you won't, because if you do there will be hell to pay. It's one thing fighting with another recruit down here, but it's another fighting with your partner."

His words don't register. "My partner?"

He reaches me and nods. "You, Cyra, are going to be Paired with Theo Graves."

18

The Pairing

The words repeat in my head

You, Cyra, are going to be Paired with Theo Graves.

I shake my head and laugh.

"You're joking, right? You're not serious?"

Ajax's face remains a picture of calm. "You were the best match during your genetics test."

"But...no. I can't be Paired with him. That's not fair...I won't do it."

"Oh, you'll do it. I imagine he'll feel exactly the same way when he finds out. You're both going to have to learn to get along."

"Get along! We need to do more than get along though don't we?! How can you do this to me, after everything..."

"It's not me, Cyra. It's just meant to be. No one has any control over the results of the genetics test, you know that."

"But, can't we swap with someone. He'll want to swap as well. I'll go with anyone else. Anyone."

Ajax shakes his head, a hint of sympathy in his eyes. "Look, I know this is tough, but it's the same for everyone. When you spend some time together,

I'm sure you'll find some middle ground. That's what it's all about. Finding some foundations to build a relationship on. You've just got to unearth them first."

I turn away, disbelieving. I've only just found out a little over a week ago that Jackson's been killed, and now this. Now I'm going to be inextricably linked with the biggest jerk I've ever met...forever. Someone who looks down on me at the best of times and downright bullies me at the worst. The only solace I'll get from this is that he's probably just as unhappy as I am. And maybe, with his powerful parents, he'll be able to change it.

The thought rushes into my head and out of my mouth. "But his parents are powerful. If anyone can switch things it will be them."

Ajax is still shaking his head. "No one can change it, Cyra. Do you know who brought in the whole idea of Pairing? It was Augustus Knight. Sure, Theo's parents are on the Council, but they're all under Knight's thumb. He's not going to give special allowances to anyone. It would destabilise his entire system."

"So, Knight's the enemy here is he? Pairing is such a stupid damn idea anyway. Why the hell did he bring it in?!"

"You know why, don't be obtuse."

I nod slowly, rolling my eyes. "To put the right people together," I mumble.

"And why?"

"So they breed offspring better suited to their duties."

"Exactly. Not everyone agrees with it, but it does work. Mostly, anyway."

"And do you agree with it?"

"I'm not going to answer that, Cyra."

"Of course not. Your duty isn't to question," I say sarcastically.

Ajax doesn't react.

"Anyway, I didn't think we would be Paired as Watchers. I thought we were like the soldiers in the military? How does it even work if one of us can see into the Void and the other can't? If one of us is called to war, or if we're stationed away from each other?"

"They're valid points," Ajax concedes. "Most probably there will be no call for war and, well, you'll be stationed together somewhere. Watchers are always stationed in their pairs because they will often share the same vision. It helps us see the details when there are two sets of eyes."

He comes towards me and rests his large hands on my tense shoulders. "In any case, the chances of two Watchers having children with the same abilities is much higher than random genetic mutations, and Knight wants more Watchers."

"Children!" I say. "I am NOT having children with him. Not gonna happen. No way."

Ajax takes a deep breath. "Take it one day at a time, Cyra. I can't give any better advice than that."

He lifts his hands off my shoulders and takes a step back. "The Pairing is a public ceremony here in Eden. Is that the same as where you're from?"

I nod my head, eyes to the floor.

"Then you'll understand the set up. It takes place at noon on Sunday in the main square. Please, take tomorrow to try to get used to the idea."

He lifts my chin up, making sure I make eye contact with him. "You've been through so much already. I know this isn't what you want, but it is how it has to be. You'll get used to it, I swear."

Then, for the first time, he steps forward and hugs me. "If you need to talk, I'm here, OK," he whispers, before stepping backwards, turning away, and walking back out of the hall.

When I wake on Sunday morning, I feel like a knife is stabbing at my stomach. The previous night I spent tossing and turning, my mind full of awful thoughts of the next day. Having to stand there, in front of everyone, as Theo and I are bound for life.

I think back to the ceremonies in Arbor, which were always small affairs. It's much like the Duty Call really, with boys on one side, girls on the other, and parents at the back. Only this time, when the names are called, both parties have to go up onto the stage, take each other's hands, and speak the oath: *I honour the Pairing, and I will honour you forever*.

It's been around for decades, so long that it's now ingrained into everyone's psyche. Yet I still don't understand why people accept it so easily. I guess, for many, it takes a lot of the guesswork out of finding a partner. That's how it used to be. People would choose who they wanted to be with and develop a relationship based on that.

Now, though, we're told who our partner will be. I

had no idea, but according to Ajax, one of the functions of the genetics test is to find out who will be the right match for you. So, not only did it curse me to this life, but it cursed me to being Paired with Theo. And there's no one to blame for it except Augustus Knight. Him and his damned scientists, playing God.

Ellie is a bag of nerves when I see her. Her situation can go one of two ways. Either she'll be Paired with Link and she'll live happily ever after, or she'll have to settle for Rupert or, at best, Kyle. Whatever the case, she'll know within a couple of hours.

There's a dress in my wardrobe, specially made for the occasion. It's simple, yet stylish, and nothing like anything I've ever worn. When I put it on and look in the mirror I look like my mother used to, although my skin and hair have lost some of their colour. Still, even now, they contrast nicely with the white dress that clings to my body, loosening at the waist and hanging to my knees.

Ellie appears, looking a little older in her make up. She wears white lipstick to coordinate with the dress, foundation on her cheeks to give them more colour and gleam, white mascara that makes her green eyes pop. She tells me that we're all meant to do the same, so helps me apply mine. Suddenly, when I look in the mirror, I no longer look like my mother. I look like a girl from Eden now.

When we arrive at the main square it's brimming with people. This is nothing like Arbor, where there's only a hundred or so school leavers and their parents. Here, there are at least a thousand boys and girls, many with their parents in the crowd. Around, I see others. Member of the public who have come to watch this special occasion. I suppose life here is meant to be social, so such an event will naturally draw people together.

The square looks different than usual though. A large stage has been constructed at the far end, with hundreds and hundreds of seats lined up in rows ahead of it. Banners and other decorations have been erected, mainly in white but with a smattering of dark blue and crimson. I see the flag of Eden, hanging above the stage and billowing in the light wind: a large band of white in the middle, with thinner bands of dark blue and crimson both above and below. Within the central white band is a basic grey sketch of the city, with it's high pylons and massive dome, and jagged waves beneath.

The seats in front of the stage are already beginning to fill. The girls, all adorned in white dresses, sit on the left, with the boys on the right. They wear black cloaks with high collars, the two sexes in perfect contrast. I catch sight of Link and give Ellie a nudge. He looks handsome in his outfit, his dark hair now carefully styled back. Just like the two of us, he suddenly looks like he belongs.

We move forwards through the growing crowd and manage to find some seats towards the back. Behind, parents dress in fine livery, mostly in the neutral colours of grey and white and black that are so common here.

We see Leeta, bustling her way towards us, a wide

smile on her face.

"Girls, you look beautiful," she says. "Are you excited? You must be excited!"

Not even the make up can hide the glum looks on our faces.

"Oh, well, good luck today. I'm sure you'll be Paired with fine young gentlemen."

Then she scurries off back into the throng to find a suitable perch to watch the proceedings.

Soon the entire square is almost spilling over. Aside from the boys and girls and their parents behind, every space is filled with onlookers. I begin to feel nervous, sitting there, knowing I'm going to have to stand up and go to the stage in front of all of these people. Knowing that they'll be as shocked as I was when they find out that young Theo Graves is to be Paired with a lowly mainlander.

There's an energy in the air. More one of excitement than nerves. I look over the sea of faces in front of me and see girls chatting excitedly as they look over at the boys, wondering who they might be Paired with. I wonder if Theo knows already. If Ajax told him as well. I hope he does, so that at least he'll have had a chance to get used to the idea. At the same time, I'd enjoy seeing his face when my name is called. That would wipe the smugness right off it.

People file onto the stage up ahead. I don't recognise any of them, but they appear to be dignitaries of some kind, perhaps those responsible for arranging all of this. Music accompanies their entrance, and the murmuring among the crowd suddenly grows quiet.

In the centre of the stage is an ornate wooden pedestal. A man walks towards it holding a scroll. He rolls it out and then turns his eyes up towards the crowd.

"Good afternoon, everyone," he says in a precise, Eden accent. "Today is the day of the Pairing. A day when all boys and all girls are bound together for life."

He talks for about 10 minutes about the history of the Pairing and its significance. Most notably, he focuses on High Chancellor Augustus Knight and how he's shaped the city and the nation into what it is today. Every time he mentions his name and accomplishments, a loud applause rings around the audience. Augustus Knight, it seems, is heavily revered here. I guess he's had plenty of time to harvest the love of the people.

I don't applaud. I don't smile and stand when everyone else does. I just sit there, arms folded, thinking of how Knight has, in fact, corrupted what it is to be free and human. Corrupted the very concept of choice. This world – his world – isn't one I like living in.

Eventually, the man on stage begins to start the official Pairing.

"When your names are called, please climb up onto the stage and come together in front of me. Join hands, speak the oath, and return to your seats."

So it begins. Names are called, boys dressed in black and girls dressed in white meet on the stage, and an almost endless applause rings around my ears. I notice a couple of people from the ship over here, girls and boys from the mainland. They always look more nervous than the natives, slightly more awkward and out of place. It's just the way those who have grown up here carry themselves. They walk with more confidence, more self assurance and poise. When I step up I know I'll stick out like a sore thumb.

It's a couple of hours before our little group of trainee Watchers is reached. By this point I'm almost so bored that my nerves have all but vanished. Ellie, meanwhile, is twitching over to my right, her breathing growing more and more abbreviated. I place my hand on hers to try to keep her calm, but she still looks like she's about to throw up.

The first to be called up is Kyle. I feel Ellie's hand grip tighter at mine as the girl he's to be Paired with is called out.

"Larna McIntosh," says the man, and Ellie's hand loosens.

Kyle and Larna approach the stage from either side, join hands, and speak the oath. Personally, I think they make quite a sweet pair, and they both look happy enough with the outcome.

Then I hear Rupert's name. It's the moment of truth for Ellie, and she's so nervous she can barely watch, dropping her chin to her chest and shutting her eyes tight.

When the man speaks the name of Lorna McIntosh, I see Ellie's head swing up quickly and a broad smile stretch over her lips. She searches the crowd for Link, who turns back as people applaud and Rupert and Lorna come together on the stage. His face says it all, a grin on it like I've never seen.

When Ellie and Link step up to the stage, I hear a smattering of laugher around me. I guess it's the sight of them. Him so tall, her so small. Yet all I can do is smile for them as they link hands and speak the oath. Ellie, at least, has got what she wanted.

I know what's coming now. The clapping dies down, Link and Ellie part ways on stage, and the man calls for silence once more.

"Next up, Theo Graves," he says.

Now I see Theo, standing quickly towards the front. People begin applauding immediately, excited to see who he's going to be Paired with.

"Theo Graves is to be Paired with...Cyra Drayton."

I stand, and hear the immediate murmuring around me. I'm so used to it by now it hardly bothers me. Soon, though, etiquette takes over and the applause begins ringing out as I make my way towards the stage.

Theo walks on the other side, refusing to make eye contact with me. When he turns in, however, I notice his eyes, both blackened with bruises, his nose swollen and set with some sort of medical tape.

Inside, I have to stifle a laugh at his appearance. On the outside, it just comes out as a warm smile, which I suppose would make sense if I was any other girl. Theo is, after all, one of the most sought after young men in the city. Strange, then, that he's the last person I want to be standing up here with.

When we come together by the pedestal, his brown eyes appear to have gone several shades darker. He looks at me with the sort of death stare that would topple an elephant, and my smile quickly fades.

For a moment we stand there, just looking at each other, our hands by our sides, until the man tells us to link them.

I raise mine first, holding them out, palms up, as the other girls did. Then he raises his, lays his palms on top of mine, and we speak the oath together.

"I honour the Pairing, and I will honour you forever," we say in unison, both our voices dull and flat.

As soon as we've spoken, he slides his palms off mine, turns, and quickly descends from the stage. And so begins my beautiful life with Theo Graves.

19
Augustus Knight

Once the ceremony ends, the host announces that we're to join our new partners. Music begins playing, everyone stands, and a long applause ensues as the dignitaries leave the stage.

Gradually, the girls and boys begin to mingle, searching for their partners through the crowd. Ellie tells me good luck, kisses me on the cheek, and scuttles away towards Link. I can see, through the sea of faces, the two of theirs meet with a kiss. It doesn't look like their first.

I stay where I am for a while, unable to move as boys and girls come together for the first time. Many kiss, many others just hug, while only a few seem unhappy with who they've been Paired with. Soon, parents begin joining them, hugging their sons and daughters and their new partners. I see smiles everywhere, hear the happy chatter of thousands of voices. Yet still I don't move.

Eventually it becomes too odd for me to be there, surrounded by new Pairings, new families. I search the top of the crowd and then see him, standing with a middle aged couple, their own eyes scanning over the throng. Theo just stares at his feet, though, his body slumped with resignation.

I think about turning away and escaping back to

my room. About defying this stupid tradition. I could leave, leave Eden, stow away on a ship and return home. I could run and never look back, face the consequences if ever they catch up with me.

But I don't.

I just stand there, staring at Theo's parents, until their eyes find mine through the mess of bodies. Smiles arch on their faces as they come forward, the sort of look that Theo has never given me.

Both have dark hair with flecks of grey, both with brown, inquisitive eyes, and perfect teeth. The crowd seems to notice who they are as they move forward, parting to make room for them, as Theo trails behind in their wake.

"Cyra, so wonderful to meet you," says Theo's father, extending his hand. I take it and he grips it firmly. "How are you finding our lovely city?"

"Well, it's great sir," I say.

"Nothing like your old home I'll bet. Where is it you came from? Agricola?"

I nod, just as Theo's mother moves in to hug me. "Cyra, darling. You look beautiful in that dress."

"Um, thank you," I say, slightly taken aback.

"I suppose we should introduce ourselves. My name is Priscilla Graves and this is my partner, Emerson. We are Theo's parents."

Priscilla reaches behind her and pulls Theo to the front, so he's right ahead of me. His eyes are still stuck to the ground, his head shaking lightly.

"Well, the two of you need to make this official. Theo, would you do the honours."

239

Theo looks up and arches his head back to look at his mother. She gives him a firm glare and he turns back to me.

"She means we need to kiss," he says glumly.

I say nothing in return as he steps closer to me, leaning in with his face. My instinct makes me want to turn away, but I hold firm under the watchful eyes of his parents. As his lips hit mine, I shut my eyes and wish for it to last no longer than a second. Thankfully, he pulls back quickly as his parents begin to applaud.

"Good on you, Theo," says Emerson. "I suppose it's not too bad for a first effort. You two will get the hang of it."

For the next hour we're paraded around the square by Theo's parents. I see jealous eyes looking at me from other girls, particularly those who I know are from Eden. They'll be wondering how on earth I managed to get Theo. What exactly our duty is that someone like me can be Paired with someone like him.

His parents, though, don't seem confused or ashamed at all. I think of what Leeta told me, how all youngsters on Eden are arrogant at first, but eventually grow out of it. Perhaps his parents, members of the Council as they are, are able to see beyond where I came from? And, I suppose, if they're part of the system that instituted the Pairing in the first place, they can't exactly start bemoaning it when their son is partnered with someone who isn't necessarily *worthy* of him.

They move through the crowd, greeting dozens of

parents with warm smiles and embraces, telling people how proud the day is for them and all parents. Most new Pairings I see seem happy together, some already holding hands and kissing each other. I notice a couple of boys snigger at Theo, laden down as he is with me. He reacts with nothing more than a snarl as we move onto the next introduction.

At one point, Leeta comes in from nowhere and gives me a hug. Theo's parents turn around to her, quizzical looks on their faces, and ask her who she is.

"Oh, I'm so sorry Councillors, I just wanted to congratulate Cyra on being Paired with your son. I was the one who took her Testing and Duty Call. I've been showing her around the city once per week."

"Oh, really, is that right," says Priscilla. "Well, in that case we'd be honoured to have you attend our gathering this evening."

Leeta looks struck dumb by the invite. "Me? You want *me* to be there?"

"Well, yes. You must know Cyra well enough by now and she doesn't have any family here. As long as Cyra would like you there that is?"

Priscilla and Leeta look at me together, the latter with wide, hopeful eyes.

"Of course, I'd love Leeta to come," I say, grateful that they'll be at least one friendly face at this event.

"Well, that's it then," continues Priscilla. "Sorry, what is your name?"

"It's Leeta, ma'am. Leeta Ashworthy."

"Well, Leeta, we'll see you at 8pm. Do you know where we live?"

Leeta nods. "The Council Chambers, although I don't know which unit is yours."

"It's unit 1," she says. "We'll see you later."

Priscilla keeps on walking, pulling the attention of Emerson away from his conversation with another couple, and Theo and I follow. Throughout all of this, we hardly make eye contact. I know there's a million and one things he wants to say to me, but he doesn't utter a single syllable out of place in front of his parents. He just smiles when he needs to and plays the dutiful partner, even putting his arm around me at one point at his parents' behest.

After another hour it's already darkening above, and the square is starting to thin out. From what I've heard, families all over the city are having parties this evening to celebrate the Pairings of their sons and daughters. Some, I know, are attending the event held by Theo's parents, most likely only the most important and notable residents of the city.

I think of Ellie and Link and wonder what they'll do. Neither have parents here, so I suppose they'll be free to enjoy the evening as they please. Perhaps they'll find a public celebration somewhere, or will take a walk under the twinkling city lights, holding hands and kissing under the warm glow of the moon. A deep surge of jealousy runs through me at the thought. If only I could have had the same with Jackson.

I feel Theo moving close to my side, his left arm

locking with my right. "We have to link arms as we enter," he mumbles, looking forward.

We're approaching a large building at the edge of the square. It stands tall and ornate against the night sky, carvings and sculptures adorning its surface. Ahead is a large opening in the shape of an arch, two guards standing on either side, rigid and upright, as still as the statues above their heads.

"What is this place?" I say, marvelling at the beautiful structure.

"The Council Chambers," Theo replies abruptly. "It's where all the Councillors live. It's where I....used to live."

Ahead, I watch as parents leave their children and begin making their way inside. Soon, we're left in a group with only other new pairs around us. Theo's parents step up to their son and nod at him.

"OK, Theo, you know what to do. Lead the rest in at the cue."

Theo bobs his head up and down as his parents begin moving into the building. After a few moments we continue forward, the other Pairings filing in behind us, arms also linked together. Inside is a cavernous space, even more beautiful than the outside, with a luxury crimson and navy blue carpet leading inwards.

To the left and right are lifts, but ahead, just a short staircase with a gallery surrounding it. As we reach the stairs, Theo stops and waits. All the others form an orderly queue behind.

Then, up the stairs, a large set of double wooden doors open. I hear a rumble of voices, of a large gathering beyond. Music starts playing, beautiful music like I've never heard before.

"That's the cue," says Theo, who begins marching forward.

We ascend the steps, and the music and murmuring gets louder. Gradually, the view through the doors beyond appears, and I see a great open space with dozens of people waiting. They're parted on either side of the door, their hands ready to applaud as their sons and daughters walk through in front of them.

Theo leads the way, and I notice his expression change immediately. He lifts his chin and a large smile appears. He nudges me and I do the same as we walk in, side by side, to the sound of rapturous applause.

Behind, a dozen or so couples follow. Children of other important members of the city, attending what appears to be its most exclusive party on this most special of days.

I see faces wash over me in delight as I enter. They don't frown at me or look down on me. Right now, I'm being properly initiated into Eden. Suddenly, I no longer feel like an outsider. I feel like one of them.

Around me the high ceiling hangs with dazzling crystal chandeliers, ornate carvings depicting the history of the city dotted around the walls. There are tables everywhere, dripping with luxurious foods and drinks, Servers carrying plates of delicacies between the crowd.

In the centre is a floor, paved from marble and

gleaming white. Theo leads me towards it as the others continue behind, the crowd of people now starting to surround us. Music fills the air and Theo turns to me, taking my hands in his.

"I assume you don't know how to dance," he says.

"Dance?! No."

"Just follow my lead, I don't want to look stupid."

We stand in the middle, other couples around us, and begin dancing to music I've never heard before. I hear clapping and see blurred faces as I twist around the room, faces filled with pride and pleasure. For a moment, despite everything, I feel like I'm actually enjoying myself. Somehow the music and the movement transport me away from myself, if only for a fleeting moment, and I feel happy.

It doesn't last long. Soon the dancing stops, people clap, and everyone begins to mingle once more. Servers appear with food, but my stomach is too knotted to eat. They appear with wine and other drinks, but I fear what I might become if I have any. Instead, I'm once again paraded around by Theo's parents, meeting people I'll never care for and having to play the delighted girl from Agricola, so blessed to have been Paired with Theo Graves.

When Leeta arrives, I finally get some respite. She looks around in awe at the place, so honoured to have been invited, if only as an afterthought. As is her way, she begins telling me about the Council Chambers, that each so called *unit* is the home of a Councillor and his partner. Unit, as it happens, simply refers to the entire floor of the building, and

245

the Graves occupy one of the largest and most lavish.

After a couple of glasses of wine, she loosens up and begins introducing herself around. By that point I've had just about enough, so manage to creep away from her unnoticed. I leave the hall behind and decide to explore, sneaking off down corridors and through other specious rooms, each one draped in luxury. Soon I find myself at the front of the building, looking out through a window at the square below. It's much quieter now than it was earlier, but some people still celebrate, dancing by the fountain, eating and drinking at the many restaurants nearby.

Here, though, it's quiet and still. I sit on the wide stone window sill and stare out at the city streets, a sight I still haven't gotten used to. The activity, the cold stone and metal, the people, so well dressed and well behaved. It contrasts so much with home. My real home.

A voice comes from behind me. It's not one I've heard before, not one I recognise. It's the voice of a man, so deep it shakes the foundation of the room.

I turn and look upon a face I've seen before, yet never in person. A face, filled with a wisdom beyond its years. Eyes of murky grey, hair as black as the darkest night. Skin so perfect it looks like it's never seen the sun.

"I've been watching you, Cyra," he says, his words sending a chill through me.

He steps forward, his entire body like a shadow, covered in a deep black suit.

"Do you know who I am?"

I nod. "You're Chancellor Knight," I whisper, just about finding my voice.

"That's right," he says. "*High* Chancellor Augustus Knight. It's a pleasure to meet you."

He reaches out his hand, pale digits slipping from his sleeve, and I take it. His fingers feel cold, almost lifeless, as they curl around mine.

"And you, High Chancellor," I say, retracting my hand as soon as his grip loosens.

He looks at me inquisitively for a moment, as if working me out. His eyes are so deep I feel like he's looking straight into my soul, into my very being. There's something in there that seems at odds with his outer visage, as if his eyes don't fit his body. They look older somehow, contrasting with his unblemished, youthful skin. Then I remember how old he is, how long he's lived here in control of this city. His body endlessly rejuvenated, yet his mind continuing to age.

"So, you've been Paired with Theo Graves I understand. Congratulations, you must be very proud."

"Yes sir, I am...delighted," I lie.

He laughs, lightly, and looks past me through the window. *Does he know I'm not telling the truth?*

"You know, I never suspected that young Theo would be a Watcher. I guess, it's hard to tell with some people, isn't it."

I don't answer. I really can't tell if he's looking for a response or just speaking out loud.

"You, though, Miss Drayton," he says, turning his eyes back on me. "Well, you just *feel* like a Watcher to me. It's deep inside you, right at your core."

"I suppose," I say, as politely as possible. "I guess I've never met a real Watcher, other than Commander Ajax."

"Ajax, yes. Very gifted man. What do you think of him?"

"He's excellent, sir. He's helped me through a lot since I arrived here."

"Yes, I know," says Knight, without elaborating on how. "It's your pain, your experiences that make you what you are, Miss Drayton. All the best Watchers have terrible pasts, just like Ajax"

I nod, my eyes switching down.

"Don't let your grief overcome you," he says. "Let it feed you, but never let it take over."

I realise that he must know about Jackson, about how I developed such a strong relationship with a boy and broke the law. The laws that he himself created. Yet he doesn't bring it up, doesn't mention it. I suppose there would be no point now.

"I'll try not to, High Chancellor. But...it can be hard sometimes."

"I understand," he says. "Yet look at what you've already achieved. You've saved a boat filled with people from capsizing. There are several other Watchers stationed on Eden, and they never saw that. You have a powerful gift, Cyra. You should congratulate yourself on it, not second guess it."

I've heard the same from Ajax time and again. By

now, whenever I hear someone say I have a gift, I hear *curse* instead.

"Thank you," I say. "I will try harder."

"Good," he says, his lips curling up and bearing his sparkling white teeth. "Now tell me, what else have you seen?"

He stares at me, his eyes as deep as the ocean beneath us.

"I don't really know, High Chancellor. Nothing clear like with the boat..."

"You know," he says quickly. "Tell me what you saw beyond the Divide."

His face stays calm. Clearly Ajax has reported this to him already.

"An army. I saw an army of people."

"What else?"

"There was a man at the front, someone leading them. Then, everything lit up behind him. It was as if they were all firing at once."

"And you don't know where along the Divide this was?"

"That's all I saw. It might have just been a dream, I couldn't tell back then. I've seen flashes since, but nothing new. I think it was just a bad dream, High Chancellor, when I first arrived here."

He stares out of the window again, his eyes gliding over the city. "It's not a dream," he says quietly. "It's much worse than that."

Then he turns and begins moving gracefully towards the door. "Enjoy the rest of your evening, Miss Drayton. And be nice to Theo. I think you two make a lovely pair."

He opens the door, the sound of ironic laughter gargling up his throat, and disappears out into the corridor.

20
The Veil Lifted

After Knight leaves, I ponder his words as I sit there in silence. Most of all, I'm troubled by what he first said to me.

I've been watching you, Cyra.

He never explained what he meant by it. Did he mean he'd been watching me across the room at the party? He can't have. He wasn't even there, not that I saw anyway. If he had, he'd have been the first person Theo's parents would have introduced me to.

Did he mean he'd been there, standing in the doorway, watching me as I stared out of the window? That's a creepy enough thought.

Or is it something even worse? Has he been watching me in another way? Watching from afar? Has he been keeping tabs on me somehow? Has he taken a close interest in me ever since I had that supposed vision of the Divide? The thought sends a shudder through my body. To think that I'm under the spotlight in any way makes me uncomfortable to my core.

For a time, I stay where I am, sitting on that window sill, looking out over the streets. The last thing I want to do is return to the party. It's all so alien to me, another world within a world. A place where, despite how I might look in this dress and make up, I'll never truly belong.

No one comes to find me. I hear no footsteps echoing down the corridor. I don't hear the creak of the door handle turning, don't see a shadow appear in the doorway. With all those proper children of Eden out there, I doubt my disappearance has even been noticed.

The minutes tick by, and I just sit there in silence, the loneliest girl in the world. I think I see Ellie and Link down below, walking hand in hand through the square. I want to call out to them, run down and join them, but all I do is watch as they fade into the distance, a single tear crawling down my cheek.

Knock, knock, knock.

The sound of pounding forces my eyes back to the door. I quickly raise my hand and wipe my eyes as the door creaks and swings open.

Through the doorway walks Theo, eyes creeping around the room. They quickly settle on me, a desolate figure by the wide, cold, window.

"My parents noticed you were missing," he says. "They told me to come find you."

"Well, you've found me." I can't help but be defensive and hostile whenever I speak to him. "I'm not going back in, if that's what you're here for."

He walks towards me, eyes a little gentler than usual. Stance less dominating and assertive. "I guess...it must be hard," he concedes, "being part of all of this."

"Hard?" I huff, shaking my head. "You have no

idea."

He moves forward and sits down near to me on the window sill, body hunched forward. I still can't make full eye contact with him for a more than a second or two. Instead I just stare out of the window, hoping for him to give up and go away.

"I have some idea," he says. "This isn't exactly easy for me either."

"Do you want me to feel sorry for you?" My words are quick and biting. "Do you even know how you've been treating me these last few months?"

He doesn't answer. How can he. There's no excuse for how he's been behaving. How rude he is whenever he knows Ajax is out of earshot.

"I guess I'm sorry about all that. We all do it. It's not like I'm the only one."

"Do what? Look down on mainlanders? Make them feel like they're nothing? Sure, I'll bet you're real sorry about that. Or maybe," I say, looking back into his eyes, "you're suddenly trying to be nice because your parents have told you to."

He wilts slightly under my stare and turns away, nodding his head.

"You're right. My parents have told me to be nice. But they're just doing it for themselves. They only ever do things for themselves."

I laugh. "You really are a spoilt brat aren't you! It's pathetic." God it feels good to insult *him* for once.

"Look, I'm trying to apologise here," he says, not reacting to my taunt. "We're going to have to get along from now on aren't we, so we might as well make the effort."

"Sure. Whatever you say."

I turn back to look outside, but feel him still staring at me.

"I know how it feels, Cyra, feeling like you don't belong."

I raise my eyebrows and look back to him. "OK, why don't you enlighten me."

He points to the door he came in through. "Back there, I don't belong any more. I've been cut from my own world, just like you. All of my old friends...they're not my friends any more. I guess what I'm saying is, I know what it's like to be taunted for being different."

I want to pour more scorn on his apology, to tell him that no matter how people treat you, that's no excuse to treat someone else badly. But I don't. Something tells me that this is genuine, that it's more than just an apology his parents have forced him to make.

"But you're not different. You have no idea what it feels like to be me in this city. Having everyone looking at me everyday like I'm a freak. Just because I grew up somewhere else. I didn't choose to come here, Theo. I never wanted any of this."

"And neither did I! Do you think I wanted to be a Watcher. I was meant to follow my parents, live here in the Council Chambers. But no. As soon as that damn genetics test found out what I could be, I became an outcast. I don't live here any more, you know. I live in regular quarters, like you. From as

254

far back as I can remember, I've been groomed to go to the top. And now, I'm probably going to be assigned somewhere else, destined to see horrible things in my sleep every night."

"Yeah, it's the same for me. What makes you so special..."

"My upbringing," he blurts out, his voice ringing around the room. "I know you won't understand it, but I was meant for something better than all of this. And now I'm cast out. Now I'm a nobody."

"Yeah, well I guess you do know what it feels like to be me then," I say. "Anyway, I'd rather be a nobody than play any part in running this country and all its stupid systems. I mean, look at this, look at us. We're now Paired for life because of a stupid test! Isn't there anyone in this city you'd have chosen to be with, if you could?"

He doesn't answer, but I can tell he's thinking along the same lines as me. This system hasn't only screwed up my life, it's screwed up his as well. I suppose you only second guess it when it deals you a bad hand.

We sit in silence for a little while, letting our tempers settle. This is already by far the longest I've spent with him alone, and by far the most we've ever spoken. And throughout, he hasn't insulted me or given me a contemptuous look once. I guess that's progress.

Eventually I can no longer stand the growing awkwardness, so get up and begin walking towards the door.

"Hey, where are you going?"

I stop short.

"I'm leaving, going back to my room. I guess I'll see you at the Grid tomorrow."

I hear him standing and moving in behind me, grabbing my arm and twisting me round. "You can't go to your room," he says.

"Why?"

"Because...you don't have one any more."

"What the hell do you mean?!"

"We have a joint room now," he says. "Didn't you know that. After the Pairing, we have to live together."

"No....I can't live with *you*."

"Yeah, I'm not thrilled about it either. But that's how it is."

"But...my things." I think of my bag with my personal items. My mother's old watch, the pictures of my family, my diary. Each are irreplaceable to me.

"It's all right, any things in your room will have been moved. They'll be there waiting for you."

I'm still shaking my head with disbelief when Theo opens the door. "Look, why don't we go check it out now. It might not be as bad as you think."

We begin walking back towards the party, before descending down the stairs. We pass through the arch and into the clear night air. It's crisp, and brings an immediate shiver to me that runs up through my body.

We return to the residential area of the city where I've been living, close to the perimeter wall. In fact, the building we enter is just next to the one I'd been in, and is pretty much a carbon copy from both the inside and out. We rise several floors in the lift, no words spoken between us. *Is this how it's going to be? Is this what my life will be like now?*

When we reach the room there's little to take in. It's larger than the room I previously occupied, although bare. Presumably, Eve is in control here too, capable of miraculously unfolding furniture from the walls. There is a bed, though. Again, it's bigger than the one I've been sleeping in these last few months. I guess it's intended for two people.

The thought of sleeping next to Theo each night enters my head and refuses to leave. In fact, the idea of sleeping next to anyone would be almost as bad. I've never felt the touch of a person next to me as I dream. It's always been me. Just me. No one else. That's how I want it to stay.

Theo is the first to speak, as if he's reading my mind. "We need another bed in here, Eve," he says. Moments later, the room has two beds, each on opposite walls, blank space in between.

"It's not so bad." Clearly he's trying to make me feel better about the whole thing. I don't get him though, and I'm sure it will take a while to properly work him out. Is he really an outcast now? Can he really appreciate what I've been going through, how he's been behaving? Or is this just a ruse, some sort of twisted game he's playing?

I see my bag on the large bed and go and retrieve it, before retreating to the bed that's just appeared. "I'll take this one," I say, and he doesn't disagree.

It's smaller, only made for a single person. It's what I'm used to. Anything larger would feel greedy.

I quickly open the bag and check to make sure the contents are still there. My fingers run over my diary, my mother's watch, the pictures of my family.

I hear Theo behind me, moving back towards the door. "I'm going back. I'll tell my parents you were feeling ill." Then he slips out of the door, leaving me alone in silence.

The tears start almost as soon as the door has shut. I thought, perhaps, I'd grown immune to feeling the pinch of change, but I haven't. Just when things begin to settle, something comes back in to send my life rocking once more.

I crawl into bed and pull out my diary. I read the pages, as I do most nights, to remind me of home, of everything I've lost. When I read the words I wrote about Jackson, I quickly drop the diary to the floor. Some things are still too painful to relive.

I don't hear when Theo comes in, but wake to the sound of breathing across the room. For a split second I'm reminded of my brother snoring above me as kids. How I'd love to see him again. See my sister too. Share in the grief for our mother. I wonder how they're coping, how they found out. I wonder if I'll ever see them again now.

The sound of odd grunts reach my ears. The mumbling of inane words and phrases. I wonder if he's having a dream or a vision. What exactly he's seeing in that head of his. In the faint light, I watch as his body suddenly rises, bolt upright in his bed, his breathing heavy. He stays like that for a few moments, before slowly settling back down.

I ask him if he saw anything when morning dawns, but he doesn't give me an answer. Instead, we dress in silence and begin our day in the Grid.

When I see Ellie I ask her how her evening was. Her smile tells me all I need to know. When Ajax stands ahead of us, however, he quickly draws a line under our personal relationships down here.

"Your new status as pairs will have no bearing here," he says. "You will continue to train as you have been, and will maintain that focus."

That's fine by me. The longer we stay down here, and the less time I have to spend alone with Theo, the better.

For the following week, we continue as before in the Grid. Weapons training, combat training, and simulation training forming the bulk of our days. Link seems to have taken Ajax's words on board, because he spares little time for Ellie during the day. On occasion, she questions me about it, but comes down each morning telling me how sweet he is once they return to the deck.

Theo seems to be living up to his word as well. He no longer offers me any taunts or insults, and doesn't even say a word to Ellie or Link. Sometimes, when the two boys spar together, I notice a few tensions rising back to the surface, but to both their credit neither of them act upon it.

The evenings, however, have become the real burden for me. Before, they were spent with Ellie and Link and Leeta and offered some respite from the Grid. Now, however, I'm forced to attend various social functions and gatherings.

For the first week, Theo and I continue to be paraded around the city, visiting the rich and powerful, eating dinners at fine restaurants, attending the most exclusive parties and events. Whenever we cross paths with one of his old friends, I begin to notice what he was telling me before. These highly bred boys and girls always greet him with firm handshakes and tender kisses in front of their parents' watchful eyes, but in private it's a whole different matter.

Theo gets looks of contempt wherever he goes. These school leavers have continued in their parents' footsteps, climbing onto the ladder towards the top of Eden. Paired with the most eligible bachelors in the city. Married into powerful families. And here's Theo, now ordered to become a servant of the state, Paired with a lowly Picker's daughter from Agricola.

I watch as he often finds himself included by the parents, but rejected by his peers. They gather together and laugh at his misfortune. Call him names under their breath. For a day or two I enjoy it, enjoy seeing him taunted and teased as he did to me. Feel some sort of vindication, some karma, for the way he treated me and my friends.

Then, as the days go by, I begin to feel sorry for him. I watch as he sinks into his shell night after night, as his own bravado is battered down by those he once counted as his friends.

Each evening, when we return to our room, we say little to each other. And each evening, I wake to him groaning in his sleep. Inside, I know, he's tortured. He tries to hide it, tries to put on a front and display this cocksure, confident presence to the world. Yet in your sleep you tell no lies, and finally I'm starting to learn the truth about Theo Graves.

That his world, like mine, is far from perfect.

21

Visions

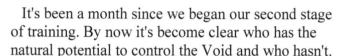

It's been a month since we began our second stage of training. By now it's become clear who has the natural potential to control the Void and who hasn't.

Link is the shining star in our group. I can tell he's Ajax's favourite too. I watch him go through simulations like they're nothing. Nothing hits him. Bullets, cars, falling debris. He's even gone through a live fire simulation and got through without a scratch. It wasn't even by Ajax's orders, but his own request.

I'm still not ready for that.

My own progress has been steady and consistent. I speak regularly with Ajax, who continues to act as my guiding light. He's incredibly passionate about what we do and the importance of developing our abilities to their fullest extent. Yet he remains frustrated with me, and expects so much.

I think, maybe, he's setting the bar too high.

I can now control the Void to a point, though, without too much trouble. I'm often able to see things a couple of seconds before they happen, which gives me a good chance of going through the simulations pretty well. It's not enough, however, to put myself up for a live fire simulation. I'm not there yet.

Theo is the only other recruit who seems capable of seeing into the Void as well. Over the last couple of weeks, he's been much more focused and far less temperamental than he used to be. Finally, I think, he's accepting that this is his life now. That he might as well grow as powerful as possible as a Watcher, knowing that political power and influence is now beyond him.

I can tell it's something he craves. Power. When you're groomed for a position of influence by two of the most powerful people in the city, you're naturally going to develop those desires.

For the others, the entire process must be incredibly discouraging. None seem to be able to control their abilities in the same way as Link, Theo, and I. Rupert and Lorna, in particular, try their hardest without getting any real results. On a couple of occasions they might see a bullet firing at them a split second early, but that's about it.

They curse and shout each time they fail, but Ajax offers them little in the way of support. I quickly realise that he's more interested in nurturing those of us who have shown potential, rather than those who may never develop those powers.

The evenings continue as before, Theo and I required to attend a variety of social functions with his parents. For the first time I'm beginning to experience the full force of the Eden social calender. Parties, plays, dinners, public celebrations. Suddenly I've been forced into the upper echelons of the city's hierarchy, required to smile politely and observe the city's etiquette on an almost nightly basis.

Leeta, of course, takes the opportunity to continue my schooling. She seems delighted at my new position and manages to wrangle her own invites to several events. Soon, people begin to know her as my adopted Eden mother, which doesn't sit particularly well with me.

Yet her own guidance proves invaluable in helping me avoid a host of embarrassing situations. She teaches me what to wear for any given event, the types of make up that are appropriate, how to eat properly without disgracing myself. I think she takes pride in shaping me into a more ladylike Edenite, although I feel I'll never pick it all up.

Theo, meanwhile, appears to hate these occasions even more than I do. It's like a kick in the teeth every time he has to go to one. A reminder of what he could have been part of. I see his old friends continue to torment him, their under-the-breath insults always so perfectly concealed from their parents. Each night he grows with more resolve, returning to the Grid the next day with a renewed focus. His personal torture, it seems, has become his fuel.

I see Chancellor Knight once more. It's the official birthday of a Councillor's son, and all members gather to celebrate with him at their home in the Council Chambers. I see him watching me across the room, flanked by a couple of guards. Even in this company, he brings security with him.

By the sight of them, they look like Watchers

themselves. It's the dark, cold stare, those eyes that seem to see everything. They stand, motionless, by his side as he sits in a throne-like chair. He doesn't stand or mingle like the others. No. People come to him.

Every time I turn my eyes up to him, they seem to already have found me. Even mid conversation with someone else, they're there. Looking at me. Searching me. I feel naked under his stare, completely exposed.

One of his guards approaches me, and I'm invited to speak with him. Theo looks at me quizzically, one eyebrow rising, but says nothing. I follow the guard, forcing my chin up and a smile onto my face. Etiquette, as Leeta has told me so many times, requires that you smile whenever you greet someone.

I feel my heart racing when I approach. For some reason I feel so much more nervous than during our first meeting. Somehow he must know, because it's the first thing he references.

"Don't be so nervous," he tells me. "Watchers should never show nerves, like they should never show fear."

I glance up at the two men to his sides, who continue to stare like statues out into the room.

"What is it you fear?" he asks me.

"Nothing," I say. "Not any more."

"So you've conquered your fears, have you? Tell me, Miss Drayton, what was it you faced in the Grid?"

I search his eyes, so deep you could get lost inside them. Within I see a deep seated malice, like a cat toying with a mouse.

He already knows. I can tell.

"Death," I say, hiding all emotion from my voice. "The death of those I care about."

His visage fails to alter. Fails to show any surprise. Any sympathy or compassion.

"So you don't fear death for yourself?" he asks.

I shake my head. I've never thought about it before in that way. My fears involve those I love dying. My own death has never been a factor.

"I don't fear anything any more," I say again.

He smiles at me. Not a warm smile. It's a knowing smile. One that says he knows I'm lying.

"Tell me, have you seen any more of your vision?" He lifts up his left hand and waves it slightly. Immediately the two guards step back a few paces, out of hearing reach.

"Nothing," I say. I sense a feeling of distrust inside him. Something tells me he doesn't believe what I'm saying.

"Are you sure of that?" he whispers.

I nod. "Yes, High Chancellor. I'm positive."

A slight grimace flows up his face. "Well, keep searching," he says. It sounds like the sort of cryptic thing Ajax would tell me. *Keep searching.* I don't even know what that means. These visions can't be controlled, so how can I possibly *search* for them?

Later that night, Theo and I sit in our room. Most nights we share a few words when we return from

266

any social function, and then go straight to sleep. Tonight, however, he seems intent on quizzing me on my brief meeting with Knight.

I can't tell if it's jealousy that drives him or not. The thought perhaps that I'm now seen to be more important than he is, given my supposed gifts as a Watcher. I'm thankful, at least, that my saving of the ship Adonia hasn't gone unnoticed at the highest levels, although the attention it's now bestowing on me makes me more than a little uncomfortable.

I tell Theo that that's all it is. That Knight is interested in hearing more about any visions I've had. I don't, however, elaborate on what I saw beyond the Divide. There's still doubt in me as to whether it was anything more than a crazy dream.

It's still not comfortable between us though. We spend all our time surrounded by other people, playing at being the happy couple. But under the surface, when we're alone, we hardly speak. It's all a charade, one that Theo's parents have forced him to endure. For all his apologies about how he treated me, for all the apparent changes he's gone through, there's still an awkwardness between us that neither of us are willing to address.

That same night I think once more of Jackson in my dreams. My mother appears too, and I wake with her watch in my hands once again. They return to me for several nights running, as apparitions in the misty night. They're trying to tell me something, warn me of something, but I can't hear them. Each morning I wake, an uneasiness growing inside me. A feeling that something isn't quite right. That something is being held back from me.

I return sometimes to Surface Level 8. Return to the same room I locked myself in. The room where Ajax found me. On those nights when we're not required to attend an event, I escape to my secret place. A place no one knows about. A place where I can hide and think and be all alone.

One night, I hear a knock at the door. I don't answer, hoping it's someone who's got the wrong room. Then I hear Theo's voice on the other side. I open it and see his eyes. They look troubled.

I step back and sit on the bed. He follows in and shuts the door, perching by the wall.

"I followed you here," he says. "Is this where you go when you want to be alone?"

"I come here sometimes," I say. "It reminds me of home."

Theo glances around the basic room. Sniffs at the smell that fills it from the corridor outside. A few weeks ago he'd have made some insulting, conceited remark. Now he says nothing, although I know what he's thinking.

"You miss it, don't you?" he asks me. "Home, I mean."

I don't say anything. It's so obvious I do. I feel my eyes welling slightly, force myself to look at the wall. I don't want him to see me crying.

"I miss mine too," he says. It's the sort of thing I'd roll my eyes at before. But now I understand that he, truly, has lost his home too.

"You've been speaking in your sleep," he says. I

drag my eyes back to him. They're sympathetic, his words tender.

"You call for your mother a lot. Did something happen to her?"

My mother's face fills my eyes. Not her when she died. Not her as she was, withered and broken by her illness. But as she used to be when I was younger. Golden and beautiful. That's how I like to remember her.

"She died, the night before I was sent here."

I glance up at Theo's face. There's a sorrow on it that's so pained, so real.

"I'm so sorry, Cyra. I...had no idea."

He walks forward and sits on the edge of the bed. "I've been such a jerk to you. And you were going through such a hard time. I'll never be able to apologise enough."

I reach forward and place my hand on top of his. It's cold, shaking slightly. "It's OK, Theo. You didn't know."

"I shouldn't have had to know. I shouldn't have behaved as I did. You must really hate me."

I don't answer immediately. Then his eyes lift and search for mine. "I don't hate you," I say.

In truth, I pity him now. He's just a product of his world, just like I am of mine. Taunting mainlanders was what he'd grown up doing, what his friends did. It's hard to judge someone when their upbringing is so different from yours.

I slide my hand off his and back to my lap. Theo's eyes stay locked to the floor, his body slumped forward. I know how he feels. I know what it's like to be so alone, discarded from your home.

"How did she die?" he asks, lifting his eyes back up.

"The virus," I say.

A frown drops down his face. "But, I thought we had a cure for that?"

"There's a cure, yeah. But only for those who can afford it."

I don't have to tell him that we weren't one of those families. He knows immediately.

A silence dawns between us. But this time it's not awkward or uncomfortable. Somehow there's a connection between us. A shared feeling of loneliness now, between the two most unlikely of people.

Eventually he turns to me and reaches out his hand. "It's late. We should go back."

I hesitate before taking his fingers. He pulls me gently to my feet, and my hand slips out of his. We walk through the corridor in silence, down passageways and past the underclass of Eden. I watch as Theo's eyes scan the people, his face no longer written in revulsion as it might have once been. Now, I see guilt there instead.

People recognise him, step to the side as we walk. They duck their heads, so used to being servants to the upper classes. I see surprise in their eyes; surprise mingled with fear. Fear that he'll shout at someone for looking at him wrong. That they'll be punished for doing nothing at all.

We reach the lifts and ascend to the deck, still in silence. It's late, the sky above twinkling with a thousand bright stars through the clear domed roof. In the total silence, I can hear the ocean. The sound of waves lapping against the metal platform of the city. I think of how long I've been here, so long now at sea, yet I'd never even know it. But now, as the city goes to sleep, I can hear the lightest sloshing of water. The sound of nature, of a world beyond this place.

Theo tells me goodnight when we reach our room, before slipping off his clothes and climbing into bed. For the first time I see his body, black and blue and littered in bruises. Marks of his new stature in the city, delivered by the boys who now look down on him.

Before I can speak, he whispers for the light to fade and the room slowly darkens as I drop into my bed.

That night, my mind tumbles in every direction. Troubled thoughts enter and don't leave. I fall in and out of dreams and find myself waking constantly, the room still dark, Theo breathing lightly in the other bed. I wonder if I'm calling my mother's name, waking him up as I've been doing in recent days.

I try to stay awake, not wanting to fall back into my subconscious, scared of what I might see, what I might say. But time lingers on, and my eyes drop again. I plunge back down the rabbit's hole, my mind now stuck on a single sight.

I see a room, dilapidated and dirty. There's a shadow in the corner, sitting on an old wooden chair. The shape of a man, hidden under a dark cloak. He looks forward and down, his head watching something on the floor.

It's so warm I can almost feel it. Feel the sweat building on my brow. Feel the clammy, hot air creeping up my nose. There's a stench in the air. The smell of rotting wood and decay.

I look to the floor, where a figure lies on a mattress. A light blanket covers him, his chest rising and falling slowly. Blood stains him, his right arm and abdomen bandaged and covered in crimson. Flies buzz in the air, attracted to a flickering light on the crumbling ceiling. The glow comes and goes, momentarily bringing the man into focus, and then shadowing him in darkness once again.

I'm drawn forward, deeper into the room. The cloaked man doesn't move. He just sits and looks to the floor, staring at the stricken figure.

A woman enters, passing as if through me from behind, like a ghost through a wall. She carries a white cloth, dripping wet with water. She blocks my view, leaning down and dabbing at the man's head. I hear the man croak as she turns to inspect his wounds. Then she stands, turns, and walks right through me once more.

Now I see him. On the ground ahead of me. The face of a ghost, a phantom only present in my dreams. The boy I watched die, over and over.

But not dead. Alive.

Jackson is alive.

22
A Plan Forming

My eyes snap open.

All they take in is darkness. The sight of the black room around me. Yet in my mind the face of Jackson lingers. Bloodied and wounded, yet alive.

Alive. He's alive.

Before I know what I'm doing my feet are hanging off the edge of the bed and I'm slipping on my clothes, fumbling in the dark. I hear Theo breathing lightly across the room and make sure not to wake him. Then I creep, quietly but quickly, to the door and push the button to slide it open.

The corridor outside is bright, the light spilling into the room. I step through and the door slides shut behind me. Then I'm off, running down the corridor towards the lift. I step inside and hit the button for the floor below. In a split second I'm out, panting as I go, my mind still swirling.

When I reach the right room I knock forcefully. I wait, listening for movement inside, and hear mumbles. A few moments later the door slides open, the room inside growing lighter, and I see Link standing in his underwear, muscled and strong. His eyes are alert, despite the early wake up call, and quickly grow with concern at the sight of me.

"Cyra...what's happening? Are you OK?" he asks.

I step forward, searching for Ellie. She sits on the edge of the bed, hair dishevelled and bags under her eyes.

"He's alive," I say, still panting. "I saw him, Ellie. He's alive."

The door slides shut with a hiss as the room continues to lighten. Ellie, meanwhile, just rubs her eyes, trying to shake the cobwebs from her head.

"What are you talking about, Cy? Who's alive?"

"Jackson. He's alive." I say again.

"What do you mean?"

"I mean....he's alive! I just saw him."

"He's here? In Eden?"

"No...no," I say, shaking my head. "I saw him in a vision."

Link moves in behind me and I feel his hands on my shoulders. He ushers me towards a chair and sits me down.

"Are you sure it wasn't just a dream, Cyra?" he asks. "How do you know it was a vision?"

I don't remember telling Link about Jackson, about what I saw. I suppose Ellie must have filled him in.

"Because I know, all right. You know what it's like, Link. You can tell when it's a vision."

He nods his head without much conviction. "Mostly, but not always. Maybe you were just seeing what you wanted to see?"

Ellie is off the bed now, her eyes brightening. She comes towards me and leans down to my level, taking my hand. "You're shaking. Are you sure you know what you saw?"

I pull my hand away from her. *Why won't they just believe me?*

"Look, I know it sounds crazy....but I know what I saw. I saw him. It was him."

Link and Ellie share concerned looks with each other, like two parents worried about their out of control daughter. *Is that really how this looks? Do they really not believe what I'm saying?*

"Cyra, I think you should go back and get some more sleep," says Link. "It's still late, maybe you're not thinking straight."

I shake my head. "No. I know what I saw!"

Now I'm standing, moving back past them towards the door. I hear them calling for me to stop, asking where I'm going, but don't listen.

As soon as the door slides shut behind me, I'm rushing once more. Back to the lift, down to the ground floor, and out of the main doors onto the street. Lights hum around me, glowing dimly as the city sleeps. A few lights are on inside buildings, rooms of early risers and those with duties that begin in the early hours. Yet the streets themselves are dead. No cars hover past. No snake-like trains glide overhead. No people hustle towards the perimeter wall, ready to descend into the belly of the city to begin another day's work.

But that's where I'm going. I rush forward, alone in the night, and under the huge opening into the wall. Inside, the trams are lying dormant, inactive until the morning rush begins. I move beneath the tracks and onto the other side. Then into the lift, hitting the button for Underwater 5, and down beneath the surging sea.

When I step out into the perimeter wall I'm standing in almost pitch darkness. The only glow comes from a few security lights set at points along the tram tracks. It doesn't bother me. I've walked this journey enough times to do it with my eyes closed, and the darkness has never troubled me.

I keep going, under the tracks, through the wall, and into the large passageway that wraps around the boundary of the level. I walk along it for a few moments before turning in, along the long corridor towards the Grid. In the distance, I can see the faint light of the door, several hundred feet away.

I'm still pacing, still rushing through the darkness. I reach the door and insert my arm into the scanner, which turns from red to blue before the door hisses open. Beyond, the Grid is still set out in stations. I move through them, past the various equipment we use for combat training and weapons training, and to the door at the end.

I knock hard when I reach it, my loud pounding disturbing the eerie silence of the huge hall. It takes no time for the door to open, Ajax's stark face staring back to me. He's so quick it's like he knew I was coming, as if he was out of bed and waiting by the door for me.

"What have you seen?" he asks quickly.

"Jackson. I've seen Jackson."

He steps to the side and ushers me in, before closing the door. His room is as bare and empty as always.

"You haven't seen Knight's Wall?" he asks, guiding me towards a seat.

I shake my head. "No....I told you, I saw Jackson."

"That can't be, Cyra. Are you sure it was a vision?"

"Yes, I'm sure. I saw him, wounded and lying on a mattress. He was being taken care of by a woman...and there was a man, sitting in the corner."

"What man?"

"I don't know. A cloaked man. I couldn't see his face. Why does that matter anyway? Do you not hear what I'm saying?! I saw Jackson. He's alive!"

Ajax leans in close to me, staring into my eyes. I know how they must look. Longing and delirious, filled with the sight of the boy I loved.

"You can't have seen him, Cyra. He's dead. You saw it yourself."

"But...maybe he didn't die! Maybe he survived."

Ajax is still shaking his head, his voice calming but sensitive. "I know what you want to think, what you want to believe. But that explosion killed him, Cyra. What you saw must have been a dream."

"But I know the difference! It *felt* real. It *was* real."

"During times of emotional trauma we sometimes see things as we want them to be. Our mind wants something so powerfully that it manifests it. Those types of dreams can appear as real as a vision. They can be hard to tell apart. I know it's been hard for you, but you need to accept it and let go. It isn't doing you any good."

"But I know what I saw...I know it wasn't a dream."

"It *was* a dream, Cyra. Nothing else makes sense."

I can't listen to this any more. Ajax, Ellie, Link; they're all just talking to me as if I'm a child. Looking at me as if I've gone mad. I stand and move back to the door.

"I'm sorry for wasting your time, Ajax," I say, my tone sardonic. "I shouldn't have come down here."

I can hear him apologising in the background, but don't wait around to listen to him. Maybe he's right. Maybe they're all right. That it was just a dream, that my mind is playing cruel tricks on me. But, even if it is, I'd hope for more support. Hope that they'd hear me out and not just dismiss me so quickly.

Later that day, I return for training. It's the last thing I want to do. I don't want to see Ellie or Link or Ajax. In fact, right now, Theo is the closest person I have to a friend.

They each come to me, of course, to apologise, but I just wave it off. Maybe I'm being immature, but I find it easier that day to ignore the lot of them. Right now, I don't care if they're just trying to look out for me. Right now, I just need them on my side. I need them to believe me.

Theo must have noticed me being a little off colour, because he asks me what's up that evening. I don't tell him. Frankly, I don't need another person telling me it's just a dream, and Theo doesn't even know about Jackson anyway. In any case, he's got enough on his own plate to worry about, without having to carry any more of my baggage.

For the next few nights my sleep is peppered with cracked images and broken forms. It's like seeing pictures, worn and creased and beginning to fade. They come throughout the night, forcing my eyes open each time. The face of Jackson, eyes closed, mouth fallen slightly open as he sleeps. His body, bandaged and stained with his own blood, lying on top of an old soiled mattress. A room, dingy and dim, its walls and ceiling crumbling, paint stripped from them and showing bare brick.

After several nights, those images form once more into a moving picture. I see the cloaked man again, sitting in the corner. I see Jackson, just as before, and the woman approach him to tend to his wounds. Once more I feel like I'm there. It's so real. Real sensations course through me. The warmth of the air. The smell of rot and decay. The flashing of the light on the ceiling as flies buzz around it.

I speak to Ajax about it once more but he spins the same record.

"They're still fragments of your dreams," he tells me. "You're thinking about it so much now that your dreams are likely to be dominated by that thought, by that sight. He's dead, Cyra. You saw it yourself."

By this point I've realised that talking to Ajax about it all is pointless. It seems as though he doesn't want it to be true. It's as if he'd prefer it if Jackson was dead, if only to make sure I keep my focus on developing my abilities. That's all he cares about really. Making sure we all develop into the best Watchers we can be. That's his duty, and little will deviate him from seeing it through.

But I can't let it rest. Not until I know the truth.

It's late that night when I slip out of bed in the darkness. It's silent in the room, the light breathing I usually hear from Theo absent for once. I guess he's sleeping peacefully, which works for me.

I carefully put on my clothes and move towards the door. When I open it, the light from the corridor outside once more spills into the room.

"Where are you going?"

I freeze in the doorway and turn around. Theo's face is now fully illuminated by the bright light, his eyebrows dipped in a frown.

"It doesn't matter," I say. "Go back to sleep and forget you saw me."

"I was never asleep," he says, sitting up. Once more, I see bruises strewn across his body. They're from more than just our training. "So what's going on?"

"I'm just...going for a walk," I lie. I know he can see straight through me, but I don't care. I make a move to keep going, but once more his voice halts me in my tracks.

"I know about Jackson," he says.

My interest is piqued. I turn around slowly.

"What do you know?"

"I heard Ellie and Link talking about you. They were saying you saw a boy called Jackson in your dreams. That he's supposed to be dead, but you think he's still alive..."

"Yeah, it's nothing..."

"I've heard you call his name in your sleep too. Like your mother. You cared about him didn't you?"

"I *care* about him," I say, correcting him. "He's still alive."

"And you want to find out for sure? That's where you're going, isn't it?"

I don't answer. If I say anything, I might incriminate myself. For all the progress Theo and I have made, I still don't trust him not to go and act the snitch and tell on me.

"So, what's your plan exactly? How do you expect to find the truth?"

I still say nothing.

"Look, he was sent for service at the Divide on Knight's Wall, right?" He doesn't wait for me to nod. "Well then, they'll be a record of him in the military archives. All military personnel, previous and current, have records down on Underwater 2."

"How do you know?"

"Because I've lived here my whole life. I've seen just about every corner of this city."

"Even the restricted areas?"

He nods. "When your parents are on the Council, you get to see everything. Trust me, if there's a record of this Jackson, it'll be on Underwater 2."

He stands now and moves towards me, pulling me back inside and checking up and down the corridor.

"Look, Cyra, you're never going to get access

there without the right barcode."

"Well, maybe I'll find someone with one and break in."

Theo laughs. "Yeah, there's an easier way than that."

Now I'm really interested. Sure, he may rat me out, but I've barely got anything to lose. "Like what?"

"A keycard for the level."

I think of Anders and how he had a keycard to gain access to Underwater 4 so he could visit Amir. Ajax arranged that. Maybe he could do the same for me?

"And why are you telling me all of this? It could get you into trouble too."

"Trouble?" he says. "Like I care. Anyway, I owe you, Cyra. For how I treated you before. If I do this, I'll feel a lot better about myself."

"Do what?" I ask.

He smiles, a devious look spreading across his face. "Help you find out about Jackson."

23
The Archives

"Here it is," says Theo, passing me the keycard. "It's activated to unlock the archives, or at least it used to be. Hopefully it will still work."

"Hopefully?"

"Yeah, well, it hasn't been used in a few years. I had to do a project at school so had access for a while. If it doesn't work, I'm all out of ideas."

"Well then, I guess it better work."

I slip the keycard into my pocket and turn to the door. "Are you sure Eve isn't hearing all of this? Won't she report us to Ajax?"

Theo appears by my side. "I wouldn't worry about it. She's deactivated right now and won't be activated until we give her an order. She can hear nothing, trust me."

"And down there? Down in the archives?"

"The same. Although she's not what we need to worry about."

I look at Theo. "We?"

"Yeah, you're not going alone. Do you have any idea where to find the archives, let alone the information you need?"

"I guess not."

"Well then, you need me don't you. Like I say, I've got a lot to make up."

"Thanks Theo," I say, but he just waves it off.

"Look, what we really have to worry about are the guards. There are always patrol guards down there, so we're going to have to get past them."

"OK. So how do we do that?"

Theo turns and moves back towards his bed. He slips a couple of strange looking masks out of a bag and passes me one. It looks like a bland, semi transparent, face. No detail to the features. No colour.

"You want us to wear these?" I ask. "Seriously?"

Theo laughs. "Guess you've never seen one before. They're morph masks. Check this out."

He puts the mask to his face, pressing the malleable material to his skin. Slowly, it begins clinging to his features, altering them slightly to change his appearance. His nose becomes a little thicker. His cheeks grow fatter. The dimple in his chin fills out. Within a few moments, he looks like a completely different person.

"So, how do I look?" he asks.

"Like you've just put on 30 lbs," I say, laughing. "You look completely different!"

"Yeah, morph masks. Try yours."

I hesitate a second before pressing the jelly-like mask to my face. Immediately I feel it sticking to my skin, feeling its way around my nose and mouth and eyes.

"Feels a bit weird, doesn't it?" asks Theo.

284

"I'll say. I feel like my face is covered in warm jelly."

"You'll forget about it in a second." I can tell he's trying to stifle a laugh. "Check yourself out in the mirror."

I turn to the mirror and see a brand new reflection staring back at me. I've lost most of my colouring, my skin now pale and unblemished. My nose has grown round and bulbous, my lips thicker and fuller than before. Everything is that little larger, that little fatter and wider. It's not a particularly pretty look.

"So this is going to help us get past the guards?" I ask. "How does that work exactly?"

"No, this is purely as a back-up in case someone sees us. Trust me, people know my face around here and I don't want to be seen. And, you know, I kinda wanted to see you wearing one. You look great, by the way."

I know he's mocking me, but it's not like before. There's nothing mean and malicious in it. It's more playful now.

"Right," I say, still inspecting my ridiculous new look, "so how do we get past these guards?"

"Well, we're going to have to work that out when we get there. We might get lucky and find there's no one around. Or..."

"Or there might be dozens of guards blocking our way?"

"Well...yeah. Like I say, let's see when we get there."

Looking like a brand new pair of people, we step

out into the corridor, both dressed in black. It's dead of night once more, and neither of us expect to see anyone on our journey down towards the perimeter wall. As expected, we move through without disruption, reaching the lifts within only a few minutes.

Theo walks with a sort of sneak to his step. I can tell from the look in his eye that he's relishing this. There's a sparkle there, one which suggests breaking the rules and being mischievous is something he enjoys. I can't say I'm the same. All I want is to find out about Jackson. This is no game for me.

"Underwater 2 isn't like the levels you've seen so far," Theo tells me as we go. "It's taller and more open. There are some huge spaces in there used for military training. Lots of military personnel live there too, so make sure you keep as quiet as possible and follow my lead."

I'm starting to wonder just what I would have done had Theo not intervened the other night. He'd asked me my plan and I hadn't told him. Part of that was because I didn't really have one. I'd thought about trying to enter the military level, but had little idea of what I'd do beyond that. Most likely I wouldn't have been able to get in or would have been caught snooping around and punished accordingly.

We pass under the tram tracks and head straight for the lifts, descending through the surface levels and down a couple of dozen feet below the waves to Underwater 2. Once more, I'm greeted with the sight of the familiar tram tracks and perimeter wall ahead of me. Beyond there, however, I have little idea as to what to expect.

It's much lighter down here than it is on Underwater 5, even at this time. I suppose it's down to the fact that people are still on patrol here and live here too.

I begin to wonder exactly where these soldiers are recruited from. Most likely the mainland regions. Stands to reason why they're cooped up down here, just like the manual workers who live on Surface Level 8. No comfortable and modern living quarters for them. Just small rooms side by side along endless passages under the ocean. If I lived and worked down here, I'd go mad within a few weeks. Sometimes just spending the entire day down in the Grid makes my head start to spin.

Theo creeps out towards the tram tracks and I follow, descending beneath them and into the inner perimeter wall. As with the other levels, there are several large doors that head into the interior of the level. We move towards one and Theo tells me to insert the keycard above the slot where you'd usually insert your hand.

It's the moment of truth. If it doesn't work, we're done. For a moment the lock seems to hum, before the red light turns green and I hear a click. *It does work.*

The door slides up, exposing the interior. As soon as I see inside I understand what Theo was talking about. It's less claustrophobic here, more expansive and open. Ahead is a massive space, stretching as far as I can see into the blackness beyond. In it are hundreds of pieces of equipment and military hardware, stacks of bags and boxes all over the place.

"It looks like storage," whispers Theo. "Last time I came here, this entire space was empty. Looks like they're stockpiling."

We scan the environment ahead and see no sign of movement.

"Are there any cameras or anything?" I ask, checking the walls and ceiling.

"I'm not sure. It's possible. People on Eden don't really break the rules, so except for the barcodes there's not actually that much security in general. People just, you know, do their duties."

"Yeah, I've begun to work that out since I've been here."

We step inside and I hear the door sliding shut behind us. "So, where are the archives?" I ask.

Theo's face screws up in thought. "It's a bit disorienting. Last time I came down here it wasn't like this. And I came down at another part of the perimeter." He looks towards a door in the distance over to the right. "I think it's through there somewhere. Come on."

We spend the next few minutes creeping through the room, stopping every so often behind stacks of boxes, cargo containers, and large military vehicles to check the coast is clear. Some of the equipment here is so huge I begin to wonder how they got it down here.

"There's a massive industrial lift that extends up to the deck over on the other side of the level," Theo tells me when I ask him.

"But why bring all this equipment here? Why not keep it on the mainland?"

"Beats me. Maybe they like to keep some safe here. It's more dangerous on the mainland. At least, that's what I've been told."

He looks at me as if asking for my own thoughts on the matter. "Well, before coming here I'd never been out of Arbor so I don't really know. You'll know more than me I bet."

We continue forward, still not catching sight of any guards, until we reach the door Theo spotted from the other side. There's no sign on it and no way of telling where it actually leads.

"Are you sure it's through here?" I ask.

"Honestly? No. But it's definitely in this general direction."

We go through the door to find ourselves in what appears to be a stock room specifically for weaponry. Row upon row of high shelves stretch out ahead of us, all filled with weapons of various kinds. I recognise many that we've been training with over the last month or so and that I'm now comfortable using. Many others, however, are alien to me.

We continue through, reaching yet another door on the far side. Theo goes to open it, but I quickly grab his hand before he's able to push the button, pulling it away.

He looks at me in alarm, but I have to act quickly. I start running to the left, dragging him with me, slipping around a shelf of pistols and stopping behind it.

"What's going on?!" he whispers. I don't answer. My eyes are stuck on the door, peeking through a gap in the shelving.

Any second now, I think to myself. *Any second.*

The door suddenly opens, shooting up as two men step through into the room. They hold torches, rhythmically swaying them from side to side, lighting up the high stacks of weapons in the gloom.

"Guards," whispers Theo, now staring forward through the gap with me.

We both stand in silence as they split, one heading to the left, and the other to the right, directly towards us. Now it's Theo's turn to take control. I feel his hand grasp hard at my wrist and begin leading me back away, darting around another shelf. Just as we sneak from his view, the guard rounds the shelf we were hiding behind, his torch bathing the spot in a bright yellow glow.

Without breathing, without making a sound, we retreat, moving further and further back behind stacks of weapons. The light of the guard continues to sway as he steps forward, whistling casually as he goes. Soon we're at the back wall, with nowhere else to hide. I see Theo crouching low to the ground and follow behind him. He's readying himself to launch himself at the guard should he come round the corner.

The guard inches closer, strolling towards the final shelf that we're hiding behind. Theo's body tenses in front of me, ready to strike like a viper.

Then a voice echoes from the other side of the room. "Anything?" it shouts.

The guard ahead of us turns on the spot, only a few feet away. "What do you think?!" His voice is so loud, so close, vibrating through me in the silence.

"Well come on then, let's take a break."

I let out a long, quiet, breath as the guard begins walking away towards the far side. Towards the door we came in through only a few minutes ago. Theo's body relaxes and he turns to me, an impish smile on his newly fattened face. "Close one," he whispers. "How did you know they were coming?"

I check to see that the guard is out of earshot before answering. "I saw them," I say. "I saw the door slide open and the two guards walk through, just like in the Grid."

"Well that saved us," says Theo. "We'd have been caught for sure otherwise."

As soon as the guards leave the room we make our way back towards the door. Theo looks at me, almost for approval, before opening it. This time, there's no one preparing to come through the other side.

We enter into a large corridor, brightly lit and with various doors leading into other expansive halls and rooms. "There," says Theo, pointing down towards a section marked 'Archives'. "Now I remember. I came down in the lift from the other end of this corridor near the perimeter. That was the quickest way in from when I was living in the Council Chambers."

I let out a small sigh of relief at the thought that he now knows where he's going. For all his uses so far, being poor with directions might well have just derailed the entire plan.

We walk along the corridor, making sure to watch for opening doors ahead. This time, however, if a guard did come through, we'd have nowhere to hide. It would be a case of surrender or fight. I know what I'd choose.

Thankfully, however, we reach the archive section without further incident. Once more we're required to enter the keycard, and both wait with bated breath for the light to glow green. It does, and the door slides open, revealing a darkened space beyond.

As my eyes begin to adjust, I notice that we're inside yet another massive area. Similar to the weapons room, here there are countless rows of cabinets, a never-ending tract of files and documents. We step inside and inspect a sign on the inside of the door, listing the various areas of the room. There are more than a dozen sections. Records for military vehicles and equipment. Battle reports and troop movements. Details of retired and discharged soldiers.

My eyes drop to the section we're here for. The section marked '*Serving Soldier Records*', located at the back right hand corner of the room. I can feel my heart rate beginning to race the closer we get, my head starting to spin with hope and dread all at once.

Theo continues to search for any sign of a guard as we go, but there's no sign of anyone. Here, in the gloomy archive room, you'd see their torch lit up like a beacon. But there's nothing. No sound of footsteps but our own light treads. No light except the gentle glow of the security lights littered at intervals around the walls.

Once we're sure we're alone, Theo pulls out his own torch and begins scouring the cabinets for the appropriate files and records.

"What's his surname?" he asks me, his voice rumbling through the silent hall.

"Kane," I say. "It's Jackson Kane."

The cabinets in the section are listed alphabetically, so it takes no time to find 'K'. "Keep a lookout, would you?" I ask Theo. Frankly, I want to do this part alone.

Now I'm sifting through drawers, searching through the surnames starting with a 'K'. Some files are bigger than others. Perhaps belonging to soldiers who have served for some time. Others are as thin as a couple of sheets of paper, most likely new recruits only just arrived. There are lots of those.

My fingers move fast, frantically, as I flick from one file to the next. Then I find it – *Kane, Jackson* – and pull it straight out.

I glance at Theo, who's now looking at me with interest as I pull the file open and run my eyes over its contents. I see a picture of Jackson, standing in military gear, a sort of snarl on his face. I guess it must have been taken soon after he arrived a few months ago.

Behind it are his vital statistics, notes on where he's been stationed, and various details about his skills, abilities, and potential aptitude as a soldier and leader. There's nothing here to suggest he's been killed. Nothing to suggest he's been involved in any accident at all.

Then I flick the page, and feel my hands tremble.

I don't even focus on the writing, on the report written at the top of the page. All I see are the big red letters.

M.I.A, PRESUMED DEAD.

I feel the file slipping out of my hand, my fingers clenching together into balls and squeezing tight. I want to let out a scream. One of anger and relief all melted into one.

Because I know, right at that moment, that Jackson is alive. That what I've been seeing in my sleep is real. Not a dream. Not a powerful manifestation. But a vision of reality. He's injured. He's missing. But he's alive.

And I know, right then, that I've been lied to. Lied to by Ajax, the man I'm supposed to trust. Manipulated by him, by Augustus Knight. Toyed with like a doll, made to believe that Jackson's dead so I let go of everything I care about. Let go of my past. Look to the future and commit myself to life as a Watcher.

I see Theo leaning down at my feet, picking up the file. He reads over the pages quizzically, shaking his head.

"Not dead?" he whispers, raising his eyes to mine. "You were right."

He neatens up the file and slips it back into the

drawer, before closing the cabinet shut. "What are you going to do now?" he asks.

I step forward, open the drawer once more, and pull out the picture of Jackson. "He's alive," I say, looking at it, "and I'm going to find him."

24

The Storm Gathers

We're rushing now, back across the level towards the lifts. We take a different route, moving down the corridor we came out onto after leaving the weapons stock room. Theo leads the way, eyes carefully scanning ahead as usual, piercing through the faint light in the distance, ever searching for guards.

I hear voices, coming to me as if on the wind. They're ghostly, unintelligible, make no sense at all.

"Stop," I whisper to Theo, grabbing his arm. It's muscled and sinewy, tightly tensed.

"What's the matter?" He turns to me, eyes focused.

"Someone's coming. I can hear them."

He's looking up and down the corridor now. There's no sign of anyone. "Which direction?"

I shut my eyes and hear the voices. Ahead, to the left. I look up and see the wispy figures of two more guards coming forward, through the door. "That door," I say. "They'll be coming through any second."

Theo's eyes dart frantically around, searching for cover, for somewhere, anywhere, to hide. There's nowhere, nothing but a long expanse of corridor behind us.

"We have to fight," he says, before darting

forward to the door.

We're there in a split second, just before the door slides open and two men walk through. They're wearing armour, carrying weapons, but aren't expecting company.

Theo steps in and sends his fist straight into one of their jaws. The man only has enough time for his eyes to widen in surprise before they close just as quickly, his body falling flat onto the cold floor.

The other guard lets out a yelp of shock before setting his eyes on Theo. He's quick to act, his fist firing straight towards Theo's face, but hitting nothing but air. Theo's below the punch, ducking down and stepping in, slipping behind his back, and putting him into a choke hold. The man thrashes and splutters for a few moments before his body goes limp, Theo gently placing him next to his friend on the floor.

"Someone might have heard," he says, turning to me. "We need to get back immediately."

We're running again, continuing on towards the perimeter wall. My blood's rushing, filling with adrenaline, as the sight of the wall grows in front of us. In a moment we're through the door, under the tram tracks, and safely inside a lift heading for the deck.

We both let out a laugh of relief. "Good thing we're wearing the masks!" says Theo, rubbing his fist. I can tell his knuckles are already beginning to swell a little bit.

"Looks like your combat training has paid off," I say. "That was impressive."

"Thanks. It's fighting Link that's done it. That guy's a brute."

It takes no time for the lift doors to open again and the rush of cool, clean air to flow inside. It's so quiet, the night still in its darkest recesses, when we enter through the inner perimeter wall and onto the deck. I look around, not quite knowing where I am.

"This was the lift I used to use when I lived at the Council Chambers," Theo says. "It's the closest one. Although, that does mean that our room is pretty much on the other side of the city."

"I guess the trams aren't going to be working for a while?" I ask.

"Nope, afraid not. We're walking."

The next 30 minutes or so is spent sneaking through the city, ducking for cover in places when we think someone might see us. Frankly, no one would know it's us anyway, and it's going to take them a while to piece together exactly what's gone on down on Underwater 2 tonight. And I don't plan on being here for much longer.

When we eventually get back to our room, we both peel the morph masks from our faces. The feeling is incredibly satisfying, like peeling dried glue from your fingers. I hand mine back to Theo, who puts them back in his bag, a seriousness dawning on his face.

"What did you mean back there?" he asks. "When you said you were going to find Jackson?"

I sit on my bed, exhausted, the adrenaline now well and truly fading from my body. "I meant just that. I'm going to find him, and save him. Did you see what the file said: MIA. Missing in action."

"So you think he's been taken? By the rebels out on the Deadlands?"

"Yeah, isn't that obvious? In my vision, he's lying in some old dilapidated building. I didn't realise before, but it's probably in an old rebel city, destroyed in the war. I can't leave him there to die. I just can't do that, Theo."

"So tell Ajax. Let the military take care of it."

I shake my head and wipe my hand down my face. "Are you serious? You think they'd do anything about it? They've been lying to me, telling me he's dead. Ajax is part of that. I can't trust him. I can't trust anyone here."

Theo stands and moves over to my bed. He sits down beside me, eyes gentle but filled with resolve. "Then I'm coming with you."

"No, I can't ask you to do that. Look, you've more than repaid your debt to me tonight. You don't owe me anything."

"It's not about that. Not any more." He stands and paces to the window and pulls the curtains open, eyes staring solemnly to the city below. "I'm sick of this place." His voice is sombre and heavy. "I don't want to be here any more. I don't belong here any more."

I stand and move to the side of him. "Those bruises on your body," I ask. "They're from your old friends aren't they?"

I watch as his face compresses in anger, deep lines appearing across his forehead. "I'll get them back.

One day I'll make them pay. All of them."

"Your friends?"

He nods. "And my parents. You can't see the bruises they inflict."

"Your parents? But, they're always so polite, so proud..."

He huffs. "Of course they are, they have to be. But it's all for show. They're ashamed of what I've become..."

"And who you've been Paired with?" I ask.

He turns to me, eyes filled with venom. "They act like it's all great because they have to. It's Chancellor Knight's system. If any Councillor disagrees with it, they're cut out, discarded. But behind closed doors, they tell me how they really feel."

"That's awful. I'm...so sorry."

He turns back to the window and gazes to the empty streets below. "This place is sick, like an apple rotting at its core. You only see it when you're cast out. Now, I'm seeing that clearly."

There's no falseness to his words. He's not lying to me. He's not trying to make me feel sorry for him or take pity on him. He's been right at that rotten core, and now that he's been removed, he can see it all for what it truly is: corrupt.

"So, when shall we leave?" I ask, almost casually. That's how Jackson and I always dealt with the heavy stuff: by being casual about it.

He twists once more and looks upon me. "Friday evening," he says quickly. "It will give us time to disappear when the entire city is distracted by the celebrations."

I understand. If we left during the week, Ajax would know we're not there the next morning. The weekend gives us a bit of time to get away when everyone will be busy celebrating the anniversary of the city's birth, one of the biggest events in its calender.

"There are merchant boats we can stow away on. They'll take us as far as New Atlantis. From there we can disappear."

We look at each other with resolve, our features hardening. He looks like he's aged several years overnight, his face growing tougher and more rugged, dots of stubble appearing on his chiselled chin.

"Will it be that easy to escape unnoticed?" I ask. Once again, I know having Theo on board is going to prove incredibly useful.

"Shouldn't be a problem. At worst, we can pay people off if we're caught. Merchants from New Atlantis have no morals."

"OK," I say. "We leave Friday."

"Friday," Theo repeats, nodding.

The next two days pass like a blur. I hear a few murmurings about the infiltration down on Underwater 2, but it seems there are no leads as to who it was. By all accounts, a full on inventory was conducted to ensure nothing was taken, the results of which were inconclusive.

Theo and I make sure to keep our distance in the

Grid, just to keep up appearances. With Ajax's ever watchful eyes on me, I don't want to give the impression that anything is wrong. I get the sense that he knows I'm up to something, but he never mentions it. Now I know how devious he's been, how truly callous and cold he is, I'll be glad to see the back of him.

I find it hardest keeping things quiet from Ellie. Part of me wants to admit to her that it was Theo and I who infiltrated Underwater 2, that I managed to find out the truth about Jackson. I want to show her that I was telling the truth all along, that they weren't just dreams and flights of fancy, but visions. That Jackson is alive, and I'm going to find him, or die trying.

But I don't say anything. I just keep on going as before, training and keeping my head down. If anything, I'm unusually quiet.

There's one more official function that Theo and I have to attend on the Thursday evening. It's a quieter, preliminary celebration for the city's anniversary, shared only by those in power. So, once more, that means spending an evening with the Councillors and Augustus Knight.

There's something liberating about knowing that this will be my final evening among these people. Theo's parents speak pleasantly with me, even though I know how they really feel underneath. I wonder if the rest of them are as two-faced as they are. Under those watchful eyes of Chancellor Knight, everyone is so deferential and courteous. Behind closed doors, it's a different matter.

I spend the night by Theo's side, keen to make sure he doesn't get too angry and react to his old friends' provocations. The last thing we need is for him to get into a fight and be put under watch. I can feel him tensing by my side at times and grab his hand for reassurance. He looks at me and smiles, that false smile he has to put on transforming into one that's genuine. I can tell, now, what's real and what isn't around here. And just about every smile in this room is contrived, plastered onto every face under the all seeing eyes of Augustus Knight.

He sits, once more, at the top of the room in his large chair, flanked by his two Watcher guards. I pray that they have no idea what Theo and I are up to, that no one has already seen a vision of our escape. It's unlikely. I've learned that visions usually tell of death and disaster, of pain and suffering. Two people sneaking out of the city should be innocuous enough.

I'm summoned to speak with him once again. I suspect he'll want to ask if I've seen anything more of the Divide, which I haven't.

I approach, and he immediately dismisses his guards to give us some privacy. His face coils into an insincere smile, and I return the look, making sure mine is about as false as I can manage without being rude. I imagine he's used to seeing false expressions of joy when people meet with him.

"Miss Drayton, how wonderful to see you again," he says. If I didn't know what he really was, I might consider him charming. "I understand you've been having some visions of your friend Jackson." He puts special emphasis on the word *friend*.

"Apparently they're just dreams," I reply. "Ajax tells me so."

"Yes, they must be. He's dead, is he not?"

He looks at me intently, those deep staring eyes so dark and endless.

"So I'm told," I say curtly. *How can he sit there, knowing he's been deceiving me, so composed and casual?*

"You know, it would be so much easier for you if you just let go. I know you'll make a great Watcher one day. But only once you fully commit."

"Yes, sir," I say. "I have accepted it."

He knows I'm lying.

"Well that's good. I notice young Theo has bruising on his right hand. I do hope he hasn't been abusing you." His soulless eyes swell with pleasure. *Does he know? Does he know it was Theo and I on Underwater 2?*

"Nothing like that, no," I say, an awkward laughter rumbling through me. "It's the training in the Grid, High Chancellor. It can get brutal down there sometimes."

He sits back, laughing. "Oh I'm only teasing, Miss Drayton. I understand the rigours of the Grid. Let's hope nothing spoils that pretty face of yours."

"We wear masks mainly when we fight, so the face is usually protected."

"Yes, I know you wear *masks*," he says pointedly.

I feel my heart rate rush suddenly. *Masks. Does he know about the morph masks?*

We share a few moments in silence, his eyes boring into me.

"Well, that'll be all, Miss Drayton. I must say, it's lovely to see you and Theo getting along so much better. Enjoy the rest of your evening with him."

With that he dismisses me and his guards return to his side. I do the little bow Leeta taught me and turn, walking back towards Theo feeling as if I'm about to throw up.

I don't tell him what he said. There's no point in making anything of it. I can't work out whether he really does know what we've been doing or whether I'm just so paranoid that I'm making it all up in my head. There's just something about him. It's like he's reading my mind or something, getting inside my head. Any time I speak with him, it's an invasive, uncomfortable experience.

That night, Theo and I speak in hushed tones about our escape. The merchant docks, he tells me, will be busy on a Friday evening, with various ships preparing to set off for New Atlantis. The city, meanwhile, will be engaged in early celebrations for its anniversary, making it easy to blend in and go unnoticed. There's no official function for us to attend until Saturday night, which is when the entire city comes together. Our absence will be noted, but questions won't be asked until Sunday. By Monday, when we fail to appear at the Grid, a full on search will begin.

"We'll be long gone by then," Theo says. "Once we reach the mainland we'll be much harder to track. We'll use our morph masks and dress appropriately. It shouldn't take more than a few days to get near the Divide."

But that's the easy part. Crossing Knight's Wall unseen. Finding Jackson somewhere across the Deadlands. That's the real challenge.

Before we sleep, we both prepare what little things we have. My mother's watch, my diary, the pictures of my family. They're now joined by the picture of Jackson I took from the archives. I pack them into my tatty bag along with the clothes I wore when I arrived here and a few rations that Theo gives me. He packs some more food and a few basic items of clothing. Most of the Eden clothes we have will look out of place, so we leave them.

It's hard to sleep that night. My mind continues to skip ahead to the following evening, playing through the scenario Theo and I have devised. *Will we be caught sneaking onto the boat? Will our plan be thwarted before it even begins?*

I lie there for hours, just thinking in the silence of the room. Across from me, I hear no sound from Theo, and know that he's awake too. I wonder if he's regretting his decision to come with me. If he'll decide not to at the last minute. Realise that this is folly, that he might die on this crusade. My crusade.

Hours pass, the minutes ticking by relentlessly, until the room begins to slowly brighten as Eve activates the morning routine. This is it. The final day in Eden. And I hope never to return.

Despite my lack of sleep, I don't feel tired that day. I'm too excited, too wired, too nervous. The hours pass like a blur as I work through my stations, paying little attention to them. Ajax reprimands me on more than one occasion for not concentrating, but I ignore him. His words of encouragement, of advice, fall on deaf ears now.

As my final day in the Grid draws to a close, however, Ellie comes to me, a quizzical look on her face. She tells me she needs to talk, leading me into a quiet corner as the rest continue to train.

"What's going on with you?" she asks me. It's an open statement, and could mean anything.

"What do you mean?" I ask innocently.

"You and Theo. You're planning something. I heard you, last night, in your room. You were talking about a plan, about leaving. What's going on, Cy?"

"You heard us? How?"

She glances around to make sure Ajax isn't close, her voice becoming a whisper. "I came to your room last night. I wanted to ask if you'd seen Knight again. Then I heard you talking through the door. So what's your plan then? You running away? There's no point, Cy. You know they'll catch you."

I've reached a breaking point with Ellie. She's been my confidant ever since I met her. The one person I could trust and talk to about everything. The person I'd confide in and tell about my mother and Jackson and everything I was going through. I've wanted so badly to tell her about the archives, tell her the truth about Jackson. To tell her goodbye, knowing I might never see her again.

In the end, I can't keep it at bay any longer. "I'm leaving," I blurt out. "You're right. I'm leaving the city to find Jackson."

Her eyebrows drop down her face. "Jackson? Cyra, why are you doing this to yourself. He's dead..."

"He's *not* dead," I say, cutting her off. "That infiltration on Underwater 2. That was me. Me and Theo. We broke into the archives, Ellie. He's not dead. It says so in his file. I can't lose him again. I won't."

Ellie's jaw hangs slightly open. "He's alive?" she says quietly, disbelieving. "So...they were visions after all?" There's a slight guilt to her voice. "I'm sorry I didn't listen to you."

"Look, it's OK. I wanted to tell you straight away. But, you have to stay quiet, OK? We're leaving tonight. You can't even tell Link you know."

"Tonight!" she shouts, before quickly slapping her palm to her mouth. Ajax looks over from the far side of the hall before turning back to Kyle, who's engaged in a simulation.

"Yes, but keep your voice down! No one can know."

"But...you can't leave. I need you here."

"Ellie, you've got Link now. You don't need me."

"I do! You're the person I come to when I need to talk. Link's not like that. He's there for me, but in a different way."

"There's nothing I can do. I have to find Jackson. I don't care about anything else right now."

Her face stiffens, her eyes setting. "Well, I'm coming with you then. If you're not here, I don't want to be here."

"Ellie, no. It's too dangerous out there. You could die..."

"I don't care about that. When I saw my mother dying in my visions, all I wanted to do was save her. I wanted so badly to leave and warn her, but it was too late. If Jackson really is alive, I want to help you get him back."

"No, I can't be responsible for that..."

"And you think they won't think I know if you and Theo suddenly disappear. It will be just as dangerous for me here, Cy. They'll do anything to find out where you've gone. I'll be safer if I leave with you."

"And Link?"

"He'll come too."

I shake my head. "No he won't. He's more dedicated to all of this than anyone."

"Yeah, dedicated to being a Watcher, but not to Eden. He hates this place as much as you do, he talks about it all the time. Please, Cyra, let us come too."

I think for a moment and look over at Theo. He finds my eyes out of instinct, and gives me a light nod. It's almost like he knows what we're talking about, that he's giving me a nod of approval.

"Pack light," I say, turning back to Ellie. "No clothes that would look out of place on the mainland. Bring some food, enough for a week at least. I'll meet you in your room at 7pm. Be ready."

I look over and see that Ajax is close. He scans us

suspiciously. "What are you girls talking about?" he asks.

"Nothing," I say. "Nothing to do with you, anyway." I try to bite my tongue, but find it hard now with him.

"Excuse me?" he asks, his face hardening.

"Just girl stuff," says Ellie. "You wouldn't be interested."

Ajax continues to eye us with mistrust, but doesn't push it. "Fine. Now back to your stations. We have one hour left today."

One hour left. It will go like lightning. My final hour in this place. This hell where I witnessed Jackson dying over and over again. And when I step out, I'll never come back. Not unless it's to burn it to the ground.

25
Escape

I knock on the door and hear the shuffling of feet inside. Within a couple of seconds, it opens and I see Ellie staring back at me. She looks at me as if we've never met.

"Um, can I help you?" she asks, frowning.

"Oh right, the morph masks," I say. "Ellie, it's me, Cyra."

She still looks confused, until I begin peeling the mask off my face.

"Cyra! What the hell?! Your face!"

I step forward, Theo moving in behind me, and the door slides shut. "It's a morph mask," I say. Theo pulls two more from his bag and hands them to Ellie and Link.

"Go on, put them on. They alter your features so you're unrecognisable."

"Yeah, I get that," says Ellie, now staring at Theo's new face. She puts the mask on, and her face quickly changes, her nose growing larger, chin more pointed, and cheeks a little fuller. In an instant she loses that youthful, innocent look she has.

"And you, Link," I say, looking up at him. He doesn't look overly pleased with any of this, but follows my orders.

"At least it will cover up that scar," says Theo, getting a glare for his trouble. I stare at him too. "Sorry, tasteless joke," he says.

I glance at the bed, where a small bag sits on top. "That's mine," says Ellie, poking at her new face and looking in the mirror. "It's all we've got. Link doesn't have a bag."

I nod. "That's OK, as long as you've got enough food. Are we ready?"

Everyone nods and Theo steps forward first, opening the door and checking there's no one out in the corridor. We descend down in the lift to the ground floor and step outside, new faces on, bags over our shoulders. When we reach the street the celebrations are already beginning. Banners cover buildings, decorations line the roads. People carry small flags of the city, many wearing its colours of dark red and blue, mingled with grey and white.

No one notices us or gives us any strange looks as we go. Just four young boys and girls, getting involved in the celebrations. As we move through the centre, things only get more busy. The central square is alive, the many restaurants around its border overflowing with customers. Everywhere people dance and eat and drink as music plays from all quarters, socialising on the eve of the city's favourite day. The highlight of the calender year.

Theo leads us on, through the chattering crowds in the main square and out onto the other side. After a further 10 minutes, we enter a part of the city I've only been to once, during one of Leeta's guided tours; the docking area in the western corner. I quickly wonder how she'll feel when she finds out Ellie and I are missing. How her rise up the Eden hierarchy will be halted now that she can no longer join me at events. I'd have liked to have said goodbye, but know that telling her would have been too much of a risk. As it is, I'll just have to remember her as she was: vacuous and naïve at times, but sweet-natured and with a good heart. Perhaps, one day, I'll meet her again under better circumstances.

We arrive at the docks, where the merchant ships arrive bringing cargo from the mainland. Here there are docking stations at various surface levels for ships and boats of different sizes. The larger ones rise up to level 6, where the city's food stores are. Others are much smaller, their cargo being taken to the lower storage levels. Most regular cargo, as Leeta taught me, is stored on Surface Level 2, while other levels have storage sections of their own. As Theo and I found out the other night, even the military level of Underwater 2 has huge munition stocks, transported down by giant industrial lifts.

"Right, so what's the grand plan then?" It's Link, who's clearly sceptical about the entire thing. By the looks of things, Ellie's had to coerce him into this.

"The ships on the docks drop off their cargo in huge containers," says Theo, "before picking up empty ones to be shipped back to New Atlantis and the other mainland ports. On their return journey there are plenty of places to hide."

"So we're going to stow away in a container?" asks Link.

Theo nods.

"Fair plan, I guess" says Link. "I just hope you know this city as well as we hope you do."

"Trust him," I say, breaking the short staring contest between the two of them. "It'll work. It has to," I add, under my breath.

We move forward towards the perimeter wall. Inside it's like the entry point where I first arrived on Eden, with a long walkway extending out towards the sea beyond it. There, I see several ships docked against the outer platform, some towering above the waves, others docked at lower levels.

Everywhere cranes and large industrial vehicles work tirelessly, removing huge crates from the ships and transporting them inside the city or onto lifts to take them to their appropriate levels. Men are everywhere, milling around like insects on the ships and out on the docks. With so many eyes, it seems impossible to get aboard any vessel.

"So what now?" asks Link. "How will we ever get past *that* unseen?"

"We're not going that way," Theo says. "Follow me."

He turns back into the city and we enter a lift, hitting the button for Surface Level 6 and quickly descending down. When the doors open, I'm not greeted with the usual sight: tram tracks ahead, the inner perimeter wall beyond. Instead all I see are countless containers in front of me. They line up into the distance, hundreds of them filling the cavernous space ahead.

Theo steps out and we follow, ducking behind the

first container and moving backwards into the maze. The smell of the sea reaches my nose. That salty, briny, scent that burns my nostrils. I turn to see a large opening leading towards the outside of the city. There's another short platform, and a ship docked against it. It's the same ship we saw from above, it's contents being quickly unloaded and brought inside the level.

"They unload to the right," Theo whispers. "All full containers are put there, with empty ones on the left to be loaded once they're done."

He leads us further back into the level, skipping between containers to stay out of sight. Soon we're onto the left hand side, the side filled with empty containers to be loaded and shipped back out of the city.

Theo moves towards one and pulls the large metal door open. Inside, it's empty, nothing but the lingering scent of fruit remaining. "Inside," he says, and we all step in. Then he shuts the door, as quietly as possible, and the world goes black.

It's damp inside the container, but smells of home. Of sweet fruit from the orchards, perhaps even brought from Arbor. Theo turns on a torch and the interior bursts to life. Link doesn't look overly pleased with his current predicament, standing grumpily with his arms crossed.

"So we wait to be loaded onto the ship and taken to the mainland?" he asks. "And how long will all that take?"

"Hard to say. They should unload and load within a couple of hours. Then it's a few more hours to

New Atlantis. The boat will dock there overnight before returning to the mainland coast."

"And how do you know all this?"

"I know everything about this city. I've lived here my whole life. You pick up things."

"And how much air is in here? Are we not all going to suffocate to death?"

Ellie puts her arm onto Link's shoulder. "Look, stop asking so many questions. Cyra says we can trust Theo, so we can, OK."

I give her a look of thanks and she nods in return. Link grunts but quietens down, before sitting up against the back of the container, Ellie settling in beside him.

I turn to Theo and lower my voice to a quiet whisper. "It's a valid point. How long will the air last?"

"Honestly, I don't know. Should be plenty to see us to New Atlantis."

"And if the ship goes all the way to the mainland?"

Theo shrugs. "It won't, but if it did we can just open the door anyway. We're not locked in here or anything. I think Link's just trying to pick a fight. He can't stand following my plan."

"Well, that's fair enough. It's not like you two are the best of friends."

"Yeah, well things are different now. I want out of this city as much as anyone, and I'm the one who knows it."

"You don't have to convince me. Just...make sure

you guys get along, OK."

Over the next couple of hours we sit in virtual silence in the dark, listening to the containers being unloaded, and then loaded, outside. As the noise gets louder, we know that they're getting closer. I pray that they won't check inside or sense that the cabinet is heavier than it should be. If they do, we're toast.

Then we hear a sudden shove and the container rocks slightly. Theo clicks on the light and I can see all eyes growing intense. Then we're lifted, turned, and begin moving. The sound of the waves and ocean grows stronger, the twisting of metal and rumbling of engines as huge machines keep working long into the night.

I feel the container being set down on the ship now, locked into place among hundreds of others. *We're safely on,* I think. *That's stage one done.*

It doesn't take long before a rumble begins vibrating beneath us, the sound of the ship's engines starting to fire. Then the unmistakable feeling of motion, of the slow churn of the ship against the waves, burrowing through the ocean.

There's a collective sigh of relief among us as we all share nervous glances. Then we sit back and relax, with nothing to do but wait.

I return to my thoughts as we go, the container dark and silent but for the sound of waves crashing against the hull, of wind whistling around us. I can't help but feel guilty, dragging these three on my crusade. Theo and Ellie seemed intent on joining me, but not Link. Despite what he thinks of Eden, I know he wants to serve and help people. Now, after this betrayal, he'll never be considered trustworthy again.

I fall into a dream in the darkness, exhaustion finally overcoming me. I see blurred images of Jackson once more, but not like before. He's no longer wounded, no longer lying on that dirty mattress. He's standing now, tall crumbling buildings around him, starring out as he's lead through the city by the man in the cloak.

I'm awoken by the feel of a hand shaking my shoulder. I look up to see Theo, his face illuminated by his torch, starting at me. "Cyra, wake up. We're here."

My eyes spring open and I sit up. The feeling of vibration is gone, the engines shut down. All that's left is a gentle swaying as the ship is pitched back and forth by the waves. Outside, there are no voices, no sounds of crates and containers being unloaded. Theo carefully moves to the front and pushes at the door. It creaks and opens a crack. He peers beyond, before pushing the door wider, the caustic smell of salt quickly rushing in.

One by one, we clamber out onto the deck of the ship. We're in a maze of containers, unable to see anything beyond. We creep on towards the railing at the ship's edge and, finally, see the city of New Atlantis grow in our view.

I've seen it before, when Leeta described it to us on our journey to Eden. Yet now, seeing it from this level, is something else entirely. The harbour is huge, a sprawling mass of ships of all sizes, docked at various points. Beyond, towers climb high into the air, linked together by passages and tunnels. In the darkness, the entire city twinkles with a million lights, as striking and beautiful as the night sky. And surrounding it all is a wall, tall enough to deflect the waves and keep the city safe from storms and pirates.

Theo continues to lead us on, sneaking forward and down onto the docks. There's little activity here, the night growing late and the vices of the city coming into full swing. New Atlantis is, as Leeta told us, a mecca for gambling, prostitution, drinking, and drugs. If anywhere is 'off the grid' and left to its own devices by Eden, this city is it. Yet it serves a purpose for those in power. A place where people are able to let off steam and enjoy themselves. A place where anonymity is everything.

With our masks on, we're as anonymous as anyone. As soon as we begin moving through the harbour, Theo starts to loosen up, his walk turning from a crouch to a stroll.

"No one here knows us, and no one would care anyway," he tells us. "Tonight, we can relax."

We move into the city, which is littered with platforms and walkways and hard to navigate without knowing your way around. Beneath the surface of the water, the shadow of the towers can be seen, plunging down into the darkness. Some levels are lit, blurred lights shimmering beneath the surface. Down there you can see out to the ocean's depths. The thought sends a shudder through me.

Around us, the people seem rough, mainly men

with several days of stubble and a mean look in their eye. Theo says they're the merchants, used to spending days on end at sea and constantly on the move. I know the type. I used to see them in Arbor. I'd even trade with them sometimes if I could find one selling medicine cheaply. Those from Eden and the other sea cities stay in another part of the city. Here, Theo says, it's more sordid and derelict. A place for those with less money and looser morals.

After about 10 minutes, we find a tower rising only a few floors up above the water. It flickers with a light that says '*cheap hotel*' and looks about the most unappealing place in the city. "This is perfect," says Theo, leading us inside.

It's grotty and dank looking. In front of us is a short desk, with a run-down looking woman behind it. A cigarette hangs from her mouth, a glass of liquor in her hand. Her bloodshot eyes raise to us as we walk in, caked in streaky, unpleasant make-up.

"Room for the night is it?" she croaks, her lungs and throat rotten.

"Two," says Theo, pulling a few notes from his bag. It's odd for me, seeing money. Where I'm from, the only currency is food. That's all I've ever traded with in the past.

"All right," says the old woman. "Rooms 7 and 8 are free. They're on the 2nd floor." She sucks in another load of smoke and sends it billowing out into the room as she hands Theo the keys.

He passes one to Link, before addressing all of us with a whisper. "We need to be up early tomorrow morning. Get some sleep, if you can."

At that, Link quickly walks off, Ellie following behind. It's obvious he doesn't enjoy taking orders from Theo. I stumble after, feeling incredibly drained, yet more at home here than I ever did in Eden. Anywhere that's dank and unkempt is more what I'm used to, what I grew up with. I'm sure, here, I'll sleep just fine.

When we enter our room I change my mind. Not because of the smell or the peeling paint on the walls, but the fact that there's only one bed, and no Eve to call upon another.

Before I can voice my concerns, Theo moves towards a wardrobe in the corner. He opens the door and pulls out a set of spare bedding, before fashioning some sort of makeshift mattress on the floor. "You take the bed," he says, "I'll take the floor."

I'm too tired to argue, even though that would be my usual inclination. Instead I just drag my feet towards the bed, and slump down onto it.

I watch Theo as he readies his bed and puts his things in order, looking every bit the confident leader. Without him, I have no idea how far I'd have got. Caught at the docks most likely. Even if I'd made it here, what would I be doing now? Finding a warm hole to sleep in for the night? Staggering around, exhausted and alone, with no thoughts of what I'd do next?

"Thanks," I say, watching him still, "for everything today. I could never have done this without you."

He looks up, his eyes still alert. "I'd save your

thanks for now. We're only just getting started."

26
The Chase

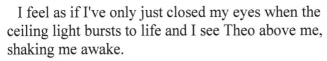

I feel as if I've only just closed my eyes when the ceiling light bursts to life and I see Theo above me, shaking me awake.

"Time to leave, Cyra."

My blurred vision clears and I see that he's already dressed, his clothes soaked and hair dripping with water. Then I hear the patter of rain against the window, tapping on the glass. Through the open curtains I see a murky, gloomy, sky. Dark clouds rumble overhead, dousing the city in a thick grey fog, periodically lit by ferocious streaks of white lightning.

"Where have you been?"

"Down at the docks. I've found a boat that will take us to the mainland, to a quiet port without much security."

"Who?"

"Just some fisherman. I paid him for passage for the four of us. He's leaving in 20 minutes."

I rub my eyes and slip out of bed, feeling the biting cold of the air outside of my blanket. "What time is it?"

"It's nearing 7am."

No wonder I feel so groggy. We've only been here

for a few hours.

I slip an extra layer from my bag and put it on, before opening a tin of beans and wolfing down the contents. I suppose we'll all be back on rations again now, scraping around for food. It's what we're all used to, except Theo. How will he cope when we hit the mainland and truly leave his world behind? I doubt he's even stepped foot there before.

I begrudgingly place my morph mask back onto my face, feeling the soft jelly stick once more to my skin. It's suffocating and uncomfortable wearing it for too long, but also a necessity. As we move inland, towards the heat and dust, I can only imagine it will get worse.

We meet Link and Ellie downstairs at reception, Theo telling me he'd already told them the plan before waking me. Once more he's proven himself invaluable. Without his wallet we'd have no way of bartering passage across the narrow sea. He knows this part of the world, how it all works. Yet when we reach the mainland, it will be new territory for all of us.

The city is dead as we step into the pouring rain. As a city of vice, it mainly comes alive at night. When we reach the docks, however, it's a different story. The harbour is thriving, heaving with hundreds of men. Large ships prepare to continue their journeys to the mainland and the other sea cities. Smaller vessels brave the weather and churn out to sea, disappearing past the outer wall and into the raging ocean.

I scan the many vessels ahead, wondering which

one will be ours. I take a sharp intake of breath when I see a stout, bearded man waving at us, standing beside a small boat which is little more than a dinghy.

"That's it?!" exclaims Link. "That's our boat?"

"It just needs to get us to the mainland. The size isn't relevant."

"Yeah, if we overturn and drown it is..."

Theo greets the man and introduces us to him. Captain Mako, he calls himself, which I doubt is his real name. I look at the boat, which is fitted with various harpoons and other odd fishing devices I've never seen.

"He's a shark hunter," says Theo as we step aboard. "Hence the name. The Mako shark is his speciality he tells me."

"A shark hunter? That's what he was assigned to be?"

Theo shakes his head. "No, this guy's not attached to any duty. He's a free man living in New Atlantis and out on the ocean. He does it for money. Shark meat is considered a delicacy on Eden."

We climb onto the boat, disappearing into a small cabin as the rain continues to drench the world outside. It's cramped, with a small kitchen and bunk bed against the side. Clearly Captain Mako spends a lot of time here.

In the harbour, the water is largely still. When we chug beyond the defensive wall, however, we're blasted from all angles. Captain Mako screams to us over the roar not to worry, that he's been in far worse weather a thousand times before. But it's little comfort for those of us who have never been this close to the water.

For the next few hours we sit, rocking from side to side, huddled together inside the small cabin. Ellie looks like she's growing more queasy as the day wears on, eventually rushing out to throw up over the side. Link goes with her, anchoring her in place to make sure she doesn't pitch over the edge into the torrent. He's attentive like that. Sweet and caring underneath that growling, brutish exterior.

"So where are we headed?" I ask Theo as we continue to rock and roll.

"A port town called Virginia Rock. Captain Mako says it's small, and won't have much security."

"You asked him about security?! Way to make him suspicious!"

"Look, it's early Saturday morning. No one is looking for us yet, OK. Anyway, Mako doesn't care. As long as he gets paid, what's it to him?"

I drop the subject. Until we get there, it's impossible to know if there will be any customs security or Custodians there to greet us. Frankly, I have no idea what to expect, and neither does anyone else. Link and Ellie, they never left their towns either until they were sent to Eden. And I doubt Theo's ever actually been to the mainland, unless on some family trip or something. So all he's going on is what he's heard or read.

After a couple of hours the weather begins to calm, the sun breaking through the clouds above. I step out of the cramped cabin and onto the deck.

The scent of rain lingers in the air, but has reduced to nothing more than a light sprinkle. Droplets tap the ocean top, sparkling under the sunshine. In the distance I see fins breaking the waves. Hundreds of them, cutting through the swell before ducking back beneath the surface.

"It's a dolphin superpod, shouts Captain Mako. It's rare to see them that big."

I watch the dolphins as they get closer, cruising alongside the boat. Some jump and flip and pull off wild stunts, splashing and playing among the waves. Free. Unlike the rest of us.

Gradually the mainland coast comes into view. It starts as a shimmer under the sun, slowly growing clearer and drawing a line between the sea and the sky. Soon I see a harbour, several boats within it, and a scattering of buildings beyond.

"Ready yourselves," says Captain Mako. "I'm dropping you off and heading straight back out."

I keep my eyes on the harbour as it gets closer, searching for security points and guards. Then I see them, two men, standing on the boardwalk heading up towards the town. A man pitches up on his boat and moves towards them. He pulls up his sleeve and slips it inside a scanner positioned within a small security checkpoint. *They're checking his barcode.*

"Did you see that?" Link's by my side, staring ahead at the two guards as the man rolls his sleeve back down and trots past them. "They're scanning codes. These masks are gonna do nothin' when they find out who we really are!"

"Keep your voice down," whispers Theo, glancing

back at Captain Mako. "He doesn't know we're deserters."

"Well he's the least of our problems!" says Link. "What are we gonna do about those guards?"

"We take them out," says Ellie. We all turn around to see her eyes set on the guards. "Link, you can take them out, can't you?"

Link dips his head. "Not a problem."

"No," says Theo. "We can't draw attention to ourselves like that."

"Well what choice do we have?" hisses Ellie. "Otherwise we'll never get past."

"She's right," I say. "If we let them scan us then Eden will know we're here. We can't take that risk. Link, can you disable them without hurting them?"

"No problem," Link says again.

"Right, then do it. And then we run."

"Run! Run where? Knight's Wall is over 500 miles away, Cyra. We need a transport."

"And we'll get one. But not here. We have no choice, Theo."

"You kids all right down there?" We all turn to see Captain Mako, his one good eye staring down at us from the wheel.

"We're fine," I say quickly. "Thanks for the ride, Captain."

"My pleasure lil' lady. Now heads up, we're docking in a few minutes."

We enter the harbour and tuck our bags over our shoulders. Link, who had been carrying Ellie's bag, goes without, priming himself for the fight.

The boat glides peacefully in through the small harbour wall and up against the wooden jetty alongside several other small boats. We step off and I catch the two guards looking at us. I don't know if it's my own paranoia, but they seem suspicious of something.

As Captain Mako begins pulling back out to sea with a wave, I feel my body tensing, my heart rate quickening. We walk, without speaking, along the pier until we meet the guards. There's no one else around, the harbour largely deserted. Hopefully our escape will go unnoticed.

"All right you four," says one guard. "Sleeves up, lets get you scanned."

I glance at Link, who steps forward ahead of us. He stretches to his full height, several inches above even the taller guard. "OK, the big one first. Left hand in the scanner."

Link stands there, not moving. "I said, left hand in the scanner. You deaf or something?!"

The guard steps forward, pulling out an electric rod from his belt. They use them in Arbor to incapacitate people, sending a charge through people's bodies that knocks them out. The rod begins flashing at the end, blue and white sparks zapping between two metal prongs.

"Left hand in the scanner, now. Or else you'll get zapped." He holds out the rod threateningly, but Link merely smiles and does nothing. I know what he's doing. He's waiting for them to act.

I see the second guard now, pulling out his own

baton, just as the first lunges forward. The speed of Link's movement is incredible, so fast he moves like a blur. Within a split second he's stepped in between the two guards and punched them both out, simultaneously, knocking them straight to the floor. They land with a loud clatter on the wooden pier, the wind thumped out of them.

"RUN!" he shouts, turning back to us.

We go, dashing forward up through the street. I hear a few shouts as people come towards us. They must have seen what was going on. We duck down a side road, past small fish packing warehouses. I see people inside, grinding out the day, humming those endless productivity songs. They look up as we pass, and I hear the songs fading out. Then we're gone, moving away down the muddy, soggy streets, passing small residential dorms and quarters.

I still hear shouts behind us and arch my head back. They're still chasing. But it's not civilians. There are more guards, armed guards, charging behind us.

Then I see Link grab Ellie to my side. He shoves her to the left as a streak of white light zooms past her, just where she would have been. A second later, the sound of a gunshot rings through the air, a bullet following behind the white line. Then more lines whip by me, cutting up the street. I follow Link to the left as the world erupts in gunfire, deafening snaps crackling through the air. We round a building and I turn to see Theo, weaving up and down as he catches up to us, ducking through gunfire, his eyes blazing.

"Stay here," shouts Link, holding Ellie up against a wall. "All of you, stay here."

I watch as Link charges back round the corner, heading back down the road towards our pursuers. Ellie turns and goes to follow, but I instinctively grab her and hold her back. "No, don't!" I shout.

"But he needs help!"

"You'll get hit," I shout. "He knows what he's doing, Ellie!"

Together we watch as Link sprints forwards, ducking and weaving. Gunfire fills the air as bullets rip into the ground at his feet, into the buildings behind him. He reaches the first guard and knocks him flat with a single punch, scooping up his gun in a single move. Then he rolls to the right, kneels to the ground, and quickly fires off several rounds. I see four men drop, almost instantly, to the dirt, each writhing and screaming in pain as they grasp at their shins.

He drops the automatic weapon to the ground and scoops a pistol from the belt of the man at his feet. Then he comes running back up towards us, sliding the gun into his own belt. I release Ellie as he comes round the corner, and she dives into his arms and kisses him, before slapping him around the face.

"What the hell was that! You could have died!"

"I've been through that before. There were only 5 of them."

"Yeah, in simulations! This is real Link!"

"And they'd have caught us if I hadn't. I had no choice."

"There's no time for this," calls Theo, checking around the corner. "They'll be calling for support. We have to get as far away as possible or we'll be overrun."

"He's right," I shout. "You two can have it out later. Come on, this way."

I begin running along the road further from the coast, the rest following behind me. The road stretches on beyond the town, the buildings thinning on either side until there are none left. A few hundred feet away I see an intersection, the road we're on linking onto a much wider one. *We need to find a vehicle right now*, I think. *Out here we're sitting ducks as soon as reinforcements arrive.*

Soon we're at the intersection, the town now well behind us. We all look left and right, searching for a car, for some sort of transport.

"There," shouts Ellie, pointing up the road. On the horizon, the blur of a hovercar approaches, zooming along the highway.

"All of you, get out of sight," she says, before falling to the tarmac in the middle of the road.

"Ellie! What are you doing!" calls Link.

"Just get back," she says through gritted teeth. "Stay hidden."

Link, Theo, and I rush to an area of shrubbery and duck in behind it. "It's an ambush," whispers Theo. "She's getting us a ride."

Through the tangle of leaves I see the car continuing down the road. It begins to slow as it approaches, then comes to a complete stop about 20 feet from where Ellie lies. A man steps out, on his own, and tentatively approaches her.

When he leans down, he gets the fright of his life. Ellie kicks his feet from under him, sending him onto his back. We all rush from the bushes and towards the car, jumping inside.

"Sorry about all this," I hear Ellie call back to the man, who's so dumbfounded he can hardly move. "We only need to borrow your car, I'm sure you'll get it back."

She's the last to get in, stepping into the passenger seat beside Theo, who's taken the wheel.

"Do you know how to drive this thing?" I ask from behind him.

"In theory," he says. "Although I've never actually done it."

"Well, let's put that theory into practice, damn it," shouts Link. "Hit the accelerator!"

Theo slams his foot to the floor and the car lurches forward, straight towards the man on the ground ahead. He twists the wheel just in time, swerving to the right.

"Full speed! Come on, go go go!" calls Link, his words frantic.

Theo lines the car up with the road, presses a button on the dashboard, and the car begins shooting forward. My head hits the back headrest, my body stuck to the seat. The world becomes a blur, the entire vehicle rumbling beneath me.

"Watch out!" shouts Link, as a car appears in front of us.

Theo swerves around it, just in time, as the car bolts on.

"Slow down," says Ellie. "We'll crash at turbo speed."

Theo shakes his head. "We need to get as far away as we can. I won't crash, I can see the hits before they happen."

The sound of sirens fills the air and I turn back to look out of the rear window. There, in the distance, two hovercars come hurtling towards us, a blue glow flashing around each of them. I watch as cars pitch off the road, sinking into ditches and bushes and crashing into trees to get out of their way.

"They're getting closer," shouts Ellie.

She's right. Despite our speed, the cars continue to gain on us, the flashing blue glow around them growing brighter, their sirens wailing louder.

Link pulls the pistol from his belt and twists around in the car. "Keep it steady," he shouts, before firing through the back window. It bursts open, shattering into a thousand shards, which scatter out onto the road behind us. The cars hover straight over the glass as Link's shots fly straight past them.

"You can't kill them!" I shout, the noise inside now deafening. Link doesn't seem to hear me. He keeps firing, his face a grimace, eyes dark and unforgiving. Yet his bullets do nothing. They merely deflect off the windscreen, creating nothing but scratches on the surface.

"They're bulletproof," shouts Theo. "That's not going to work."

"Well do you have a better idea?!" Link roars furiously.

Theo doesn't need to answer. He spots a train ahead, zipping along a track from left to right. It extends far into the distance, dozens upon dozens of carriages linked together and blocking the road.

"Don't even think about it!" shouts Ellie, but Theo's already made up his mind. He doesn't slow down, doesn't hit the brakes. He keeps going, the train looming closer. Behind, the two cars slow, expecting us to plummet straight into the side of the train and send it crashing off its tracks.

But we don't. Timed to perfection, the car zooms through a gap between two carriages, shooting straight through onto the other side and leaving our pursuers stuck behind thousands of tonnes of moving metal.

We all let out a cheer as we hit the tarmac. "That'll slow 'em!" roars Link, reaching forward and shaking Theo's shoulder. "Nice one!"

"It's not over yet," Theo responds, eyes still keen and stuck to the road. Behind us, the train still blocks our pursuers, stretching far into the distance. Through the gaps in the carriages I can see them, turning and driving in the opposite direction as the train.

"They're gonna drive around it," I say. "Get off the road or they'll catch up with us again."

I can tell it's already in Theo's mind. He speeds off the road, kicking up dust and dirt as he rumbles over open plains. In the distance I can see hills, covered in green trees, blocking our path inland. It looks just like Lignum, the region Ellie grew up in.

I turn to her and see her eyes glazing over at the sight. The rolling hills, the beautiful, earthy greens and browns, just like the colour of her eyes and hair. I imagine she's thinking of her mother, thinking of home.

A jolt snaps me from my thoughts as we skip over a series of rocks. "Sorry," calls Theo, "that came outta nowhere."

"So how are we gonna get through those hills then?" asks Link, still checking behind us regularly for any sight of a blue glow. "Can we get through those woods in this?"

"Ellie?" I ask.

She shakes her head and turns back to us. "Not likely. It'll be too dense for this. We'll need to get back on the road if we want to go through."

"And do we want to go through?" asks Theo. "I mean, is this the right direction."

"As long as it's inland, yeah. We can make a better plan when we rest for the night."

No one says anything in response to me. Maybe they're regretting being here after the morning we've had. I wouldn't blame them for that. There's even a part of me that thinks I should have just stayed in Eden. Jackson could be anywhere beyond the Divide. There's thousands of square miles of nothing out there. *How the hell do I expect to track him down?*

Theo slows the car as we near the wooded hills, before stopping entirely behind a formation of rocks. The howling of the wind abruptly ends, the world suddenly falling silent. We listen for a moment, but hear no sirens in pursuit, no vehicles following. We've lost them, for now, but that won't be the end of it.

"We need to change vehicles," says Theo. "They'll be tracking this one now. Ellie, ready to play dead on the road again?"

Ellie nods. "Always."

We drive on a little, searching for a minor road where we might be able to catch another fly. After another 10 minutes, we come across a narrow track that winds down from the hills. Theo stops at the side of the road, and we all step out. "Pretend you've broken down," he says. "We'll do the rest."

Leaving Ellie by the car, we creep off into the thicket to hide. It doesn't take long for us to hear the sound of a car rumbling along. This time, however, it's not a hovercar but an old fashioned one with wheels. It's larger, too, beaten up and tattered. A truck, similar to the sort I'm used to seeing back home.

Ellie does her job well, picking on yet another Good Samaritan. This time it's a couple of men who Ellie won't be able to subdue. As they go about figuring out what's wrong with our fully functioning car, however, the rest of us sneak inside theirs. All Ellie has to do is dart off when the two men aren't looking and jump on as we rumble off into the hills.

I feel a little bad for stealing another car, but we have no alternative. It's only temporary, and I'm sure the vehicles will get back to their owners eventually.

For the next few hours, we make good progress, though, despite the far slower top speed in this tin can. We pass hills and woods, rivers and waterfalls, just like on my initial journey out of Arbor all those months ago. I'm reminded of those days, when everything was constantly changing around me. Of how far I've come, we've all come, in only a few short months. It seems like a lifetime.

Day soon fades to night, the sun dipping below the hills and smothering the green tops of the trees in a celestial orange hue. The woods thin around us, and Theo cruises off the road into the darkening bosk. When we're far enough in, he stops the engine, and the world falls silent.

"So," he says "this is the sort of thing that happens on the mainland is it?" He turns around to look at us, a flippant smirk on his face. "I think I'll go home now."

We all laugh, despite the day we've had. Sometimes, there's nothing else you can do. So that's what we do. We laugh, and tell jokes, and build a small fire. We cook some food and sit together, like four friends on a camping trip, and for the first time in our lives feel completely free.

We enjoy it while we can. Because underneath it all we know that tomorrow, when the sun climbs over the horizon, things are only going to get worse.

27
The Mainland

A small group of men run through the dirt, keeping low to the ground. They carry weapons at their shoulders, move in a tight formation. Their clothing is old and weathered, their mouths and heads covered in black rags to protect against the billowing sand.

The dust swirls around them, kicked up by the wind, obscuring their vision ahead. Gradually, a shadow looms in the distance, standing high into the air, built of thick rock and metal. The men keep moving, darting quickly across the desert, until they reach the face of the palisade.

One searches the stones, feeling with his hands along the surface. Then he stops and presses hard, and a single rock moves deeper into the wall. There's an immediate cough of smoke, and then the grinding of stone against stone as a small door slides open. The men step inside, one by one, disappearing into the blackness.

The man who pushed on the stone is the last to enter. Before he does he turns, looking back out towards the desert, and I see his eyes, only his eyes. They flash blue, squinting in the sun, and then he turns and fades into the darkness beyond.

Jackson.

I wake, my eyes opening in a flash. I hear light breathing around me as the others sleep under the night sky. Our fire has burned itself out, only a few glowing embers remaining that give off a faint orange light.

In it I see Theo, eyes shut, chest gently moving up and down. I look for Link, who's on the other side of the fire. His back is turned to me, but I can hear the rumble of his breath as he sleeps. Finally, I guide my eyes to Ellie. She isn't sleeping. Instead her eyes are wide and unblinking, her green irises glinting under the pale moonlight.

"You're awake?" I say. She seems to snap out of a trance. "What are you thinking about?"

She turns her eyes to mine, a grave look on her face. "Today," she says. "About what happened at the dock."

A sudden wave of guilt fills me. "I'm sorry about that. For dragging you and Link into this."

"No Cy, it's not that," she whispers, crawling a little closer to me. "I chose to come with you, you can't blame yourself if anything happens to us. It's not down to you."

"But all of this, it's all about me, about finding Jackson. None of you should be punished for that. Or worse," I add.

"It's about finding Jackson for you. But for the rest of us, it's about freedom. Don't you see that?"

"Freedom? But how can we ever be free if we're always running? It's no life, Ellie."

"And being a Watcher of Eden is? I'd rather take

my chances here. We can find Jackson and then disappear, just the five of us. No rules, no duties. Just us, together."

I had no idea she felt like that. That she believed all of that was possible. Beyond finding Jackson, I've spared little thought as to what we'd do after. In truth, I've only ever been taking this step by step, never quite knowing where my feet would land next. But freedom. Disappearing. I like the sound of those words.

I feel a weight lift from my shoulders. The thought that Ellie, and perhaps even Link, are enticed by the thought of freedom is liberating, unshackling me from my guilt of dragging them out here with me.

"So...what about the docks then?" I ask. "What's troubling you?"

"Well, Victoria Rock isn't a big town. It's tiny, actually. I can understand there being security at the port, but why were there five other Custodians there with automatic weapons?"

"Maybe they were passing through? Or maybe Knight's beefing up security along the shore for whatever reason. The entire military is being expanded, Ellie. Down on the military level on Eden there were stocks and stocks of munitions and military vehicles. Maybe it's the same on the coast."

"Maybe," says Ellie, thinking. "I just think it's too coincidental. Like they knew we'd be there."

The thought strikes me like lightning. "You think another Watcher saw it happen?"

Ellie nods. "I think someone saw us attacking those two guards, so they had reinforcements ready.

I guess, had it been anyone else, they'd have caught us. But then Link goes and takes them out."

"But they won't know it's us will they?" I ask.

She shakes her head. "They will, Cyra. When they realise the four of us are gone they will. Only a Watcher could have done what Link did, what Theo did when he drove through those train carriages. They'll be coming after us now. All eyes will be on us."

Her words are portentous, sending a shiver running up my spine. "Then we have to get across the Divide as soon as possible. Then we'll be out of reach."

I watch her now as she scans the woods around us, her green eyes piercing through the darkness. I wonder if she's been up all night, keeping watch. It's not something any of us thought of, to take it in turns to keep lookout. Perhaps she's the wisest of us all.

"You should get some sleep, Ellie," I say. "You look tired. Have you slept yet?"

She shakes her head vacantly, still searching the trees. "Not yet. I thought I saw something before, through the trees down the hill. Then it went away, but I haven't been able to sleep since."

"What was it?"

"Just a shadow moving in the darkness. A bear, I think."

The thought of encountering a bear hadn't even crossed my mind. Or wolves for that matter. With us now fugitives of Eden, I suppose the beasts in the woods were the least of my concerns. Not Ellie though. She grew up in a place like this. Her mother was killed by a bear. And suddenly I know why she hasn't been able to sleep.

"You should get some shut eye, Ellie. I'll stay awake and keep watch, OK?"

She's still staring out into the gloom, but nods lightly, before settling her head down onto her bag. For a while she just lies there, eyes open, before slowly her lids slide shut and fail to reopen.

I fall into my own thoughts as I sit up and begin my vigil. *Freedom*. It's not something I expected to hear from Ellie. But then, what other choice is there now? We're deserters. Such a thing is punishable by banishment, or worse. So when they catch up with us, will they simply discard us onto the other side of the Divide anyway? There would be some irony in that, I suppose.

Something tells me, however, that things won't be quite so easy. We all possess special gifts. We've been told that by Ajax on more occasions than I can remember. Rare gifts. Powerful gifts. Gifts that make us important. With so few Watchers, we won't be considered so expendable. So we'll be forced to keep watch somewhere. Chained, drugged maybe, and compelled to live out death and destruction in our dreams each night.

Yet what's the difference? We'd have been condemned to such a life anyway. Perhaps we'd have more freedom and privileges. The opportunity to enjoy the city or region we're assigned to. To go to social functions and dinners and have a life beyond our visions. But at the end of the day, it all comes down to the same thing. Whether we'd have stayed in Eden or get caught here now, we're all still slaves of the system. Assets. Nothing more.

A stirring by the fire snaps me out of my thoughts.

I turn to see Theo, sitting bolt upright, his eyes open and suddenly wide awake. He glances all around us at the woods, completely alert, as if awakened by a gunshot.

His eyes find mine and he speaks, whispering in the dim light.

"We have to leave."

"What's going on?" I say, my heart beginning to pound.

"They're coming. I've seen them, their lights in the darkness. They're searching for us. They know we're here."

I turn in every direction now, quickly rising to my feet. I see nothing out in the woods, though. Nothing but the shadows of trees, rising up high into the air.

"Wake them up. We have to go."

I watch as Theo jumps to his feet, grabs his bag, and darts towards the truck. Within a moment I hear the engine rumble, disturbing the silent night, and begin to chug lightly. Headlights burn bright into the darkness, illuminating the eerie woods ahead, before quickly being doused.

I don't even need to wake Link or Ellie myself. The sound of Theo starting the truck is enough to send their eyes opening like an owl's, wide and unblinking. "What's happening?" Link asks. He looks all around us, searching for an enemy, for any sign of danger.

"Theo says they're coming. Searching the woods. We need to go, right now."

Ellie goes to stamp out the final glowing embers of the fire, but I stop her. "Leave it as a decoy," I say, before we all rush towards the truck and jump inside.

I join Theo at the front, who doesn't hesitate to move as soon as we're in. With the lights off, he slowly drives through the forest, steering around trees and fallen branches and back towards the road.

I stare in the wing mirror and see flashes of light behind us suddenly appear in the gloom. Of armed guards, moving through the thicket, approaching our dying fire from down the hill. There are at least ten lights, each swaying in a different direction. *They're searching for us.*

The road ahead comes into sight, a gap among the shadows of the trees. Theo speeds up and we break through the blanket of foliage above, straight out into the glowing moonlight. Behind, I hear calls, voices shouting, and notice all lights turning our way. Some point down to the ground, following our tyre tracks. Others shine through the trees, searching the forest beyond.

But it's too late. We're already onto the road, accelerating down the other side of the hill. Around us, the woods remain thick, the road ahead winding to the left and right, limiting our view.

"You saw them?" shouts Link from behind us. "Did they have transport?"

I see Theo shake his head. "I only saw them coming with their lights, carrying guns. They looked the same as the guards at the dock. They must have known we were hiding somewhere in the woods, but didn't know the exact place."

"Probably thought they'd catch us napping."

"No such luck."

We drive faster, the road ahead beginning to straighten out. Beyond, it diverges, several other tracks leading off in various directions.

"We need to get off this road in case they're following," I say. "Take the left one."

"Why left?" asks Theo.

"Why not?" I respond. "It's not like we know where we're going anyway."

Theo does what I say, pulling to the left and down a narrower track surrounded by overhanging trees. We drive for a while in almost total darkness, too afraid to put on the main headlights, using the moonlight as our guide. Gradually, however, the woods begin to thin, until we enter a large swathe cut down and with nothing but stumps remaining.

"It's just like Lignum," Ellie says. "We must be somewhere in the region."

We pass a small town, hidden in a valley below us, a track leading to it from the road. A single light blazes in the middle of a small square, surrounded by wooden shacks. It looks more like an outpost than a town. Perhaps somewhere Choppers stay when they're working in the area.

Other similar outposts and settlements appear,

peppered among the huge fields of tree trunks and giant piles of wood. We drive for a couple of hours, taking various turns where we can but always aiming to travel westwards. And all the time, our eyes scans the path behind us, the horizon ahead, searching for any hint of our pursuers.

Eventually, the skies begin to brighten, lighting up the blanket of grey mist that hovers at the tops of the hills. Cars begin to appear on the roads, small towns and forest camps spring to life in the valleys and higher up on the hillside. We keep moving, gradually leaving the rolling slopes and forests and descending onto flatter lands stretching miles into the distance.

We drive for several hours, always wary of any vehicle that passes us or lingers too long at our rear. On several occasions, we slide down quieter paths and hide in the shadows of old, disused buildings and factories, driven off by the glowing sight or screaming noise of a blue siren on the horizon. Each time, however, we watch as they pass by, in pursuit of someone else or called to resolve a problem somewhere nearby.

By midday, we're all exhausted and starving, so stop in an old barn for some food. By chance, we stumble across another car, keys handily stashed in the flap above the driver's seat. When we get moving again, we leave our truck and continue in a battered and rusted old station wagon, our progress slowed further by its plodding top speed.

We pass by miles of old, desolate ruins. Old cities, once filled with people and busy with industry, now stricken and bare and lifeless. Ravaged by war and the virus that sunk its teeth into half the people across the nation.

Crumbling buildings stand high into the sky, their once proud outer walls now covered in moss and vines and retaken by nature. Old cars litter the streets, blocking off roads and forcing us to deviate our path.

All eyes scan the world around us, shocked at the bleakness and devastation of it all. "I didn't know there were places like this on this side of the Divide," says Ellie. By the looks on everyone's faces, they didn't either.

"Except the Graveyard," I say. "It's just as empty, isn't it? I guess there aren't enough people to sustain cities as large as this now."

We drive on, passing other smaller towns that appear to suffer from the same affliction. Empty, lonely, no sight or sound of a living soul for miles. Large factories stand tall, once important production centres in the region. Now they sit bare and abandoned, long fallen into disuse.

"I guess we must be getting close to the Divide," says Theo. "All of these places must have been hit hardest by the fighting. All the functioning regions are nearer to the coast."

"Well, if that's the case we should stop and rest. We should be safe here. Looks like there are plenty of places to stay out of sight."

We search for a little while before finding an old deserted town in the middle of an open plain. The place is largely intact, though, with several beautiful farmhouses bordering its outskirts. I'm reminded of Jackson's home back in Arbor. Of the timber panel walls, painted white. The slanted roof and brick chimney. The veranda at the front. Only here, the wood is rotting. The paint stripping. The beams threatening to break down and collapse.

We find a suitable house and park the car undercover and out of sight. As we step out I can already feel the heat increasing as we move inland, the air warm and close and clammy. Up in the heavens the skies start to rumble, the clouds descending and trapping the heat and humidity below.

We quickly move into the house, its insides bare and stripped of furniture, and have a quick forage for food. There's nothing. We move upstairs, hoping perhaps to find a comfortable bed or two for the night, but it's empty.

I hear Ellie call from below and find her outside at the back of the house, peeking out of a trap door. I follow her down a short ladder and find a shelter of some kind. It's cooler down here, and there are a couple of sofas, so we call the boys down to join us.

"Must be a bomb shelter," says Link.

"Or a hurricane shelter," adds Ellie.

"Well, whatever it is it works for me," I say.

A growl of thunder booms overhead as we start peeling the morph masks from our faces and stash them in our bags. Then we conduct another quick search for rations in the cupboards and shelves built into the walls of the shelter. Aside from a couple of old tins of beans, there's little on offer.

"We'll need to scout for food if we're going to cross Knight's Wall tomorrow," says Theo. "I'd imagine finding some here will be easier than there."

"And how exactly are we going to do that?" Link asks bluntly. It's become obvious over the course of the day that he's grown surly and disgruntled. Perhaps because of a lack of sleep. More likely due to our current predicament.

"Well, we'll spread out and check different houses. There's gotta be plenty of food around here. Tinned maybe, but it's better than nothing..."

"No, I mean how are we gonna get across the damn wall! We've got guards on our tail and we're heading towards the most heavily militarised area in the country. There are loads of bases along the Divide, and tens of thousands of soldiers manning it. So, how are we gonna get across?" There's a bite to his words that I know is intended for me. His eyes even flash on me as he asks the question. Despite what Ellie said, I know none of this is what Link wants. He, unlike the rest of us, would rather be back in Eden.

"We'll scout it and find a way across. It stretches for hundreds of miles. There must be some weak, unmanned points."

Link huffs. "Yeah, you think so? Well there ain't. The thing is several storeys high and there are no breaks. Nothin'."

"We'll find a way," says Theo. "We've gotten this far, haven't we?"

"This far was easy. Now we're choosing self

banishment, and for what?" He turns to me, head shaking. "Do you even think he's alive, Cyra? And where is he if he is? There's a million square miles out there. We could live a thousand lifetimes and never find him."

"Hey," says Theo, stepping forward and pulling Link's attention back on him. "Leave her alone. She never asked you to come. If you want to go back, go back. I just never figured you for a coward."

"A coward?" Link's eyes begin burning, his breathing starting to grow more heavy. "*You* are calling *me* a coward?"

"What do you mean by that?" Now it's Theo's turn to boil, his eyes narrowing.

"I mean you've been a coward from day one in the Grid. You couldn't cut it down there..."

"Yeah, and you can't cut it now!" Theo bites. "You want to go back to Eden, then go back. Go be a lapdog to Ajax and Knight and everyone else."

They stand against each other, fists clenching, teeth grinding, eyes piercing. A rumble of thunder shakes the house above us, but no one moves.

Then I see Link's lips curl into a smile, a sneer spreading across his face. "She'll never love you, you know. Do you even know who Jackson is to her? You'll be discarded as soon as she finds him."

"What are you talking about?" snaps Theo.

"I've seen the way you look at her. She doesn't look at you the same way."

Theo shakes his head and laughs awkwardly. "I don't know what you've seen, but you're way off base..."

"No, I'm not," whispers Link, drawing even closer as he lowers his voice. "This isn't gonna end well for you, Theo. Best you run back to mummy and daddy right now."

It's the final straw. Theo swings, his fist as fast as lightning, but not quick enough. Link deflects it with his arm, reaching forward and clasping Theo's throat with his spare hand. He pushes and drives him back against the wall, smacking it with a thud as another rumble of thunder booms overhead.

Ellie and I are quick to act, shouting for them to stop, rushing forward and pulling at Link's arms. But he's too strong, too big. He shrugs us both off and the two men go crashing to the ground with another heavy bump.

Fists fly as they roll on the floor. I hear more thuds and boom of lighting. Blood begins spilling as we continue to attempt to separate them, dripping from noses and split eyebrows.

They finally split, both panting and breathing heavily, primed to pounce once more.

Then I hear more thuds. But none of us are moving.

Dust falls from above, accompanied by the sound of creaking wood. We all raise our eyes and listen. Footsteps. Above us. And we freeze.

Then I see it. I don't know what it is at first, and by the time I work it out it's too late. The sight of a wispy white cloud, filling the air at our feet and quickly rising. My mind clicks into gear, but it's too late.

"Gas!" I cry.

A cannister rips through the wooden door at the top of the ladder. It hits the floor and stops in place, before sliding open and releasing a thick, green cloud. We all lift our sleeves to our mouths and hold our breath, but there's nothing we can do.

Thick, putrid fumes slip up my nose, burning the inside of my nostrils. My eyes water, my vision blurring, but I try to hold my breath. I step gingerly forward, and hear the sound of bodies slumping to the floor behind me. I turn and see both Link and Theo, still catching their breath from their exertions, fall first. Ellie drops to Link's side, hand over her mouth, eyes beginning to well.

She shakes her head as she looks at me, before sucking in a breath. The result is immediate, her body going limp, her head falling onto Link's chest.

Now it's just me. Inside, my lungs burn, my head spins. I can't hold on, have to breathe. I step forward, my body already weak, and reach up the ladder. I rise a step, then two, and remember nothing more.

28

An Old Friend

Heat.

It's all I feel.

Warm, clammy air licking at my skin, filling my nose. It's suffocating, smothering my entire body in a sweltering blanket.

My eyes open to the sight of bare brick walls. A dim light shines above me, buzzing quietly and casting a faint glow on my surroundings. I'm on a small bed in a corner of a cell, cast iron bars rising from the concrete floor and into the ceiling. Beyond, I see a corridor, and another cell on the other side.

I sit up and drop my feet to the hard floor, my head spinning. I reach back and touch the back of my skull. A large swelling protrudes from its surface, aching horribly. I stagger a bit as I move towards the bars, winding my fingers around them and peering out into the corridor outside. There, to the left and right, I see cell after cell, stretching off into the darkness.

I call out, my voice croaking and cracking.

"Ellie! Theo! Link!"

I hear no reply. I strain my vision, but see no people in the other cells. No one calls back except my own voice, echoing down the empty corridor.

"Hello!" I call. "Can somebody hear me?! Is someone there?"

I shout several times, my words ringing in my head like tiny knives picking at my brain. Yet still there's no reply. No voice. No sound of footsteps approaching. Nothing but the endless buzzing of the light above me.

I return to my bed and return to my thoughts. The gas. The shelter. We were caught like flies in a web, so easily tracked and discovered in the end. How stupid was I to think it would be any different.

My head continues to throb, my vision still slightly blurred. I continue to rack my brain for the last thing I can remember – climbing that ladder. I was up one step, then two, and then nothing. I had to breathe. Had to suck in that poison. Then everything went immediately black.

I must have fallen back to the floor, hit my head. I feel a slight ache in my back, a stiffness in my neck. But it's all muted, all drowned out by the lingering scent of gas in my veins.

Darkness begins to overcome me again and I start drifting in and out of consciousness. Each time I close my eyes, I see flashes of orange and yellow and red. Flashes of blowing sand and the hard, parched earth. Of the high fortress wall, standing like a bastion against the broken world beyond. Of men, tiny atop it, lights flashing from the tips of their weapons.

Each time I wake, my mind is filled with another horror. A young man's leg being blown off. Bullets ripping through flesh. Faces of fear, exposed to the terror of battle. But one strikes at me more than any other. The sight of a blanket of fire engulfing thousands of men, all burning against the blood red, setting sun.

I open my eyes a final time, the drug now wearing thin in my blood. My mouth feels parched, my throat dry and sore, my head still throbbing lightly. Hours must have passed, but I don't know how many. Down here, in this strange dungeon, there's little to tell me whether it's late or early, night or day.

"You're awake?"

The voice comes from behind me, and I quickly turn to look into the room. In the corner is a shadow, the shape of a man, sitting on a stool, watching over me. He's shrouded in darkness, dressed in a cloak. I can't make out his features, but recognise his voice.

He stands and moves towards me, stepping under the buzzing light. It falls on him like a spotlight, illuminating his face, his eyes, his shining blond hair.

I think I must be dreaming, still caught inside my own imagination. He continues forward and kneels ahead of me, a bright smile arching across his golden face.

"Jackson," I whisper, my voice nothing more than a croak. I shake my head in disbelief, raising my hand to his face. *Is he real? Is this just a dream?*

"It's me," he says. "You're safe now."

"But...how? It was you? In the shelter?"

He nods, rolling his fingers through my hair,

feeling the bump at the back of my head. "I'm sorry about the way we did it. The gas was a knock-out agent. They wanted all of you to come without a fight."

"The others...they're OK?"

"They're fine, all of them. They're being kept separately for now."

It's only now that I glance to the front of the cell. Behind the bars stand two guards. They hold automatic weapons, wear dark brown desert clothing and armour.

"Where are we?" I whisper, finding it hard to catch up. "I thought I'd been caught by Eden."

"We're in a free city, Cyra. Miles beyond the Divide."

"Beyond the Divide? But...how?" I stare at my surroundings again, as if they'll give me some indication. I knew I wasn't back on Eden, not in a place like this. But beyond the Divide; how could that have happened? And why is Jackson helping the rebels?

"I'll explain everything soon," says Jackson, his eyes smiling and shining blue. "But first..."

He pulls me in for a hug, squeezing me tighter than ever before. His hands run over my back, fingers pressing hard against my flesh. "I saw you," I say into his ear, my eyes beginning to well. "I saw you from Eden. You were injured, lying in a basement. I can see things Jackson, visions of the future..."

He pulls back, but there's no surprise in his face. "I

know," he says. "You're a Watcher."

"You...know what I am, what I can do?"

That's impossible. How could he know? How did he find me?

"The rebels have them too, Cyra – Watchers. One saw you and your friends. We knew where to find you. I can't explain it. I don't understand it. But as soon as I heard, I had to come get you."

I think of my vision the other night. Of the men moving through the secret door in the stone. It *was* Jackson. He knew where the secret passage was through Knight's Wall. Only he knew how to open it.

"You're working with them?" I ask, glancing back at the guards outside the cell. I lower my voice, lean in close. "We have to get out of here," I whisper. "We have to save the others and escape."

Jackson twists his neck and looks at the guards. They talk between themselves, apparently oblivious to what we're saying. Then he turns back to me, his eyes like steel.

"There's no escape from here, Cyra. It's safer here. You can't go back."

"What do you mean? What's happening Jackson? Tell me the truth."

Jackson glances again at the guards, before moving to sit next to me on the bed.

Then he starts talking, telling me his story. How he came to be here. His experience with the rebels. His journey to find me, to save me.

He was caught in an ambush, he tells me, during a

routine patrol. During his time training he had learned that rebel attacks had died down over the last few years. Yet there was talk of an uprising, of forces massing far beyond the Divide. That those in power knew that something was coming and that's why the military was being expanded.

He learned of the Watchers through rumour among the soldiers. People whispered of them, these people who could see things that were yet to come. Word spread that the wall was being prepared for war, that something unseen was coming.

Patrols were ordered to scout the parched earth beyond the Divide. They'd go deep, searching for rebels, but would never find any. That was, until Jackson's unit were ambushed. He was caught in an explosion, shrapnel cutting into his abdomen and arm. He thought he was going to die, his life cut short out there on the wasteland.

But he didn't die. He woke in a basement, a woman tending him. Every day a man came and spoke with him. The cloaked man. The man I saw in the vision, sitting on a chair in the corner of the room.

He wanted information. Information about the new fortifications, about any weak points along the Divide, about the number of soldiers being trained. But Jackson said nothing. He kept his mouth shut, expecting them to torture him and interrogate him. But they never did.

He recovered quickly, but was kept in a cell. The man kept coming, kept asking questions. Not just of the military, but of life in the regions. Eventually,

Jackson began to speak. Not of the military, but of home. They'd talk for hours about the disparity of life. Of the Duty Call and Pairing. Of the strict rationing and the hardships that those on the mainland face on a daily basis.

Jackson learned about the rebels. Learned how the old urban legends of barbarism and cannibalism were untrue. Those legends that parents would tell their kids, who'd then tell their own kids when they grew up. Urban legends spread down from Eden to make people fear the rebels. To make banishment sound like the worst punishment imaginable, all so that kids would grow up behaving and never questioning their lot in life. All a system of control to keep the regions in order.

Yet the banished were always taken in. Picked up by the rebels, they'd be cared for and join the free people, starting a life without boundaries and restrictions. A life of fairness and equality in their joint fight for survival.

Gradually, leaders came together from the ashes of war. The virus that was thought to have wiped them all out left them only scattered and divided. Years passed, however, and they began to unite, their numbers swelling.

"Up there, there are thousands of them. Tens of thousands. Just here, in this city," says Jackson, his voice rising with passion. "And there are others, Cyra. Other cities, other settlements spread across the country. This war is coming, and it's real. Nothing's going to stop it."

"I know it's real," I say. "I've seen it."

My words have an immediate impact on Jackson, his eyes narrowing, his ears pricking up. I'm reminded of when I first told Ajax about the army beyond Knight's Wall, out on the Deadlands.

"You've seen what?"

"I've seen an army outside the Divide. Back in Eden, it's all they wanted to know about. Chancellor Knight questioned me on it. They're desperate to know where the rebels will strike."

"And what did you tell them?" he asks quickly.

"Nothing. All I ever saw was a random part of Knight's Wall. I had no details to give."

"And Knight. You've met him?"

I nod. "A few times. He made out you were dead, Jack. Just so I'd commit to my training, commit to Eden. That's why I came to find you. I saw you in my visions. I needed to know the truth."

"He knows who I am? But why do I matter?"

"Because you matter to me. He was using your death to make me let go, all so I'd see clearer visions of the attack."

A pensive look rises over Jackson's face. "So it was you? You were the Watcher who saw the army? That's why the military is being expanded?"

I shake my head. "No, that makes no sense. The military was being expanded before I ever left for Eden."

"So there's someone else. Another Watcher must have known about it. There's no other explanation."

Jackson stands now, and turns towards the guards. "Open it up," he says, and they do as ordered. And there's me thinking he was a captive here. It looks more like he's been fully enlisted to the rebel cause.

As the barred door opens with a metallic squeak, Jackson steps towards me, lifts me to my feet, and hugs me once more. "I'm sorry to leave like this. There's so much more to say." He runs his fingers over my palms, as he used to back home, and kisses me on the cheek. "But I have to report in. I'm acting as liaison with you and your friends."

"You've met them?" I ask.

"Not yet. But I will. Don't worry, Cy, you won't be down here for long. It's just a precaution. Get some more rest. I'll be back soon."

With that, he turns, and begins marching quickly down the corridor, flanked by the two guards. I hear the grind of a heavy door around the corner, which closes with a thud, and then the entire floor falls silent once more.

29
Leaders

I'm shaken out of a nightmare. One filled with the sight of men burning, screaming as their bodies are blanketed in flame. Thousands of them, scorched by the breath of the devil.

Jackson's eyes peer down on me, glowing blue in the dim light. "It's time to go, Cyra. They want to see you."

I'm lifted groggily to my feet, my head still swimming, and step out of the cell. Once more there are two guards waiting outside. They allow Jackson and I to pass before following in behind us.

"Are they your personal escort or something?" I ask.

Jackson laughs. "Not exactly. They're more my protection against you lot."

"Protection. You don't need protection."

"Not against you maybe. But the others, we weren't sure."

I glance back at the guards. "You know, if Link or Theo wanted to get past you they would. I take it they were cooperative?"

"Well, you could say that. Ellie was nice."

We reach the end of the corridor and pass through the heavy metal door. Beyond is a staircase that winds up past several other floors, each of them filled with long corridors and cramped cells.

"Sorry for keeping you down here, Cy. It wasn't my idea. I told them you could be trusted, but they're a little skittish right now."

"And who's they?"

"The Leaders. The people running this show. They're scared of Knight's spies."

"Well, we're not spies, I can assure you of that."

"I think it was Theo they were more worried about. You know, being the son of two Councillors."

"That means nothing," I say, slightly defensively. "We all wanted out of that place, him as much as anyone."

Jackson makes a sound of agreement, but doesn't look overly convinced.

After half a dozen floors we emerge into a large open hall. Inside are hundreds of people, sitting around eating at tables. A line forms against a long counter at the end where food is served onto trays. It reminds me of the canteen at school, only much larger.

The people are covered in tatty clothing, similar to back home in Arbor. I suppose, after living in Eden, everything seems slightly worse now outside of the city. Slightly more gritty and grubby. The clothes, the food, the cracked walls and faded paint. Yet there's a buzz in the air. One of excitement. Of hope and promise. One that only freedom can bring.

"I had no idea there were functioning towns and

cities in the Deadlands," I say, staring around at men and women and children of all ages and races. "Back home we're taught that it's nothing but scavengers and cannibals."

"Nor did I. You quickly understand their cause when you're exposed to it. I don't think Eden wants the general public to know. These people are just like us, Cyra. They used to be our countrymen. I suppose if the people across the regions really knew the truth, they might not be so compliant."

We pass out the back and into the open air. Buildings rise above me, stretching down rubble strewn streets. Many are caved in and destroyed, many others remain largely intact. Around one is a contingent of guards. Men and women dressed in armour and carrying heavy automatic weapons.

We move towards it and are ushered inside. Once more, I get some odd looks from the guards outside. It's something I've well and truly gotten used to by now.

The space within is no different from anywhere else I've seen. It's crumbling and broken, the walls and ceilings gradually being retaken by nature. We move through the large lobby of what seems to be an old hotel, before continuing through into the back. We pass more guards as we go, staring with their inquisitive, watchful eyes.

"Ignore the stares," whispers Jackson. "They're just wary of anyone from the other side of the Divide."

"And especially from Eden," I say.

Jackson dips his head but doesn't answer. The idea

that these people really think I come from Eden is mildly insulting. I guess, now that my blonde hair has faded and golden skin grown more pale, I look more like one of them.

We walk down another corridor before appearing in an open room. Here it seems more intact, an old banquet room used for special occasions. Large and open and ornately decorated with stone sculptures on the walls and moth-eaten drapes hanging from the ceiling.

Jackson guides my eyes to the far end, where three people sit on simple wooden chairs. Each wears a cloak that obscures their face, patiently awaiting my arrival.

"They want to speak with you alone, Cyra. Go to them. I'll be right outside."

He runs his fingers over my palm and then leaves the room, the two guards leaving with him. I turn back to the three Leaders and begin walking towards them. None of them speak as I go. None of them move. They just wait as I approach, the echoes of my footsteps bouncing around the walls as I get closer.

"So this is the girl with the vision," says the man on the left. His words ring out and stop me in my tracks, ten metres away from them.

"Your name is Cyra Drayton, is that right?" he continues.

I nod.

"And tell us, why were you and your friends so far from Eden?"

I swallow hard and find my voice. "I came for Jackson, sir. I was told in Eden that he had been killed. Then I saw him in a vision, wounded but alive. I...I came to rescue him," I admit.

"Thank you for your candour," says the Leader in the middle. A woman, her voice tender but firm. "But Jackson needs no rescuing."

"I understand that now, ma'am."

The woman nods, but her features remain obscured beneath her hooded cloak.

"Jackson told us you've had visions of an army outside the Divide. Our army. What have you seen?" It's the woman once again. The Leader on the right has yet to speak, but looks to be a man by his size and shape.

"I've seen the vision for months, ma'am. I saw Knight's Wall and soldiers on top of it. There was fighting, gunfire, explosions. Then, beyond the wall on the Deadlands in the distance, there was an army, led by a man in a cloak."

The three Leaders turn to each other. "When did you first see this?" asks the Leader on the left.

"When I first arrived in Eden more than three months ago."

"So you've seen a long way through both time and space. You must be gifted."

"So I'm told."

"And you've seen the same vision since?"

"Yes, but mainly in fragments, sir. Is that your plan? To attack the wall?" I ask. I know I'm speaking out of turn, but I don't care right now.

They share looks again, and then the woman answers. "We have discovered a weak point that we will target. We intend to strike secretly and without warning. Yet...you say you've seen fighting?"

"Yes, ma'am. Fighting, death, destruction. And...fire. I've seen thousands of men blanketed in fire."

"Our men?"

I nod. "I think so. They all die."

"Then we are to call off the attack." The Leader on the right speaks for the first time, his voice cutting through the air like a scythe, deep and penetrating.

"Call it off?" says the other man, turning to him. "We've planned this for months, years. We can't call it off now."

"There's no other choice. If what Cyra says is true, we'll be walking into a trap. Knight has some powerful agents at his disposal, we all know that. Who's to say he hasn't worked out where the attack will come, that he hasn't set a trap to destroy us before we even strike? We all know what the man is capable of."

"Yes, but this is our one chance. How can we let it pass? If we strike right now, we can penetrate and overcome their weaker bases. We know they're still fitting out the military and recruiting more soldiers. Most of them are young, only partially trained. They're not hardened or experienced. Now is the time to strike..."

"But you can't!" I shout, my words breaking their debate, dragging all eyes back onto me. "You can't kill them. They're good people, they didn't ask for any of this!"

I think of Jackson being dragged away for service along with plenty of others from my school. How it must have been the same all over Agricola, all over Fossor and Lignum and the other regions. "They're just kids, you can't kill them!"

"This is war, Miss Drayton," calls the Leader on the left. "Casualties are part of it."

"No! You'll die and they'll die if you go. I've seen it."

"You don't even know what you've seen, or where. These visions of yours, they're not real until they happen. They're only possible versions of the future and can be changed. Your testimony will help us greatly, and we thank you for that. But we have no choice. We have to strike."

A silence dawns on the room. I think of Jackson outside, how quickly he's converted to this cause. Is he willing to kill his own people, the people he trained with, went to school with? Young soldiers, dragged from their families, terrified of the threat of looming war. Was it his information that helped them discover the weak spot at which they'll strike? Has he doomed thousands of people to their deaths?

I hear my name and raise my eyes back up to the Leaders. The woman in the middle lifts her hands to her cloak and pulls back her hood. She has greying blonde hair, wizened blue eyes, darkly tanned skin riddled with wrinkles.

"We understand how you feel," she says softly. "Many of us here once lived in the regions, banished for minor crimes. We know the people there are good. We know that they're innocent. And that is why we're trying to free them, Cyra. We're not conquerors or invaders, we're liberators. We will not kill needlessly and it pains us to have to take such drastic steps. But they are steps that must be taken."

"Needlessly?" I ask, letting out a breath of air. "And what about the Graveyard? What about all the thousands who died from the nuclear weapon you sent into an innocent city?"

The woman holds up her hand as the man on the left begins his retort, cutting him off. "Is that what you believe? Is that what you've been told?" she asks calmly.

I don't answer for fear I'll say something out of turn. All I do is nod.

"That bomb was not sent by us, Miss Drayton. We had no access to such weapons. It was the work of High Chancellor Knight."

I can't help but screw my face up in disbelief, shaking my head. For all the man's manipulation and elitist policies, he's surely not capable of murdering so many innocent people. Would he really kill his own countrymen? Destroy one of his own cities?

"It may be difficult to understand, but it's the truth," continues the woman, seeing the look on my face. "The bomb brought people together under a common goal when dissent was brewing. It gave the people a reason to hate the rebels, to unite against them."

"But, killing his own people?" I'm still shaking my head. "Not even Knight could do that."

"You've been lied to your entire life, Cyra. The truth is far from what you know, what you've been told. It's true, I can assure you of that."

"And how do you know it's true?" I question.

"Because I was there," she says, her voice impassioned. "I was once of Eden myself. I asked too many questions about the source of the bomb and was banished, sent out beyond the Divide to die. I was taken in, fed, watered, cared for. I discovered a people leaderless and divided, scattered to the winds by the war and the virus that came soon after."

I watch her eyes, and see no lies inside them. Only pain, memory filled with torment and heartache. A single tear drops down her cheek and she quickly raises her hand to brush it away.

"Your ruler is only interested in keeping power for himself, Cyra. Augustus Knight is as ruthless as they come, and will stop at nothing to get what he wants. He's ruled for nearly a hundred years, and has shaped this country as he's seen fit. If we don't stop him, no one will. We have no choice."

Her words hang in the air, and a silence once again dawns. Knight's treachery runs deeper than I'd ever have imagined. But if this is true, surely he's capable of so much more. Surely this entire rebellion is folly....

As I prepare to speak again, my mind filling with a thousand questions, a sudden sound fills the room.

It comes without warning. A loud, ear piercing wail that cuts straight into my brain.

Then there's a heavy thud behind me, and I turn to

see the doors swing open. The wailing siren grows louder and several guards rush forward, guns held up to their shoulders.

"What's happening?" shouts the Leader on the left, standing from his seat.

"We have missiles incoming, sir," shouts one of the guards. "We need to get you all to safety."

"But that can't be! We're hundreds of miles from the Divide!"

The guards continue rushing on towards the Leaders, moving straight past me as if I'm not there. I swing my eyes to the back of the hall and through the open doorway, seeking Jackson. He's there, rushing down the corridor, eyes lit in alarm.

I begin moving towards him as he explodes into the room, his voice calling out so that everyone can hear. "They're coming!" he shouts. "They've found us."

Jackson grabs me by the arms and stares into my eyes. "You have to get underground, Cyra. This place isn't safe."

I turn back to the guards, who are progressing through the hallway, flanking the Leaders as they rush forward. A shaking rises up through my feet, the entire building beginning to tremble as an explosion sounds from outside. Dust falls from above, cracks appear in the walls, and a roar fills the air.

BOOM.

Another explosion rips through the wall on the left, fire pouring in through a gaping hole as the hall jolts and rocks. Jackson's arms rush around me as I watch the Leaders collapse to the floor, driven off their feet by the force of the blast.

"We have to help," I shout, ready to dart forward, but Jackson holds me back.

"No, Cyra, it's not safe!"

Another shock-wave runs up through my body as I rip myself from Jackson's grasp. I can hear him behind me in the roaring din, calling for me to come back.

The guards lift the Leaders to their feet, pulling them on as rubble begins dropping from the ceiling, segments of it torn off by the violence of the explosions around us.

They're 30 metres away and still coming, stumbling over rubble and fallen debris. I watch, unable to help, as a slab of stone comes plummeting down onto one of the guards' heads, crushing his skull in an instant. His body goes immediately limp, dropping to the floor in a heap.

Then I see it. The sight of the ceiling caving in completely, ghostly and crumbling right at my feet. I stop in place, unable to press forward, knowing it's coming. Soon, in seconds, the entire ceiling will collapse.

I scream forward, urging them to rush past me, but it's too late. They're close, so close, only feet from me when the sky comes crashing down. It drops so fast they have no time to react, no time to move or escape.

Tons of concrete and stone come collapsing down on top of them. I watch in horror as they turn their eyes up to see their death looming. Rock meets skull and bone in an explosion of red blood. Bodies are crushed into the stone floor, their screams immediately cut short.

There, in front of my eyes, they're all crushed to death.

30
The War Begins

All are dead but one.

A single Leader remains, the one on the right. He darts off to the side before the ceiling comes down, dodging around broken stone and brick. He moves fast now, his cloak flowing behind him as he goes, miraculously avoiding all falling debris.

I stand, struck dumb as the world falls down around me, staring at the crushed bodies at my feet, at the blood weeping from their burst veins. Then I feel a hand on mine, a voice calling into my ear: "We have to go, Cyra!"

The Leader pulls me back and my mind snaps into focus. I twist around and pace towards the door, towards Jackson. We all rush down the corridor, just as the rest of the building begins to collapse behind us. Dust and smoke fills the air, fire licks at our backs, and an endless rumble continues to shake the foundations of the city.

We burst into the lobby, and see a hive of activity. Guards file out from other rooms in the building, some limping, others bloodied and burnt. They pour through the large front door, weapons ready to fire.

Beyond, outside on the streets, I see a war raging. Soldiers hide behind barriers, firing at an unseen enemy. Artillery guns boom, sending explosive missiles back at the incoming forces. Fire swirls in the wind as explosions rattle the city. Buildings crumble and burst into a thousand bits in the distance, crushing people beneath them as they topple to the ground.

I turn to see Jackson directing people, his face already growing dark with ash and smoke. Then he swings back to me, eyes bulging, and shouts: "we need to get out of here." He turns to the Leader. "We need to get you to safety, sir. Get you to the tunnel."

I grab Jackson's arm, his wide eyes locking again with mine. "The others," I shout, as another explosion rocks the building. "I have to get them out."

Jackson sends his eyes to the entrance, grimacing at the sight of the war zone out on the street. He seems to hesitate, working out what's best perhaps, before speaking. "OK, follow me."

Ducking low, we exit out onto the street, Jackson at the front, the Leader and I just behind. By now the Leader has pulled his cloak from his face, yet his features remain hidden beneath a veil of soot and dust and black ash. All I can make out are his eyes, keen and blue and lit within his dark visage.

The sound outside is cacophonous and deafening. Bullets whiz like fireworks. Missiles shoot with loud rushes of air, pounding into buildings with almighty booms. I see the faces of men and women, screaming in pain and fear and anger, yet fighting on.

Around me my senses grow finely attuned to the danger. Any time a bullet threatens to get near, I see its ghostly form appear seconds before it rushes by. I pull Jackson back just before one rips through his neck, the bullet tearing into the side of a building and ripping off a chunk of brick with a loud crack.

But there's no time to thank me. I see his eyes glow with gratitude but nothing more. He continues on, and we follow, keeping to the side of the street, largely unexposed to the fighting.

Soon we're back at the canteen, rushing through to find families cowering together under tables and up against the walls. The place is shaking, but mainly intact, yet to be hit by the bombing. If it does, though, all these people will die.

The Leader knows this. He steps forward, jumps up onto a table, and calls for the people to retreat, to get to the tunnel. I see scared faces grow with resolve at the sight of him, alive and fearless, standing like a beacon of hope above them. They begin moving, emerging from under their tables, rushing out of the building and further down the street.

"What's the tunnel?" I call to Jackson.

"It's an escape route into the mountains. A contingency in case this ever happened. They told me that it leads for miles to a safe location."

He begins fiddling at his belt, pulling out a set of old fashioned metal keys. "I have to stay with the Leader, to protect him," he shouts. "Your friends are on levels three, four, and five below us."

I nod, snatch the keys from his hands, and quickly

turn towards the door. I rush straight through, kicking it open, and begin galloping down the stairs. One level. Two levels. Three levels.

I turn in and push through another door. Ahead of me lies a long corridor, cells extending into the darkness to the left and right.

"Ellie! Theo! Link!" I call out.

I hear Ellie's voice, echoing from the other end, and rush into the gloom. Tremors run up through me as I go, the floor beginning to shake and rattle. Ellie's face appears, up against the bars of a cell, eyes lit up and wide.

"What the hell's happening?" she shouts as I approach.

"The city's under attack," I say, stuffing the key into the lock and twisting quickly. With a metallic click the barred door falls open and Ellie rushes out.

I hug her briefly. "Are you OK?"

She nods. "I'm fine. Where's Link?"

"On another level below. Come on."

We turn together and run back towards the door, down the stairs, and onto level 4. Ellie calls for Link. I call for Theo. Then we hear a reply, a rugged, course voice in a cell nearby. Link's there, fingers wrapped tightly around the bars. I see his knuckles, bloodied and torn, and know he's been trying to get out.

When I open the cell, Ellie jumps into his arms. They kiss and hug for an all too brief moment before another boom shakes the walls, sending a shower of dust down onto us.

"Link, get Ellie upstairs. Jackson's there with a Leader. We need to get them out to safety."

I begin rushing back to the door as they follow in behind me. "Where are you going?" shouts Link.

"Theo's down below. I need to get him. I'll meet you up top."

My lungs are burning now as I clamber down another level, taking several steps at a time. Once more I enter a long corridor, cells on either side, darkness beyond. I shout out again, this time only for Theo, and hear his voice down the hallway.

"I'm down here, Cyra," he calls as I run towards his voice. When I reach his cell and open the door he bursts forward, arms wrapping straight around me and hugging me tight. I grip him back as the world continues to shake above us, dust sprinkling down from the ceiling.

Then he pulls back and kisses me on the lips. A short kiss, soft and tender yet filled with passion and urgency. I hardly have any time to react before it's over. Yet I don't feel the urge to pull away.

"Sorry, I just didn't want to die without knowing what it's like to kiss a girl," he says. "Not like at the Pairing. I mean, properly kiss a girl."

His smile defies the current state around us. The shaking walls, the ceiling dripping with dust and broken stone, the endless sound of rumbling and explosions above. I can't help but smile back.

Then we start running: back down the corridor, up the stairs, and back into the canteen. All hell has broken loose. The ceiling at the far end has caved in, the searing sun now pouring down from above.

Crushed bodies lie everywhere, unable to flee before the missile tore through the building, sending hundreds of tons of concrete on top of them.

"Cyra!"

Jackson comes rushing towards me, blood trickling from his head. Behind him the others stand, weapons scavenged from dead soldiers in their hands. Link keeps watch at the back, his eyes on the hall, ready to warn us of any falling rubble or stray bullets.

"That's everyone," I shout. "Now where's this tunnel?"

"Down the street. The entrance is in an old subway."

"OK, let's go."

Jackson leads the party once more as we step back out onto the street. Dead bodies lie all around us, ripped apart by bullets or bombs or deadly shrapnel. Behind us, the fighting continues to rage, the city booming with a chorus of explosions and the endless rat-a-tat of machine gun fire.

People flee from all directions as the Leader calls for them to escape to the tunnel. Soldiers run the other way, rushing towards the fighting in defence of the city. Part of me wants to turn and join them. But I know it's all futile. All of these soldiers are going to die.

The streets grow quieter as we get further away, the zipping and fizzing of bullets past our ears fading. Jackson leads us to the right and I see people disappearing underground into the tunnel in the distance, a few hundred feet away from us.

But there are two who aren't moving. Two men, standing still in the middle of the rubble-strewn street. They aren't trying to flee or escape into the tunnel. They're just standing there, tall and upright, staring straight at us.

"STOP!" I shout.

Jackson and the others spin around to me. "What's wrong?!"

I stare forward at the two men ahead. I've seen them before, and they're not from around here.

"They're Watchers," I shout. "I've seen them guarding Knight."

We take a collective intake of air, and I see genuine alarm spread over the faces in front of me. "What the hell are we going to do?!" cries Ellie. "We can't get past *them*."

"Yes we can," says Link, his eyes narrowing. "Theo and I can handle this."

"No Link!" shouts Ellie. "They're fully trained Watchers. You'll have no chance!"

"We have to try," says Link calmly. He turns to Theo, who looks equally determined, and nods.

"Jackson, can you flank around us to get to the tunnel?" asks Link.

Jackson nods. "We can take side streets."

"Then do it. Don't wait for us. When you get around, go straight into the tunnel."

"No, Link!" shouts Ellie. "Just come with us."

Link takes Ellie's face in his palms and kisses her. "They're here for us. We need to make a stand now. Go, Ellie. I can't fight if I'm worried about you."

"Thank you, Link," says Jackson. "Cyra, you're coming with us."

I find all eyes falling on me. Go with Jackson and Ellie and the Leader, help them get to safety? Or make a stand with Theo and Link, and probably get killed or captured in the process?

"Cyra, come on," says Jackson. "We need to go!"

I glance up once more at the two Watchers ahead of us. They stand, patiently, waiting for us to make our move. Jaws like stone, eyes dark as the night, bodies wrapped in black. I have no idea what the limits of their powers are. But I can't leave Theo and Link alone.

"I'm staying here. You go, I'll see you at the tunnel."

"Cyra, no..."

"I have to, Jack! I'm not going to change my mind. I'll see you at the tunnel."

Jackson shakes his head, moves in towards me, and tries to grab my hand and pull me away. I resist, pulling back.

"Go with them, Cyra," says Theo. He turns around, eyes pleading. "Please, help them escape. They might need you."

"You *will* need me," I say.

"Get the Leader to safety. That's more important. Go, Cyra."

He turns back towards the two Watchers and he and Link begin walking forward. I start to go with them, but still feel Jackson holding me back. "Come on, Cyra, there's no time!" he shouts, but I just watch as the two of them walk away. To death or capture. Not to victory.

"Come on, Cy!" shouts Ellie. "Come on!"

I still watch Theo and Link marching forward as I'm dragged away towards an alley by Jackson and Ellie. The two Watchers begin walking forward too, casually strolling towards them. Then, just as they're about to clash in the middle, I'm pulled around the corner and out of sight.

I have to fight the urge to go back now as we rush down the dark alleyway, caught in the shadow of two tall buildings. Jackson urges me to the front to look out for danger as we go, but my mind is all over the place. A section of the wall crumbles in front of us, but I don't see it coming, my focus and concentration shot to pieces. We stop just in time as the wall falls down, clambering over the pile of bricks before more of the building begins tumbling down just as we pass.

"Focus, Cyra!" shouts Ellie behind me.

We carry on, emerging into the light of another wide street and turning left. Ahead now I see more fighting as the soldiers of Eden continue their advance from all angles, enclosing the city in a vice and squeezing tight.

We stay to the side and keep on going, my senses returning to me. White wisps cut through the air in our direction, explosive clouds appear seconds before they turn into reality. I lead the party on, weaving a path through the dangers before they cut us down.

Jackson and the Leader fire as they rush forward,

shooting without mercy at the forces ahead. But in my head all I can think of is school. Boys, only 16, forced out here to do battle against an enemy they've been told awful lies about. Boys from Arbor and Agricola and all across the mainland. Innocent boys with mothers and fathers and brothers and sisters.

I don't shoot. I can't. I dodge through gunfire and turn us back inwards, up another alleyway heading back towards the street we left Theo and Link on. Jackson calls for us to run faster, that the tunnel is just ahead at the end of the alley to the right. We leave the rebel forces fighting, and dying, in the detritus. Bodies falling on either side, the blood of youngsters spilling into the grime.

The light at the end of the alleyway grows fierce, and we burst back out into the blistering heat. The streets are now emptied of fleeing civilians, the entrance to the tunnel close to our right. I don't turn that way, though. I turn left, searching up the street for Theo, for Link, for the two Watchers sent here to take us.

The street is so filled with smoke and dust that I can hardly see ahead. Jackson calls behind me to keep going, to get to the tunnel, but I keep staring forward, searching for my friends.

"Go," I say. "Get Ellie and the Leader to safety. I'll see you down there."

Jackson tries to pull me again, but this time I rip my hand from his and turn my eyes to him. "GO, JACK! I have to check on my friends!" I roar, my voice splitting the air. "I'll be OK. I swear it."

He stares into my eyes for a few seconds, but must

know my mind is made up. Then he turns, quickly, and pulls Ellie and the Leader towards the tunnel.

I stand alone now, staring back into the fog of smoke and soot. I hear grunts ahead, the sound of fighting echoing through the shattered streets. I begin walking forward into the cloud, lifting my sleeve to my mouth to prevent my lungs filling with smoke. I can only see a few metres ahead, shadows of rubble piles and old battered cars slowly appearing in front of me.

Then I see a body. The shape of a man lying on the ground. I rush on and bend down to examine him, and see blood pouring from a bullet hole in the head. But it's not Theo, and it's not Link. It's the face of one of Knight's Watchers, the back of his skull split open and emptying its contents onto the dusty earth.

The sight is repulsive, but brings a sudden feeling of hope to my heart. If they bested him, they can best the other. I keep going forward, faster now, as the fighting grows louder.

And then I hear it.

A voice, close by to my left. That deep, resonating voice that rumbles right through my body. Calm and cold and devoid of any emotion.

"Stop right there, Cyra."

I turn to my left and see a shadow appear through the mist, dust swirling around him. Dressed in black and with that chiselled face, cut from stone. Eyes of deepest grey, like slabs of cold slate.

Ajax.

I lift my weapon and point it straight at him, only a few metres away. His face doesn't change, doesn't flinch. He just stares into my eyes and slowly shakes his head.

"You're not going to shoot me, Cyra."

I raise the gun to my shoulder and stick my finger to the trigger, pulling lightly. But he just stares at me, and whispers again. "You're not going to shoot me."

Then, suddenly, his eyes dart into the fog ahead, towards the continuing sounds of battle. In the blink of an eye he moves forwards, slipping behind me before I even know it. I feel a sharp tug at my back and feel myself being flung backwards through the air several metres, landing with a thud on my back. As I hit the ground, I see the spot where I'd been standing explode in a thousand shards of cement and stone as a ball of fire swells in the mist.

I feel Ajax by my side, crouching low to the ground as the fire lifts into the air and fades. "Don't move," he tells me again, before darting forward into the smoke.

My head spins. My ears ring. My eyesight blurs slightly around the edges. But through the clearing mist I can now make out figures, the shapes of bodies. One rushes towards me and I brace for an attack, trying to focus to see what danger it will bring.

Then I see Theo's face, bruised and bloodied, but alive. He emerges through the smoke and is quickly by my side, lifting me up into his arms and flinging me over his shoulder. He begins staggering towards the tunnel as I continue to watch the smoke clear behind him.

"Link?" I croak, but he doesn't answer.

He doesn't need to.

In the distance, caught under a pile of rubble, I see him. Eyes closed, body unmoving, blood dribbling from his lips. Theo continues to run forward as I bounce on his shoulder, my vision blurring around me.

"Link..." I croak again.

But again, Theo says nothing.

Then, just before we descend down into the tunnel, into the darkness, I see Ajax. He moves forward, the other Watcher to his side, and stares down at Link. He crouches to his body, brushing blood from his mouth, and I see his head drop. His star pupil. The boy he trained for months, who only wanted to help people. Now lying dead in the middle of the street.

31
Revelations

I wake to silence.

The booming of explosions has ceased, the relentless rattle of gunfire ended. All that remains is a light ringing in my ears, and the sound of weeping nearby.

I scan for the source and see Ellie, sitting up against a bare rock wall, her head tucked into her knees. Theo sits next to her, arm around her for comfort, eyes staring at his feet.

My head aches as I shakily shift on the bed and drop my legs to the floor. My feet hit hard rock with a muted thud, and Theo's eyes raise up to mine. He looks at me for a few moments, a sorrow on his face, before gently slipping his arm off Ellie's shoulder and coming towards me.

When he reaches me we hug, and I feel warm tears running down my cheeks. Tears of relief and happiness at seeing him alive and unhurt. Tears of grief and anguish at the thought that Link is dead. At the sight of Ellie, distraught and broken-hearted on the floor. I want to go to her, hug her, tell her it's going to be OK. But I don't. I can't. Nothing can take away her pain right now. The sort of pain and fear and desolation that no training in the Grid can prepare you for.

Theo releases me, and we sit together on the bed. He whispers to me in the silence, telling me what happened, his face growing in anger and sorrow and regret all at once.

He tells me how he was knocked out during the fight, leaving Link alone. He came around to find that one of the Watchers was dead, lying prostrate on the floor, his head blown apart. Nearby, Link was still there, fighting hand to hand with the other Watcher in the swirling smoke.

Then the explosion hit, tearing the ground from under them. I see a tear building in Theo's eyes as he tells me how Link saw it coming a split second early and pushed him out of the way of the blast. The rubble came down on him instead, just as Ajax came rushing through.

Theo knew there was no fighting them off alone. So he ran, found me lying there in the street, picked me up, and headed for the tunnel. He trails off as he speaks, shaking his head.

"He saved me," he says. "After everything I've done, *he* saved *me*. I don't deserve to be here. I should be dead, not him."

I hug him again and tell him he's done nothing wrong. But he won't hear it. "I've done more wrong than you know," he says, before standing and walking off into the darkness of the tunnel.

I follow him with my eyes as he goes, but don't move from the bed. I just sit there, the sound of Ellie's sniffs and sobs still filling the cave, unable to move, unable to think. Numb from everything that's happened. From everything I've seen and done.

Eventually I go to Ellie and sit beside her. I don't say anything. I just wrap my arm around her and pull her towards me. Her head rocks to the side, settling on my shoulder, and a fresh stream of tears falls from her eyes.

Then I think of Jackson, almost forgotten among the turmoil. I know he's safe. He must be or Theo would have said something. Yet I can't see him. Him or the Leader in the cave.

I tentatively ask Ellie if she knows where they are. She tells me, through her sniffs, that they went ahead to help people escape the tunnels. It's a labyrinth down here, apparently. And there's only one way out that few people know about.

We sit in silence for a while as Ellie's sobs begin to dry up, exhaustion taking over her body. I stand and help her towards the bed, laying her down on the thin mattress and stroking her head until she falls asleep. In sleep, perhaps, she'll get some respite from all this. I only wish that were true.

It's a while later that the silence is finally broken, the sound of gentle footsteps coming from the darkness. I lift my head to see Jackson appear from the dark shroud down the tunnel, his pace quickening as he sees me. I stand and rush towards him, jumping into his arms and gripping him tight.

When I finally let him go I see that half his face is caked in dried blood and soot, his eyes worn and weary. I run my hands through his hair and feel a cut, sticky with blood. He grimaces as I touch it but assures me it's just a scratch.

We sit against the bare rock and Jackson tells me

where we are, his voice low and empty and completely drained. "Deep in the mountains," he says. "Down one of an endless series of passages. We'll stay here for tonight. Tomorrow morning, we need to keep moving."

"Moving where?" I ask.

"To the other side of the mountains. There are more cities in the east, Cyra. This isn't the end."

I let out a breath at the thought that there's more to come. More fighting, more war. This, I know, is only just the beginning.

We sit in silence for a little while, a heavy weight on top of us both. It's not like before, back home, where we'd make light of our troubles if ever they got too serious. Nothing back then seems serious now. Over three short months, things have changed forever.

So we just sit, and don't speak, except to talk about what we might do or where we might go. For all his apparent knowledge of this place, of this cause, I know Jackson knows very little. The path that lies ahead of us will be determined by the Leader who still lives. The beacon of hope who these people will look up to now. Will he choose to retreat into the recesses of the Deadlands to live in peace, or fight for something more and risk losing everything? Whatever he chooses, me and Jackson and Theo and Ellie are stuck along for the ride. There truly is no going back now.

Soon Theo reappears. His eyes pass over us, still slightly shell-shocked and forlorn, before quickly turning away. He finds a darkened corner of the cave and settles in against the wall, looking a million miles from the boy I first met. I go to speak to him, to make sure he's OK, but all he does is keep his head low. He, like all of us, just needs time to process all of this.

The minutes and hours pass, and I sense Jackson growing more agitated. He spends most of his time looking down the tunnel, listening intently for any sound of footsteps coming our way. The Leader told him he'd make sure that any stragglers knew where they were going before returning to us. That meant going back towards the entrance and the chance of encountering more Eden soldiers.

Then, from nowhere, the Leader appears, walking almost silently through the darkness. Jackson rises to his feet quickly and moves towards him. They whisper for a few moments in private before Jackson returns to me.

"He wants to speak with you alone," he says.

I stand and walk towards the Leader, his face still darkened by soot and shadow. I join him at his side and we begin walking down the tunnel, lit only in places by dim lights built into the rock ceiling.

To the left and right, small alcoves have been cut into the rock, fitted with beds and shelving containing tins of food and other rations.

"This place has been used for decades as a sanctuary against the threats from outside," says the Leader. There's something about his voice that's so familiar, so comforting. "The tunnels were built during the last war for the people to hide in and escape through if they needed."

We continue on, passing other passageways and tunnels leading in various directions into the mountains. The place looks like a maze, impossible to navigate except by those who know the way.

Soon we come to a large opening, a wide cavern with several linking tunnels leading off from it. In the middle is a stone table, and a spotlight shining down on it from above. The Leader moves towards it and I follow. On top is a stone basin, filled with water that drips from the ceiling above.

"Please, wash," he says.

I dip my hands into the cool water and lean down to splash my face. Immediately my fingers fill with grime, dark liquid dripping down from my face onto the table. The Leader passes me an old cloth and I wipe my face clean, staining the fabric black.

"That's better," says the Leader. "Now I can see you properly."

His eyes twinkle with memory as he looks at me for a few moments. Those blue eyes, sparkling behind his mask of dirt and grit.

"You did well today, Cyra," he says. "You saved lives."

I shake my head. "I didn't save anyone. I should have seen the attack coming."

The Leader steps forward, drawing closer to me. "You can't blame yourself for that. No one saw it coming."

"Not even you?" I ask.

He looks at me questioningly. "No, how would I..."

"Because you're a Watcher too," I say quickly. "The way you dodged that ceiling when it fell. The way you moved through the street. You can see into the Void, can't you?"

Slowly his head begins to nod. "You're right. I can."

"And was it you who saw me? Me and my friends coming to find Jackson."

He nods again. "That was me," he says.

It's a question I've been wanting to ask Jackson. Something unsettling in my mind that I can't figure out. The fact that they knew it was me in that underground shelter. Only someone who knew me could possibly know that.

"But how did you know it was me?" I ask.

The Leader hesitates for a moment, before turning away. I watch as his hand slips into his cloak, pulling out something shiny and metallic. He looks at it for a moment, eyes deep with a lingering sadness.

Then he turns back to me, and I see what he's holding. In his hand is my mother's watch, the face cracked and broken.

"This was your mother's watch," he says. It's not a question. He runs his finger over the cracked surface, just like I've done a thousand times.

"How...do you know that?" I whisper.

He doesn't answer, but moves towards the basin. He places the watch on the table and drops his cupped hands into the water. I watch on as he washes his face, the dirt and soot quickly clearing and revealing his tanned, weathered skin. His slightly crooked nose. His firm, dimpled jaw, covered in a shroud of dark stubble.

He raises his face back up to meet mine, a smile arching at the corner of his lips.

"We have a lot to catch up on, Cyra," he says.

And then I see him. See the man I knew. The man I loved.

The man who was taken from me when I was a child.

The man who I thought was long dead.

My father, Drake.

THE END

Book 2 – City Of Stone is out now!

To hear about the author's latest discounts and new releases, sign up to his newsletter at www.tcedgebooks.com

21648584R10221

Made in the USA
Middletown, DE
13 December 2018